JUST ONE LAST
CHANCE

THE INSPIRING STORY OF ARTIE CALL AND THE
MOST AMAZING FANTASTIC CAR IN THE WORLD!

OTHER BOOKS BY JERRY BORROWMAN:

Life and Death at Hoover Dam

Compassionate Soldiers

How 4 Feet of Plywood Saved the Grand Canyon

and other inspiring books
Visit www.jerryborrowman.com

JUST ONE LAST CHANCE

...PIRING STORY OF ARTIE CALL AND THE
...ZING FANTASTIC CAR IN THE WORLD!

...dium without the

...ucts of the

...OWMAN

Acknowledgments

I'd like to thank Richard Losee and Kevin Marsh for giving me the unique opportunity of riding in a fully restored 1929 Duesenberg as part of my research for writing this book. Richard is a private collector of vintage automobiles and Kevin the chief restorer. As you will learn in the course of the story and in greater detail in the Author Notes at the end of the novel, the Duesenberg J Series was considered the finest automobile in the world in the years of the Great Depression.

I also want to thank Jon Bill of the Auburn/Cord/Duesenberg Automobile Museum in Auburn, Indiana, for his hospitality and insights during my visit to Indiana during the writing of the book. Like Richard and Kevin, Jon responded to every question and helped me appreciate the quality of the cars from this remarkable era.

Both Jon and Kevin were kind enough to do a technical edit of the completed manuscript to provide historical accuracy regarding the vintage automobiles talked about in the book.

The primary task of the writer of historical fiction is to bring the past to life for his or her readers. I hope that as you read my story of Artie Call you will feel what I have felt and imagine what it would be like to experience both the best and the worst of America in its time of greatest despair.

I'd also like to thank my friends and family who gave me suggestions on this story as it was being developed, with special thanks to Val Johnson and Kirk Shaw for their professional edits of the book prior to submission.

CHAPTER 1

Old Man Marchant

Boise, Idaho—August 1932

Joey Weston couldn't believe he was doing this.

But there he was, once again, trailing behind Artie Call as they moved stealthily toward the barbed-wire fence that separated the alley from Mr. Marchant's backyard. Artie had left it up to Joey whether he wanted to come along or not. After a moment's hesitation the younger boy made his decision and crawled noiselessly up to Artie's side. Artie glanced at him and smiled then lifted the top wire with his left hand while his foot pressed the lower one to the ground, giving Joey room to quickly scramble through the opening. Then Joey returned the favor from the other side.

As they closed the twenty feet or so to the small ditch that ran through the old man's yard, they heard some tuneless singing in the crackled old voice that had yelled at them so many times before—which is precisely why Mr. Marchant was such a frequent target. He yelled at them even when they didn't deserve it, as well as when they did, sometimes even reporting them to the Boise police. Of course this required them to get even with him in some even more insidious escapade. It was an ongoing test of wills that grew ever more daring with each encounter. Tonight's prank held out great promise for being the best ever.

Crawling up to the garden where Mr. Marchant was busy pulling weeds, they were relieved to see that he had his back turned to them. Even Artie had to admit that he was a diligent old fellow who loved his garden, so it wasn't unusual that he'd be completely lost in thought at a moment like this. That's what made him vulnerable. Although Joey wasn't a particularly imaginative boy, even he could picture the mayhem that was about to ensue, and by making the assumption that their victim would live through it, he was able to snicker at the thought of what was coming. As bad as the noise would be, it was the irrigation water that filled the trenches between the rows of the corn stalks that made the opportunity perfect.

Artie shushed Joey, and it took a moment to register that he had started singing the same tune that Mr. Marchant was singing as he knelt blissfully unaware in his garden. Fortunately, Marchant was very hard of hearing, so his chance of hearing Joey was limited. The only thing that could betray them is if he were to randomly stand up and change positions. Then he'd see them and the whole thing would be ruined. But with only a few seconds to go, that wasn't likely.

In the semidarkness, Artie pointed to the row directly to the right of Marchant as they slowly crept closer. At just the right moment, Artie came up off his knees into a crouching position, pulled the mammoth firecracker out of his pocket, and coolly struck a match to the fuse.

Joey would have tossed the firecracker immediately the instant it was lighted and then would have bolted out of there, but Artie rather calmly allowed the fuse to burn its way down toward the igniter while waiting for just the right moment to toss it. Just when Joey thought his heart would burst if they didn't get the heck out of there, he saw Artie gently toss the firecracker into the water, a foot or so in front of Mr. Marchant. There was a terrific explosion as the thing went off, the light and sound of which was so startling that Joey instinctively covered his eyes with his arms. Fortunately, Artie grabbed his arm and shook it; otherwise Joey would have missed seeing the magnificent waterspout that erupted from the muddy garden with at least half the column of water and mud cascading right down onto Marchant's face. What Joey wouldn't have missed was the almost simultaneous sound of Marchant's terrified shriek, followed by the old man rocking back on his haunches so forcefully that he fell over backward, his back on the ground, his face covered in mud, his feet up in the air, and his mouth uttering words that you don't ever hear in Sunday School.

At first Joey thought the firecracker might have hurt Marchant, but such was Artie's skill that only water and mud struck the old man. The explosion itself was directed away from Marchant so that the blast neither burned him nor injured him. Rather, he was simply the beneficiary of an unexpected late-summer shower. Based on the gigantic roar that erupted from Marchant, it was apparent that it wasn't an entirely welcome shower. Artie and Joey burst out laughing.

"Why you . . . you little criminals! I'll get you for this!" The words exploded out of his mouth. And with that, Marchant rolled over to his stomach as he tried to wipe the mud from his eye. It was the mud that gave them the chance Artie was counting on, and having had time to enjoy the whole thing, he took off on a full run with Joey just behind.

"I can't see you, you little hooligans, but I know it's you, Artie Call! You and Joey Weston!"

"At least he didn't die," Joey called out with relief in his voice.

"No, but he's plenty mad," Artie replied happily. When they reached the garden fence, they had enough speed going that Artie reached out his left hand and placed it firmly on one of the posts while vaulting up and over the barbed wire. Joey was too short to pull that off, so Artie quickly wheeled around and slapped his foot on the lower wire while lifting the top wire. Joey dove through and bounced up quickly on the other side and turned to run off with Artie. At this point, Mr. Marchant had stood up and had started chasing them, running in a stilted gait, reminiscent of a wounded bear. But then he paused and roared, "You've gone too far this time! There's only one thing good enough for you right now!"

They'd heard that line from Mr. Marchant before. In fact, they'd heard it enough times to know exactly what it meant. On one occasion they'd even felt what it meant. Quite simply, Marchant was on his way to the kitchen to retrieve his shotgun, which he kept loaded with rock salt for occasions just like this. Jagged rock salt propelled through the air by exploding black powder hurt like the dickens when it hit, even if it didn't kill. The salt could easily shred a cotton shirt while embedding the crystals deeply into the skin, where the blood of the wound promptly started to dissolve it. Now *that* was a feeling neither Joey nor Artie would ever forget.

What happened next was totally unexpected.

As they turned under full acceleration to make their getaway, they ran headlong into a solid object—well mostly solid. It yielded a bit as they hit it. The shock of the impact was so startling that the hair on both their necks stood up and in spite of themselves they let out a surprised yelp of fear.

"What the—!" Artie blurted out as he tried to figure out what he'd hit. Then he heard the voice he hated most in the world.

"Well, well, what have we here? Artie Call and his cohort, Mr. Weston."

Artie looked up defiantly at Mr. David Boone, the local banker and neighborhood busybody. Artie tried to scramble away, but faster than lightning Mr. Boone reached out and grabbed him by the collar.

"And what exactly are you up to, Mr. Call? From the sound coming from Marchant's kitchen, I'd say it's not anything good. In fact, I'd bet you've been up to your old tricks again, harassing a poor old man. What did you do to him this time—chase his cat or break his sauerkraut pot?" He smiled a false smile.

"We didn't do nothing!" Artie said. "We heard poor old Mr. Marchant cry out like he needed help or something, but when we got here, he'd already gone into his kitchen. You know he doesn't like us much, so we decided to get out of here."

Boone nodded. "Yes, and I'm the new President of the United States." The fake smile was gone, and now Artie shivered at the cold glare in his eyes. "Come on, you two, let's go find out what you've been up to." Artie did his best to get away, but Boone was way too strong. Before Artie could get any traction, Boone had lifted him up and off the ground. Even though he was fourteen years old, Artie was smaller than most boys his age and weighed hardly a thing, something that was a constant source of annoyance to him.

"You let me down!" he shouted as he tried to kick Boone. But Boone was too strong and he managed to twist Artie just in time so that the kick hit Joey, who let out a yelp.

"Now see what you done!" Artie shouted furiously.

Boone pulled him up close, with Artie facing away from him, but fully constrained by Boone's powerful arms. "I'm sorry about that, because when he's not with you, Joey is a nice boy. But he *is* with you, so I suspect he's part of this." After Artie stopped struggling, Boone slowly let him down to the ground but maintained a firm grip on his shirt collar and the collar of his bib overalls. "Now let's go."

Even though he hated it, Artie knew that there was no escape, so as sullenly as possible, he shuffled along as they approached the house, quickly trying to think of what he'd say to deflect the old man's wrath. It was just at that moment that Marchant came storming out of the kitchen with his shotgun pointed directly at them. "I'm going to shoot you for sure, you little hooligans!" he shrieked. The site of the enraged old man was startling enough that Boone instinctively raised both arms while shouting, "Don't shoot, Wilford! Don't shoot! It's me—it's David Boone!"

But Marchant did shoot, not directly at Boone, but rather at the backside of Artie Call who had used Boone's surprise to wriggle free and head off. Fortunately, it was getting dark, and the blast missed by a mile. Well, at least it missed Artie. But it didn't miss Marchant's horse, which let out a startled whinny and then tore off through the garden, upsetting a bushel of ripe toma-toes that Boone had set by the gate when he stopped to interrogate Artie and Joey. Boone ran after the horse, shouting at the top of his lungs for it to stop, at the same time cursing the night air as the poor, frightened animal continued to wreak havoc on anything that got in its way. A second blast from Marchant's gun simply added to the melee, particularly since some of the pellets found their way into David Boone's backside.

Joey ran for cover, happy in the knowledge that Artie had made his escape into the twilight. And yet he knew that it wasn't over. Mr. Boone could be mean, and he was certain to be mad tonight. Still, as he thought about the look on Marchant's face, all covered with mud and water, he couldn't help but laugh.

CHAPTER 2

Getting By

"Okay, you got what you're supposed to do, Artie?"

Artie's heart was pounding, but he nodded in the affirmative.

"Good. Just to make sure you don't mess it up, your job is to keep asking questions while I take care of the cash drawer. As soon as I'm done, I'll come back and ask the clerk a question so you can drift away and lift a loaf of bread or whatever else it is you want. Meanwhile, Jake will come in the front of the store and he'll ask to buy some hard candy, which will take the clerk to the counter. That will give you and me a chance to get out the door without anyone getting suspicious."

"Are you going to take all the cash?" Jake asked.

Reuben shook his head in disgust. "Of course not. If I did, he'd know in a second the very next time he opens the cash drawer, and he'd call the police right on the spot. It wouldn't be real hard for him to put two-and-two together, would it, and they'd be onto us in no time." Reuben smiled. "The trick is to be patient and not get too greedy. I'll lift just enough that we get a good payoff, but small enough that the clerk won't notice anything until he closes out his drawer at the end of the day. By that point, he will have helped dozens of people, and he won't know who to blame. With any luck, he'll blame himself for miscounting."

"All right," Artie said breathlessly. "Let's get it over with."

"You're sure you don't want any of the money? You never take any money when we do these deals."

Artie shook his head. "Just food. That's all I need."

Reuben shook his head. "Seems kind of stupid to me, but it's all the better for me and Jake. With that, the three boys started sauntering toward the Ada Street Market.

* * *

"Is that you, Artie?"

"Yes, it is—I'm home!"

Artie's grandfather startled him by coming into the kitchen. Artie tried to hide what he was doing, but his grandfather saw him.

"Is that food you've got there?"

Artie nodded. "Yes, sir, it is. Just some bread and some cans of soup. I thought you might like some soup for supper."

His grandfather got a confused look on his face. "I don't remember giving you any money for food."

"That's all right. I had some."

"But how did you get the money?"

Now Artie's heart really did pound. He hated lying to his grandfather. Even worse, he hated deceiving him like he was about to do. But he couldn't have him asking questions. "You gave me the money this morning, Grandpa. Don't you remember? You said that you thought soup would taste good, so I should stop by the store and get some."

His grandfather's face fell. "I did? I don't remember. . . "

This was the critical moment. Sometimes his grandfather would get all sad and bothered because he didn't remember, and other times he'd get angry and accuse Artie of lying to him. That was always kind of tough, because his grandfather believed in giving a person a good slap if they did something he didn't like.

"I guess I'm getting old, Artie." His grandfather smiled. "I honestly don't remember a thing."

"That's okay.. . " Artie was immeasurably relieved that Grandpa was going to be good-natured this time.

"Truth is, I don't know where I would have gotten any money, anyway. But I'm glad I gave it to you this morning. Why don't you show me what you got for us?"

Artie let out a sigh of relief and displayed the cans and the loaf of bread.

"It's not a lot, is it? Not for a growing boy like you."

"It'll be enough, sir. I got your favorite—Campbell's tomato soup. And I got some cheese so we can have a cheese sandwich with it."

His grandfather sat down heavily in the chair. "You're a good boy, Artie. You take good care of your old grandpa. Since your grandmother died . . ."

Artie knew that he would tear up over this. Even though there were lots of things his grandfather couldn't remember, lately he never forgot about his wife dying. It seems like that was when it all started to go downhill for them.

"It's okay, Grandpa. Hey, could you tell me a story about my dad when he was a little boy? You remember, how the two of you used to go fishing?"

His grandfather's face brightened. "He was a good one, Artie. Maybe the best fisherman I ever knew. Even as a sprout, he could pull 'em out of the river . . ."

And with that, Artie started to fix dinner, relieved that his grandfather had gone to a happier place in his mind. Artie thought it odd that his grandfather could remember things that happened fifty years earlier with almost perfect clarity but couldn't remember to put his trousers on before going out in the cold.

CHAPTER 3

When Justice Can't Be Just

September 1932—The Old Boise Courthouse

"He needs to go to reform school!"

Even with the heavy oak door fully closed to the hallway where Artie was sitting he could hear Wilford Marchant's voice as it shrieked inside the judge's conference room. It was a high-pitched voice that had much the same effect on the nervous system as fingernails on a blackboard, and he felt the skin crawl on his arms as the old fellow yelled this phrase for at least the third or fourth time since the meeting had started.

"He's pretty angry, isn't he?"

Artie turned to Aaron Nelson, who vied with Joey Weston for the rank of Artie's best friend. While Joey was a small, immature boy who quite easily fell under Artie's charismatic spell, Aaron was the exact opposite. He was the best student in school and a leader in the church's youth group. He wasn't popular in the sense of being good looking or witty, but everybody liked and admired him. So much so that no one even made fun of him for not being athletic. It's like Aaron had managed to carve out this special space for himself where everybody, both kids and adults, respected him for how smart he was. The only smirch on his character was that for some unfathomable reason he had befriended Artie Call. Nobody could figure that one out. Artie overheard some adults debating the issue of Aaron and Artie's friendship one time. Some took the position that Aaron did it strictly out of a sense of duty since he was Artie's youth group leader. Others thought that maybe Aaron liked Artie because he secretly wished he could be a little bad sometimes, and just knowing Artie let him feel some of the thrill vicariously. For his part, Artie couldn't figure it out, either. Aaron was nothing like him. Yet Artie loved the kid and was grateful that they were friends. Somehow it was always Aaron who stood up for him, even when he didn't deserve it, and it was his loyalty that had saved Artie on many previous occasions.

One time Artie had asked him why he liked him, but Aaron just shrugged and tried to avoid replying. But when Artie pressed, he finally just said, "For crying out loud, Artie, you know as well as I do that you're not bad. You'll grow out of all this stuff. Now leave me alone! I get to like whoever I want to, and that's the last I'm going to say about it." And when Aaron said that he wasn't going to say any more, he meant it. Two Buick roadsters pulling with all their might couldn't get anything more out of him. So Artie left it alone. But still he wondered. He even wondered if Aaron was right about him growing out of it.

Pastor Wyndham, from church, said, "But we can't just take him away from his grandfather. He needs Artie!"

This made the hair on Artie's neck stand up. The thought of being taken away from his grandfather was his greatest fear, and the very fact that Pastor Wyndham had to say something about it meant that there was a chance it would happen. In spite of the policeman standing across the hallway, Artie jumped up when he heard that. "I've got to go in there, sir! They can't take me away from my grandpa. Please!"

"Sit back down!" said the policeman firmly. "When they want your opinion, they'll ask for it." Artie glared at the man, but he proved equal to the glare, so Artie finally sank down on the bench and put his elbows to his knees and rested his head in his hands.

"It's okay, Artie," said Aaron. "Pastor Wyndham knows what's best for you. He won't let them take you away."

Artie didn't look up. "But I really did it bad this time. Joey and me were caught red-handed. Mr. Boone caught us." He looked up urgently. "What can I do, Aaron? Grandpa needs me?" In spite of his best effort, he couldn't stop the tear that suddenly freed itself from his eye to streak down his cheek.

"I think it's going to be just fine," Aaron said softly. The young man seemed to think for a while. In a gentle voice, he said, "It doesn't help that you hang around with Reuben Kinley and Jake Carter, you know. That makes people think maybe you're like them."

That made Artie sit straight up, and his eyes flashed as he turned to respond. "Listen, Aaron, you're my best friend. But even you can't tell me who to spend my time with."

Aaron shrunk back a bit. "I'm not being judgmental, Artie. I'm just trying to think of ways to help you get what you want. And both of those guys have been to reform school, and some people think they need to go back. So when you spend time with them, a lot of people assume you're going along with their plans. That won't help you stay with your grandfather."

Even though it made him angry to hear Aaron say this, he knew he was right. He just didn't know what to do about it.

"How did you get to be friends with them, anyway?"

Artie squirmed on the bench. "At first they were nice to me. Grant Hugley was trying to beat me up one day, and Reuben threatened him. Well, that was enough to send Grant packing for home. Then they just started hanging out with me. It was kind of fun, at first, since everybody was scared of them. It made me feel kind of big. And then, they . . ." Artie hesitated.

"Then they what?"

Artie squirmed some more. "They just helped me out of a little jam. That's all. So I can't just turn on them, even if they are kind of mean."

What Artie couldn't tell Aaron, or anyone else for that matter, is that Reuben and Jake had taught him how to steal food so that no one would even suspect him. That had become pretty important since his grandfather had lost all his money to the con man that had come through selling pots and pans. They already had plenty of pots and pans, but the man had sold him more than fifty dollars' worth. That was a lot of money, and since his grandfather didn't like taking money out of savings they didn't have anything left for food. So Artie felt forced to stealing from the local grocers to keep food on the table. He didn't like it, but he didn't know what else to do. That's really why he'd befriended Reuben and Jake.

But now, as his mind quickly played its way through this little scene, he got a sick feeling in his stomach, both because of what he was doing and because now those two could use it to threaten him. When he'd told them thanks for helping him, they said something that made his blood go cold. "Don't thank us. Someday we'll need you, and you owe us. You owe us real bad. So you better not let us down." It was at that moment that he realized that they hadn't really been his friends, like they'd pretended. He'd once heard a story about a man who made a deal with the devil and who couldn't get out of it later. That's sort of how he felt about Reuben and Jake. But now he didn't know what to do.

He was about to say something to Aaron to try to make up for yelling at him, but just then the heavy old door creaked on its hinges, and he looked up to see Pastor Wyndham motion for him to come in.

"Can Aaron come too?" asked Artie.

"I'm afraid not this time, Artie." Then he stood there holding the door. Artie turned and looked at Aaron. He couldn't go inside with things unresolved. "I'm sorry I yelled at you, Aaron."

His friend smiled. "It's no big deal. Now go in there and try to keep your temper in check. They want to help you. So don't go getting your pride all up."

"I'll try." With that, he accepted Aaron's hand and then turned and walked to the pastor. He felt his pulse calm down when Pastor Wyndham put his hand on his shoulder as he guided him into the room.

Sitting at the front of the courtroom behind a huge mahogany desk was a man with gray hair. Artie figured that he must be the judge. Then there was Mr. Boone, Mr. Marchant, the Pastor's wife, and Joey's mother. She was head of the Women's Auxiliary. Artie's grandfather was supposed to be there, but Artie had intercepted the summons before his grandfather received it. He'd put it in the trash to be burned so that his grandfather wouldn't know this was going on.

The pastor steered Artie to a spot directly in front of the judge. When he got there, he didn't know what to do, so he simply dropped his arms and folded his hands, his gaze down so he didn't have to look at the judge.

"Artie Call?" The judge had a nice enough voice.

"Yes, sir."

"Kindly look up at me, please, Artie." The judge didn't say this harshly, so Artie reluctantly raised his eyes. "I'm Judge Farnsworth. We're here to figure out what's best for you. Won't you please have a chair?"

Artie sat down heavily. He didn't want anybody figuring out what was best for him. He was doing fine on his own—if only people like Old Man Marchant would mind their own business. But he knew he was up against something bigger than usual, so he resolved to keep his temper like Aaron had told him.

"Artie, you've been charged with assault and battery. Do you know what that means?"

Artie shook his head from side to side and mumbled something inaudible.

"Sorry, but we have to keep a record of what is said in here—that's what my clerk is doing over there, writing down everything we say. So you'll have to answer my questions with your voice, not just a nod of the head. Do you understand?"

Artie nodded. Then catching himself, he replied, "Yes, sir, I understand."

"Good. Now, it's very important that you understand what you're being accused of, so I'm going to spend a few minutes to work through it with you because you are so young. I think you indicated that you don't know what it means to be charged with assault and battery."

"No, sir."

"Assault means a threat to inflict physical harm on a person, which makes them feel fearful for their safety, while battery means that you actually hurt them by causing some kind of physical injury."

"But I didn't hurt Mr. Marchant. Not really. I made sure that he wouldn't get hit by the firecracker. All he got was splashed with some water and maybe some mud on his face!" Artie had gotten so riled by the accusation that he had instinctively stood up partway out of his chair.

Rather than argue, the judge waited a few moments to respond, which made Artie feel uncomfortable and embarrassed. Only after Artie sat back down did the judge proceed. "I understand what you're telling me, Artie, but if you listen to the first word I described—assault —do you think it's possible that what you did might have scared Mr. Marchant? After all, he didn't know it was coming, and he couldn't really know whether or not you were going to throw it in a way that would hurt him. Do you think that maybe that could make a person feel frightened?"

Artie wanted to say no, but he knew that the judge was right. He was clearly guilty of assault if it meant making someone feel scared. Of course, it didn't really make sense that such a thing was against the law, since a lot of people made him feel scared, but that was a matter for a different time. So he answered simply, "Yes, sir. I can see that it did."

"He should go to reform school! I don't know why we have to take all this time. He's a hooligan!"

The judge looked up sharply. "Mr. Marchant, you will not speak out in my chamber without permission! Do you understand?" He said this very loudly so that even Wilford Marchant would hear. Artie didn't dare turn to look, but he could hear the old man sit down heavily in his seat.

The judge turned his gaze back to Artie. "Now, since you've admitted that you're guilty of assault, and since the physical act of throwing a firecracker where it blew water and mud up on Mr. Marchant's face is clearly battery under the law, then we don't need to go any further along those lines. It's true, isn't it, that you did what these men accuse you of? Do you admit that?"

Artie felt a sense of panic inside. He'd just been convicted of committing a crime, and Mr. Marchant was probably right that he'd go to the reformatory. He didn't want that. He'd heard terrible stories about the place and what the big kids did to the littler ones. But there was nothing he could say other than, "Yes, sir. I did what they said I did." But then he got another quick feeling of panic and added, "But Joey didn't do anything. He didn't want me to do it, and he even tried to talk me out of it. He just came along because he's my friend. He's not guilty of either assault or battery. You're not going to send him to reform school, are you?"

Judge Farnsworth shook his head. "No, Artie. We're not going to send him to reform school. We already figured out that Joey didn't take an active role in this. But I think it's very respectable that you stood up for him." Artie didn't know how to take this, so he just looked down at his feet again. He realized how embarrassed he was by his shoes, since everyone else in the room had well-polished shoes and his were dirty and scruffy.

"Artie, please look at me again." Reluctantly Artie looked up, even though he didn't want to. What he wanted to do was to jump up and run from the room and keep running until he reached the new Union Pacific Depot up at the top of Capitol Boulevard. Then he'd jump a freight train and get himself so far away from Boise that they'd never find him. He actually thought about trying it for just a moment, but then he remembered the policeman who was standing just outside the door, and he knew it was hopeless. So Artie looked up.

"What I need to know is what causes you to do all these things to Mr. Marchant. Can you answer me that question?"

The last thing he intended to do was to tell the judge or anybody else why he hated Mr. Marchant. Some things were personal. It's just that simple. He'd sooner go to jail or even to reform school before he'd do that.

"I take it by your silence that you don't want to tell me?"

"No, sir," Artie mumbled.

"Well, then, I'll have to do some detective work to see if I can't figure it out for myself. Because it's only when I know the answer to that question that I can decide what we need to do with you. So I think we should start at the beginning."

"The beginning? What do you mean?"

The judge smiled. "I thought that might raise your curiosity. Here's what I mean. Since everything we say is going into an official transcript—that means it will be written down and a copy kept in the court records—we need to get a clear picture of who you are and what your circumstances are. All of that will help me in making my judgment. Some of what we talk about may be hard for you to listen to and may even make you angry, but it's very important. So what can you tell me about yourself?"

This was an unexpected turn in the conversation, and Artie didn't quite know what to say. He wasn't used to having an adult talk to him like a person, other than Pastor Wyndham maybe, so he didn't know exactly how to reply.

"Maybe I can help you. In an informal session before this hearing started, Pastor Wyndham told me that your mother died when you were just four years old from a bad case of the flu. Do you remember your mother?"

Something happened that Artie had not counted on. He had always done anything to prevent the hurt feeling that came to his throat when he felt like he was going to cry. He didn't want to show emotion, but thinking about his mother made it impossible not to. Doing his best to choke down his tears, he said, "I kind of remember her. I remember a woman singing to me when I was real little, and I also remember sitting by her feet while she ironed my dad's shirts. It was warm there, and she used to tell me stories. And I remember . . ." Artie's voice choked up at that point.

"You remember, what?"

"I'm not sure if I remember it, but it seems like I remember my mom being really sick and telling me that she loved me." This was too much, and in spite of his best efforts, Artie couldn't suppress a sob. It made him angry that the judge would do this to him, and his cheeks flushed, making the tears feel hot as they ran down his cheek.

"And then I was told that your father did his best to care for you but that maybe he had some problems."

Artie looked up furiously. "My dad didn't have any problems. He got sick, that's all. He just got really sick! People don't have any right talking about my dad!" Artie rose up out of his chair at that point, wanting to hit somebody or something. Once again the judge could have become angry, like he had with Mr. Marchant, but he didn't. He just sat there calmly until Artie finally sat down.

"Whether you like to remember it or not, your father had a problem with alcohol. I know that because he had to appear before me once."

"But he wasn't bad—he was just sad. He was really sad that mom died. That doesn't make a man bad."

"No, Artie, that doesn't make him bad. In fact, I liked your father very much. Everybody I know liked him. He was a kind and gentle man. We all felt sorry that he was so sad. Still, it made it hard for him to care for you."

"He did all right." Artie looked up at the judge as he said this. He was glad the judge had said nice things about his father, but he wanted it very clear that he had been just fine when he lived with his father.

"I'm glad you feel that way. It had to have been a terrible blow when he died in the automobile accident."

Artie knew he was supposed to say something for the record, but he couldn't. So he just shook his head and took some deep breaths.

"That's when you went to live with your grandparents, isn't it?" Clearly the judge wanted to get him talking again.

Artie looked up. "It seems like you know my story pretty well already. I don't see why we need to go through all this."

"It's for the record, Artie. And so I can try to understand how you feel about things. I don't ever want to pass judgment on a person until I know something about them. Now, you went to live with your grandparents and from what I understand, they were pretty good people."

"My grandpa is *still* a good person. It wasn't our fault that my grandma passed away last year." Talking about his grandmother made Artie feel panicky again, like he was going to cry yet another time. The truth is that Grandma was the best person he had ever known, and he loved her like a mother. But then she died. And that's just what people did. They made you love them, and then they died.

"I don't know if you know this, Artie, but your grandmother and I were very good friends. She was one of my school teachers when I was a boy. We all loved her. I can only imagine how hard it was on you when she died, too."

Was the judge trying to make him cry? He was saying all these nice things, but he had to know that it was the kind of stuff that made a person feel bad. The last thing a kid needs is to have other people see him cry.

"Can you tell me what you're thinking, Artie?"

Artie looked up reluctantly. Aaron's warning sounded loud and clear in his mind, and he knew he had to keep his temper. "It made me and my grandpa feel bad."

"So since you know what it feels like to feel really bad why is it that you do mean things to Mr. Marchant?"

So this was where the judge had been heading him to all this time. It made Artie angry to think that he'd just been trying to find a way to get him all mushy and sad so that he'd open up and tell the truth about something that was none of his business. Still, he knew he couldn't just sit there, so he finally said, "I don't know why I do it. I guess it just shows that I'm bad."

The judge sat back in his chair and stroked his chin. It bothered him that Artie was doing nothing to help his case. He suspected there was a reason, but it was obvious the boy wasn't going to say what it was. It was one of those times when a young man gets himself backed into a corner where he can't get out. But it still didn't leave the judge much room to compromise.

"Well, Artie, I'm in kind of a tough spot—" Just then the judge was interrupted by a hand in the air. While it wasn't at all usual to have spectators want to say something, this was a juvenile session, so he decided to let the woman talk.

"Yes, Mrs. Weston? Can you shed some light on this?"

Joey's mother cleared her throat nervously. Artie guessed that she wasn't used to spending much time in a courthouse. In fact, this was probably the first time. She had probably gone there to defend Joey. Knowing that Joey was in trouble made Artie feel even worse. "Your honor, sir, it's just that . . ." her voice choked off.

"Why don't you come up here closer where I can hear you more easily? In fact, if you don't mind, I think I'll have my clerk put you under oath so we can make a record of what you say." Artie saw her face blanch, but she bravely stepped forward and accepted the Bible that the clerk held out. She swore to tell the truth and then sat in a chair not more than three feet from Artie.

"What can you add, Mrs. Weston?"

"Well, your honor, it's just that Artie often plays with my boy Joey. Most of the time it's just harmless fun, but every now and then Artie gets them in trouble."

"I understand that. It's why we're here today."

"Yes, sir. Well, it's just that when Joey does get in trouble, I ask him why Artie does these things. It seems almost out of character for him, because he always acts very polite and well behaved when he comes to our house."

"And what has Joey told you?"

Mrs. Weston looked at Artie nervously as if she was pretty certain that he wouldn't want her to tell what she knew. At first Artie wasn't concerned, but then it dawned on him what she might say, and he stood up quickly.

"I don't want her to tell you anything. You can go ahead and send me to reform school, but don't listen to her!" He looked up at the judge desperately.

The judge motioned for Pastor Wyndham to go sit next to Artie. "I'm sorry," the judge said, "but I have to know everything I can. And it seems like Mrs. Weston knows something that may be important. Even if you don't want us to hear it, I'm going to let her speak."

Artie let out a strangled sort of groan and then slumped forward in his chair. He somehow knew that everything was lost.

"Well, Mrs. Weston?"

At this point, everyone in the room was leaning forward to hear whatever it was she had to say. The mystery was intriguing. "It's just that one day Joey told me that Mr. Marchant called Artie's grandfather stupid and said that he was losing his mind. Mr. Marchant said that he had a good mind to tell people that Artie's grandpa was going senile. It seems like it was after that that Artie started doing all these mean things to him."

"It's true!" shouted Wilford Marchant. "The old buzzard is going senile! He nearly burned down his house a few weeks ago. He ain't fit to have no child living with him! He's a danger to society, and he needs to be put in an old-folks home. I said it, and I meant it!"

"I told you to be quiet, Mr. Marchant. I don't care how old you are; you will still show respect in my courtroom!"

"It's not true!" Artie couldn't stop himself from standing up. "My grandpa is just fine. All we want is to be left alone. That mean old coot has threatened to make up terrible stories about my grandpa. That's why I had to make him stop. They're lies!" Pastor Wyndham was doing his best to get Artie to sit down. His thin little body was trembling with rage, and the judge knew that they'd finally plumbed the depth of the matter.

"Artie. Sit down!"

Artie did sit down, the misery showing in his face. "Please don't put him away, judge. He's the only thing I've got. He needs me. He's a bit forgetful, sometimes, and he doesn't always know everything he should do, but he's not senile."

"He hits the boy!" said Marchant, as though speaking under his breath, but still loud enough that everyone could hear.

"What's that, Mr. Marchant?" When Marchant looked up surprised, the judge motioned for him to repeat himself.

"He hits the boy—I've seen it. He gets turned around when he's outside, and when the boy tries to get him straightened around, he whacks him. I'm no fan of Artie Call, but he doesn't deserve that. His grandpa used to be a nice man, but not anymore. He's getting more and more mean every day."

"Why didn't you tell us this before? Clearly this has bearing on the case. I gave you the chance to tell your side of events earlier, and you didn't bring this up. All you said is that Artie should go to reform school."

Marchant got a tortured look on his face. Now it was his turn to be embarrassed. "I didn't tell you, because he threatened me. The boy told me that if I ever told anybody anything about his grandpa that he'd find some way to hurt me. I know it sounds foolish, but I'm getting old and the last thing I need is to have some young thug angry at me. I thought if you just put him away, I'd be safe. But in case you didn't put him away, I didn't want him mad at me for telling on his grandpa."

As he looked across the courtroom, Judge Farnsworth saw a site that he could never could have imagined when he first got his law degree. Artie was sobbing in the center chair under Pastor John Wyndham's arm while Mrs. Wyndham was as pale as a ghost. He saw Mrs. Weston's hands trembling from the strain of telling her part of the story, and even David Boone seemed shaken. Wilford Marchant was both defiant and frightened. And now they expected him to somehow make everything right.

But he wasn't quite ready. "Artie, I need you to talk with me, just a little bit more." Pastor Wyndham helped Artie raise his head. "Are the things that Mr. Marchant has just said about your grandfather true? Remember that you're under oath, and you swore to tell the whole truth."

The misery on Artie's face troubled the judge. This boy that everyone judged to be so tough and hard was possibly the softest one in the room. After losing everyone who mattered in his life to an early death, Artie had to watch his grandfather start to decline. Even so, Artie had been hell-bent on protecting him, even if it meant taking on the meanest man in town. It was true. Wilford Marchant was mean and always had been. Kids had called him "Old Man Marchant" even when the judge was a boy. The only thing is that until Artie came along, no one ever had the courage to stand up to him. And now he knew why Artie did. It was for someone else.

"Artie? Was Mr. Marchant telling the truth?"

"It's only kind of true. It's true that he gets confused and does things he shouldn't. Like last week he started a fire without first opening the flue. That's not such a bad thing, except that he'd put green wood in the stove, and before you knew it, the house was filled with smoke. There wasn't any real danger of him starting a fire—it just looked like that. I was able to get things straightened out with no trouble. But it shook him up kind of bad, so he swatted me. It wasn't hard, though. I've received a lot worse. And sometimes he gets a little mean when he gets confused, and he yells at me. But I'm not the only kid who gets yelled at or hit once in awhile. Most everyone does, so I don't see why you have to hold that against him."

Artie looked up with pleading eyes. "I know you should send me to reform school, but if you do, I don't know what will become of my grandpa. He needs me."

Judge Farnsworth drew in his breath and released it slowly. "This certainly brings some interesting new information to light. I'll need to do more investigating. In the meantime, for your grandfather's own safety and yours, we're going to ask a doctor to look in on your grandfather. He might not like it, but I think it's what we have to do."

"Yes, sir."

"And since that may take a few days, we need a place for you to stay."

"We'd be glad to take him in, your honor." Artie looked up in gratitude at Pastor Wyndham.

"I know you would. But with seven children of your own and with so many in your congregation out of work, that doesn't make any sense. No, we'll have to find a foster home. In the meantime he can stay here in the county jail. We'll keep him apart from the adult prisoners."

In what was turning into a very unusual hearing the judge saw another hand go up. "Yes, David?"

"The boy can come live with us for a time. We have room, and it might do him good to be in a regular family situation."

Artie wheeled in alarm. The last person he wanted to live with was David Boone. He hated Artie. And Artie felt the same way about him. This was probably just a ploy to get at Artie.

"Your honor!" shouted Artie, but the judge shushed him.

The expression on the judge's face settled. "It seems like this is the best course. I award temporary custody of Arthur William Call to Mr. and Mrs. David Boone. I also order the sheriff to transport Artie's grandfather to the state hospital for a mental health evaluation. The future disposition of this case will await that evaluation."

Artie raised his hand, and Judge Farnsworth reluctantly acknowledged him.

"It's just that he doesn't want go to an old-folks home. And the state mental hospital is even worse. He told me that he'd sooner die. Please don't send him there."

"Unfortunately, Artie, we sometimes don't get a choice in such matters. Sometimes we have to go to a place for our own good, rather than where we want to."

Even as he said this, the judge realized that no one in the world understood that better than the fourteen-year-old boy sitting in front of him. The boy who had been shuttled between adults his whole life, undoubtedly with people telling him it was for the best each and every time. This boy had a terrified and defeated look in his eyes.

"One last thing. While you may not like my decision, you need to behave at the Boones'. That's the only way I can help you. Do you understand?"

"Yes, sir," Artie replied, sullenly.

Although nearly everyone had something else to say, the judge was finished with the proceeding, and he picked up his gavel and banged it on his desk.

CHAPTER 4

Life in the Boonedocks

October 1932

"Artie, mind your manners!"

This was perhaps the ten thousandth time that Artie had heard this injunction from Mrs. Olivia Boone since he arrived at the Boones' three weeks earlier. The Boones were, to put it kindly, a "formal" family. They had just one daughter, Monica, who was twenty-four years old. Monica was not, in Artie's opinion, attractive in the least. But her looks exceeded her personality, which was stuffy and conceited. She had thrown a temper tantrum—worthy or a five year old—when she learned that Artie was moving in, but her father had quickly squelched the reaction by explaining that it was their civic duty and that if Artie was to have any chance of becoming a productive member of society, he needed the company of a "good" family like the Boones in order to overcome the bad effects of so many undisciplined years with his no-account father and grandfather. When Artie protested this characterization, "Mr." Boone, as Artie was instructed to call him, promptly introduced him to a new regimen that was intended to improve his moral character.

"Interrupting adults is simply not acceptable, young man, and we must find a way to help you appreciate that fact. So at 7:00 PM tonight, you and I will go out into the yard to cut a good, strong willow branch, and at 8:00 PM., before bed, we will use the switch as a whip. For this first infraction you will receive three stripes. Do you understand?"

When Artie attempted to protest, the number was raised to four. When he asked why he had to wait until 7:00 PM, he was told that it was to give him time to anticipate his punishment so that he would reflect on it more seriously and perhaps feel a greater anxiety from his disobedience. Since he didn't request permission to ask this question, the number of stripes was raised to five. Even though he was burning up inside, Artie finally understood the trend that was developing so he relented to Mr. Boone. He only hoped he could bear the stripes without wincing or crying out.

After that first night, Artie had done his best to avoid provoking the family, but it seemed like he was always running afoul of rules he didn't know about or understand. For example, it was only after he started wiping some leaves off Mr. Boone's Model-A Ford that he learned that one isn't supposed to touch the car, even to bring about a good result. For scriptural support, Mr. Boone recounted the story of the man who attempted to steady the Ark of the Covenant from falling to the ground and who lost his life for the effrontery of acting out of his place. Wiping leaves off the car wasn't worthy of that severe a punishment, but it did earn Artie two stripes. Then there was the rule that one never took a drink from the outside well since touching one's lips to the bucket must inevitably contaminate the whole container. Three stripes. The worst punishment was reserved, however, for the times when Artie sneaked away to be with friends like Joey or Aaron. Mr. Boone had explained that he should see no one but the family for at least four weeks so that he could learn proper discipline, but that was too much for Artie and he'd been caught on two occasions when leaving or returning to the home. Five or even six stripes was the payment for that most serious of offenses.

"It really makes him angry when you don't yell or cry when he's spanking you." Artie nearly jumped out of his skin at the sound of Monica's voice, coming from just a few inches behind him. She must have sneaked up on him while he was standing on the back porch, smarting from his most recent beating.

"What?" Artie asked, even though he had heard her the first time. He just couldn't believe she was talking to him about her father.

"I said that it makes him really angry when you don't make any noise. He wants you to react so that he knows he's getting through to you."

Artie couldn't tell if she was pleased by her father's increasing anger or if she was trying to warn him. Something in his mind told him he should be careful how he responded, but he decided he didn't care. He was angry enough that he was glad to have someone to talk to, even if it was a member of the Boone family.

"I know it does. Last week when he caught me coming home late because I'd stopped to see Joey, I decided that no matter what happened, I wasn't going to make a sound—not a single, solitary sound. I didn't want to give him the pleasure of knowing he was hurting me. But a lot of good that did."

"I know, he just kept hitting you until mother finally stepped in. He must have hit you twenty times."

"Twelve. I counted them. But with a green willow whip." Artie's face burned at the thought, since he'd had to drop the backside of his trousers so that the whip could strike him on his bare butt. It had been very hard to sit in a chair the rest of that night and the next day.

"So why do you do it? Why not just cry and act hurt so that he quits?"

"Because . . ." Artie couldn't finish because he really didn't know why he didn't go along with the game.

Monica continued, almost as if in a trance. "He just kept hitting you and hitting you until you were bleeding. And his face was dripping with sweat, so it had to be hard on him, too. But you didn't say anything, so he just kept on."

Artie didn't know what to say now, so he just stayed silent.

"He never beat me, you know."

"I know. He tells me that. You were always perfect."

"No, I wasn't. He just didn't want me to tell stories to people. He thinks Boones should be perfect naturally, without having to work at it. If he had had to hit me, that would have been a sign of family inferiority, so that was never going to happen. But he hits you because he's convinced that it's perfectly acceptable for him to discipline a delinquent. In fact, I think he wants you to tell people so they'll see how firm he is and how hard he's working to make you turn out all right. It's all about how people think about him. You know that, don't you?"

Artie pondered that for a moment. He hadn't ever thought of it like that. He wasn't even sure what it meant, so he finally just shook his head.

"Well, it is. He doesn't care a thing about any of us, except for how we make him look. It's all about his reputation. I didn't get beatings, but I got lectured. *Boy*, did I get lectured. And the disappointed sighs when I received something less than the best score on a math test or something." Her voice had grown cold, and the pace had quickened. It was almost scary how angry she was, and Artie wished that she wasn't telling him all that.

So he tried to defuse the situation. "Still, I guess it's my fault. He does have rules, and I should obey them."

Monica shook her head as she came out of her thoughts. "Rules? Yes, my father has rules. All kinds of rules—for me, for mother, and now for you. But none for him. No, he gets to make the rules. But someday . . ."

Their discussion was interrupted by Mr. Boone shouting from somewhere inside the house, "Olivia, where is that girl? She has a job interview tomorrow, and she should be rehearsing what she'll say! She's going to fail this interview if she doesn't pay attention, just like all the others."

Artie turned and looked at Monica, frightened for her. But when he saw her blushed and crestfallen face, he felt sorry.

"Sometimes I think you're lucky," she said through clenched teeth. "All he does is whip you. I know it hurts when it happens, but at least it heals. Some things never heal . . ." The look on her face was dark and foreboding, but she didn't say anything else. Instead, she pursed her lips, turned, and disappeared inside the house.

* * *

November 1932

Dinner was served promptly at 6:00 p.m. each night, never one minute earlier nor one minute later. The meal always consisted of a single piece of bread with butter, a preserved vegetable like green beans, a modest helping of meat such as chicken or meatloaf, and, happily, some kind of dessert with milk. Usually dessert was bottled fruit, but occasionally the cook was allowed to turn the fruit into a pie, which Artie loved. Once each week they went out for ice cream and on one occasion Mr. Boone took them to a restaurant. That was something Artie had never experienced before. They became impatient with him when he couldn't decide what to order, but he'd never been given so many choices before, and he simply didn't know how to decide.

The Boones' house was perpetually quiet, except for the one radio show they liked to listen to each evening from seven to eight. Aside from that, the women sewed or did needlepoint, and Mr. Boone read books and reports. Often he read religious books, which seemed to have great appeal to Mr. Boone. At 8:30 p.m. they assembled for reading from the Bible for fifteen minutes, and then Artie was sent to bed in a huge, old brass bed on the enclosed back porch. It was very cold out there, but the Boones explained that it was good for Artie and would force him to stay in his bed until morning. They explained that they would try to find a heater but that he'd just have to get by in the meantime. Artie shrugged and said that he wasn't going to live there that long, anyway, since he'd soon be back with his grandfather. Mr. Boone simply scoffed and told him that it was highly likely that his grandfather would be certified incapable of living on his own. So that was that. When Artie grew defiant over that, there were more stripes. But far worse than the whipping was the thought of living with the Boones forever. In his wildest imagination, Artie could not picture himself staying with them, even through the rest of the winter.

One evening, Mr. Boone instructed Artie to stay at the table after the ladies had retired.

"Yes, sir," he said nervously.

"I think you'll be pleased to know that I've arranged a job for you at Derkin's Hardware Store. You'll help Mr. Derkin load supplies onto trucks or wagons, fetch supplies from the back room, and do anything else that he asks you. You can work after school and on Saturdays. I assume that's all right with you." It was not a question, even though it looked like one on paper.

"I'll be glad to work for Mr. Derkin." Artie liked the idea that he'd have someplace to go after school, rather than home to the Boones'.

"Of course you have to keep up with your school work, since that's most important. You'll need to do your homework as soon as dinner as finished."

"Yes, sir."

"Good. I'll tell Derkin tomorrow. Stop by my office on your way home from school, and I'll introduce you to him. He can tell you when to start."

* * *

"Hello, Artie."

Artie froze at the sound of Stephanie Lewis's voice.

"I said, hello, Artie."

Stephanie's friend laughed at his discomfiture.

"Uh, hello."

"I like your new clothes," said Stephanie pleasantly.

Artie glanced down at the new shirt that Mrs. Boone had bought him and his freshly pressed trousers. The Boones sent all their clothes out to a Chinese laundry, and they always came back stiff from the starch. It scratched him a lot, but now all the irritation seemed well worth it. "Thanks." It was obvious that Stephanie wanted to talk, but Artie didn't know what to say.

"Well, I guess I better be going."

"Yeah. Okay." Artie shook his head in self-disgust. Her girlfriend laughed, again, but Stephanie smiled at him. As she started away, he called out, "You're dress is real pretty, too." She turned and smiled again. And Artie nearly collapsed from the lack of breath.

* * *

"I told you I'm sorry! But you really have to go. That's my final answer!" When the man standing at David Boone's desk didn't leave, Boone added, "I said go!" For a moment, Artie thought the man was going to hit Mr. Boone, the way he glowered at him. But then the fellow said something under his breath and turned and shoved his way toward the door, knocking Artie to the floor as he went by him.

For his part, Boone was flushed. He stepped forward and extended a hand to help Artie up. "I'm sorry about that. Are you all right?"

"Yes, sir." Artie's eyes were as round as saucers. He wasn't alone. Many of the customers in the bank had a shocked expression. When David Boone seemed to sense that, he cleared his throat and then said in a loud voice. "It's all right, folks. Just a little misunderstanding. It's all cleared up now, and everything is fine." Boone then excused himself to go to the lavatory.

Artie sat down in the chair next to Boone's desk, where he watched the crowd start to chatter. It died down quickly when Boone emerged a few moments later. Artie noticed that he'd straightened his clothing and looked like nothing had happened.

"Now, then, I think we need to go see Bill Derkin."

"Yes, sir. But why was that man angry?"

"Angry? I don't think anyone was angry. I just needed to clarify some points for the man. That's all."

Artie wanted to protest that he seemed pretty angry to him, but Boone's face masked any emotion he might have been feeling, so Artie let the matter drop.

"Now, let's be off. I don't have a lot of time. A bank's a busy place, and the manager needs to be here."

* * *

As Thanksgiving weekend approached, Artie found that he thoroughly enjoyed his job at the hardware store. He liked all the bustle and noise and loved to listen to the men talk as they came in to buy supplies or tools.

Besides, Mr. Derkin treated him very well, even allowing him to talk with Joey or Aaron occasionally on his break. Apparently that was even all right with Mr. Boone, since he could see them talking from his window in the bank directly across the street from the hardware store The only thing he ever said was, "Don't spend so much time talking to your friends that Mr. Derkin needs to correct you."

Artie had replied, "Yes, sir," and resolved that he would take Mr. Boone's advice. The last thing he wanted to do was to lose the job and have to go straight home after school.

Of course, living with the Boones also meant that Artie had to start going to church again. He'd never gone during the years he lived with his father, apparently because his father was embarrassed by his alcoholism. Then when his grandmother was alive, he went every week. He liked church, even though he often got in trouble because he had so much restless energy. For example, when he got excited, he almost couldn't help but stand up, which was distracting to both the teacher and the other students in his Sunday School class. If he knew the answer to a question, he was so impatient to answer that he often blurted out the answer out before being called on, which was another infraction. But his most serious offenses fell in the range of touching, poking, and generally aggravating other kids. When asked why he did it, he couldn't explain, but it often caused him to be put out in the hall. Aaron and Joey were the only two who had accepted him in spite of his behavior. And his grandmother. Even though she had sometimes shown her disappointment, she had been his advocate no matter what the provocation. After her death, Artie and his grandfather kept going for awhile, but when his grandfather started getting forgetful, Artie simply stopped reminding him that it was Sunday, and they soon started missing meetings on a regular basis. When no one followed up to see why they weren't there, the habit stuck.

But David Boone was a resolute member of the congregation, and Artie understood from the outset that he was expected to go. Mr. Boone even took him to buy a new suit, shirt, and tie. He cut quite a figure in the suit, which made him proud to go. This time he resolved that he would do everything possible to be orderly, since he could only imagine the rebuke he'd receive if he messed up at church.

* * *

December 1932

"Excuse, me, sir, but have you heard anything about my grandfather? I was hoping that maybe he'd get out of the old-folks home in time for my birthday.

"Your birthday! When is your birthday?" Olivia Boone sometimes had a shrill voice when taken by surprise.

"December twelfth, ma'am."

"How old will you be?"

"Fifteen."

"Oh, for heaven's sake. I suppose we'll have to do something for it—"

"Your grandfather will not be getting out," David Boone said, not hesitating to cut his wife off.

"You mean this month?" Artie watched Boone's reaction and then said in a more emotional voice, "or that he'll never get out?"

"Never," Boone said in an absolutely flat voice. "Judge Farnsworth has declared him mentally incompetent and a danger to himself and society, so he'll be a permanent resident of the home."

Artie's eyes flashed. "But he can't do that. He can't just lock someone up when he hasn't broken any laws!"

Boone stood up abruptly, almost knocking over his chair. "Stop shouting this instant, young man! You know we have rules of behavior in this house!"

Artie shrunk from the force of Boone's rebuke. But he did register the irony that while shouting was forbidden for Artie, it was apparently perfectly all right for Mr. Boone.

"I'm sorry," Artie mumbled. "But it's just that I think that it's unfair—"

"I'm afraid that what you think doesn't matter. There are laws to protect people, including protecting them from themselves." Boone had regained his composure just that quickly.

"But…"

Boone softened. "Tell me truthfully, Artie. Do you think your grandfather can function on his own? You visit him often enough."

Artie swallowed hard. "No, sir. But, he'd have me."

"And you need to be in school and at work, so you can't be there with him. Who would watch him while you're gone?"

Of course Artie had no answer for that, since there wasn't one. "But he doesn't like it there," he said softly.

"Well, it may not be for long. It seems that when people start to deteriorate mentally, their body quickly follows."

"David!" Olivia said. "That is not a very kind way to talk to Artie about his grandfather."

Boone rolled his eyes. "You heard him, Olivia. He's about to turn fifteen years old. I would think that he could take the truth in a straightforward fashion by this age."

Artie sat quietly. He really didn't have anything to say—he was so saddened by this news. Sad for both his grandfather and for himself. In a very real sense they were both prisoners of Judge Farnsworth, who could tell them where to live and with whom.

"Well, maybe he will live a long time—who knows?" Boone said this in a condescending way as if he had to suffer his wife's and Artie's sentimentality. "But from a financial point of view, it would be better if he doesn't linger. We'll have to start selling his property to pay for his care. Right now, we can sell the farmland he owns and keep the house, just in case. But it won't take long before it's all gone, and he'll be living on charity. If he dies fairly soon, however, there may be something left for you, Artie. If there is, we'll put it in a trust fund for you. After all, the worst thing that could happen would be for you to get a lot of money all at once. As irresponsible as you are, you'd waste it in no time."

"I don't want Grandpa to die so I can get money! I want him to move back to his house so we can live together again. That's all I want."

"Well, I don't think that's likely to happen. So whether you like it or not, you're likely to get an inheritance."

Somehow Boone made it sound like his grandfather's bad health was a good thing, which left Artie fuming, but he didn't want to get in a fight.

"Can I visit him? Has anybody told him? If not, I think I should. He might not feel so bad if it comes from me."

"Of course you can," Mrs. Boone quickly answered. Apparently even she was frightened by the thought that the simple gesture would be denied.

While Mr. Boone looked at her sharply, he didn't contradict her. "I'll take you there tomorrow. Just to make sure he understands."

Artie wanted to shout at him that he was perfectly capable of explaining things to his grandfather without David Boone's help, but he squeezed his jaws closed so that he wouldn't say something that would prevent him from visiting his grandfather. He would visit him as often as possible from now on, no matter how bad his memory got.

Later that night, when he was given permission to visit Aaron for an hour, he told him all about it.

"What a rotten thing to say. He's treating you and your grandfather like you're children."

"I know, but it won't last forever."

"What do you mean?"

"I mean that I've come up with a plan."

Sometimes Artie's plans weren't all that well thought out, which is probably why Aaron pressed him.

"I need to stay in Boise while my grandpa's alive. And I need to stay on Boone's good side so I can go see him. But when he does . . ." Artie's voice caught. "When he does pass on, then I'm going to get out of Boise once and for all."

"And how will you do that?"

"I'll jump a train. My grandpa's the only family I've got, and when he's gone, there's nothing to keep me here. Maybe I'll go to Portland or Seattle. I hear there's work in the lumber industry. Or fishing." He looked up at Aaron seriously. "It's gotta be better than here."

"What about California?"

Artie nodded. "California might be nice. They say it stays warm all year round. I'd like that." Artie was thoughtful and then asked Aaron, "Where would you go if you decided to run away?"

"Me? I'd go to California for sure. That's where they make movies, you know."

"You want to make movies?"

"I don't know if I want to make them. But I want to do something with them. There's a lot more to a movie than just standing people in front of a camera, you know. Somebody's got to buy the stuff that shows up in the film, somebody else has to build the sets, and there are always the people who own the theaters where they're shown. I think I'd like doing any one of those things."

"Hmm. I wish I knew what I wanted to do with my life, like you do. You're pretty lucky, I guess."

"So?"

"So, what?"

"So where are you going to go when your grandfather dies and you run away?"

Artie shook his head. "I'll probably figure that out when the first train rolls out of the switch yard. Wherever it's headed is where I'll go."

Normally Aaron would object, but somehow this sounded pretty reasonable given Artie's personality. If you don't care where you wind up, then what difference does it make which train you catch?

"But you've got to be good to the Boones in the meantime so you have a place to stay."

"I know. But it's hard. Their schedules and rules are about making me crazy. But I'll do my best."

"I think you're going to be all right," said Aaron tentatively. "Something will happen to Mr. Boone so that he lets up on you." Aaron's voice had an odd quality to it when he said this. Artie was surprised at just how much animosity Aaron had for David Boone. But he decided not to press the point.

"I hope so. I hope I don't just go crazy or something." He looked up and smiled. "Thank heavens the food is good. At least that makes it tolerable."

CHAPTER 5

Reuben and Jake

February 1933

"Hey Call!"

Artie's blood ran chill as he heard the grating voice of Reuben Kinley. He pretended not to hear.

"Artie! Wait up!"

This time it was Jake Carter, whom, if he had to choose, Artie preferred. Recognizing that it was hopeless, he stopped and turned around. They were in an alley behind Grove Street, and Artie had just finished making a delivery for the hardware store.

"Hi!" said Artie, as casually as he could.

"Have you been avoiding us?" asked Jake a bit breathlessly as they caught up with Artie.

"What?"

"Of course he has," said Reuben with a sneer. "He's a suit and tie guy now that he lives with that old banker and his family of misfits."

Artie was surprised at his own reaction to Reuben's words. He found himself irritated that Reuben was making fun of the Boones. In spite of the harsh treatment he sometimes received from Mr. Boone, the family was generally nice enough to him, and they made certain that he had whatever he needed. Even Monica wasn't as bad as he thought at first, particularly since she'd started talking to him on the porch. But it made no sense to say something positive about them to Reuben, since he'd just twist it.

"Cat got your tongue?" Reuben slapped the side of Artie's face as he said this, which made Artie's temper flash instantly. But as much as he wanted to slam his fist into Reuben's face, he'd seen a number of kids get beaten up by these two before, and he knew he was no match for them. So he mentally vowed not to let Reuben provoke him.

"I bet you've figured out how to rob Boone's bank by now. You're going to let us in on it, aren't you?"

Artie turned to Jake with an astonished look on his face. "Like you think Mr. Boone ever takes me to any part of his bank? He can hardly stand me, so why would he take me to work?" The last part was maybe a little bit of a lie, since Artie didn't really believe Mr. Boone couldn't stand him. He just probably didn't like him all that much. And there had been the one time he went to the bank before being taken to the hardware store, but he only got inside as far as Mr. Boone's desk. But the tone of the conversation forced him to draw the lines pretty hard.

Reuben sighed and looked around restlessly. "We don't have time for this. Look, Call, here's the deal. You're in the perfect position to skim some goods from the hardware store. We've been wanting to get into that place for months, and now you're on the inside. They've got some pretty good stuff, and you can help us get it."

"What?"

"What?" Reuben repeated in a mocking voice. "You really are a brilliant guy, Artie. You have the best answers I've ever heard. You should be a lawyer someday."

"I won't do it! They pay me to work there, and I won't steal from them."

"Oh, I see" said Reuben, rocking back again with a smile. "I get it. You want to keep it all for yourself. You don't want to share anything with your old pals."

"I'm not keeping anything for myself. It's not fair to take things from some-body who pays you."

"Ah, but it's okay to steal food from strangers?"

Artie's face flushed. He had known that this would come back to haunt him. He also knew that if these two snitched on him, he would almost certainly go to reform school, and he didn't want to go there while his grandfather was still alive. Still, in spite of the risk, he repeated, "I won't do it!"

He thought Reuben was going to hit him, but then he saw Reuben's eyes grow wide, and he turned to see a policeman enter the alley from behind him. "You're real lucky that he's here, Call, or I'd have pounded you." Reuben looked around quickly, trying to figure out the best way to make a nonchalant escape.

He turned back to Artie. "Okay, you win. We won't make you take from the hardware store. But this isn't over. You still owe us, and you told us as much.

We're gonna collect one way or the other, either by getting your help on a job or by watching you go to jail."

"You'd go with me!" said Artie with something of a tremble in his voice.

"And that would make it even more fun, wouldn't it!" Reuben sneered when he said this, and Artie caught his meaning immediately.

"What are you no-accounts up to?" The voice of the police officer cut through the air.

Reuben stepped away from Artie. "Just talking to an old friend, officer. Nothing illegal about that, is there, sir?"

The officer looked at Artie suspiciously "Nothing illegal about talking, but Artie has a job to do, and you're interrupting him." The policeman touched Artie's shoulder with his night stick. "You better get on your way. These two will do you no good."

"Yes, sir. Thank you, sir." Artie cast a sideways glance at Reuben, who simply smiled back at him. As Artie made it to the end of the block and turned onto the main street, he felt like he was going to throw up. He hated that Reuben and Jake had power over him, but he didn't know what to do about it. It was at that moment that the words of his Sunday School teacher, Mrs. Neeley, came to mind, and he decided to try a silent prayer. *"Please, God, help me."* He didn't know what else to say, so he decided to trust God to figure it out.

* * *

March 1933

Sunday was rapidly becoming one of Artie's favorite days. Not so much because of church, although he didn't mind that, but rather because Mr. Boone had given him permission to spend the whole afternoon with friends. Each afternoon between Sunday School and evening service, he could go over to Aaron's or Joey's house for Sunday dinner. Mr. Boone made it sound like this was a great sacrifice on the part of the Boone family, but Artie suspected they were happy to have him out of the house for awhile. Either way, he was happy to spend time with his friends and their families. Besides, he often stopped by the old folks home to visit his grandfather.

While talking with Aaron about how he liked going back to church, one Sunday afternoon, Aaron added, "Of course, there's also Stephanie Lewis."

"What?"

"You say that a lot, don't you?"

"What? I say what?"

"Yes, you say 'what'."

Artie shook his head to try to clear. "What do I say a lot?"

Aaron laughed. "When people take you by surprise, you always respond by saying the word *what*. That's what I'm saying."

"Well, thank you for pointing that out! I'll be sure to change it from time to time with statements like, 'Oh, my goodness, Aaron, you just took me by surprise. I don't know what to say for a minute or two while I try to organize my thoughts."

Aaron laughed. Which was exactly what Artie hoped for. He wanted to divert the subject from Stephanie Lewis. She was easily the best-looking girl in all of Boise. Artie suspected that she may be the best looking girl in Idaho, or the United States, or perhaps even the whole world, for that matter. It bothered him that his face sometimes got warm when he saw her, and it was even more embarrassing that he became tongue-tied every time she said hello to him. He'd never once been able to have a normal conversation with her. And if Aaron had noticed it, others had probably noticed too, which was embarrassing.

Aaron recognized Artie's consternation about Stephanie, so he didn't follow up. Instead he started talking about whether Artie was going to be able to play baseball when practice started in March.

"I'll have to ask Mr. Boone. I know he expects me to keep my job at the hardware store, so I probably won't have time."

Aaron nodded. "That's too bad. You're good at baseball and one of the best runners we've got. Still, it's a pretty good job. How long have you been there?"

"Almost six months. I get a raise if I stay at it."

"Do you get to keep any of that?"

Artie knew that Aaron was disgusted by the fact that Boone didn't let him keep much of the money he earned. The rule was that he had to put fully one-half of what he earned into a savings account at the bank, and only then could he use the rest to buy clothes for school and things like that. But even though he wished he had more spending money, Artie recognized that it was a good thing to have this kind of discipline. Particularly since there was enough left over for an occasional malt or soda.

Artie looked up at the clock. "Well, I guess I better get going. I want to stop by and see my grandpa before I go home."

* * *

April 1933

Artie crumpled the note that had hit him from behind. It was from Reuben, and it said simply, "Meet us tonight at ten behind your old house. You better be there, or else."

He shook his head as he walked down the street. It would be easy enough to get away, since the Boones had started trusting him. He could easily slip off of the porch where he slept, leaving a mound inside the covers of the bed just in case they checked. Hopefully he wouldn't be gone long and could be back and safely in bed with no one taking any notice.

But getting away was the least of his worries. He wondered what scheme the two guys had cooked up and what role he was to play in it. The rest of the day was pretty agonizing since he had to pretend that everything was normal when it most decidedly was not.

Making things worse, it was Wednesday night, and he had to go to the church youth group meeting. When he got there, he found that Aaron was in an unusually talkative mood, Joey was cheerful, and neither one could understand why Artie was so subdued. They tried to tease it out of him, but of course there was nothing he could say. So he did his best to limp through the program without being too obvious, but it was hard.

Finally, the meeting ended and he raced home. A little after nine, he excused himself to go to bed early since he was tired. Mr. Boone raised an eyebrow at the unexpected change in Artie's routine but didn't say anything other than good night. When he got to the porch, Artie took care to undress so as to not raise any suspicion, but then he tucked his pants and shirt under the covers. Once in bed he pulled his pants back on and waited. At a quarter to ten, he listened with relief as he heard each of the members of the Boone family climb the stairs to their bedrooms. One of the luckiest discoveries he'd made early on is that there was one squeaky stair that always gave a distinctive squeal when stepped on. That was Artie's early warning when someone in the family was going either up the stairs or down, and it had saved him from getting in trouble on more than one occasion.

As he slipped off the back of the porch, turning around and glancing back at his bed to make sure his artificial body under the covers looked natural, he quickly left to the street. The other big break he had in living with the Boones is that Mr. Boone didn't like dogs. He thought they were filthy creatures who carried disease, so Artie never had to worry about disturbing some barking dog. At around ten, he slipped up to the outbuilding behind his grandfather's house and waited. A little after ten, he heard a rustling by the building, and he braced himself for whatever was coming.

"So you decided to save your life, huh, Call?"

Artie didn't reply. The fewer words he shared with Reuben, the better.

"Not in a talkative mood? Boone has probably beat it out of you."

"What do you mean?" Artie asked sharply.

Reuben snorted. "You think people don't know that he whips you? Everybody knows. He brags about it. He likes to tell people that he's going to turn you into a regular citizen yet." He looked at him with a sneer, his face rather ghostly in appearance in the light of the full moon. "Is that true? Are you planning to become a regular citizen? A true-blue American?"

"What I'm planning is my business. Now what do you want from me?"

"Temper, temper," said Jake. Clearly they were both enjoying this.

"That's all right. He can get mad all he wants. As long as he does what we tell him. You'll do what we tell you, won't you?"

"I suppose that depends on what you tell me."

"None of that," said Reuben sharply. "We gave into you once. But not again. This time you'll do exactly what we tell you with no guff or arguments. Otherwise we inform Mr. Manning about what happened to all that food last spring. And don't get any ideas. He won't turn us in, because it will be our word against yours – which is two against one."

"That and the fact that he's afraid of Reuben," added Jake with a forced laugh.

Artie felt sick to his stomach. He knew it was true. They could easily send him away for good.

"So what am I supposed to do?"

"You promise you won't snitch?" Reuben asked forcefully.

"What? Snitch? I'm no snitch."

"You better not be, because if you did something stupid like telling anybody what we're going to do, we'd have to hurt you. And I'm not joking. We'd really hurt you." There was an ominous sound to his voice, almost as if he hoped that Artie would do something stupid.

"I'm not a snitch! Now what do you want?"

Reuben looked around, and Jake went out on a short scouting party to make sure nobody happened to be within earshot. When it was established that the coast was clear, Reuben scooted right up next to Artie in a way that made Artie's skin crawl. "All right, Call, here's what's up. Do you know that rich widow Mary Wilkerson?"

"The one who lives up on Warm Springs Avenue?"

"That's the one."

"What about her?"

"Well, we have it on good authority that she has gold coins stored in her basement. Her husband made his fortune in mining, you know. At any rate, we have a pretty good idea where she keeps it. So we're going to break in and steal some. Not all of it so that she gets suspicious. Just enough that we can get out of Boise once and for all and live in style."

Artie felt his heart pounding as never before. When he glanced down, he saw that his shirt was shaking. "So what do you need me for? I don't want any gold."

"We figured that, which is one of the reasons you're perfect for the job. We don't have to give you a cut. The other reason is that we have to get into the basement. She has a cellar door that's locked from the inside. So we need someone to get in through one of the small basement windows and open the double door from inside."

"And that's where I come in—you need somebody little."

"Brilliant, Mr. Call. I told you he was smart, Jake. You've underestimated him all this time."

"But how will we even get close? The rich people on Warm Springs have lots of servants who work for them, and there are dogs at nearly every house. It's almost certain that somebody will hear us. Heck, she probably even has a telephone so she can call the police!"

"Maybe too smart." Reuben looked at him piercingly. "We've figured out that every Tuesday night she goes out to attend meetings of the Women's League of Boise. Because she's gone, she gives her housekeeper and cook the night off, and her chauffeur gets to have some private time while she's at the meeting. So from seven to eight-thirty, the place is empty. It's the perfect time."

"What about the dogs?"

"Dogs like meat. And we'll have plenty of it. They'll be fat and sassy and quiet."

Artie just stood there for a time. "Well?" demanded Reuben.

Slowly Artie looked up and directly into Reuben's eyes. "If I do this, are we square? Will you leave me alone from now on?"

"Why would we do that? Having a small guy on the team makes a lot of sense."

"But you said you want to leave Boise."

"Maybe not right away. What if it turns out that we're all really good at this?"

Artie fixed his gaze even more steadily. "Here's the deal. If you make me do this, then you have to promise me that we're square. We'll shake hands on it. Otherwise, I'll turn myself in and go to reform school, but I'll turn you in as well. And you'll go to the penitentiary. That will be a lot worse than where I'm at."

Reuben lunged for him, but Artie was way too quick. He rolled out of the older boy's way, making enough noise in the process that Reuben stopped his attack.

"I'm not making deals with you, Call!"

"Then I'm not doing it. And the two of you will never fit through that window!"

Reuben growled, but it was Jake who finally said, "We don't need him after this, Reuben. If he wants to go off and live a stupid, boring life, why should we care?"

Reuben glowered, but finally replied, "Yeah, who cares? All right, Call, I'll shake on it. This is the one job that will make us even. After that, you're on your own. But part of the deal is that you don't want any of the gold, right?"

Artie spit on his hands and rubbed them together. Reuben and Jake did the same, and the three of them shook on it. The deal was sealed.

CHAPTER 6

An Afternoon
at the Egyptian

April 1933

"I promise that he'll be with me all afternoon, Mr. Boone. If he leaves, I'll call you. Besides, the head projectionist is going to be there, so we can't get into any trouble."

Boone looked at Aaron with pursed lips. The request was clearly out of the ordinary, particularly since Mrs. Boone had serious reservations about movies and variety shows. She was often heard to say things like, "The women simply aren't modest enough. They wear those revealing clothes and short hair, and well, it's just scandalous, really. . ." But the truth is that having Artie locked up in the projectionist's booth all afternoon on a Saturday seemed like a pretty safe venture, and it would get him out from under the Boones' feet for a few hours.

"You're a fine young man, Aaron. While I don't understand what you see in Artie, I guess I can trust you."

Boone turned to Artie, "If you break one thing in that theater, you'll be working to pay it off until you're thirty. Do you understand me?"

"Yes, sir," Artie mumbled.

Boone wanted to grab Artie by the cheeks and make him look at Boone directly, but he knew it would be futile.

"All right, then. But be home by six for dinner." He saw Artie flash a quick grin to Aaron, which was even more irritating, but he decided not to press it. "Well, be off then, so you don't make Aaron late for work!"

Artie turned and started to jog to the front door but then hesitated. Turning back to Boone, he said, "Thank you, sir." Catching the look in Boone's eye made him glad he'd thought to add that; otherwise, who knows what level of grief he'd have had later on.

Once out of the house, they walked quickly to the corner. "What a creep!"

"What do you mean? He's letting me come."

"Big favor. It gets you out of his hair. I hate the way he talks to you. He treats you like a little kid. He treats both of us that way."

Artie shook his head. "It seems to me he treats you fine. 'You're a fine young man, Aaron . . .'" Artie did his best to imitate Boone's ponderous speech.

"Exactly, he says nice things, but then he goes on to say that he doesn't see why I like you—which is condescending to both of us." Artie didn't know what condescending meant, but it had to be pretty bad since Aaron was far angrier than Artie thought he should be. Boone was in a good mood today, at least for him.

"Well, if it's okay with you, I'd just as soon forget about Boone. I'm just glad to get out of there. Besides, he does buy all my food and stuff."

Aaron cast an irritated glance Artie's way. He knew that Artie had to defend him since he lived there. But he still didn't like the way he treated Artie. He started to say something sarcastic but then thought better of it. "You're right. There's no sense spending the precious few hours you get out of that house thinking about a creep." Aaron turned and slugged Artie. "Race you!" And with that, Aaron took off running as fast as he could. He was no match for Artie, but it changed the mood and left them both breathless as they reached the corner of Main Street and Capitol.

Artie couldn't help but grin as he looked down the busy street. There was just something to love about all the activity in town. He liked it a lot more than the quiet street where the Boones lived.

Aaron glanced down at his watch. "We gotta hurry. Hank gets really cranky if I'm late." So they started jogging the two blocks to the Egyptian.

The Egyptian Theatre was one of the cultural highlights of Boise. Located on Main Street, just south of the Capitol, it had an elaborate façade of giant Egyptian guards, pyramids, and mummies, all made out of plaster of Paris. Inside, the walls were painted in rich colors, like pink and blue and gold, and the lobby was made to resemble the inside of King Tut's Tomb. Artie was never able to figure out if it was real gold, or some kind of fake, but all of the statues had gleaming golden belts and headdresses that gave them an exotic appearance.

It was a marvel to attend a movie there, particularly since the talkies had come out a few years earlier. Artie loved the talkies—the few he'd seen—since it had been hard for him to read the subtitles on the screen during the silent movies. Somehow the words got jumbled up and out of order when he tried to read. His teachers, and even his grandmother, often became exasperated with him when he'd read the letters in a word backward, thinking that he did it just to be obstinate or contrary. He didn't know why he did it—he just read them the way he saw them, but it made him feel stupid. Which is why he liked talkies, even though it meant he didn't get to hear the organ music that used to accompany the silent pictures, which he had also liked a lot.

Today held more than the usual excitement since Aaron's father had helped Aaron get a part-time job as an assistant projectionist. When they arrived in the projection room at the top of the backstairs, they were met by Hank Grimwald, chief projectionist.

"Thank you for letting me come, Mr. Grimwald."

At age twenty-five, Hank Grimwald hardly thought of himself as a mister. "It's Hank, and just mind your manners and don't touch anything."

Artie turned and winked at Aaron. This was exactly what Aaron had predicted Hank would say.

"Hands in my pockets, I promise."

Hank scowled, finished the complicated splice he was making on a length of film, and then looked up. "Well, since you're here, I guess I ought to show you how all this works. Are you interested in the mechanics of things?"

"I love knowing how things work," replied Artie, perking up.

"All right, then. Well, go over and bring me that silver canister—the one marked No. 1."

Artie hefted the large canister of film and carried it over to Hank, who set it on a table next to the projector. "We use 35-millimeter film in this projector." He opened the canister and removed the large reel. "The first step is to spool the film on the top reel," which he did with some effort. Once the film was threaded through the projector, Hank started a laborious explanation of how projectors work. Even though Hank was one of those people with a monotone voice, Artie was fascinated by the intricate detail of how the projector worked to convert still-frame photos into a moving, talking picture. Hank was very pleased at the attention, which caused him to go into even more detail than usual in explaining how they would go through more than two miles of film in a two-hour movie, how the exciter lamp converted light and dark images on the side of the film into sound, and how they had to form two perfectly sized loops above and below the shutter so that the sound matched up with the image on the screen. Probably many would have found this boring, but Artie listened in rapt attention.

When he finished loading the film, Hank turned to Artie triumphantly and declared, "We've got a double feature, today, so we'll probably have seven canisters to work with."

Artie smiled. "A double feature?"

"*Around the World in 80 Minutes* with Douglas Fairbanks Sr."

Artie laughed. "In eighty minutes? Nothing can go that fast."

"It's a travelogue. He goes to places like Japan and Singapore and India. So it's like the audience gets to see all those places from around the world, but the movie only takes eighty minutes."

"That's kind of clever."

"Yeah," said Aaron, "but he really only goes to Asia and India, so he doesn't really go all the way around the world." Aaron was clearly a bit annoyed by the false advertising.

"I think it's boring," said Hank, reasserting control over the conversation. "At least the main feature is the *Little Rascals*."

"The Little Rascals? I love those guys!" Artie said cheerfully.

"Well, enough of the lesson. We've got to get ready to show a movie. Why don't you help Aaron get the second reel loaded onto the second projector, and I'll start warming up the tubes in the audio amplifier. We've got the house-lights up, the curtain is ready to raise . . ." and with that Hank continued to go through a mental checklist of everything they had to do in the next ten minutes, or so, to get things underway. Fortunately for Artie, Hank had forgotten his original warning not to touch anything.

"This is so great," Artie said quietly to Aaron. "Thanks for getting me up here."

"Hank likes you. I've never seen him take that much time with people. Who knows, maybe you could get a job someday."

"Wow!"

"Want to watch me ignite the carbon rods?" Hank asked Artie. "That's one of the best moments in the whole job."

"Carbon rods?"

Hank smiled. "That's what creates the light—an incredibly high-powered arc of electricity between two rods. The light is so bright it would blind you if you looked at it directly—brighter than the sun!"

"Wow!" said Artie again. "Yeah . . . I'd like that a lot." Artie gulped and then moved over to the projector to watch Hank in action.

CHAPTER 7

Warm Springs Boulevard

Tuesday was the most miserable day of Artie's life. He tried saying a silent prayer that something bad might happen to Reuben and Jake, like maybe a comet would fall out of the sky and hit them or something, but he realized that he was in no position to be saying prayers. He'd agreed to assist in a robbery, and he was absolutely certain that God wasn't coming anywhere close to him that day. So he gave up and spent a miserable day at school, followed by a solemn dinner where he was even more quiet than usual, followed by a request to go visit Joey. He hated that the most since he was lying to the Boones and indirectly involving Joey in the whole mess. But Mr. Boone didn't take any notice and said he could go.

Perhaps the only good news in the whole thing was that it would all be over that night, and he would be free of those two creeps once and for all. Of course the only way it would really be over is if they followed through and left town. He'd never hoped for something so much in his whole life.

As he found his way to the rendezvous point, Reuben and Jake showed up wearing dark clothes with their faces blackened. When they saw Artie's surprise, Reuben laughed and said, "You didn't expect us to show up in Sunday suits, did you? We talked it over and decided that if anyone gets spotted we want it to be you—what with your light-colored hair and all. You'd be recognized from half a block away."

Artie shook his head but said nothing. "Let's get it over with then."

"Don't get impatient, Call. Thing like this are to be savored. It's not often that a person gets a chance to make their fortune in a single night. You've got to learn how to enjoy life."

"I'll enjoy life when I'm done with you."

"Watch your mouth. You think you're pretty smart and better than us. But you aren't. You're just as bad as us. Maybe worse, because you pretend to be good."

Artie felt his face flush at the rebuke. It made him angry, in part because he suspected it was true. At the very least, he had no room to talk.

It took nearly half an hour to make the trip over to Warm Springs Boulevard. Reuben had intended to arrive at a quarter to seven so they could watch Mary's elegant Cadillac depart from the old carriage barn, but his planning was a bit off, and they arrived at five minutes after seven. The house was dark except for a single light in one of the upstairs rooms.

"Maybe somebody's home," Artie said. He was hopeful that someone was home since it would mean they wouldn't have to go through with it. But he also dreaded someone being there for the opposite reason, because calling it off tonight would do nothing more than postpone the robbery for another week, during which time he'd have to agonize about it all over again.

"The old lady always leaves her light on. We've checked that out the past two weeks to confirm it." He grinned. "She probably thinks it discourages burglars!" He and Jake had a good laugh at that.

"All right, get out the meat," Reuben ordered Jake, who quickly complied.

"We had to save a pretty penny for this, but it should be well worth the investment. Of course we'd have stolen it if you'd still been part of the team." As they approached the metal fence, the dogs began barking furiously, but Jake quickly tossed a couple of steaks over, which quieted them immediately. In a moment the three boys were up and over the fence and then Jake, trembling in fear, held out additional pieces of meat for the dogs to devour. Reuben made sure that both he and Artie did the same thing, which quickly calmed the dogs to the point that they allowed themselves to be petted.

"Okay, that takes care of that. Now let's get on with it." The grounds were very large, but it was a cloudy night so that it was easy to make it across the grass without being seen.

"There's the window," said Jake in an excited voice.

"Well, get it open!" Jake recoiled at Reuben's rebuke but quickly went to work prying the small basement window open. He'd been practicing so that he could do it without leaving any obvious marks. Their hope was that the woman wouldn't have any reason to suspect that she'd been burgled and that it might be months before she found out about it. As Jake was working away, Artie felt himself shivering in the dark and not because it was cold. Finally, Jake told him it was open, and Artie flipped over to his stomach and slid into the darkness, feet first. He expected to hit the floor at any moment, but even after his head was in the window, his feet still dangled. He flopped around a bit to see if he could feel something but ultimately concluded that he simply had to drop. When he did, his left foot hit something before his right foot, and he couldn't help but tumble to the ground. He did his best not to make a noise, but the fall inevitably made a noise that made his heart race even faster. He waited for a couple of moments to make sure there was no noise from upstairs and was relieved when nothing stirred. Once he knew he was firmly in place, he took out the flashlight that Reuben had given him and turned it on. Rotating the beam around the room, he saw that he was in a very large space—much bigger than he'd expected. To his left a stairway led up to the house. To his other side, the brick wall opened up, revealing the first few steps of the stairs that led outside. Walking as quietly as possible, he made his way to this opening and up the stairs, putting his hand overhead to feel for the doors that would open horizontally to the outside. Next he found the lock, which was remarkably similar to the one that Reuben had made him practice on, and with a special awl and hammer that Reuben had given him, Artie quickly broke the lock. He slid the bolt to the open position and, using all his strength, started to push open the heavy door above his head. He almost lost his balance when the door was suddenly flung open from the outside.

"All right, you did it!" Even Reuben sounded excited.

"Can I go?" he asked while standing in the open stairwell.

"What? Are you crazy? Of course not! We need help carrying the stuff out. The job isn't over until everything is put back together. Which even includes you replacing the old lock with this one. We need to keep up the show." At this news, Artie's heart sunk because it meant he'd have to crawl out the window somehow. It also meant he'd have to stay to the bitter end. But, there was nothing to do about it so he made his way back down the stairs.

With three flashlights it was easier to see, and Artie waited to the side as Reuben made his way around in the unfamiliar setting. Artie had no idea where Reuben had gotten his information about the gold, but he certainly seemed confident in his motions. After two or three minutes, Reuben made a circling motion with the flashlight beam on the ceiling, which was the signal for Artie and Jake to close to his position.

"This is it!" said Reuben proudly. Artie dropped his gaze to a dusty old steamer trunk that looked like it hadn't been disturbed in years. "Just where she said it would be?"

"She?"

Reuben whirled on Artie. "That's none of your business. Don't ask any stupid questions, or you'll learn far more than you want to know. Do you understand?"

Artie nodded.

Very carefully Reuben felt under the lip of the trunk. In a few moments, he was able to find the release and lift the lid. When he did, they saw some old newspapers and dusty bags. Reuben carefully lifted the first bag and opened it. He smiled—a very broad, triumphant smile. It was easy to see why. The bag was filled with gold coins, just like he'd expected. He handed the bag to Artie and started rummaging in the chest for more. Artie felt the hair on the back of his neck tingle as he held the bag. Part of him was exultant to think that he was holding the equivalent of a small fortune. This was the sort of pirate treasure that little boys dreamed about. But far more overpowering than his lust was a deep fear that they would be discovered and that he would go to prison—not the reformatory, but prison. This had to be grand larceny, at the very least.

"All right," Reuben said finally, "there's not as much as I expected, but there's still plenty. There are three empty burlap sacks at the top of the stairs. These bags are heavy enough that it will take two or three trips. I want you two to carry the bags out and put them in the larger burlap sacks. Let's be fast about it, and then we'll have Artie seal the door up again."

Even though he hated what they were doing, Artie was in full agreement with Reuben that they ought to hurry. The old basement had a musty smell, and he felt like maybe it was haunted or something. At least that would explain why his stomach was so nervous. Each time he made it to the top of the stairs where he could smell the fresh air he was relieved. On one trip he actually thought about bolting and getting out of there, but he knew that Reuben and Jake would beat him up for that.

As he picked up the last sack, he heard Reuben closing the trunk. Reuben was so well prepared that he even pulled out a small sack of dust from his pocket which he sprinkled over the trunk to make it look like it was undisturbed. And then the three of them started for the outside stairwell.

Just as they reached it they were blinded by the flashlight beam that poured down on them.

"What the hell . . ." said Reuben. But before he could say anything else, they were startled by the woman's voice behind the flashlight. "What's going on down there? Who are you?" They looked up to see an elderly woman coming down the stairway.

"Stop!" she shouted. "Stop! Thiefs!" Her voice was shrill but authoritative, and for a moment everybody just froze. Artie dropped the bag he was holding and was startled at the metallic sound it made when it hit the floor.

The noise must have startled Reuben, as well, because all of a sudden he shook his head and ran headlong toward the screaming woman.

"Help!" she shrieked when she realized he was going to tackle her. Reuben didn't slow down. Artie had never seen a look so frightening as the one that filled Reuben's eyes right then. He looked like he'd gone crazy.

"Stop!" the woman shouted again, but by now she must have known she was in trouble and had turned to go back up the stairs.

"Oh, no you don't, you old witch. I'm not going to let you call the police on us!" Reuben was in a frenzy, and as he bounded up the stairs, he grabbed her by the waist, and the two of them came tumbling back down the stairs. Reuben started slugging the poor woman's face as she cried out in pain.

Almost as if he was detached from his body, Artie seemed to watch himself as he tore across the floor shouting, "You leave her alone! Do you hear me?"

In an instant he was on top of Reuben, pounding as hard as he could on the back of Reuben's head. When Reuben turned in surprise, Artie was able to land a major blow right in his jaw which caused the older boy to yelp in pain.

"I'll get you, too!" Reuben shouted, and he lifted Artie into the air and threw him seemingly effortlessly. As Artie fell back against a pile of boxes, he felt a sharp pain in his left arm and heard the sickening sound of his bone snapping.

"Help us!" Artie shouted to Jake. "Don't let him do this!" At the edge of his peripheral vision, he could see that Reuben had renewed his attack on the woman, so he did his best to struggle up and into a standing position. He hoped that he could kick Reuben to get him to stop. But he didn't need to, because suddenly Jake was on top of Reuben, pulling him off.

"Come on, Reuben, we've got to get out of here!"

Reuben turned on Jake with a fury, but when he saw that Jake was holding a hatchet, and that it looked like he had every intent to use it if necessary, he backed down.

"We can't just leave her," Reuben said.

"Yes, we can. We can get out of here right now and leave her. She's unconscious. Maybe she's dead."

Reuben growled, but he picked up his flashlight and started to move. Turning to Artie he said, "I'll get even with you when we're out of here."

"I'm not leaving. I've got to call someone to help her."

"You're not staying!"

"Yes, I am!" Artie knew he was in trouble, but he was done taking orders from Reuben.

"Come on," Jake urged. "Leave him if he wants. He won't know where we go anyway!"

"Fine!" Reuben shouted. "You stay here and be a Boy Scout. But you're going to pay for it."

Artie knew that he would. But he was not going with them. That much he was certain of. As a last minute thought, Reuben walked over and slugged Artie hard on the side of his head. Then, Jake and Reuben made their way to the stairs and were up and out of sight in a matter of seconds.

In spite of the searing pain in his broken arm, Artie made his way to the woman, where he gently lifted her head with his right hand. "Are you all right?" At first there was no movement. "Ma'am, are you all right?" He shook her head even more gently. Finally there was a slight stirring. "It's okay. You can wake up!"

Her eyes fluttered and then opened. At first they looked at him with incomprehension and then with alarm. "You're one of the crooks! You're trying to kill me! Let me go!" She struggled mightily, but she didn't have the ability to even raise her head.

"No, no, he's gone. The person who was trying to hurt you is gone. I chased him away. You're safe now. But I need to call for help. How do I get to your telephone?" "But you're one of them! You don't want to help me! Help!!"

"Please, ma'am. I was one of them, but I didn't hurt you. And I want to help you now. Please tell me how to use your phone."

When Mary Wilkerson figured out that she couldn't get up by herself, she calmed down just a bit. "Why would you want to help me? You wanted to steal from me?"

"Ma'am, please. You can think whatever you like about what we were doing, but I am not someone who would hurt an older person." His voice choked up. "I had a grandmother, and I have a grandfather . . . Please believe me."

Mary took a few breaths to calm down. "I guess I don't have much choice. The telephone is in the parlor. Go to the top of the house stairs and turn to your left. You'll pass through the foyer into the parlor. The telephone is on the wall just beside the door."

"All right. Let me lay your head down so I can go." He took his jacket off and put it under her head.

"Well, what are you waiting for?" she said sharply.

"It's just that, well, I've never used a telephone. I don't know how."

She rolled her head slightly. "Oh, for heaven's sake. It's very easy. Just lift up the earpiece from its cradle on the left side of the box. Then turn the crank on the right side four or five times. That sends a signal to the operator, who will come on the line and ask you what number you'd like. Tell her there's an emergency and that she needs to send medical help. And tell her that she needs to send the police!" Mary said this last part in a very stern voice.

"Yes, ma'am." And with that, Artie was up the stairs in a bound. Fortunately, the lights were on, since he nearly slid off his feet as he tried to gain traction on the highly polished wood floor. But after quickly orienting himself, he found the phone, lifted the earpiece, and frantically turned the crank. When the operator came on, he didn't even give her time to ask for a number. He just shouted "There's an emergency out here on Warm Springs Boulevard. You've got to send a doctor or something. You've got to hurry!"

"Slow down," the operator said, followed by, "Who is this? Why are you calling from Mrs. Wilkerson's phone?"

"It's Mrs. Wilkerson who's been hurt." Artie found that he was trembling from fear, but he persisted.

"All right, all right. I'll send somebody out right away. But who is this, and what happened to Mrs. Wilkerson?"

"It doesn't matter, does it?"

"Yes, it does. I need to know so I can tell if this really is an emergency or if you're playing some kind of joke."

Artie shook his head. For a moment he thought about just hanging up and disappearing into the night. He had tried to do the right thing, after all. He thought maybe he could jump a train and get out of Boise, although he wouldn't get on the same train as Reuben and Jake. But after just a moment to think about it he knew he couldn't take the risk that this operator wouldn't believe him.

"My name is Artie Call. Some people busted into Mrs. Wilkerson's home, and one of them hurt her real bad. I was with them, but I chased them off. Now won't you please get help?"

This apparently convinced the operator, and she said to hold for just a moment. Artie could hear her talking in the background to somebody else. Her voice was faint, but he made out that it must have been the hospital or something. Her voice came back into his earpiece at full strength, which startled him. "All right, an ambulance is on the way. How will they find you when they get there?"

"Just tell them to come in the front door and go straight to the basement. The door's open. Mrs. Wilkerson's just lying there, but I'll be with her. You told them to hurry, didn't you?"

"I did. Now why don't you go see how she's doing, but leave the earpiece hanging so I can hear when the ambulance arrives. I can talk to them if they need help."

"That's a good idea. Okay, good-bye." Artie dropped the earpiece and started away but then got a cold feeling. He stopped in his tracks, paused a second, and then went back to the phone. "Hello! Hello!"

"I'm here, what is it?"

"Mrs. Wilkerson said that you should send the police as well. The people I was with stole some money from her besides hurting her."

"I've already called them. They're on their way, as well." Artie felt a stab of pain in his stomach. But he didn't have time for that, so he just dashed off to the stairway.

"They're on their way!" he cried out. But Mary Wilkerson didn't hear him. No matter what he did, Artie couldn't get her to wake up.

CHAPTER 8

The People vs. Artie Call

May 1933—The Old Boise Courthouse

The last time Artie had been before Judge Farnsworth, the judge had smiled at him. There were no smiles in the courthouse today.

"And so, your honor, in spite of Mr. Call's involvement in the robbery, it's also well established that he took on great personal risk in challenging Reuben Kinley and Jake Carter, even though they are much larger and stronger individuals. It was his action in fighting off those boys that saved Mrs. Wilkerson's life. She has testified that he treated her with kindness and respect and very quickly took action to summon medical assistance. He even followed her instruction to call the police with full knowledge that it would likely result in his incarceration. Given these mitigating circumstances, as well as his age, we ask for leniency, your Honor. We hope you'll give him another chance."

"And yet in spite of all he did for Mrs. Wilkerson, she continues to press charges against him? How do those two sentiments reconcile?"

Artie's defense attorney dropped his gaze for a moment. Naturally Artie had been in the city jail since the night of the attack, even though he'd stayed faithfully by Mary Wilkerson's side until the ambulance arrived. He'd answered all the questions put to him by the police and even walked them through the basement, showing them how things happened during the course of the robbery and battery. It was even on his tip that they captured Reuben and Jake in the Nampa railroad yards, attempting to make their escape. Still, Mary Wilkerson was unforgiving.

Artie's attorney said, "I'm afraid you'll have to talk to Mrs. Wilkerson about that, your Honor. My client has confessed to everything related to his role in this ugly event and did his level-headed best to make things right when the burglary turned to assault and battery. He knows that what he did is wrong, and he feels terrible about it. Which is why I'd ask you to consider whether it really makes sense to lock him up with true criminals and hardened boys who will likely teach him even more dirty dealings."

The judge looked at Artie in a way that surprised him. "I'm not sure the defendant has confessed everything. I believe he's withholding some vital evidence that would assist the court in reaching its verdict."

"I don't know what this is, your Honor," Artie's attorney replied.

"Because this is not a formal trial, perhaps you'd allow your client to return to the witness stand one more time for direct questioning?"

Bill Holden, the attorney, didn't even look at Artie before replying, "He'll do it, your Honor."

But Artie didn't want to answer any more questions. He just wanted it to be over. But he shuffled up to the stand, anyway, frightened for whatever it was that Judge Farnsworth was going to do to him. He'd pretty well resolved himself to the idea that he was going to be sent to reform school, so he didn't see why this was necessary. But he wasn't in charge. He was never in charge.

"Artie, do you understand that you're still sworn to tell the truth?" Judge Farnsworth asked.

"Yes, sir."

"Then will you answer my questions?"

"I'll try."

"Why did you go along with those boys even though you've testified that you didn't want to?"

Artie felt his heart leap up in his throat. He'd thought about this question and had come up with a pretty good lie to tell. He figured he could simply tell them that Reuben and Jake made him do it because he was little enough to get in the window. From what he could tell, neither one of them had ratted on him yet about stealing. But the more he thought about it, he figured that it wouldn't work, because either one of those snakes could turn on him eventually. Still, he wasn't ready to confess to it yet.

"I dunno."

"That's not an acceptable answer. You said you'd tell the truth."

"I said I'd try," said Artie defensively.

The judge sat up in his chair. "I won't argue with you, Mr. Call. I'm trying to find every way I can to be lenient with you because of what you did in standing up to those two cretins. But if you're not willing to help me by answering my questions, there's not a lot I can do."

Artie felt miserable, but he just sat there. So the judge picked up a sheaf of papers and prepared to render a judgment. There was little question what it would be.

"Excuse me, your Honor!"

Judge Farnsworth looked up sharply from his desk, only to see Aaron Nelson raise his hand. The judge shook his head in irritation.

"You're Aaron Nelson, aren't you?"

"Yes, sir, I am."

"Well, do you not understand that a person can't just raise his hand in a courtroom? A person has to have standing before the bar to do that! Only an officer of the court can address the bench."

"Yes, sir. I did know that, but it's just that I know something that I think will be helpful to you."

"He doesn't know anything, judge!" Artie was instantly agitated—so much so that his hands trembled.

"Sit down, Mr. Call! Now!"

Artie turned and looked at the judge. "But he doesn't know anything."

"Perhaps not. But I'm interested to hear his story. Of course, I can't do that directly. Mr. Holden, perhaps you would consider calling Aaron Nelson as a defense witness before I render judgment."

"Of course, your Honor. With your permission, I'd like to call Aaron Nelson to the stand." He motioned for Artie to come down, which he did reluctantly. When he passed Aaron on the way to his seat, Artie glowered at him as he mouthed the words, "Don't do it," but Aaron proceeded directly to the chair.

After being sworn in, Aaron took his seat. "Well, let's try to find out what Mr. Nelson knows," said the judge.

"Yes, sir." Bill Holden had a puzzled look on his face as he tried to figure out what questions to ask. Finally he gave up and just said, "Mr. Nelson, why don't you tell us what you know about Artie Call that may be relevant to this case." It was a dangerous thing to do since Aaron might have information that would incriminate Artie even further. But since Artie was unwilling to help in his own defense, the attorney judged that it wasn't likely to do much harm.

"It's like this, your Honor. Artie told me in confidence once why he was stuck with Reuben and Jake."

"And you're willing to break that confidence now?"

Aaron dropped his head. "Yes, sir, although Artie will probably hate me for it. But he had a reason for doing what he did, and I think it needs telling." The judge looked up at Artie, who was glowering at the floor.

"Go ahead."

"Well, sir, Artie told me that about a year ago he and his grandpa were really hungry, so he was rummaging through some garbage cans on Grove Street behind the butcher shop to see if he could find some food. Apparently Jake and Reuben came along and teased him about it. When he explained that he and his grandpa didn't have any food, they told him that they'd help him steal some. According to Artie, they said that they did it all the time. Well, Artie didn't want to, but he was really worried about his grandfather, so he let them show him how to open the lock at the back of the store. They even showed him how to take pieces of wrapped meat in such a way that it wouldn't be very noticeable. Then they showed him how to steal from the bakery and the green grocer, and before long they'd turned him into a scavenger. Sometimes they'd even work together so that Reuben and Jake could steal money while Artie got food." Aaron dropped his head. "At any rate, Artie did this for a time because he didn't have any other way to get food. His grandpa had lost all their money to a conman, buying some expensive pots and pans, and Artie didn't know what else to do."

The judge shook his head at Aaron's words. "And what does this new information, which at this point seems to incriminate Mr. Call even further, have to do with the break-in at Mrs. Wilkerson's?"

Aaron looked up at the judge. "It's just that when you took Artie away from his grandfather to live with the Boones, he tried to stop doing things with Reuben and Jake. He even told them he wouldn't steal from the hardware store. That made them plenty mad, but they didn't make him do it. What they did tell him is that he owed them and that if he didn't pay up, someday they'd turn him in. So when they decided to break into Mrs. Wilkerson's home, they needed somebody small who could get through the basement window, and they told Artie it was time to pay up. Since he wanted to stay close to his grandpa while he's in the old-folks home, Artie decided to go along with them rather than get ratted out and sent to reform school. I think that's why he was there that night." Aaron said more earnestly, "He didn't want any of the gold or anything. He just wanted to pay off his debt to Reuben and Jake so they'd leave him alone."

The judge looked at Bill Holden, who simply shrugged his shoulders. This case seemed very much like an onion. After peeling off one layer, you found another. And each layer wanted to make you cry.

"Thank you, Mr. Nelson. You can step down."

As Aaron stood up, he looked directly at Artie. "I didn't want to tell your secret—and I know that it was a terrible thing to do—but you wouldn't stand up for yourself. I did it because you're my friend." Then Aaron, who was usually unflappable, wiped his face with his sleeve and went straight down the aisle and out the door.

"Artie, come back up here."

Artie looked at the judge defiantly and refused to budge. One of the court bailiffs finally helped him to the stand.

"Why didn't you tell me this when I asked you?"

When he didn't answer, the judge said, "I can have you put in jail if you don't answer."

"It's just that I didn't want anybody to know about it. It's already bad enough about people thinking that my grandpa is crazy and everything. I just figured that if people knew that I was clear down to stealing food, they'd think even worse of him. Aaron had no right to tell you!" Artie looked up at the judge defiantly. "And it didn't do any good anyway, did it? Because you still have to send me away. It doesn't matter whether it's because we were hungry or not—it was still stealing!"

Once again Judge Farnsworth found himself shaking his head. "I'm afraid you're right. But I'm glad Aaron told me. At least it helps me understand. It also gives me hope that someday you'll turn out all right." Of course, there was nothing Artie could say to this, so he just sat there with his head dropped forward.

"It's time for me to render judgment."

"Excuse me, your honor!"

Judge Farnsworth turned sharply to his right to see who dared to interrupt him, yet again.

"Mrs. Wilkerson?"

With help from her chauffeur, Mary Wilkerson stood up.

"Well, what is it, Mrs. Wilkerson?"

"I drop the charges."

"What?"

"You heard me. I want to drop the charges against Artie Call."

The judge looked at her sharply. "And why, may I ask, have you had a change of heart? You've been the one who has insisted on all this."

The normally imperious Mary Wilkerson softened. "Because of the boy's grandfather. I didn't know about that. Any boy who is willing to go to reform school rather than embarrass his grandfather deserves a second chance."

"I wish it were that easy. But now we've learned that his stealing has been more extensive than this one incident. I'm sure the prosecutor will need to deal with that, as well."

"Your Honor, perhaps the state can resolve the issue for you?"

The judge turned to the prosecutor. "Yes, Mr. Jones?"

"In view of this new information, we desire to drop the criminal assault charges. And while the burglary charges remain, including the new evidence of additional stealing that's been brought forward, we recommend leniency on the part of the court. Perhaps something can be worked out to repay the injured parties."

"So you're suggesting that we just let him go?"

"No, sir. There needs to be restitution. And perhaps community service. We even recommend jail time, with credit given for time already served."

Judge Farnsworth sat back in his seat and took a couple of deep breaths.

"I'll accept your withdrawal of charges, but I can't give up the option for reform school unless a suitable home is provided in the community for Mr. Call by someone who will supervise him closely and report periodically to the court." He looked out into the audience where David Boone was sitting. "Mr. Boone, you last had custody of Artie. Are you willing to take him back?"

Boone stood up slowly. "Your Honor, I feel the same thing that everybody else is feeling and I'd like to help. But the truth is that it was very hard on us having another person in our house. I think Artie tried to fit in. I tried very hard to discipline him. But it just didn't work out. Now with this terrible event with Mrs. Wilkerson . . ." He shuffled uneasily. "It's just that I have a reputation to uphold, your Honor, and Artie is the type of boy that brings undue notoriety to himself . . ." Finally, with a defiant look, he said, "I just don't think we can go through it anymore. I simply can't trust him."

This time the judge nodded. "I understand, David. You shouldn't feel guilty. You've done more than most of us."

At that point, Pastor Wyndham started to stand up, but the judge motioned him to sit back down. "You don't need this either, so don't even raise the issue."

Judge Farnsworth sighed. "Well, I guess that after everything we've been through, we're back to the same point. Much as I hate to do it I have to render judgment . . ."

"Your honor, I'll take him!"

Farnsworth was astonished. "Mrs. Wilkerson?"

Mary Wilkerson had stood again. "That's right. I'll take the boy. He needs a home, not a reformatory. And I can certainly provide for him. I'm not saying it will be easy on him, but I'll take him."

"But, your age . . ."

"My age has nothing to do with it. I'm healthy and fit, and I have enough staff that he'll never be left unattended. In fact, he can help out around the place. I think he'll find himself yearning for simpler days." Mary Wilkerson set her jaw with a determined look that would make Gibraltar itself look weak.

"Well. This is something I need to consider." Judge Farnsworth sat back in his chair, wishing for a moment to clear his thoughts.

"Perhaps you ought to ask Arthur," said Mary Wilkerson sternly. "After all, it's his life we're discussing here."

"What do you think, son? Would you like to live with Mrs. Wilkerson?"

Artie shook his head in disbelief. Finally, he looked up at Mary Wilkerson to see if she looked sincere. What he saw was a woman who somehow reminded him of his grandmother, even though Mary Wilkerson was much more confident and domineering. He decided he could live with that. "I guess I would, your Honor. I'll do whatever she tells me."

For the first time in the town's collective memory, Mary Wilkerson smiled. It was just for a moment, though, because as soon as Mary saw people looking at her, she quickly adopted her stern look again and said defiantly, "That's taken care of, then. Of course there will be rules!" Then she sat down.

Judge Farnsworth leaned forward in his seat. Carefully he fixed his gaze on the audience and looked over everyone in the room. The courtroom fell into a hushed silence under his baleful gaze. In a very deliberate and solemn tone, he said, "I'm about to say something, and if anyone—and I mean anyone—interrupts me, I'll have every person in this room thrown in jail. Do I make myself clear?"

No one made any noise, but nearly everyone nodded their heads.

"Good. This is the judgment of the court. Arthur William Call is sentenced to three months of community service for the crimes of petty theft and burglary. He is also required to make restitution to all shop owners and grocers who may have been damaged by his criminal activity. Further, he is condemned to five days in jail with credit for time served. All other criminal charges are withdrawn. Mr. Call will be on probation, for a period of not less than twelve months and not more than twenty-four months from this date forward. Should he live up to the terms of his probation all records of this proceeding will be expunged on his eighteenth birthday. Finally, since the defendant is a juvenile, I appoint Mrs. Mary Wilkerson of Warm Springs Boulevard as his sole legal guardian." Judge Farnsworth then turned to Artie, "Do you understand what I just said, Mr. Call?"

Artie gulped. "Yes, sir. I think I do."

"If not, I'll explain it to you later." He turned to his court recorder and declared in an authoritative voice. "So be it!" and with that he rapped his gavel on his desk with such force that it startled everyone nearly right out of their chairs.

"Adjourned!"

Artie was surprised and pleased with the decision. But his mood fell a bit as he saw the scowl on David Boone's face as he walked past him to the door. Boone just shook his head and glowered.

CHAPTER 9

Mary Wilkerson

Artie had been far too intimidated to say anything as he rode home to Mary Wilkerson's house in her amazing V-16 1931 Cadillac Madam X Sedan with its stylishly raked-back windshield and it's forward opening suicide doors. In his wildest dreams Artie never thought he'd get to sit in a Cadillac, let alone ride in one. As he thought about it, he had sat in a Cadillac once—for approximately ten seconds before he and Joey had been thrown out of the dealership. But now he got to settle deeply into the luxurious leather seat next to Mary's driver, Ray McCandless. As he gingerly touched the handle that was used to roll down the side window he cringed when he heard Mary cough in the backseat, frightened that she was going to yell at him. Of course she'd have every right to yell since this car cost so much money. He was pretty well terrified of doing anything that would hurt it. Having always loved cars, he'd pressed his nose up against enough dealer windows to know the price of nearly every car on the market, and this one was a dazzler at more than $4,000. That was so much money that it might as well have been a million dollars, or a hundred million dollars, since he knew that he'd never in his whole life earn that much money.

But Mary was simply plumping herself in the backseat when she coughed, and Artie was happy to know that it wasn't directed at him. Still, she made him nervous so he shrunk down as far as possible so that his head didn't stick up above the back of the high seat. He thought that was the best way to respond to his new and unfamiliar situation – but a whack on his left ear put that idea to rest. "Sit up straight, young man. You'll ruin your posture slumping down like that. Have you no pride?"

"Sorry, ma'am." Artie straightened up until his back ached. It was kind of difficult for someone his size to sit up straight in the seat since it was so deep that it made his feet hang forward, rather than down to the floor. As he shifted uncomfortably, he happened to glance over to Ray, who winked at him. Artie didn't know exactly what to think about that but thought that maybe it was a good sign.

"My, how that judge carried on. It seems like he could never come to a decision—still, he had a lot of things to sort through so I suppose we should excuse him; he is an officer of the court, after all, and deserves our respect, but the man simply didn't maintain order in the court the way he should have."

Artie wondered how she could say all those things without pausing for a breath. His brain wandered, as it often did, and he imagined her coming to the end of one of her long sentences, suddenly grabbing her throat and gasping for air in desperation before passing out and dying right on the spot. He did his best to suppress a smile, which was a good thing when he heard her continue.

"But goodwill and tolerance aside, it's still true that he used up the whole afternoon so that we don't have time to go and get you any decent clothing. That suit you're wearing is threadbare and shabby. And it's at least ten years out of style."

Instinctively Artie blushed and turned a quick glance at Mary. But he did manage to stifle his response. Even so, Mary had good enough eyesight that she caught his look to which she replied, "No offense intended, for heaven's sake. It's not your fault you don't have anything nicer to wear—I understand that. At least you had the decency to put on a suit, which is so much better than what many of the young men wear today. Why, some men today are positively indecent wearing those sport jackets with trousers that don't match when they go out in public."

"But the whole purpose of a sport jacket is so that men can go to a sporting event in something a little more relaxed than a suit. It seems a nice contrast to me," said Ray.

Mary huffed at Ray. "Don't you go lecturing me on how a person should dress in public. If I didn't insist on keeping your wardrobe up-to-date and fresh, you'd probably drive me around in your coveralls."

Now it was Ray's face that flushed, but this time Mary didn't seem to notice. Or if she did, she apparently didn't care. She started talking to Artie. "At any rate, Arthur, tomorrow I want you to get up early and help with the chores that our cook, Bethany Jones will assign you, and then I want you to take a bath so we can go out and buy you some decent clothes. I won't have any dependent of mine going out in public dressed indecently!"

"A bath?"

Mary Wilkerson tipped her head to the side, "Yes, a bath. Is that a problem?"

"But a person only takes a bath . . . well, when . . ."

"When? When do people take a bath?"

"Well, maybe on the weekend before church. Tomorrow's only Wednesday!"

Mary rolled her eyes and fanned herself as if she was going to faint. "Did you hear that, Ray? The boy takes a bath on a schedule, rather than when he's dirty."

"I think that's the way most people do it, Mary."

"Well, you're a lot of help, aren't you?" She rolled her eyes again, this time as if to bring Artie over to her side at Ray's expense. "I guess that tells me just what I'm up against." Mary shook her head to compose herself and then said rather firmly, "Arthur, please turn around and look at me."

"Yes, ma'am."

"Arthur, I'm afraid your life is going to change from now on. I think it will be for the better, although you may not agree. That doesn't matter. I'm responsible for you now, so I have to raise you the way I think is best. And one of those ways is to insist that you keep yourself well-groomed and well dressed. At the very least, that means a bath once a week, but more often if needed. Even birds groom themselves in a birdbath when they get dirty, and if they can do it, so can you."

"But how will I know when I should do it?"

Ray laughed. "Oh, don't worry. Mary Wilkerson will tell you."

Mary shook her head and glowered. "The unemployment rate is very high, Ray McCandless. I turn away two or three good men nearly every single day who come to the house looking for work."

"Yes, ma'am. I appreciate that. But would you really want to trust your cars to that lot—vagrants and hobos?" Before he really aggravated her, though, he added, "But you're right that this is a good job and Artie should be as clean as those little birds."

Mary tipped her head to the side, recognizing his impertinence, but she let it slide. That surprised Artie and made him wonder just how Ray had come to get this job and what made him feel like he could speak so boldly to his employer. After all, she was right in saying that there were lots of people looking for work who would love the chance to drive a beautiful car like this one.

Artie's mind had started to wander again when a sudden shift in Mary's voice jolted him back to the present as she said, "And another thing, Arthur.

While we're at it, I should tell you that you'll be expected to use proper English when you speak around the house. You seem to be a polite boy, always calling me ma'am and such, so that's not a problem. And while you speak fairly well, at least as well as most young men of your generation, we're going to start correcting your grammar so that you can speak even more correctly. That will make a great difference in your prospects as an adult."

Artie turned his head quickly so she wouldn't see him roll his eyes. He had been left largely to himself over the past two years, and he didn't know if he wanted someone dominating him again. In fact, he was just about ready to tell Ray to turn the car around when he thought better of it. An image of his grandfather came to his mind, and he knew that he didn't want to be away at the reform school way over in Blackfoot, on the other side of the state, where he'd never get to see his grandfather again. Even though he didn't always know Artie, when he went to see him, he still seemed happy to have his company. So Artie bit his tongue and said quietly, "I'd be pleased to take your correction, ma'am."

If Mary sensed his hostility, she didn't say anything about it. She was about to continue when Ray made a slightly sharp left turn that startled Mary, which, to Artie's relief, shifted her focus from him to Ray.

"Ray McCandless! Can't you be more careful than that? You know how I get disoriented when you go careening around corners like a drunken man!"

Ray pursed his lips before replying. "I'm sorry, Mary. I was trying to avoid running over a cat."

At first Artie was surprised because he hadn't seen a cat in the street. But he hadn't been looking forward, either. The hood of the Cadillac was unusually long, so it was possible that Ray, who was taller, saw something he hadn't. But Artie became suspicious when he happened to see the side of Ray's mouth turn up ever so slightly in a grin. He watched as Ray glanced at Mary in his rearview mirror. When she dropped her head for a moment Ray mouthed the words, "She loves cats!" Artie almost burst out laughing but managed to disguise it as a cough. Still, he couldn't help but smile.

"Well, you should have spotted the cat much earlier than that. Still, a little discomfort on my part is more than justified to save the life of a little dear. Just please be more careful from now on."

"Of course. I'll keep my eyes peeled."

Even after just a few minutes together, Artie felt like Ray was the kind of person that wouldn't mind talking to someone like him.

"Well, we have many more things to talk about, Arthur, but right now I'm too upset to think about it. We'll be home in a few minutes, anyway. When we get there, you'll get out of the car and open the door for me. Usually that's Ray's responsibility, but it makes no sense for him to have to come around the car when there's a perfectly healthy fifteen-year-old who can do it. Ray deserves respect too, you know."

"Yes, ma'am. I'd be happy to do that."

"And then when you've helped me up the stairs and held the door into the house, you can come back for your suitcase, and Ray can show you where you'll be sleeping. I think he should stay in the apartment above the garage, don't you, Ray?"

Ray hesitated. "That's certainly one way of doing it."

Mary frowned. "But you think there's a problem?"

"It's just that with all the temptation this boy has had to face in his life, and not always successfully, it seems a bit risky leaving him out there by himself, at least for awhile." Ray turned to Artie and added quickly, "Not that we don't trust you."

"It's all right," said Artie. "I don't deserve any trust. For all I know I might get it into my head to run away—and just think of all the trouble that would cause. I think poor old Judge Farnsworth would have a heart attack if he had to see me in court, again."

Ray laughed, but Mary was not amused.

"Well, that's a fine thank-you. We invite you into our home, and you're already thinking of running away."

Before Artie could reply, Ray interrupted. "Besides, since I live at my own place, there might be some value to having Artie live inside the main house, particularly given the recent problem of the break-in. Now that all the lowlife in Boise know about it, others might get an idea. Artie could be a real help should anyone else decide to try it again."

"And what makes you think he'd help me? It wasn't exactly his idea to come live with me in the first place!"

Artie's face flushed, and he cleared his throat. But he didn't say anything. Ray did instead. "I believe he's already shown by his actions that he's willing to help you, Mary. That really wasn't very kind."

Now it was Mary who blushed. She started to say something, caught herself, and then continued quietly. "Ray's right, Arthur. It's not fair to ask you to adjust to all of this on your own. And it would be good to have you in the main house. So we'll find a room for you on the first floor where you can help Bethany and our house maid Judy with chores and other assigned duties like going downstairs to tend the backup furnace in the winter. The first floor is the perfect place, after all."

For a moment, Artie wondered if she'd taken him on out of the goodness of her heart or just for his value as a slave laborer, but when he thought about how she talked to Ray, he realized that it was just her way of saying things and that it wasn't meant to be mean or cruel. Besides, with times as they were, he'd be lucky to be a slave—at least he'd have food to eat and a warm place to sleep. In fact, it would be a lot warmer than the porch of the Boones' house.

"I'd be happy to stay wherever you tell me, ma'am."

"That's settled, then." At this point, Ray turned the car onto the gravel driveway that would take them back past the house to an imposing three-car garage. Only one of the garage doors was open, so Artie couldn't see what was behind the other two. But he wanted to see what was there. Ray had spoken of "cars" not just "car," and Artie couldn't help but wonder what else they had. As he looked at the imposing house on his right, which was truly magnificent, his heart skipped a beat just to think that he'd be living here.

"And one more thing, Arthur."

"Yes, ma'am?"

"After we get you cleaned up and suited in new clothing tomorrow, I think we should take time to go visit your grandfather."

Artie was surprised and embarrassed when he felt his throat tighten up, and he had the momentary feeling that he might cry or something. That would be terrible. But he managed to squeak out, "Thank you, ma'am. That would be real nice."

"*Really* nice," she corrected gently.

"Ma'am?"

She smiled. "I told you I'd correct your grammar. The correct way to reply is to say 'that would be really nice.'"

"Yes, ma'am. That would be really nice."

She leaned up and patted his head. "I don't need to correct your thank-you, though. You said that perfectly." She smiled at him, and he found it easy to smile back.

CHAPTER 10

Ray McCandless

July 1933

"Hand me an 3/8-inch wrench, Artie."

Artie glanced through the neatly organized wrenches hanging from the wall behind a workbench and selected a gleaming chrome wrench. A month earlier, he wouldn't have had any idea how to tell the difference between an 1/8-inch wrench, an Allen wrench, and a monkey wrench. But Ray had been patiently teaching him about tools and about how to keep things organized in a shop so that you could always find what you were looking for without having to shuffle through the tool kit. "A well-organized toolkit is essential for the professional mechanic," he liked to say. He'd said it so often, in fact, that Artie could recite it from memory each time Ray started into the phrase.

"Very good," Ray said cheerfully, and Artie watched in fascination as he gently tightened the clamp that secured one of the radiator hoses of the Cadillac. "That should do it!" Ray stood up and carefully wiped his hands on one of the laundered rags he kept in small piles around his work area. Artie noticed that unlike other mechanics, Ray never wiped his hands on his clothing, and in fact always managed to keep his clothes looking clean and crisp. He looked more like a doctor in an operating room than a mechanic in a garage. In fact, everything in Ray's world from the engine compartment to the tools in their chest to the garage itself looked as neat and clean as Mrs. Wilkerson's front parlor.

"What do you think?"

Artie looked inside the motor compartment of the Cadillac in wonderment. "I think that's the biggest engine I've ever seen in my life."

"At 452 cubic-inches with sixteen cylinders, she develops upwards of 180 horsepower at 3600 rpms!"

"Rpms?"

"Revolutions per minute—that's how many times the engine turns around in a one minute cycle."

Artie's jaw dropped. "You mean to tell me that it turns more than 3,000 times each and every minute you're driving? That's impossible. I mean it seems like it would burn up from heat or start breaking into pieces with parts flying everywhere."

Ray smiled. "We don't drive that fast all the time. Do you see this big oil pump here?" He pointed past the elegantly chrome-plated valve covers to a round cylinder mounted toward the back of the engine compartment. "This keeps a constant bath of oil washing over the moving parts to reduce friction. The faster you go, the more oil it pumps." He then motioned for Artie to move forward to the front of the compartment. "Meanwhile, the radiator circulates water to draw off excess heat from the engine block. The water moves out of the tank through the hoses I just tightened, where it circulates inside the engine block to absorb the heat of the engine. Then it returns as super-hot water to the radiator, where air blows through all these tiny fins to cool it off again. Between the oil and the water, you get a constantly circulating flow of fluids to keep the engine operating within tolerances."

"Wow!"

"It's actually good for an engine to run fairly warm, since gasoline operates more efficiently at high temperatures. You get better performance."

Ray stood back and looked at the engine for a moment then reached up and closed the engine cowling, securing it at the bottom. "This is one beautiful automobile, isn't it? The Fleetwood body is the best in the business, as far as I'm concerned." Ray walked over to a chair that he kept to the side of the garage and motioned for Artie to come near. "Why don't you run into the house and get us a soda."

"But it's still morning, and Mrs. Wilkerson said she didn't like me drinking soda in the morning."

"You go to Bethany and tell her it's for me. Tell her I need two because I'm powerfully thirsty. She'll know it's for you, but she won't say anything. And if anybody asks her about it, she can truthfully say it was for me. I don't always agree with Mary, and since you're working for me today, I think I should be the one to make the decision."

Artie smiled. "Yes, sir!" And with that, he raced off to the kitchen. Once inside the kitchen he told Bethany exactly what Ray had told him to say.

Bethany, who was a rather rotund widow with light brown hair, harrumphed. "Indeed. I'm sure Ray wants *two* drinks." Artie did his best to keep a straight face but couldn't. Still, he didn't outright laugh; he just smiled. Bethany put her hands on her hips and winked at him as she turned to the refrigerator.

"Thanks!" Artie said as Bethany handed him the sodas. He bolted out the door and ran to the garage, where he waited eagerly as Ray carefully used a pair of pliers to pry the bottle cap off his bottle of Coca-Cola and then he repeated the process to open a cream soda for Artie. Artie took a big gulp, perhaps too quickly, because the carbonation burned his throat as it went down.

"Slow down, Artie, so you can taste the flavor. It'll be awhile before you get another one, so you should take some time to enjoy it."

Artie wiped his lip and said, "Yes, sir."

"Can I ask you a question?" asked Artie after taking another gulp of cream soda. "Ask away."

"How did Mrs. Wilkerson get to be so rich?" He looked up anxiously. "I mean if it's okay for me to ask something like that."

"It's all right to ask. From what I gather, she was always pretty well off. She grew up on Grove Street when that was still the most prominent street in Boise. Her father was a well-respected doctor. When she tells stories about those days, Boise was even smaller than it is now, and her house was one of the largest in town."

"So she inherited her money."

Ray leaned back in his seat. "Yes, but that turned out to be small potatoes compared with what she has now. She married into it."

"So her husband was rich."

"Not when they got married. In fact, he was seen as something of a rascal by most people. He was born in Portland but didn't seem to fit in so well there, so he moved down to Boise when he was old enough to leave home. I think he was planning to go to Denver, but while he stopped here, he heard about gold mining up in the hills near Idaho City, so he set off to make his fortune."

"So, he made it in gold?"

"Some. But that was really just the beginning. He was smart enough to see that gold miners had a lot of money but few places to spend it. So he and a friend went into the grocery business to sell to the miners. When you're stuck up in the hills for weeks and months at a time, you'll pay nearly anything for good food and liquor. He did pretty well at that, which gave him enough money to buy into a teamster company to haul supplies from Boise up into the mining areas. And that made money, as well. So then he bought some big stands of timber which he later sold to Boise-Cascade at a big profit. He made enough money on that deal that he bought into a water company to build canals out into the far reaches of the Boise Valley and the surrounding farms, and that did good, particularly when they built the Anderson Ranch Dam on the Boise River so that water flows were more predictable. Finally, he started buying car dealerships. He owned the Auburn Motors, you know?"

Artie's eyes widened. Auburn was one of the best names in the business. "No, I didn't know that."

"He became one of the most highly respected businessmen in the city. Once he had plenty of money, he built a couple of the downtown office buildings, a theater, and all sorts of things."

Artie whistled through his teeth. "So she really is rich."

Ray nodded.

"But how is it that she didn't lose all her money when the big depression hit, like everybody else?"

Ray shook his head. "I'm not sure about that. She said something about short selling stocks, holding onto mining certificates, and things like that. I know that her husband, George, didn't like to use debt, so all the buildings were paid for. Even with rents down, she still makes pretty good money from her real estate. But the truth is that she keeps most of that to herself."

"But she's still rich?"

Ray laughed. "She doesn't think so. To hear her carry on, we're all on the verge of bankruptcy, which is why she let the gardener and butler go last year. The truth is she could easily afford them, but I think she's embarrassed that she still has money when everybody else is up against hard times. So she's let the place run down a bit so that folks don't get envious. But I know enough to see that she's got money in lots of places."

They were quiet again for a time.

"How did he die?"

Ray looked up. "Die? Who?"

"Mr. Wilkerson?"

"Ah. He got consumption about ten years ago. He was always a really athletic man, very trim and fit, so it took everybody by surprise. He used to brag that he'd never had a sick day in his life. Then one day he was walking into the dealership talking with a customer, when he started coughing uncontrollably. It was so hard for him to get his breath that he passed out. That's when they noticed that there was blood in his handkerchief. We called the ambulance, but there was nothing they could do at the hospital. He died just a couple of days later. It was a terrible shock to everybody, but most particularly to Mary. She was completely heartbroken, even though she didn't show much emotion at the funeral."

"Did they have any children?"

Ray looked at Artie with a quizzical look. "You certainly ask a lot of questions. Why is that a concern of yours?"

Artie looked abashed. "I'm sorry. I shouldn't ask so many questions."

Ray softened. "I suppose you ought to know the story since you're going to be with us for a while. She never did have children of her own. But her younger sister had a boy. When his parents died from gas poisoning from a leaky lamp in their house, he came to live with her for a while. He was a really quiet boy, not very talkative. I think his parents' death was very hard on him. And, truth be told, Mary didn't know how to be a very good mother. She thought it was her job to keep him all buttoned up and strict, so she was really hard on him."

Artie got a sick feeling in his stomach. "So what happened?"

Ray was very serious now. "What happened is that he developed a gambling habit, and he sneaked out of town when he couldn't pay his debts. Mary had bailed him out a couple of times and refused to give him any more. Naturally, Mary was worried when he disappeared, so she called the police."

"Did they find him?"

Ray nodded. "In Pendleton, Oregon. The police recognized him from the description that was telegraphed to them, and they approached him in a café to talk to him. But he was an impulsive kid, and he pulled a knife on one of the policemen. They say that he cut the policeman. But we don't know." Ray went quiet.

"So did they arrest him?"

Ray looked at Artie very seriously. "They shot him. Shot him dead right there on the spot. When Mary heard the news, she collapsed right onto the floor. She was taken to her bed for more than a month and she kept saying over and over how she'd done it to him even though she didn't care about the money. It was a very hard time."

Artie was crestfallen. "So when Reuben attacked her . . ."

"I think that's why she was so hard and unforgiving about you. She'd been hurt once before and didn't want to get hurt again."

Artie sighed. "But she isn't being too hard on me now. I mean she's strict and everything and makes me take a darned bath like every other day, but she's not mean."

"I think that has a lot to do with you. You talk a lot more than her nephew did, and she likes that."

"Likes it—she's always telling me to quiet down and that children are meant to be seen not heard."

Ray laughed. "Do you believe her when she says that?"

Artie smiled. "No, I guess not. I think she just likes to play tough, but she's really pretty nice."

Ray grew serious, again. "That's why you've got to be good to her, Artie. She's had her heart broken two times now, and she doesn't need any more trouble. It would be an awful blow if you did something dishonest."

Artie's face darkened. "I want to be good. But sometimes I get notions inside my head, and I just do things. I don't want to make her sad."

Ray reached his arm and put it around Artie's shoulder. "I think you'll do fine. I've been surprised at how good it's gone, actually. She's trying a lot harder this time to let you have some room to run. I'm pretty sure she felt like she was way too strict before, and that's why Will ran away."

"Will?"

"Her nephew."

"Oh. Well, I'm going to do my level-headed best to stay on the straight-and-narrow path that she talks about so much."

Ray chuckled. It sounded funny to hear somebody so young use a word like *level-headed*. He knew it was because Artie heard it from Mary all the time. She really was trying hard to make it work this time, and he suspected that she was coming to love the boy. That pleased Ray, because Mary was genuinely happier than she'd been for a long time. But it also worried him since Artie was hardly tamed at this point.

"What about you?"

"Me? What about me?"

"How did you come to work for Mrs. Wilkerson? It seems like she thinks of you real highly, like more than a regular employee."

"*Really* highly . . ."

"Oh, yeah. I mean, yes—*really*, highly." Artie held Ray's gaze, not willing to let go of the question in spite of the correction. "Well?"

"It's kind of a long story. I was born in the east and was trained as an engineer, like my father. At first I worked on construction projects back in New

York City and Washington, DC. But, eventually I decided I wanted something different, so I moved to Detroit."

"You've seen New York City and Washington, DC.?" There was a sound of total awe in Artie's voice. "Like you see in the movies with all those buildings and cars?"

Ray laughed. "Yes, just like that. Cars and elevated trains and subways, great big bridges like the Brooklyn Bridge, and skyscrapers like the Flatiron Building next to Madison Square Garden. I've seen them all."

"But why would you leave that to come to B*oise?* I mean, there's nothing here, is there?"

"I'm not so sure that's true. But let me finish my story, and maybe it will make sense."

"Sorry."

"As I said, I decided to go to Detroit. Construction is fine, but what I really love are mechanical things. I'm Scottish by heritage, and most of the great steamships are designed and maintained by the Scots, you know. I actually have family over there, and I went there one summer to work in a shipyard."

"So why'd you end up in Detroit?"

"Well, if you get seasick really easily, you have to find something besides steamships, so I decided to go into automobiles, and Detroit's the place to do that."

"So you built *cars?*" The sound of awe returned to Artie's voice.

"Lots of them. First I worked for Ford Motor Company, but I didn't really like working on an assembly line. So then I moved to the Chrysler factory when they first broke off from General Motors. I got a job doing some basic design work. I really liked it and figured that I'd pretty much found my home. By then I was in my early fifties so I thought I'd work there until I retired or died."

"What happened?"

"George Wilkerson is what happened. He was rich by that time—rich enough to buy really magnificent automobiles like this Cadillac here. Somehow he got it into his head that he should start a car manufacturing company right here in Boise. He reasoned that labor was cheaper out here in the west and that he could find a niche market for small roadsters."

"Niche market?"

"In this case a niche means a small group. What he wanted to do was find a car that appealed to a certain type of buyer, like movie stars, who would pay top dollar for very fast sports cars."

"So did he start the factory?"

"He was lining up the money to do it when he came to Detroit to buy a new car. It was on that trip that he asked people who they could recommend to help him get something started. Someone recommended me, and so one day I got an invitation to go to his hotel for breakfast. It didn't seem like there would be any harm in that, so I went."

"And he talked you into coming to Boise?"

"Talked me into it? He practically browbeat me into it! He was a powerful talker, old George Wilkerson. Once he got started, it was almost mesmerizing. He'd start out in a low voice and slow pace that would soon grow to almost a roar as he got more and more excited. It was like watching a thunderstorm build in intensity. He told me tales of how beautiful Boise was and how the mountains would remind me of my time in Scotland and what a great opportunity it would be to get in on the ground floor of something like this. He promised me that I could design a car of my own, even put my name on it, but I reminded him that there was already a Ray Motor Car company. Well he just laughed and said we'd have to name it a McCandless."

"You decided to come out here so you could design your own car?"

Ray smiled. "I did. Came out six months later when he felt like he was ready to start designing a factory."

"But wouldn't it have been hard to start a new company out here where most cars are made in Detroit?"

"It was a gamble, of course. But back in those days, there was a lot more motor car companies than there are today, and it was easier to get your foot into the market. They were scattered in lots of places in the country, so it wasn't as far-fetched as it sounds."

"What happened, then?"

Ray shook his head. "What happened is that I came out to Boise and spent nearly a year working on plans. George set up an office for me in the back of his car dealership where I split my time between drawing up designs for the car and writing down ideas on how I thought the factory should look."

"That had to be pretty neat—designing your own factory."

"It was. I had some pretty good ideas on how to organize things."

"Well, when we finally thought we were ready to start building the factory, he got all the bankers together, and they agreed to loan him the money he needed. He'd just finished a building and had used up all his ready cash. We had architectural drawings and everything. Then he got sick, and that was the end of the factory."

Artie blew through his teeth again. "Wow, that was bad luck."

"It was the end of that dream. The bankers pulled their offer of loans as soon as they heard that George had died."

"So why did you stay around?" Artie felt a bit uneasy at this point for fear that Ray might want to move back to Detroit.

"I thought about moving on, but Mary asked if I would stay on to run the dealership. She really needed my help, so I did that for two years before we decided to sell it. After that, I was almost sixty years old with no real place to go, so Mary asked if I'd like to take over the care of her cars. She has some really spectacular automobiles, and I like the weather here in Boise, so I decided that it wouldn't be such a bad idea."

"That's why you can talk to her the way you do. You're not really just a chauffeur but an engineer?"

"I suppose that's it. Plus, I'd been pretty frugal with my money through the years, and so I have plenty of my own money to retire on if I wanted to. Mary knows that, so she doesn't press me too hard."

Artie was thoughtful. "I'm sorry you didn't get to build your car. And that the dealership got sold."

"Those things turned out for the best. It was pretty easy to get a car company going in the 1920s, but this depression would have wiped us out—along with Mary's fortune—if we had built the factory. As for the Auburn dealership, it was just a few years after we sold out that sales of Auburn automobiles slowed down because of the Depression.. So that would have been bad news, as well."

"What happened to the man who bought the dealership?"

"Fred Grover was fine. He decided that selling top-of-the-line cars wasn't such a great idea, anyway, since you had so few customers who could afford them. He talked to General Motors and got hold of the Chevrolet line. He was able to use the same building and shop, just sell a different kind of car. He's still got problems with the Depression, but at least they're still in business, and he's still selling cars."

Artie took a deep breath. "That's good. I'm glad he's okay."

Just then they heard Bethany's strong, if somewhat shrill, voice call out that she had made some fresh blueberry muffins.

"We better get going," said Ray. "Even though we spent a lot more time talking than we did working, I'm still hungry."

"Me too!" Artie liked it when Ray rested his hand on Artie's shoulder as they walked together toward the house.

CHAPTER 11

Crime or Sin?

"I can't believe that Hank gave me a quarter. And just for being there for three hours. That's pretty darn good money!"

"You helped out a lot," Aaron said. "Hank doesn't like lifting the film canisters, so he's happy to put it off on you."

"Well, it's fun to be up there with you and Hank, and I think I've watched you guys enough that I could thread one of the projectors myself if one of you dropped dead or something."

Aaron laughed. "I hope that doesn't happen. But I wouldn't be surprised if Hank offered you a part-time job. He's been seeing his girlfriend a lot lately, and I think he wants a little more free time."

"That would be great!" Artie's eyes danced at the possibility. He still liked his job at the hardware store, but running the projectors would be a lot more interesting.

"Well, don't say anything just yet. Hank likes to make things his own idea, and if you suggest a job, he might say no just to prove he's in charge."

"I can wait. But still, the thought is pretty exciting."

As they continued their walk to Aaron's home on Jefferson Street, they stopped at the grocery store so Aaron could pick up some baking soda for his mother. While meandering down an aisle where there were candy bars on display Artie hesitated for a moment, making a swift movement to the display, and then kept walking and talking.

"Very nice, Artie. You slipped that candy bar out of the bin and into your pocket so quickly that I almost don't trust my own eyes."

Artie looked up with a shocked expression directly into the eyes of David Boone, who held out an open hand.

"Let's see it!"

"I don't know what you're talking about," Artie stammered.

"Come on, I know you've got a candy bar in there." Boone reached over and grabbed Artie's arm, jerking it so suddenly that his hand emerged from his pants pocket holding a Butterfinger bar.

"Well, well, well. Just as I thought. So, Mary Wilkerson's protégé is still nothing more than a common thief."

Artie's face flushed and he started stammering, trying to explain himself.

"Just a minute, Mr. Boone," Aaron said sharply. "Why don't you ask Artie to pull the quarter out of his pocket that he was going to use to pay for the candy bar."

"What?" asked Boone, clearly flustered by the unexpected interruption from Aaron.

"That's right—you can't accuse somebody if they were really planning to pay. Go ahead and show him the quarter, Artie. Go ahead!" It was almost an order.

Slowly, Artie reached back into his pocket and pulled out the quarter that Hank had given him for helping in the booth that day.

"See!" said Aaron defiantly. "You can't be accused of stealing before you've even left the store."

David Boone frowned and started to say something but stopped. Then, after a moment, he smiled. "Fine, Aaron. If you want to cover for him, go ahead. But we both know that he would have stolen that candy bar if I hadn't seen him. You can protect him if you like, but I don't know why." With that he turned and started to the door. But just as he reached the end of the aisle, he turned and faced both of them again. "This isn't the end of this. You'll do something again, and then you'll have to face up to it. I'll see to it." With that, Boone strode out the front door, apparently forgetting whatever it was that brought him into the store in the first place.

Very quietly Artie went to the counter and paid for the candy bar then waited outside for Aaron, who emerged a minute or so later. They started walking down the street in silence. Finally, when Artie couldn't take it anymore, he said, "Thanks, Aaron."

Aaron didn't look up. Instead, he said very quietly, "He was right, wasn't he? You were going to steal the candy bar?"

Artie stopped dead in his tracks, his face clouding up instantly. He thought about denying it, but decided that the last thing he could do was lie to his best friend. So he just nodded.

By this point Aaron had stopped as well, and now he turned and looked directly at Artie. "But why? Why would you steal something when you have money? The darn candy bar only costs three cents. And I know that you have even more than the quarter since you get paid by the hardware store."

"I . . . I don't know." Artie looked down at his shoes, unable to look Aaron in the eyes. "Maybe it's because I've always done it and now I don't know how to stop."

"That's not a very good answer. It's not right to steal, whether you have the money or not. It's just not right."

"I know." Artie was miserably.

"Look at me," Aaron said firmly. But Artie didn't look up. "I said look at me!" This time it was clear that Aaron was angry, which caused Artie's temper to flare, as well.

"What?" he asked ferociously, his eyes flaring.

Aaron gaped back at him, surprised at the intensity of this new look. But it just served to make Aaron even angrier. "Don't you talk to me like that! I just stood up for you back there. And I took you to work with me today. I don't need this kind of guff from you."

Artie inhaled sharply. He hated being caught. He hated being guilty. He hated being himself. But he didn't want to get crosswise with Aaron, so he took another deep breath and backed down.

"I'm sorry."

"Look. You know that I can't stand Boone. But this time he's right. Why do you do this?" Aaron was glad that he'd brought his own temper back into control. "You've got to figure out why you do this if you're ever going stop. You want to stop, don't you?"

Artie walked over and sat down on a bus bench, motioning for Aaron to join him. "I don't know why I did it. I just did. One second we were walking down the aisle and the next thing I knew, I'd snatched up that stupid candy bar."

"Did you think about it at all? Did you take even a second to think to yourself, 'I shouldn't do this?'"

"Of course I did," Artie said sullenly. "But I did it anyway."

"I don't understand. I know that you're a good guy, but then you do something like this."

"Maybe I'm not a good guy. Maybe I am naturally bad, like Mr. Boone thinks. I go along for weeks at a time thinking I'm all right, and then I do something stupid like this. I don't know why you stick with me."

"Look, Artie. I can't tell you what's going on inside your head. All I know is that you have to get this under control. You came this close to going to reform school, and I'm afraid that even one mistake like stealing a three-cent candy bar will really get you there. That would be pretty stupid, wouldn't it? Going to jail for three cents!"

When Artie didn't say anything, Aaron hesitated for a moment, trying to decide whether to say even more. He knew he could hurt Artie with what he was thinking and didn't particularly want to do that. But maybe it was needed to get through to him. When Artie still didn't say anything he decided that he should. "If you go to reform school, you won't be able to lead the kind of life your grandmother and grandfather would want you to lead."

Artie shook his head but still didn't say anything. He didn't have to, since Aaron saw tears trickle down his cheeks. He'd hit Artie where it hurt most, and he felt kind of bad. But even though he felt bad, he still decided that he wasn't going to do what he usually did at a time like this, which was to try to cheer Artie up and tell him it would work out okay. The truth is that it might not work out okay if Artie didn't straighten up. So instead of saying anything, he just waited.

Finally, Artie looked up and said, "I'm sorry. I let you down. It's so stupid that I do this. I've been giving up half my paycheck from Derkin's to pay back the food I stole, so it's not like I don't know that it's wrong. But I don't know how to stop. What's even more crazy is that I don't do it very often—in fact I haven't done anything like this since living with Mrs. Wilkerson. But it just happened so fast. What do I do?"

"I dunno." Aaron was thoughtful. "Maybe you should go talk to Pastor Wyndham. He knows how to help people. And it seems to me that this is as much a sin as it is a crime. At least this time you paid for it. The pastor can help people with sins, you know." Aaron braced for the reply since Artie had stopped going to church a long time earlier when his grandpa got sick, and he'd even bad-mouthed some of the other kids at church, saying they all looked down on him. He honestly had no idea how Artie would react to this suggestion.

After a very long and uncomfortable pause, Artie finally looked up. "I suppose you're right. There's something going on inside me that I don't get. Maybe the pastor can help." He didn't smile like he usually would. But he did try to conclude the conversation. "Thanks for covering for me. Boone would have had me in handcuffs by now."

"I hope you don't ever give him an excuse to do that."

Aaron stood up. "Let's go. We can grab a snack at my place."

"Thanks." Artie stood up and started shuffling down the street.

"By the way, I didn't think you liked Butterfingers. I thought you liked Baby Ruth candy bars."

"I like Butterfingers," Artie said peevishly. Aaron knew it was a lie.

"Your grandpa likes Butterfingers, doesn't he?"

"Mind your own business. I said I'd go to the pastor, so let's leave it at that."

Aaron didn't know what to say, so he kept walking. He cast a sidewise glance at Artie and saw that his face was flushed again. That had to be one of the biggest disadvantages to having blond hair and a light complexion. All of a sudden Artie looked away and said, "Listen, I'll have to pass on that snack. I better head home." With that, he took off on a run.

Aaron shook his head, feeling bad for Artie. But he didn't feel bad for what he'd said. Something needed to happen to help him stop this stupid stealing.

Chapter 12

Grand Prix Racing

August 1933

Artie awakened at sunrise to make sure he was ready when Ray got there to pick him up. He'd been looking forward to this for weeks. Pulling on his Levis and an old shirt, he quietly opened the door and tiptoed down the hall to the kitchen. He planned to cut himself a piece of ham and put it on some bread for breakfast. Artie didn't want to wake Bethany or Mary, so he very quietly made his way to the kitchen door. He should have opened the door slowly, but he was in a hurry so he hit it pretty forcefully, making far more noise than he had wanted to. But the noise of the door was nothing compared to the noise that Bethany made when the door slapped her on the back. She let out a frightened yelp of surprise that startled Artie so badly that the hair on the back of his neck stood up as he let out his own yell. The two of them stood there laughing when they figured out what had happened. Then they both sobered up pretty quickly when they heard Mary call out asking what was wrong.

"Nothing, ma'am!" Bethany called back. "I'm just up getting Artie some breakfast before he and Ray go off on that crazy race of theirs." Artie smiled at her and mouthed the words, "Thank you," as he slipped past her into the kitchen.

"You didn't need to get up," Artie said quietly. "I was just going to make a ham sandwich for breakfast."

"A ham sandwich? You call that a breakfast when you and Ray are going to be gone for the whole day? I won't send a boy off starving. You'll have a proper breakfast of eggs and pancakes and bacon. And bottled raspberries." Artie loved bottled raspberries. "Besides, I'm making sandwiches for your lunch."

Artie knew better than to argue with her. Bethany took great pride in both her cooking and in her kitchen, and she was, as far as Artie was concerned, the best cook in the whole world. It seemed as if there was nothing she couldn't cook, and she worked very hard to find interesting new recipes. That sometimes caused a little problem between Bethany and Mary since Mary liked a fixed routine. Mary would have been perfectly happy to have the same thing every Monday, like beef stew, and the same thing every Tuesday, like fried chicken, and so on. But Bethany was always mixing it up on them. Mary might have said more if she didn't know that Bethany was the best cook in Boise and that at least a half a dozen other prominent families would love to hire her away from Mary. So she mostly kept her peace.

"Thanks! I didn't even think about lunch."

"Or dinner, I suspect. Do you honestly think you're going to find a five-star restaurant out there in the middle of the Idaho desert while you and Ray go driving around in that big Chrysler of his?"

"My, what a sight you two make at this hour of the morning!"

Artie almost dropped the cup of milk he was holding at the sound of Mary's voice.

"Now, why didn't you go back to sleep?" Bethany asked accusingly. "Artie just happened to startle me earlier, and I let out a little scream. But that's no reason for you to get up."

Mary moved over to one of the chairs and sat down. She was wearing an elegant burgundy bathrobe.

"I was awake already, anyway. You two and your caterwauls just gave me a reason to get up instead of lying there in my bed. Besides, who wants to eat breakfast alone?"

"I have plenty," Bethany said easily. "Just give me a minute to fix some eggs."

A few moments later, Mary accepted the large plate of over-easy eggs and two strips of crisp bacon that Bethany put in front of her and then reached over for a couple of pancakes, which, to Artie's horror, she put right on top of the eggs. She then poured syrup over the whole mess before taking a couple of bites out of it. For someone who was almost seventy years old, she still liked to eat a lot. After eating perhaps a third of the food on her plate, she looked up at Bethany. "Maybe you wouldn't mind driving me into town today, since Ray is off on his adventure."

"I could do that, as long as you let me drive that little Ford truck that I'm used to. I'm not comfortable driving those big cars that Ray takes you around in."

"The Ford will be fine."

"What do you plan to go shopping for?"

Artie always had a feeling that Bethany was a bit impertinent with Mary, but somehow she usually got away with it.

"I need a new dress, if you must know. I looked absolutely dated and foolish last week at the club. All my dresses are out of fashion."

Bethany shook her head in disgust. "You're not thinking of getting rid of all those beautiful dresses, are you? There's a fortune up there, and it would be a terrible waste."

"You watch yourself, Bethany. What I do with my clothes is my business!"

Bethany shrunk back, knowing full well that she was in the wrong for speaking out like that. But the look on her face made it clear that she hadn't changed her opinion on the subject.

"Besides, I'm not going to get rid of all those dresses. I plan to call my seamstress and have her come over and remake the ones I like so that they look better on me. And I'll donate the rest to charity. I'm sure there are a number of people who could use some good quality clothing as winter sets in." Mary said this with a smug tone in her voice, as if to put to Bethany in her place.

Bethany nodded. She seemed to like the solution and was glad that Mary had found a way to end the dispute.

"I was thinking that maybe you'd like something new, as well."

"What?" said Bethany in genuine surprise. "You'd buy me a new dress?"

"For fall. All the young people get to buy new clothes for school, but what about us? I think we're coming up on the most wonderful time of the year in Boise, and we should celebrate it with new clothing, don't you think?"

Bethany almost sat down in the chair she was standing next too. This was not the Mary Wilkerson she knew. It struck her that maybe it was because she liked getting out more, now that Artie had joined them.

"Well, thank you. I'd like that."

"Good, it will be a lot more fun to shop if I have someone with me."

Mary finished off her food while Artie was finishing boxing up all the sandwiches and potato salad and other things that Bethany had made for their lunch.

"I know you've got to go, Arthur, but would you mind going out to get the newspaper for me?" Mary asked.

"Not at all!" He raced out of the house. It wasn't entirely true, since he'd heard Ray's car come into the driveway, and he didn't want to make Ray late. But it wasn't too much of Mary to ask so he waved to Ray, and then bounded back up the steps with the newspaper. He was so excited at this point that he could hardly wait to get started. A Grand Prix race right there in Boise! And he got to ride with Ray through the whole thing.

* * *

"So what does *Grand Prix* mean?" Artie asked Ray as they made their way west across the Fairview Bridge on their way to the fairgrounds, where the race was scheduled to start. "And why is it pronounced 'Pree' when it's spelled 'Prix?'"

Ray laughed. "Because it's French. This type of racing started in Europe, and it just means that the race will be run on regular roads between towns rather than on a race course like the Indianapolis 500."

"Have you ever seen the Indy 500? I've watched some of the movie reels about it, and it looks like they must be going a thousand miles an hour."

"More than a hundred miles per hour actually, and yes, I have seen it."

"Wow! Was it really great?"

Ray laughed again. It was so refreshing to see the world through a teenager's eyes. He nodded his head. "All that and more. There are some of the finest automobiles in the world at the Indy. Studebaker, Willys-Overland, Chrysler, Ford, and even a Mercedes-Benz from Germany on occasion. There are Italian cars and French cars. It's pretty exciting."

"So why did you pick a Chrysler?"

Ray patted the door on his Chrysler Imperial. In his mind it was the finest American roadster outside of the Auburn. And it didn't cost nearly as much as the Auburn. "I think Walter Chrysler is an engineering genius. He worked for General Motors for years, learning everything there is to know about making cars, and then, once he was a millionaire, he set out to make his own car. I'm not saying GM and Ford don't make good cars, but Chrysler is famous for its engineering. This one has won some of the toughest races in the world, if not coming in first place outright, at least it's finished first in its class. It's been clocked at more than a hundred miles per hour, which is far more than most of the roads we'll be driving on today can take."

They drove on for a few moments, Ray lost in thought. Artie knew that Ray was thinking hard—mentally reviewing each and every step of the work he'd done on the engine and the car to get it ready for today's race. A race of this type was as much a test of endurance as of speed. In fact, it was clocked in segments, rather than at the end of the course. That way, cars didn't have an incentive to engage in dangerous behavior trying to get ahead of one another. It also meant that they could each have their own starting time so that there wasn't too much traffic on the small country roads at any given time.

As they pulled up to the fairgrounds, there was a huge cloud of dust in the parking lot where the various racers and spectators were congregating. Auto racing was becoming an increasingly popular sport as each competitor did his best to soup up his particular car. The competition between the car manufacturers was intense since each win in a major race tended to have a positive impact on sales. The fans loved it because they could live vicariously through the exploits of their favorite drivers. For people who had very little money, this was an inexpensive way to see some great automobiles in action.

As Ray parked his car, a couple of his friends came up and started chatting with him about the course. Artie hung back from the group, doing his best to listen in on what they were saying without getting in the way. But he was quickly lost in the automotive talk of such things as bore and stroke and compression ratios. Ray had given him some books and magazines to study, and Artie felt like he was starting to understand, but this was still too deep for him. Still, he marveled at how these guys seemed to know every single detail about every single engine and car in the race that day. Ray had already told him there would be around twenty competitors.

"Hi, Artie!" Artie turned around to see Joey come bounding up to him.

"Hi, Joey. What are you doing here?"

"My dad decided to come out. Ever since you've started working with Mr. McCandless, my dad has taken an interest. I think he'd like to be a mechanic if he could."

Artie nodded. "I think that's what I want to do. I'll probably drop out of school in a year or two so I can get certified. Ray says that after doing an apprenticeship here in Boise, there's a General Motors school in Salt Lake City that is recognized all over the country. It would be pretty neat if I could go there."

Joey accepted this without comment. He never thought that far ahead, but he liked the fact that Artie was excited about something. "How's your grandpa doing?"

"He's all right, I guess." Artie's countenance darkened a bit. "The doctor says that his heart is as good as a fifty-year-old's. It's only his mind that seems to have gone. So he might live like this for a long time."

"I guess it's good that he's feeling all right."

"I suppose so. But I know that he doesn't like the thought that people have to watch him all the time. Whenever I go to visit him, he begs me to take him home. When I start down the hall to leave, he calls after me to come back, almost like he's pleading. I really hate that."

Artie was about to change the subject, because this one was so painful, when Ray yelled over to Artie to come join him. They were getting very near the start of the race. "Gotta go, Joey. Wish us luck!"

Joey smiled. "You bet. I hope you get the trophy."

Artie jogged over to Ray, who guided him into the circle where the drivers were assembled. Each driver was allowed one passenger and one mechanic. Most of the drivers chose an experienced driver as their passenger, just in case, but Ray told Artie that it was all right if he came along, even though he couldn't drive. That was a pretty big sacrifice. Henry Grinnell was joining them as the mechanic. He worked at the local Chrysler dealership, which was sponsoring Ray. It was Ray's car, but the cost of the entry fee and a lot of the custom parts that Ray used on his engine were paid for by the dealership. They figured it was good advertising to have a Chrysler in the race, particularly since Ray was one of the best drivers in the Intermountain West. His convertible was kept in perfect condition, so it showed the car off at its finest.

"Welcome everyone! Is this the perfect day for a race?" People cheered and clapped at the sound of the race coordinator's voice coming through the loudspeaker. "I think the weather should remain hot and dry, so aside from some overheated radiators, there shouldn't be any reason that everyone can't finish the race and come back safe and sound tonight." The crack about the radiators was no joke. With the high temperatures of the last few days exceeding 95 degrees, it would be hard to keep the engines running, particularly if they got bogged down in sand, slowing down the flow of air through the radiator.

"Drivers step forward and draw a number out of the bowl!" Ray stepped up with the other drivers and came back with a folded piece of paper. "We'll start out in the number ten position. Right in the middle of the pack."

"Is that good?"

"It's got its advantages and disadvantages," Henry replied. "The other cars will pack down the road for us, which is good, but we'll also have to put up with a lot of dust. We're likely to have to pass some of the cars that take off in front of us, and that's always a little bit ugly as they try to block us." His face lit up in a grin. "But that's what makes it all worth doing, isn't it, Ray?" Ray nodded. "Besides, it doesn't really matter where you are in the order. You've still got to cover the same amount of ground."

"Now that everyone has their number, let's review the route." Each of the drivers had been given a map. Even so, they listened intently as the race coordinator went over the details. First, they would continue west on Fairview through Garden City and all the way to Caldwell, to the west of Nampa. That would be their first call station where their time would be logged. Then they'd head south to Marsing on the Snake River where they'd cross the river to pick up their second chit. They'd recross the river and work their way to Nampa for stop number three. Next, they'd follow the railroad tracks out to the small railroad town of Kuna, which was their next to last stop. From Kuna it was northeast to Boise and the finish line. All in all, it was approximately ninety miles of racing, mostly on dirt roads. The chances for flat tires, broken axles, overheated radiators, and even cracked cylinder blocks were great, and it was almost impossible odds that all the cars would make it. That's why the race officials had a number of tow trucks set up in each location to go out and rescue anyone who got into trouble.

"Artie, you're in charge of the water and the food. We'll have to put it in the backseat with you."

"Check!" said Artie, imitating Ray's habit of going through a checklist.

"It's going to be harder than you think. I'm not just talking about water for the three of us, but also water for the car. We've got two ten-gallon cans stowed on the grill behind the rear bumper, plus two ten-gallon gasoline cans. As we use the water up, you'll have to replace it at each of the stops. After all, Henry and I are old men, and we shouldn't have to lug those things around, now should we?"

Artie smiled. "Of course not. That's why you need me along." But he knew full well that since he was the smallest of the three, they would help him when the time came. This kind of banter was just Ray's way of working off energy.

As Artie climbed into the backseat to rearrange all their things, including the food and tool boxes, he heard a great cheer erupt from the crowd. He looked up to see the first car take off, everyone waving to them as they went by. It was a Chevrolet roadster. He knew enough from Ray to know that it wasn't likely to be a real threat, not because it was a bad car, but because the driver wasn't aggressive enough. Artie wondered if they could make up enough time to catch it. That was unlikely with their number ten starting position.

"You can go talk to Joey if you like. We've got nearly an hour to wait. So go ahead."

Artie stepped out of the car and went over to where Joey and his dad were. "Once everybody takes off, we're going to drive into town to work in our garden," Joey said. "But we'll be back by late afternoon. I hope you're in first place by then."

Artie replied, "Nobody will know for sure, since they have to bring in all of the time logs and add them together."

"You know what I mean," Joey said.

"I know. I hope we win, too. But even if we don't, it's going to be a great adventure."

* * *

"Is there anything we can do to help him?" Artie asked urgently.

"A flat tire just takes time to change. Henry knows what he's doing and will have it changed faster by himself than if we got in the way."

"It's just that we're losing time," said Artie nervously.

"We know that, Artie. It's all part of the race. We're not the only ones to have trouble." Artie wasn't consoled, but he was smart enough to know when to stop pestering Ray. After all, Ray was doing a great job of driving, and by the time they had reached Caldwell, they'd passed three of the earlier cars in the race and were told that they had the best time on the first leg of the journey up to that point. By the time they crossed the Snake River at Marsing, they were running neck and neck with the DeSoto that had started out in the number six position.

After a quick lunch, the race organizers made them wait to put some spacing between the competitors again, since there had been a rather ugly incident between car number four and five when number five tried to pass on Kartcher Road. It seems the earlier car didn't want to be passed, so it made some rather wild maneuvers to block number five. Unfortunately, in its attempt to block the passing car, it swung a little wide at one point and its front wheel went down into a ditch. From the reports, it made a rather comical scene as the three occupants were hurled up and over the hood of the car as it came to an abrupt halt. It was only comical because they all managed to come out of it without serious injury somehow. But it was still bad enough that the race organizers didn't want anything else like that happening again.

After that wait, they were on their way to Kuna when they got a flat.

"I'm afraid the rim is bent!" Henry said in a frustrated voice.

Like a small rocket, Artie was off the rock and over to Ray in an instant. "What does that mean, Ray? Are we out of the race? Can it be fixed? What are we going to do?"

"Quiet, Artie!" It wasn't said in a mean way, but it was enough to stop Artie in his tracks.

"We have two spare tires but only one spare wheel. It just means that we have to be a little more careful from now on since we will be out of the race if we damage another rim. Now, help Henry get this wheel off while I get the replacement off its mounting,"

"Yes, sir!" Artie immediately moved to help Henry, who was sweating profusely as he manhandled the large rubber tire and wheel. Artie helped him lift it up and off the rim and then wheeled it over to the car. He noticed that it kind of wobbled as he rolled it, which is why they'd had to stop. Ray had swerved to miss some kind of animal on the road and hit a rock in the process. While Henry and Ray mounted the spare wheel, Artie went to work letting the air out of the tire on the damaged rim so they could use it on another wheel if needed. It was amazing how much they could accomplish out in the wilds with Ray's and Henry's tool kits and a hand pump.

Looking up a few moments later Artie saw that they almost had the new wheel on. He was frustrated at how much time it was taking but knew that it was unavoidable. Finally, loading the damaged rim in the trunk, Ray called out for everyone to load up. Artie's head flew back as Ray popped the clutch. From that point onward there was a real urgency to Ray's driving. Artie didn't know how fast they were going down Black Rock Road, but it had to be pretty fast, given how long it took the train on the tracks to their left to catch up to them. Ray had told Artie that the train often reached speeds of sixty or seventy miles per hour through this stretch of track where the land was level and the roadbed in excellent condition. He couldn't help but turn around in the backseat and watch as the huge passenger engine came lumbering up behind them. They were so close to the roadbed that he felt the blast of steam on his face as some of the exhaust steam from the driving pistons escaped out the side. The ground trembled under the Chrysler Imperial as the monster lumbered past. It was fun to wave to the passengers inside the train, who were startled to see a car moving that fast on the dirt road. Still, the train was pulling ahead of them when suddenly it seemed to slow and they began to gain on the engine again. Turning to look ahead, Artie saw that they were approaching Kuna, which meant the train had to slow down. They would, too, eventually, but for now they sped on ahead. Artie laughed as they passed the engineer and the fireman, who waved to them from the cab of the engine. This had to be the most exciting moment of his life. For a few moments they were the fastest thing in Ada County! Then they started to slow down as they got closer to town. However, they still turned crazily onto King Road at what could only be thought of as a very dangerous speed. If any pedestrians had stepped out onto the road, Ray could never have stopped in time to avoid hitting them.

"I see it up ahead," said Henry, his words calm even though Artie could sense the tension in his voice. "You probably ought to back off now."

Ray turned to him briefly but didn't slow down.

"I said back off, Ray, or I'll get out here. You're supposed to obey the local laws."

It took a moment, but then Ray finally let off on the accelerator, and the car immediately began to lose speed. In a few more moments, they came to a stop at the little park across from the dry goods store. Henry got out of the passenger side without a word, and Ray got out from his. Artie was going to follow him, but Ray slammed the door. So Artie changed sides and climbed out of Henry's door.

"You better get the water cans filled back up," Henry said to Artie. Ray had gone over to the judges table to officially sign the log and to pick up his chit.

"Is everything all right?" Artie asked Henry.

Henry looked at him evenly. "He gets like this sometimes. He's really competitive, you know. You don't usually see it because he stays away from things like this. But I think this race bothers him. I've got to talk with him, because he's taking too many risks." Henry paused, obviously upset at the conversation he was about to initiate. "Why don't you go over to the store and buy us some candy?" Henry handed him some money, and Artie took off across the street.

When he got back, Ray came directly for him, which was a little frightening. He braced himself when Ray said, "I'm sorry, Artie. I got a little out of control back there. I do that sometimes. Henry talked to me, like he always does. I'm better now. Do you still want to ride with me, or do you want to go back with one of the judges?"

"I want to go with you." Artie couldn't help but sound a little frightened still.

"All right, why don't we get going." Artie started around to Henry's side of the car, but Ray called for him to climb in from his side. As he did, Ray patted his shoulder. "It'll be all right. We don't have to win. We just need to finish."

Henry climbed in the car, acting like nothing had happened. "With fair roads we're maybe ninety minutes away. Let's pray for no broken axles or other calamities." And with that they were off.

Artie relaxed as Ray took a more cautious speed through the town and onto the main road. He shouldn't have relaxed. It's approximately thirty miles from Kuna to Boise following the grid that made its way across the mesa toward the valley, and it was to be the most exciting thirty miles of Artie's life.

CHAPTER 13

A Photo Finish

It wasn't really a photo finish, since it was a timed race, and it didn't really matter what order the cars came in. But it made for a much better headline in the *Boise Statesman* the next day.

After leaving Kuna, Ray had stayed true to his word and had driven with at least a modicum of sanity. That is, until they reached Meridian. There they caught up to Leon Skandler and his mechanic, Ron Franken. Leon was driving one of the new Lincoln KB models that had been stripped down to the lightest possible weight with the engine modified for just this type of extreme racing. Through the years Leon had been Ray's biggest critic while Ron Franken was Henry's biggest competitor in the car business.

"You know he's got a 447-cubic-inch V-12 engine in that monster!" Henry yelled over to Ray. "It develops 150 horsepower!"

Ray nodded. "This year's Indy 500 pace car. We'll have our hands full with this one," he said grimly.

The Chrysler had a smaller displacement at 384.8 cubic inches and featured a straight-eight engine block. But with the custom-built, aluminum, high-compression head and the Stromberg carburetor that Ray had added to it, he'd managed to juice it up to 160 horsepower. Each team had won at a couple of races, and this one had the potential to be a tie-breaker. Of course, neither team could know where they were in the standings, but since they'd each had a breakdown, they had to be pretty close to each other. Besides, the main race aside, they were now in exactly the same spot, driving for exactly the same finish line. What had started out as a twenty-car Grand Prix could now be reduced to a simple drag race.

Or not. Ray didn't have to race Leon. In fact, he was committed to not racing him since it was only likely to end up in a fight. But when Ron called over to Henry that a Chrysler Imperial like Ray's didn't stand a chance against a Lincoln, and that Walter Chrysler was an imposter, *and* that Henry Ford was the only true automotive giant in the industry, Henry very quietly told Ray to take the gloves off and let Leon have it. And that's when the fun began.

The map called for them to head north toward Eagle and then turn right on Fairview, where they would retrace their way back to the fairgrounds. That's where the final timer was waiting, as well as the crowd. By now the early cars should be returning, so the excitement would have built up by the time they got there. And since local traffic was being blocked off of Fairview for the end of the race, they could open the cars up all the way. It was the perfect opportunity for a race within the race.

"Are you both sure you're all right with this?" At the moment, Ray was still in front of the Lincoln, pushing upward of sixty miles per hour. Henry nodded, and Artie shouted that Ray should go for it. With the top down, it was hard to hear very much in the backseat at that speed, so Artie had to lean forward and strain if he hoped to hear their conversations. Once Ray had clearance, he floored it, and Artie was thrown back in his seat as the Chrysler let out a guttural roar. Artie pulled himself forward to look over Ray's shoulder, where he watched in fascination as the speedometer inched its way past eighty miles per hour. He was now going faster than he'd ever gone in his life, and it was thrilling. The road wasn't really designed for this sort of thing, but Ray yelled out that he was of the opinion that it was easier to hit the road at top speed since the car reacted less to the bumps in the road as it skimmed the surface. Artie didn't know if that was true or not, but he was convinced that they became airborne on more than one occasion.

As they reached the brow of the bluff that marked their descent into the Boise River valley, Artie's breath was taken away as the car flew out over the edge and started its descent. He was so wrapped up in just trying to stay inside the car that he was totally unprepared for the draft of air that hit him as the Lincoln made its move. They blasted past with their horn sounding. Artie gasped as he saw Ron nearly bounced right up and out of the passenger seat when the Lincoln hit a particularly deep rut in the road as it was passing them.

From the way Ray reacted, it was pretty clear that he'd been surprised by the maneuver as well. But no matter what maneuvers he tried, he couldn't prevent Leon from getting past him. Now it was the three racers in the Chrysler who had to eat dust as the powerful Ford-built Lincoln tore down the road.

Artie leaned forward, expecting to hear Ray cussing or something. But instead Artie saw him laughing as he yelled over to Henry, "You've got to give credit where it's due. That Lincoln chassis is taking a real beating. If he can keep the wheels on the road, we're going to have the ride of our life trying to keep up."

Artie was very glad that Ray was taking the competition in a good-natured fashion, rather than the way he'd acted by the train. The dust was pretty thick, so Ray backed off enough that at least they weren't going to choke to death, but then he matched the speed of the Lincoln precisely.

The air cleared enough for Artie to see that in just a matter of moments, they would reach Fairview Avenue, so Artie braced for the corner, but not quickly enough. It was there that he learned Ray's strategy for getting the lead back as he cut the angle of the corner, tearing out some rather large sagebrush plants as he made the turn. Artie was thrown violently against the side of the backseat, arms and legs flailing, but he managed to keep himself inside the car. When he was able to pull his head back above the level of the seat, he let out a cheer, since the Lincoln was now behind them again. Leon was waving his hand furiously, but Ray just calmly lifted his arm and waved back.

Now that they had turned onto Fairview, they had approximately seven miles to go. At more than seventy miles per hour, that wouldn't take long. Fortunately, the road was paved through this final stretch, and the surface was much better than anything else they'd experienced since leaving it earlier in the day. The road was sometimes labeled the Old Oregon Trail Highway, so it was the best maintained of any road in the valley. At this point they knew that traffic had been taken off the road so it was all theirs. It also meant that Leon could use the other lane to pass them if he could muster the speed to do so. So now it was an all-out free-for-all.

Artie felt Ray shift into the highest gear and then felt the car slowly gain speed. When he leaned forward to look over Ray's shoulder, he was shocked to see the speedometer passing ninety miles per hour. It seemed like the occasional trees off to the side were nothing more than a green blur. Periodically Artie turned around to see how the Lincoln was doing. It was hanging in there pretty well, but it appeared that the Chrysler had a slight edge in top speed, because they continued to lengthen their lead ever so slowly. In a matter of a few minutes, they started seeing cars parked along the side of the road with spectators sitting on the hood to cheer them on. It was thrilling to see people waving happily at them. It didn't take long to figure out who were the Chrysler fans and who were the Lincoln and Ford fans. But at this rate, it didn't matter that much because nobody was in view for very long before Ray had blown right past them.

Henry turned around and motioned for Artie to lean forward. When he did, Henry shouted in his ear, "This is the trickiest part. We're going to go full speed past the finish line, but then we have to stop pretty fast, so brace yourself." Artie nodded and slid back into the comfortable seat, bracing his legs.

Slumped down as he was, he couldn't see the difference in the road surface, but he felt it. All of a sudden the noise from the tires changed, and he felt the car start to wobble. The change was scary enough that he expected Ray to slow down, which he did, but not very fast. Now Artie was panicked, because at the rate they were losing speed, it was very likely the Lincoln would overtake them. Deciding to brave being thrown around, he rose up in the seat to see what was happening. What he saw scared the wits out of him. It seemed that a summer thunderstorm had just dropped an unbelievable amount of rain on the road, making the road extremely slippery. At the speed they were traveling, they could easily slip and flip if Ray wasn't able to bring the car under control. Artie kept hoping he'd hit the brakes to slow them down, but Ray didn't do it. At one point Artie saw Ray lift his hands right off the steering wheel. That seemed crazy, but the slight turning slide they'd started into quickly evened out, and Ray was able to reassert control. Artie had no idea what was happening to the Lincoln, and frankly he didn't care. He just wanted to get out of it alive. As they approached the finish line, he saw spectators scattering. Obviously they had all figured out that both cars were in trouble, and they didn't want to get in the way if one of them went off the road. Finally, Artie turned to see if Leon was still there and was happy to see that he was all right. But the big old Lincoln wasn't slowing down as fast as the Imperial, and the narrow lead they'd built up was quickly evaporating. Artie thought that was either very brave or very stupid. But as they got closer, he saw that it wasn't by choice that they were going that fast. Leon had a panicked look on his face, and Ron had covered his eyes.

"Brace yourself, Artie!" There was a commanding tone in Ray's voice. Artie looked forward and saw why. Up ahead, just past the finishing line, there was a mound of something on the street. Ray had to get the car stopped, or they'd hit that and fly straight up into the air, undoubtedly turning the car over as they did.

"Now!" Ray shouted, and Artie felt the brakes grab. The car immediately began to slide, and Artie felt them go into a spin. In one of those crazy moments when it seems like everything slows down, he felt the car do a complete loop in the road. Then Ray managed to hold it straight for a moment, but then it started spinning again. Still, Ray reacted to each turn of the car in such a way that it held level, rather than flipping. It had to be a miracle, but somehow they were slowing down. Somewhere in his mind, Artie registered that they slid past the finish line, even though he wasn't sure which way the car was facing when they did. In his mind's eye he was also aware that the Lincoln went flying past them at high speed in a desperate skid.

And then it was over. The car came to an abrupt stop as the brakes finally found a piece of dry pavement. Artie was thrown forward against the front seat, and he heard a sickening thud in the front seat. When he was able to pull himself up, he saw Ray slumped over the steering wheel.

"Ray!" he shouted. "Ray!" and he got ready to scramble over the seat to help him. Fortunately, Henry was already moving over to help Ray so Artie stayed where he was. Then he watched in horror as Henry sat Ray's limp body upright in the seat. There was blood coming out of his nose, but Artie didn't see any cuts. "Ray!" he shouted again.

"Artie, get out and run for help," said Henry.

Artie stood up and jumped over the side. "Wait a minute," Henry called. "He's waking up."

Artie came running back. "Ray! Ray, are you okay?" There were tears streaming down his face now. "Ray, you've gotta be okay."

At that point, Ray rolled his head in Artie's direction and smiled and said something very softly—too softly for Artie to hear very well. It sounded something like, "Did we win?"

"What?" Artie looked desperately at Henry, who shrugged his shoulders to show that he didn't understand him either.

"I said, 'Did we win the race?'"

Artie was so terrified about Ray's getting hurt that he wasn't in the mood for this, so he slugged Ray's arm. "Darn you, Ray! You scared me half to death."

"I think I was half dead. That was pretty exciting."

"I'd say," Henry added with relief.

"Well?"

"I don't know," said Artie.

By this time, some of the spectators and officials came running up to the car. "Is everyone all right?" one of the judges called out. "A little worse for the wear, but we're alive. What about Leon and Ron? Are they okay?"

The judge looked over to the north and said, "It looks like they're all right, but their Lincoln didn't do so well. They didn't get stopped in time and hit the load of sugar beets that came off a truck when the storm first hit. It's quite a mess."

Artie looked over to see Leon and Ron standing outside their car shaking their heads. Leon even kicked one of the tires.

"Who won?" Ray asked firmly of the judge.

"You know we won't have the answer to that until all the cars get in. Did you get a concussion or something?"

"No, I didn't get a concussion. At least I don't think so. But I mean who crossed the line first, me or Leon?"

The judge's face darkened. "Is that what you two were up to, you old coot? You know there's not supposed to be any head-to-head racing."

Ray sat up straight. "No, of course not. It's just that Leon was so close that I lost track of him. I didn't mean anything by it."

"Darn you, Ray McCandless, you could've killed yourself and these two with you."

"But we made it." Ray took a deep breath. "Why is that I can't make myself want to get out of the car? And why are my hands and legs shaking so much?" They both laughed, and the judge helped him up and out of the car, where Ray stood on wobbly legs. Artie laughed to see him so unsteady. It was the laugh of someone who had been scared to death and who was relieved that his friend was all right.

"It was exciting . . ." he said under his breath. And then he laughed as Joey came jogging up to him. There would be lots to talk about after this race. That much was for sure.

* * *

"Don't the two of you make a fine spectacle," said Mary the next morning over breakfast.

Artie ducked his head. He knew she was referring to the photo that had been printed on the front page of the *Statesman* that morning. Right there in glorious black and white, it showed the Chrysler Imperial crossing the finishing line just inches ahead of the Lincoln. The fact that they were going backward at that point is what gave the picture such a dramatic effect.

"It was just plain foolish of us," Ray said. He didn't see how Mary could fault him for that analysis.

She snorted. "Try to weasel out of it by being honest, will you? You could have killed yourself. And Artie and Henry with you."

"It was his driving that saved us," Artie said defensively. Somehow he felt like he needed to stand up for Ray. "There was no way we could have known there was water on the road, and Ray drove like a magician as he brought the car to a stop."

Mary scowled, but she didn't say anything else about it but kept looking at the paper.

"Actually, Ray, I think you owe your victory to Arthur!"

"And how's that?" Ray asked in surprise.

"Well, the paper says that you won by a nose, and as I look carefully at this picture, it's quite clear that Arthur was leaning over the backseat, with his head in the wind. It seems to me that it had to be his nose that won, since you went over the finish line backwards."

Ray laughed. "Why, now that I think about it you're right. It was Artie's nose that won it for us. Good work, Artie." He let out a full-bellied laugh.

"But we really only came in third place, overall. Probably because of that darned flat tire," Artie said.

"Ah, but we beat the Lincoln, Artie!" Ray smiled.

"And that obnoxious Leon Skandler has to finally admit that his precious Lincolns aren't everything after all."

Ray looked up with a surprised look on his face. "Why, Mary Wilkerson! I didn't know you had it in for Leon."

"You know perfectly well that I have no use for Lincoln owners. They're so smug. It's about time someone gave them their comeuppance. I just wish you'd done it in a Cadillac instead of an Imperial. Still, it humbled him nonetheless."

Ray turned and grinned at Artie. Life was pretty good, bent rims and mud-caked Chrysler Imperials notwithstanding.

CHAPTER 14

A Bad Day at Church

"You look quite handsome, Arthur. What's the occasion?"

"Aaron thinks I should go to church."

Mary nodded approvingly. "I think that's a very good idea. It means you get to use that suit I bought you."

Artie looked down. His suit really was something, a Hart Schaffner & Marx that had been tailored to fit his slender frame like a glove. The weave of the pure wool jacket was smooth and soft—softer than anything he'd ever felt. It made him feel great to have it on, but he worried that he'd be way overdressed compared to most of the people at church. There was the Depression, after all, and fine suits were low on the priority list.

"So what time are you supposed to be there?"

"The main service is at 10:30 AM. Then it's Sunday School."

"Are you going to ride your bike or walk?"

Rather than answer, Artie just stood there uncomfortably.

"Well, is something bothering you?"

"It's just that things didn't go very well the last time I went to church. In fact, I was kind of asked to leave."

"Ah, so you're a little worried to go back and face them?"

Artie nodded.

"Well, you have every bit as much right to be there as the next fellow. Church is for sinners, after all." Mary thought that should satisfy him, but apparently it didn't because he just continued to stand there. "Is there something else?"

"It's just that you told me once that you're a member of the church, too."

"What?" At first she started to laugh, but when she saw that Artie was serious, she said, "Oh, you're not suggesting that I go to church with you?"

"It would be a lot easier if I had someone to sit with. People wouldn't talk about me as much if you were there."

"I should say not! They'd all be talking about me." She looked at Artie, who didn't move but who didn't really press her either. "Listen. I went to church as a little girl and even as a young woman. But when I married my husband, he told me that he didn't want to attend. Even though his parents were church goers in Portland, he was always something of a rebel, and he had given up on going. He left it up to me to decide whether I wanted to be go or not. For a few years I tried. I admit that I enjoyed the services and the people. But my husband was always working so much that Sunday mornings turned out to be a really good time for me to be with him. So eventually I stopped going to church and I haven't been back for more than forty years. I couldn't just start going now. I'm way too old to make that kind of a change."

"But you said that church is good for people. Why wouldn't it be good for you? And you'll be all alone here if I go without you."

Artie worried about pressing her, but he really didn't want to go alone. It only seemed fair that with all the changes he was having to make, it might not be so bad for Mary to make a change or two in her life. Perhaps it was a sign of the growing strength of their relationship that he was willing to press her.

"Artie," she said with a bit of desperation in her voice. The very fact that she said Artie indicated how discombobulated she was by the conversation. "Arthur," she caught herself, "My husband was a very good man. And he wasn't irreligious. In fact, even though very few people know this, he still paid tithing to the church all the years of his life. He just didn't like the social aspect of it."

Artie whistled. "That must have been a lot of tithing!"

Mary smiled. "That is none of your business. But yes, I suspect that it did make something of an impression on the financial clerks who had to account for it."

When Artie didn't say anything, Mary added, "He has one of the best gospel libraries of anyone in town—maybe the very best, for all I know. He read from these books when he wanted a Sunday church service. Now that he's gone, I do the same thing."

"Well?" Artie said, "Are you coming?"

"I thought I just answered that question. I study gospel books on Sunday."

"But you just told me that you liked the services when you went. Besides, I'd *really* like the company."

Mary flushed, and she found herself in real danger of hyperventilating. She hadn't bargained for this when she agreed to take Artie in. But she knew that he'd changed their lives for the better in the time he'd been there. Now he was asking a favor—one of the very few he'd asked.

Taking a deep breath, she said, "All right, I'll go with you. There are likely some people who will faint dead away when they see me, but I'll go for you."

Artie burst into a grin. "That is great! It'll be like I have a family, just like everyone else."

Hearing him say that pleased Mary far more than she cared to admit. "Well, you better call Ray to see if he'll drive us. He usually doesn't get out here much on Sunday. You'll probably get him all upset."

"I could drive you." Artie smiled mischievously.

She harrumphed. "That will be the day. Imagine me being driven around Boise by a fourteen-year-old."

"I'm fifteen. Besides, I'm sure I could drive if I got the chance."

"Fifteen and mouthy. Well, I'm sure the day isn't far off when Ray will spoil you even further by teaching you, but I can assure you that I don't want to be with you on that first ride. Now, call Ray and see if this is even possible, and I'll go upstairs and see what I might possibly have to wear." Artie walked over and helped her out of her chair.

"I have no idea what women are wearing to church these days, so I'll probably look completely out of place. I should have had more warning . . ."

Artie smiled, knowing full well that she had dozens of beautiful dresses to choose from. He suspected that she would really enjoy the opportunity to dress up and be with people. If not, she would have said no. He knew from personal experience that she was more than capable of declining when she didn't want something. Still, she was going, and he felt good to think that she would do that for him.

* * *

"Stephanie! Please come over here right now!"

Stephanie turned from Artie, startled by her father's voice. She'd been having a nice conversation with Artie about how surprised everyone was to see Mary Wilkerson at church. A lot of people didn't even know she was a member of the congregation, and it was surprising to know that one of Boise's wealthiest citizens belonged to their little church. Somehow it made them all feel a little special, and everyone had been so nice to her when she and Artie arrived. But now she'd gone off to the adult class, and Artie and Stephanie had been walking to their youth class.

"What is it, Daddy?"

"Just come here! Now!"

Stephanie's countenance darkened.

"I'm sorry, Artie. I'll catch up with you in class."

Artie dropped his head. While she may not have known why her father wanted to see her, he did. Standing next to Mr. Lewis was none other than Mr. David Boone, who stood there with a scowl on his face. As if to confirm his fears, Artie saw Mr. Boone point at him and say something to Stephanie and her father. Stephanie turned and looked at him, as well, and Artie could tell that she was upset. Obviously, Boone had told her father something bad about Artie, and now she was being told that she shouldn't talk to him. It was an old story, but one that still hurt.

Without waiting to see if she could rejoin him, Artie made his way to the classroom. Unfortunately, the only person in the class who would have much to do with him was Joey. When he walked into the room, Joey motioned for him to come and sit by him. Artie started over in that direction, not noticing that John Redmond was sitting just inside the door. It was a costly mistake. As Artie started across the concrete floor of the basement room, John stuck his foot out. Artie didn't see it and went sprawling, which caused the other kids to laugh. The teacher wasn't there yet to quiet them.

Artie scrambled up and turned to face John, ready to slug him. "Why did you do that?" Artie asked angrily. At least part of the anger was prompted by the fact that he couldn't think of anything smarter to say.

"What do you mean, Call? I thought I was being nice not to slug you for hurting my foot. You're pretty clumsy, aren't you?"

John was never a very graceful bully. When Artie made a move toward him, John stood up. He was a good six inches taller than Artie and probably fifty pounds heavier. "Oh, my!" John said thickly. "Did you get that pretty suit of yours dirty?"

Artie looked down and saw that his knees were scuffed up. That really irritated him, and he was tempted yet again to get into it with John.

"Come on, Artie. It's church. Just ignore him."

Artie turned and looked at Joey. He was right, of course. So in spite of his anger, he turned without a word to John and moved over to his seat. Naturally, that irritated John, who was enjoying his moment of notoriety.

"Hey, Call! I hear that your hundred-year-old grampa has gone crazy in the head. Is he stark raving mad or just a drooling lunatic?"

With a roar the could be heard two classrooms away, Artie lunged and smacked John square on the nose before tackling him and knocking him down onto the floor. Artie started pounding him as soon as they hit the floor and managed to land some pretty good blows before John brought his superior strength to bear to wrestle himself free. The tables were turning just as the teacher, Sister Noolan, came in and shrieked. Fortunately, for Artie, her shriek was the rough equivalent of an air-raid siren, and the sheer blast of it was enough to scare both John and Artie right out of their wits. John rolled over on his haunches, which gave Artie a chance to scramble up and away.

"Back again so soon, and you're already in a fight!" she yelled to Artie. Her next move was going to be to tell John that he was just as bad, but Artie didn't stick around long enough to hear it. Like a cat that gets its tail caught under a rocking chair, he tore out of the room at top speed, raced down the hall and up the stairs. The last thing he heard was John cursing, undoubtedly because of his bloodied nose, which, given the blood on Artie's shirt, must have been injured pretty badly by his first blow.

Once outside, Artie didn't stop running until he got to the Cadillac, where Ray was reading a magazine.

"What happened to you?" asked Ray as he surveyed the mess that was Artie's suit and shirt.

"I don't want talk about it," Artie replied. "I just want to go home."

"What about Mary?"

"You can wait for her. I want to walk, anyway. Aaron's idea about coming to church was about as stupid as anything he's ever come up with. I need to cool down."

Ray decided against questioning him further. "You'll be all right?"

"Yeah, I'll be fine."

"What about the blood—are you hurt?"

"It's not my blood."

"Ah." Ray nodded. "Then you take your time. I'll make some excuse for you. Why don't you stop by my house on the way home so you can clean up as best as possible? There are some coveralls in the hall closet that should fit. Just leave your suit by the back door, and I'll take it to the laundry tomorrow to see what they can do with it. It should look as good as possible before Mary sees it."

Artie shook his head and tried to stop his hands from trembling. He still had so much adrenaline coursing through his body that he wanted to hit something, or take off running, just to work it off.

"Thanks, Ray."

"The house is open. Maybe I'll see you before you head back to Warm Springs?"

Artie nodded and took off in a jog.

* * *

When Artie got home later that afternoon, he decided he had to go straight to Mary and apologize for making her go to church. He felt responsible for getting her into the mess, and he was very embarrassed that on her first day back he'd been thrown out. He could only imagine how angry she must be. He really didn't want to face her, but he'd learned early on that the best thing to do with Mary was to tell her the whole truth when he did something wrong and to let the consequences follow.

Rounding the corner into the parlor at full speed, he expected to find Mary reading the newspaper, which was her favorite activity for Sunday afternoons. He skidded to a halt, however, when he saw who was in the living room with Mary. He regretted coming into her line of sight, because it made it pretty much impossible for him to reverse course and get out of there.

"Come in, Arthur, and join us," said Pastor Wyndham.

Artie hesitated and stood with his arm resting on the door jam. "Please, Arthur. Pastor Wyndham has taken time away from his family just to see us. Won't you come in and sit down?" Mary phrased it as a question, but it was really issued as a command. It irritated Artie that he was probably going to get yelled at for making such a commotion at church. But still, he obeyed.

"Artie, I'm very sorry for what happened to you today. Are you all right?" Pastor Wyndham had one of the most soothing voices Artie had ever heard. No matter what happened, he always seemed calm and collected. A very tall man at nearly six feet, he had a large chest and powerful arms, all of which complemented his deep bass voice. With any other face, he'd be quite imposing. But his smile was the type to warm even the coldest day, and his eyes were gentle and reassuring. Still, Artie wasn't in the mood to talk. Church had been a disaster; taking Mary was a mistake; and he hadn't gotten the chance to ask the pastor for his help, anyway so it was all a colossal waste of time. And that didn't even count what had happened to his suit.

"The pastor asked you a question. Please answer him."

Artie nodded.b

"I heard the story of what happened. John was completely out of line to trip you and to then insult your grandfather. I'm sorry he did that. You certainly had every right to be angry with him." Artie did his best to disguise his surprise. He figured that since he was the one to bolt—and the one who had been arrested and everything—that he'd be the one to get the blame.

"I had a talk with Aaron after church. Together we realized that it had been a long time since I've talked with you. That's my fault, of course. But I'd like to correct that now. I'm hoping that we can get together sometime to have a chat."

Artie still didn't look up, but he appreciated that the pastor had found a way to talk about getting together without revealing to Mary that it was really Artie who wanted to meet with him. Some things needed to remain private.

"Arthur, I wish you'd talk with the pastor. He's trying very hard to be nice."

Artie looked up at her, his eyes flashing for just a moment. He wasn't used to having people try to get in the middle of his affairs. It was his business as to whether he wanted to talk to the Pastor or not. Then he realized that Mary was probably just acting like any mother would do, so he decided it was okay.

"Thanks," he mumbled. "But there's really not that much to talk about."

Pastor Wyndham raised an eyebrow, clearly indicating that he knew better. But rather than challenge Artie, he took a different tack. "John's father was furious with him for being so disrespectful in the church. I'm afraid that John often says things to provoke people without realizing just how hurtful he's being. It's something that he and I have been working on." Artie looked up, suspecting that Aaron had already told him why Artie wanted to meet with him. This was the Pastor's way of saying that he worked with people on their problems. Something in the pastor's voice made it impossible for Artie not to look at him. As soon as he made eye contact, Pastor Wyndham smiled and added, "It seems like John still has a ways to go." That actually got a quick grin from Artie.

"I'm sorry you had such a bad time at church. I know how much you hoped it would be a good experience," Mary said sincerely.

"I'm sorry I made you go and that I got in a fight like that. I'm sure it embarrassed you."

"I wasn't embarrassed a bit. When I heard about what had happened, I demanded to know who had started it. Once I knew that you were only defending yourself, I'm afraid that I became a bit imperious myself. That John fellow got a tongue lashing to equal what you did to his nose!"

Artie laughed, in spite of the seriousness of the circumstance. He'd been on the receiving end of Mary's tongue lashings just often enough himself to know that John probably preferred the bloody nose, and the thought of it was pretty hilarious.

"Listen, Artie. We're very glad that you came to church today, particularly since you brought Mary with you. I've hoped for years that she'd come back to church. In fact, I've wanted that ever since I was hired as the pastor. I hope we can talk you into trying it again. I'm sure that John will treat you better." He looked at Artie kindly.

"I don't know," Artie mumbled. "As I thought about it this afternoon, I kind of resolved myself to going it alone, without church. I mean I've got Mary here—Mrs. Wilkerson, I mean—and Ray, and I get along fine." He looked up, "No offense, Pastor, because I know I can count on you to be nice. But Mr. Boone doesn't like me there, and Stephanie . . ." His voice caught for a moment. "Well, it's just that I don't think it is right that I should have to hide behind you and Mrs. Wilkerson. If the kids don't want me, or their parents, then why should I make everybody unhappy?"

It was probably the most frank assessment of a situation the pastor had ever heard. He wished he could tell Artie that people didn't feel that way about him and that everyone in the congregation wanted to welcome him back, but the simple truth was that there was bad blood between Artie and David Boone, and he also knew that Stephanie's father had been upset that she was talking to Artie. It had been a long afternoon as he sorted it all out, and he'd had to exercise uncommon patience not to tell everybody off. He'd finally gotten some measure of control by asking everybody involved whether they thought Jesus would have treated Artie the way they had. It seemed like that was the only thing that finally got them to consider the pastor's point of view, which was that he had a young man who desperately needed the church but who found it to be a hostile and unwelcoming place.

"I can't really speak for Brother Lewis or Brother Boone. I'm sure they have their reasons to be concerned about what happened. But I do know that everyone feels bad that your day was so unhappy. We'd really like to make a place for you in the congregation." He stood up. It was a lot to ask of a fifteen-year-old. The pastor wasn't sure he personally would come back if the same thing had happened to him at that age. But he also knew that this was probably the most crucial time in Artie's life—when he would either overcome his anger and hurt and hang in there, or he would leave organized religious activity forever. So he decided not to give up just yet.

"Tell you what, Artie. Evening service starts at 7:30 PM. Why don't you come and meet with me at 6:45 PM. Then you could sit with Sister Wilkerson through the services. After that you can decide if you want to come back. If you'll come tonight and give it a try, I won't pressure you again, no matter what you decide." The pastor turned and looked at Mary, realizing that he'd committed her to coming back to church, even though she might not want that. But she nodded ever so slightly.

"Can I think about it?" Artie didn't look up, but he did rub his hands through his blond hair.

"Of course you can think about it. I'll be there one way or the other." He turned to Mary. "It was so nice to have you join us today, Sister Wilkerson. You can't imagine how many people remarked at how excited they were to see you."

Mary nodded and took his hand. "I'll walk you to the door."

Before she even had to prompt him, Artie stood up and extended his hand to the pastor. "Thank you for coming to talk to me, sir."

The pastor took Artie's small hand in his great big hands and held them for a moment. His hands were warm and strong, and Artie felt something stir inside him as the pastor held them. Then Pastor Wyndham released his grasp and started walking to the door. Just as he was about to disappear from sight, he turned. "By the way, that was a nice jab you got in there on John. I'm not sure his pride will ever recover from it." And then he was gone.

Artie smiled. *It was a good jab.* Then he must have decided that a smile wasn't enough for such an accomplishment. So he laughed. It felt good to laugh.

CHAPTER 15

Driver's Education

In December, Artie Call turned sixteen years old. The *second* thing he did on that day was take advantage of Mary's permission to start driver's lessons from Ray. Not many teenagers had such a privilege, since cars were few and far between and gasoline was expensive. But there were plenty of vehicles at the Wilkerson's.

The *first* thing he did was enjoy the first birthday party of his life. It really was special since parties and presents were simply beyond the reach of nearly everyone because of the current economic circumstances. Mary wanted it to be a unique experience, so she asked Artie where he would take people to dinner if he could choose any restaurant in Boise. She soon had a reason to regret it since Artie said that it would be really neat if they could go to the Automatic Restaurant on Grove Street, one of the new innovations in food service that captured the imagination of young people. The idea was that food was prepared cafeteria style and then put on plates that were loaded into individual bins on the wall that separated the kitchen from the eating area, and then patrons would put money into a slot to buy each type of food they desired. A small glass door would open when money was deposited and the person could pull out, for example, a piece of blackberry pie or a fresh turkey sandwich or a dish of macaroni salad as desired.

"It looks like a row of post office boxes," Mary had said dismissively.

"And the food isn't nearly as good as I could have made for your darned old party," Bethany had added.

But Artie didn't care. The Automatic was the most popular place in town, and he was thrilled to have that as part of the event. For her part, Mary had gone to the bank to get a handful of nickels and dimes that she distributed freely to Artie's friends to get whatever they wanted. That, in and of itself, was something worth taking note of since even a nickel was dear to many families.

After the meal, they drove back to Mary's home, where she passed out presents— not just to Artie but to everyone who attended. That was a great success. Then they played games in the parlor and had a tasty birthday cake that Bethany had made.

Finally, for the last event of the evening, Mary had purchased tickets to the Egyptian to watch the latest Laurel and Hardy movie—a delightful comedy that made everyone laugh. Ray then shuttled everyone home, since a light snow had dusted the area, and he thought it would be nice for the kids to have a ride.

"That was the best party ever," Stephanie said to Artie as he walked her to the door.

"Thanks for coming," he said shyly.

"I wouldn't have missed it. The food was great, the games were fun, and I loved the movie."

As they stood at the door, Artie was uncomfortable. He glanced out of the corner of his eye and saw that Ray was sitting patiently in the Cadillac, pretending to read something with a flashlight.

"I'm glad your dad let you come." The instant he said that, he regretted it.

But Stephanie replied rather easily, "I think the pastor had something to do with it. My dad's not really bad. He just gets nervous about me."

Artie nodded. Then the conversation stalled once again. "Well, I guess I better go," said Artie. "Thanks for coming. Oh, I said that already."

Stephanie laughed. Then she stepped forward very quickly, and before he knew what had hit him, she'd given him a light kiss right on the lips. "Thanks again, Artie," she said quickly as she stepped inside the door. "Tell Mrs. Wilkerson that I loved it and tell her thanks for the present." The door closed, and Artie was left standing alone on the porch, his face burning and his heart pounding. He decided right then and there that he really liked birthday parties.

The next day, Artie hounded Ray to give him his first driving lesson. Fortunately, there was no snow on the ground, so after grumbling just a bit, Ray got down to the very serious of work of teaching Artie how to drive. It was harder than it appeared, particularly with a heavy automobile like the Cadillac. After a few failed attempts in which Ray expressed his certainty that Artie would burn out the clutch, they'd switched to the much lighter-weight Ford pickup truck. But there was still a problem.

"Artie, you need to let out the clutch while pressing the gasoline pedal. As the clutch starts to engage, you've got to give the car more power so it doesn't stall!" Ray said this with very measured tones—tones indicating he was at wits' end.

"I just can't do it!" Artie said this as the truck engine raced, the clutch engaged precipitously, and the car lurching forward a few feet until the motor quit.

Ray took a deep breath. Artie started to get out. "Where are you going?" asked Ray.

"I'm walking home. I can't do this. I'll never be able to do this. So I'm not going to try anymore."

"You get in this car right now!" That stopped Artie in his tracks, but he didn't get back in. He just glowered.

"This isn't only about you. It's about me. I've trained many people to drive a car, and so far I've never failed. I'm not about to begin with you. So get your sorry little rear end into the passenger seat!"

Artie fumed, but he went and got in. Ray easily started the motor and put it in gear then took off like a shot. "Where are we going?"

"You'll see."

Artie could see it would do no good to ask, so he just sat stewing as they made their way west toward the foothills. To his surprise, they made a right turn to go up the mountain toward the military camp. At the base of a small incline, Ray pulled to a stop and took the car out of gear while engaging the parking brake.

"All right, come and get in behind the wheel."

"But . . ."

"No buts—just come get in."

Artie did as he was told. "Now here's the deal. I think it will be easier for you to do this on an incline because you'll feel the clutch start to engage as the car starts pulling against gravity. Once you feel it start to grab, that's when you'll increase the pressure on the gas. Slowly but surely you'll let the clutch out to the point that it's got enough force to hold the car against the pull of gravity. We'll then take the brake off, and you'll give it progressively more gas while slowly letting out the clutch. Now let's try it."

"But I don't see how . . ."

"You don't have to see anything—you just have to do what I tell you!"

Artie took a deep breath and pushed the clutch in just like all the other times."

"Now, start to let the clutch out very slowly until you feel it start to pull."

Even though he had tried dozens of times already, he went ahead and did as he was told. Surprisingly, this time he felt what Ray had described. At a certain point, he felt the car start to strain against the brake.

"Is that it?" he asked excitedly.

"That's it. Now give it just a tiny bit more gasoline."

Artie followed his instructions.

"I'm going to release the brake, so it's up to you to hold the car in position. You've got to keep your foot steady on the gas pedal." Artie assured him he could at least do that. As Ray started to let the brake go, Artie felt the car start to lurch forward, which panicked him, and he was tempted to pop the clutch, but the hmph he heard from Ray persuaded him to keep his foot right where it was. To his delight, the engine didn't stall, the car didn't lurch forward, and suddenly the brake was fully disengaged.

"Do you feel that? You can sense that the engine is turning against one side of the clutch with enough force to hold it?"

"I think so."

"Well, this is what we've wanted all along. The trick is now to give it just the right amount of gas so that the car starts moving in time with the motor. Too much gas, and the clutch won't be able to take the strain, and it will kill the engine. Too little gas, and there won't be enough power, and *that* will kill the engine. But just the right amount of power *and* clutch will help us start to go forward."

Slowly but surely, Artie advanced the throttle and then moved his clutch foot out a bit. He felt them start to creep forward, so he gave it a little bit more gas and then a little less clutch, and suddenly, to his joy, they really did start to move.

"It's working!" he shouted jubilantly.

"Don't lose your concentration—more gas and let it out all the way. Artie pressed down about two-thirds of the way on the accelerator while releasing the clutch pedal, and they started moving steadily up the dirt road.

"That's it! You're doing it, Artie. Now just keep going!"

Artie felt a thrill unlike any other. They gained speed on the road, and soon he was feeling the confident power of the motor pulling them along easily. "Go ahead and practice some steering maneuvers," Ray said, "and then we have to learn how to shift!"

"To shift?" The horror returned to Artie's voice, which prompted Ray to roll his eyes and sigh.

* * *

It turned out, of course, that shifting was easier to learn than starting from a dead stop. Once Artie had learned to engage the clutch in one gear, it was easier to do it again, particularly since the shift to a higher gear is done while the car is moving.

After that, Ray's only worry was how to avoid running into Artie, since he'd ask to go driving whenever the two were together. Artie pestered him about it constantly. Still, Ray was patient and spent the weeks leading up to Christmas going out with Artie as often as he could. After a month of driving lessons, just after the turn of the new year, Ray was finally confident enough to let Artie take the truck out on his own, but only when the roads were dry, and with Ray shadowing him from behind. But after a week or two of that, Artie and the little Ford became inseparable. Like most teenagers, he was constantly pestering Bethany for an excuse to drive to the store or badgering Ray to let him go to the auto parts store to pick up some part or tool that he needed. In fact, the only person he didn't pester was Mary. He simply wasn't ready to take her driving.

When Ray asked him why, Artie replied, "Are you kidding? She criticizes your driving sometimes, and you're the best driver in all of Idaho. Can you imagine what she'd have to say about me?"

Ray laughed. "I see your point." But then he added, "I don't think you need to worry too much. She usually says things to me just so she'll have an excuse to talk. I think she'll be nicer to you."

But it wasn't enough to convince Artie. It was Mary who finally forced the issue.

"Arthur, when are you going to show me your driving skills?"

"Um . . . I could take you out in the Ford if you like."

"I don't want to go out in the Ford. I want you to drive me in my car. Now, when can you be ready to do that?"

Artie turned to Ray, who shrugged his shoulders. "I think a couple of weeks of practice, and he'd be ready."

After they finished lunch, Ray and Artie walked out to the garage. "Will you go out with us the first time?" Artie asked hopefully. "Just in case something goes wrong."

"Nope! There's only one way for you to get through this and that's to face up to it squarely. So you'll have to do it on your own."

Artie gulped, but he relented and spent the next two weeks learning to drive the mammoth Cadillac.

As the calendar changed to February, Mary asked him if he was ready. In his own mind, Artie thought he might take her out on a Monday evening, when the roads weren't crowded. But Mary declared that she wanted to go out in the daylight, so it had to be on a Saturday, when he wasn't in school.

"But there are a lot of people out on the street on Saturday. What if I mess things up?" asked Artie desperately.

"Then you'll have to figure out how to un-mess them," Ray replied. When Artie gave Ray a why-won't-you-help-me look, Ray softened. "Look, you can do this. You've practically worn out the clutch on the Cadillac—not by driving it wrong, just by driving it so much. You're as ready now as you'll ever be."

Artie shook his head. "All right, I guess I have to face up to it sometime." So when Saturday arrived, Mary climbed into the car and settled herself in. Artie asked Ray one last time if he didn't want to join them.

"No, I'll stay here by the phone for the call from the hospital."

"The hospital?" It took Artie a moment to figure out Ray's implication. "I don't know why I like you sometimes. The only one who will be going to the hospital is you when Mary tells you how much more she likes my driving than yours! You'll have a nervous breakdown over that!" Ray laughed.

* * *

Aaron had been allowed to join Artie's first excursion as a chauffeur, although he had to sit in the backseat with Mary, rather than in front with Artie, since Mary thought he'd be too much of a distraction. She'd forbidden Joey to come along, asserting that he was far too excitable and that he'd make her a nervous wreck. Artie felt bad for Joey but understood Mary's point of view.

The drive had gone very well, except for one stop sign that was obscured behind some drooping tree branches. That made for an exciting moment, but Artie's quick reflexes had helped him to quickly maneuver them out of harm's way. Aside from that, he'd driven at exactly the right speed—perhaps even a little slower than the speed limit. He'd been extra cautious before starting out from the intersections to make certain that he had plenty of time to accelerate gently so he wouldn't jerk Mary's head, something she often complained of with Ray, and he always started braking way in advance so the car would come to an even, steady stop. In their training sessions, Ray had put a glass of water on the floor with instructions that Artie had to be so smooth in his braking that he never spilled the water. Artie had drenched a number of towels until he got used to that one.

The only lighthearted moment of the trip came toward the end, when Artie chose to turn down a street that Ray never used when he drove Mary to the store. Much to Artie's surprise he saw Ray sitting in his Chrysler Imperial about midway down the block. At first he was delighted and threw Ray a happy wave to indicate that all seemed to be going well. But then he got suspicious when he happened to glance in the rearview mirror where he saw Mary tip her head to Ray. That was when it dawned on him that for all of his tough-guy attitude, Ray had been shadowing them. Rather than be mad, he was happy that Ray cared.

Probably the happiest moment of his life was when he pulled the Cadillac safely into Mary's driveway on Warm Springs Boulevard, bringing it gently to a stop by the house. Jumping out and moving quickly to the side door, he opened it and then extended his hand to help Mary step out.

"Well?" he asked expectantly.

"You did very well, Arthur." That's all she said before calling for Bethany to come help her into the house.

"You did very well," Artie repeated happily as Aaron piled out of the seat behind her. "Did you hear that?"

Aaron nodded.

"What did you think?"

"I think you did fine."

That made Artie grin but only for a moment. The grin was replaced by a frown as he said, "*Good* and *fine?* That's not saying a lot. What did you two talk about back there?"

"We didn't talk." Aaron looked suspicious."Oh yes, you did. I saw you. Now what did Mary really think?" Artie's countenance had darkened considerably.

"She really did say that you were doing a good job. I think it's fair to say that she was nervous. There were only one or two times when I thought her fingernails would draw blood on my arm, but I didn't say anything."

"Why? Why was she nervous? I didn't do anything bad."

"Oh, come on, Artie. Take a compliment when you get it. She said you did fine. Besides, if you think about it, wouldn't you be nervous getting in the car with a sixteen-year-old driver for the first time?"

Artie started to come back at him, but then he paused and decided that Aaron was right. Then he laughed. "Sorry about your arm. But it was kind of neat to be driving around town in a big old Cadillac like that, wasn't it?"

"It was downright incredible. The thing I liked best was seeing the expression on people's faces when they realized that you were driving. I thought Old Man Marchant was going to swallow his dentures, he gawked so much."

"I did too!" Artie laughed delightedly. "Of course, I couldn't take my eyes off the road very much, so I'm sure I missed a lot of people seeing us, but what I did see was pretty funny."

"I bet you didn't miss seeing Stephanie . . ."

"No, I didn't miss that. I felt bad I couldn't wave to her, but Ray had already told me that Mary's greatest fear is that I'd get distracted whenever I see another kid and I'd be a sloppy driver, so I had to keep my eyes straight ahead. I need to go see her to tell her thanks for waving at me."

"So will you ever get to take the car out without Mary? You know, just to go do things you want to do?"

"Nah. Not the Cadillac. I'm lucky enough to take out the truck. I don't want Mary to have to worry about me in that big old car of hers."

"Speaking of Ray, here he is."

Artie looked up to see the powerful Chrysler pulling into the driveway. Artie jogged over to the garage, where he parked. "So what kind of report card are you going to give me?"

"Report card?"

"Yeah—report card. I know you were shadowing us. I assume you're here to pretend to have coffee with Mary, but you're really going to talk about me. So what are you going to say?"

"You think you're pretty smart, don't you?" Ray looked around. "All right, since you asked, I think what I'm going to tell her is that it's a pretty sloppy chauffeur who leaves the car dusty and out of the garage at the end of a trip."

Artie's eyes grew wide, and his mouth dropped. "But . . . but, I just got here. You know that I was planning to drive it over and clean it."

Ray smiled mischievously. "Well, then, if that's the case, I think you better get going." His smile narrowed. "And while you're cleaning up the Cadillac, I think I'll have coffee with Mary." He winked at Artie as he turned to leave. "By the way!"

Artie turned to look at him again. "Yeah?"

"Why don't you give the Chrysler a wash while you're at it?" He tossed the keys while saying this, taking Artie by surprise. But his reflexes were fast enough that he snatched them out of the air.

"And why would I want to do that? It's a nice enough car and all, and could certainly use a wash, but why would I want to do you a favor after you were spying on me?"

"Suit yourself," Ray replied easily. "But if I knew someone was about to fill out a report card with Mary, I'd want to get on their good side. But you do things your own way, don't you?"

"Did you want a wax job with that car wash, Mr. McCandless, sir?"

Ray smiled and tipped his finger to his head. It was the very same maneuver Artie had seen in the rearview mirror.

"It's a conspiracy," he said darkly to Aaron.

"But I think you won."

Artie nodded. He felt great inside.

CHAPTER 16

The Surprise of a Lifetime

February 1934

Mary said it so nonchalantly that it didn't really register at first. Her invitation for Ray to join them for dinner should have signaled that something was up, but it didn't. Besides, even if they had been suspicious, nothing could have prepared them for the invitation Mary had just extended.

It was Ray who reacted first. "Just a minute, Mary. Did you just say what I thought you said?"

Mary huffed. "How on earth can I know what you think I said?"

Ray looked at her through lowered eyes. "What I think I heard you say is that you've been asked to go to the Auto Salon in New York City as a guest of the Auburn Motor Company."

Mary nodded, while taking a long sip of cool water. "I'm glad to see that your ears are working, after all. I was worried that perhaps you were going deaf from all that crazy racing you do."

Ray scowled but not too severely. If the first part of what he heard was true, then it was likely that the second part was also true, which is that she wanted Ray to come along to drive her around Manhattan while she was there.

"And did I hear you say that you wanted me to come along as well?" Bethany asked with a hint of disbelief in her voice.

"Oh, for heaven's sake! You both heard me perfectly well. I want Ray to come and be my driver, and I want you to come to help me get around. I'd take Judy, but with her new baby, that doesn't make sense, does it? I know it will be two old women going around together, but I'd sooner have two of us than to be all by myself."

Ray burst into a grin. "Well, this is a surprise. I haven't been to New York City in more than twenty years. The truth is that I miss the place."

Bethany wasn't as excited, the anxiety showing on her face. "I've never been to New York. I haven't even been outside of Idaho. I can't imagine what you're thinking in wanting to go there."

Mary played it easy. "Of course you don't have to go, if you don't want to. I'm sure I can hire someone else to help me."

Bethany looked up sharply. "Oh, no you don't. You invited me and I will hold you to it." She started clucking under her breath about Broadway and how she'd always wanted to see Central Park and other things like that, all the while nervously cleaning up dishes and taking them to the sink—even those that hadn't been used yet, like the dessert plates.

"You're awfully quiet, Arthur."

Artie didn't look up. "Yes, ma'am."

The tone in Artie's voice made Ray think about what had been said so far, and it dawned on him why Artie was so quiet. "What about Artie, Mary? What are you going to do with him while we're off in New York?"

"It's all right," Artie said. "I can probably live with Joey or Aaron while you're gone. I'm sure their parents wouldn't mind."

"What would you do if you could choose?" asked Mary.

"I guess I'd choose Aaron. He'd probably be better at getting me to do my homework."

Mary laughed. "But is he as good at getting you to do homework as I am?"

Artie looked up.

Mary smiled. "I want you to come with us, too, Arthur. You've just turned sixteen, and Ray is teaching you to drive, and with all of that to your credit, I think you should get out and see a little bit of the world."

"But what about school?" Artie regretted asking the question as soon as the words were out of his mouth. What did he care about school compared to a trip to New York City? "I mean, I'm sure it's okay. I've already gone a long ways in school, anyway . . . longer than a lot of kids."

"Oh, hush. You're not getting out of school until you graduate from high school. So you can forget that nonsense. But there's more than one way to complete your assignments, and I've already talked to the school about the trip, They've agreed that if I'll personally supervise your instruction while we're gone, they will make arrangements for you to stay with your class when we get back."

Artie's eyes grew wide. "You'll be my teacher?" When Mary nodded, he added, "Wow! You're kidding . . . I mean, that would be great, but you don't really mean that I get to go . . .?"

"Arthur. Stop that mumbling! I mean exactly what I said. I want the three of you to come to New York City with me. With a week of travel time to get there by train, and a week to get back, plus two or three weeks in the city, the whole thing will take at least a month. More than likely it will be six weeks."

She pretended to be annoyed by the smiles and looks of disbelief around the table, but everyone knew that she had relished their reaction.

Finally, it was Artie who broke the tension by letting out a whoop. "New York City! I never thought I'd get to go to someplace important like that in my whole life." His exuberance made everyone laugh. But it was clear that all in attendance were just as happy as he was.

"I can't wait to tell Aaron. He'll be jealous, of course, but I'll tell him everything about it when I get back."

"But what will we do for a car?" Ray asked.

"We'll have to take mine, of course. Cars travel by train, too, you know."

Ray nodded. "It's too bad someone doesn't rent cars to people. That would be handy."

Mary shook her head. "That's a foolish idea, Ray. How could they ever charge enough money to make such a notion worthwhile? It doesn't make sense to me."

"I suppose you're right. Still, it's got to cost a lot of money to ship a car both ways."

"I was thinking of shipping the Cadillac just one way. In fact, one of the reasons I want you to come along is because I'm thinking it would be smart for me to sell the Cadillac while we're in New York City. It seems to me we're likely to get a better price there than we are here in Boise. I'd like you to help me with that."

"Sell the Cadillac? But you love that car. Besides, it's less than two years old."

"I know," she said breezily. "But if I'm going to buy a new car, I don't see why we should keep two of them. Times are tight, you know."

Ray cocked his head to the side. "A new car?" Then he looked at her suspiciously. "What do you have up your sleeve, Mary?"

"Oh, for heaven's sake. Can't you put two and two together and come up with four? We're going to New York City to attend the New York Auto Show.

The members of the board of directors of the Auburn Automobile Company are my friends and have invited me to the Salon. Perhaps I'll want to sell my car and buy a new one." She smiled coyly. "Now what kind of car do you think I hope to buy?"

Ray crinkled his brow. Artie loved it when he did that since he looked so serious. "But the front-wheel drive Cord has been pulled off the market," he said. "And I don't really see that an Auburn is that much different than what you have."

"So?" Mary said impatiently.

"Well, then the only other car in production right now, aside from the Auburn, is a Duesenberg, but that's way too expensive and you wouldn't buy . . ." All of a sudden it was Ray's eyes that grew so large that Artie thought they might actually bug right out of his head. "You plan to buy a *Duesenberg*?"

Mary smiled. "Perhaps. At least I'd like to look."

Now Artie was worried that Ray might hyperventilate. "But . . . but," he stuttered, without really coming to a conclusion.

"May I ask just what a Duesenberg is and why it's causing poor Ray here to have a heart attack?" Bethany asked.

"It's just a fairly well-known car that is quite popular in some circles, and I think that I ought to have one. My husband was good friends with E. L. Cord, and so I should do something to show my confidence. It's really nothing more than that."

Ray rolled his eyes. "Popular in some circles? Now there's the understatement of the century."

Artie knew that this must be something really big, even though he didn't know much about it. He'd seen pictures in the magazines but had never paid much attention to them. But for Ray to be acting like this was something... "What do you mean, Ray?" he asked.

Ray continued to shake his head in disbelief. "The Duesenberg is only the most popular car for Hollywood movie stars, like Clark Gable, Douglas Fairbanks Jr., and Greta Garbo. It's more expensive than a Rolls-Royce and faster than any car ever built. It comes with a 265-horsepower engine. They even make a supercharged version with nearly 320 horsepower!" He looked around the room, exasperated that the other three weren't as impressed by the technical details as he was. So he decided to try a different tack. "Have you heard of Ab Jenkins, Artie?"

"Of course. Everybody has. He drives the fastest cars in the world."

"Exactly?"

"So?"

"So he drives a Duesenberg."

Artie's eyes widened. "Oh!"

Having won Artie over to the significance of the Duesenberg, he could see that Bethany was still unimpressed. "The base model costs $13,000, Bethany. I've heard of some that sell for as much as $25,000 with the body. I seriously doubt that there are any *houses* in Boise that cost that much." Then to polish it off, "And not only that, but Gary Cooper owns one." He knew that Bethany was a huge fan of the soft spoken movie star.

"Oh, my. Gary Cooper?"

"Wow!" Artie whistled.

Ray and Bethany laughed. Even Mary couldn't maintain her scowl in the face of such childlike wonder.

Then very quietly, almost under his breath, Artie added, "We get a new car." Mary was unexpectedly pleased by his use of the word *we*.

"So I take it that you're all willing to come along?" she asked everyone.

"Oh, I think that's a safe bet. When do we leave?" Ray quickly confirmed.

"That's the biggest problem. We need to leave in six weeks. I'll need help making all the arrangements. David Boone has agreed to hire a property management company to watch over the house and grounds. Perhaps you could make arrangements to store the automobiles in a public garage, where they'll be safe?"

"Henry would be glad to do that for us."

"Bethany, you'll need to help me pack for it, although I'm sure that none of my clothes will be in fashion, and we'll have to buy new ones once we get to New York. I'll send a telegram to the Auburn people today confirming that we'll attend, and they'll take care of our accommodations."

"Meanwhile, Ray, if you can look into railway tickets and renting space on the train for the Cadillac." She sighed. "I just don't know if we can get it all done. There are so many details to follow up on."

"Don't worry. We'll get it all done. I'll take care of the car and tickets."

"Can I do anything to help?" asked Artie.

"As a matter of fact, you can. We need to clean the house from top to bottom, secure the house and outbuildings, make sure that the hot water system is on to keep the house at a decent heat so the plants don't die while we're gone . . ."

"Is it cold in New York City?" Artie asked.

"A bit colder than Boise. But April in New York can be a delightful time of year." She sighed deeply as if remembering times past. "Many of the trees will be in bud, some of the flowers popping through the ground in Central Park. The street vendors will have steam coming up from their grills, and the museums will have new exhibits opening. The city will be bustling with life."

Ray's smile faded just a bit. "It might not be exactly as you remember it, Mary. The economic downturn has hit New York even harder than the rest of the country."

Mary nodded. "I know. It will be very different but mostly because George won't be with me. He loved the city and knew all its nooks and crannies. He could find ethnic restaurants in obscure corners of town, great delicatessens with the most wonderful sandwiches you've ever tasted, as well as these delightful little vaudeville houses where you could enjoy the most wonderful variety shows imaginable. I'm afraid I'll be lost without him."

"Will we get to go to vaudeville shows?" Bethany asked.

"We'll go to full-scale production shows on Broadway. I hear that both the Gershwin brothers and Cole Porter have new shows going on now."

Bethany closed her eyes as if in an ecstatic trance. "This is truly a dream come true. I think I'll die of excitement waiting."

"Do you think we can see those big skyscrapers?" Artie asked.

Mary raised an eyebrow. "And what do you know about skyscrapers? I didn't know you were interested in New York City."

"I saw a documentary on the building of the Empire State Building while helping Aaron one night at the Egyptian. They say it's like a million stories tall, or something. And they have a place up near the top where you can look out over the city."

"A million stories tall. That is the most absurd exaggeration I've ever heard," Mary noted.

"Well, do we get to go see it?" Artie was not one to let things like that pass.

"I don't know. Perhaps—if we make it to New York first. You heard how many things we have to get done. If we don't get moving, we won't have to worry about seeing anything at all." With that she started to rise.

But before she could get away, Ray said, "Before we all head off to work on our tasks, I think we should pause." Mary turned and looked at him quizzically. Ray held up his glass of water. "I'd like to propose a toast to New York City and to our magnificent hostess who has so generously agreed to take us there. To Mary Wilkerson!"

Artie led them in a hip-hip-hooray while Mary blushed. But this time she didn't pretend to be annoyed. As they finished she smiled and raised her glass to theirs.

CHAPTER 17

A Dark Day

Late February 1934

"Where is that boy?" Mary asked for perhaps the one-hundredth time. Bethany felt like she would have to strangle her if she asked it again.

"I've told you that I don't know anything more than you do."

"Oh, for heaven's sake! I don't really expect an answer when I say that. I'm just nervous and have to say something. It's not like him to do something terrible like this. He's never been late for an appointment, not once. And now it's 8:30 PM and he's still not here. Don't you think you should call the police again?"

That last sentence said more than anything else about how distraught Mary was. The fact that she asked Bethany's advice, rather than simply commanding her, showed just how unsteady Mary was.

"Why do you think he would do this? He knew that we were having dinner with the Glens, and he made us all wait until the food was cold . . . He said he was going to stop by Aaron's on his way to the Glens' house, just for a moment to ask a question about homework, but he promised that he'd leave there in plenty of time to get to the Glens', but Aaron says he never showed up. You know that Aaron's a reliable young man, so I think we can trust him to tell us the truth. And I thought that I could trust Arthur. It must be that he's hurt, or been in accident; otherwise he would have called. I'm just sure of it. I never should have let him drive that pickup by himself . . ."

Bethany knew that chattering like this was Mary's way of dealing with anxiety. It was Bethany's preferred way of handling nervousness as well, but in the

present case it did her no good since she couldn't have squeezed a word in edge-
wise even if she had a crowbar.

"Oh, my." Mary inhaled deeply and then let out a long sigh. "It better be
something serious, or I'll have to kill that boy with my own bare hands."

Just at that moment they heard a noise in the driveway and saw red lights
flashing through the kitchen windows. "Oh, dear," Mary said desperately. "The
police are here. Let's go out and see what they've found."

Mary and Bethany strode quickly to the back door and were relieved to see
that Artie had gotten out of the Ford pickup and was talking with the police
officer. After a moment, the two turned and came up the steps.

"Well, here he is, ma'am. He's pretty upset, and I wasn't able to get the story
out of him. Do you want me to come in and help you sort it out?"

Mary looked at Artie sternly, but he was looking down at his feet so that she
couldn't see his face. She was so furious with him right now that she thought
she might need the policeman to restrain her from slapping the boy. But instead
she took two deep breaths and then said evenly, "No, thank you, Ian. I think
this is something for our family to work out. I hope we didn't put you to too
much trouble."

"Not at all, ma'am." He glanced over at Artie, quite clearly disgusted. "You
know we have more important things to do than chase you down."

Artie shrugged and Officer McKenzie turned and walked back to his car.
Mary waited until he was safely inside the car and then she said, rather abruptly,
"Bethany, I think I'd like you to join me in the parlor. Arthur, take your things
to your room and then come join us."

Artie nodded and glanced up for just a fraction of a moment before turning
to go to his room. She only caught a glimpse of his face, but what Mary saw in
that briefest of moment alarmed her. He had been crying, and the look of sheer
desperation on his face was unlike anything she had ever seen. Quite frankly it
frightened her. Which is why the next five minutes felt like an eternity as she
sat nervously in the parlor waiting for him. After what seemed forever, and just
before she was about to stand up to go check on him, she heard his door creak
open and closed. Soon Artie was in the room, his head down.

"Please take a chair right here," said Mary firmly. "And please look at me
when I talk to you." She wasn't really sure she wanted to see his face, but she knew
that to get any kind of an answer, she would have to be able to hold his gaze.

"Now, then. I think I should first take the keys to the truck." She braced for
his response, but he rather meekly reached in his pocket and took out the keys.

He handed them to her without looking up. She had hoped that this action would provoke him to start talking, but it didn't.

She had to try again. "May I ask what you have to say for yourself? Why did you leave us stranded at the Glens' with no idea of where you were or what you were doing? Dinner was late, and we excused ourselves early because we were too worried about you to visit with them. What has happened that caused you to behave this way?"

Artie looked up miserably. "I'm sorry, ma'am. I had . . . I had." He stopped.

"You had what? What did you have that justified you embarrassing us like that in front of our friends?"

He dropped his head. "I'm sorry. I was wrong."

"I appreciate your apology, but it still doesn't tell me what's wrong."

Artie shook his head, as if weighing a response, but in the end he just sat there. With visions of vandalism or burglary in her mind, she was very anxious that he'd gotten himself into trouble and didn't know how to get out of it. So she decided she had to force the issue.

"Arthur—look at me! I said look at me!" Reluctantly, Artie looked up. She expected to see defiance, but instead all she saw was misery.

"I am your guardian, and I need to know what's happened."

Artie's countenance hardened. "It's just that I had someplace I thought I needed to go, so I went. It was wrong. I shouldn't have done it. You trusted me, and I left you in a bad spot. That's all. I'm sorry. But like you say, sorry isn't always enough."

He started to stand up to leave.

"Artie," Mary said softly. That was enough to stop him in his tracks.

"I appreciate that you're trying to fix the problem you created by punishing yourself. But that's not how families work. I think I've done enough for you that I deserve better than to have you dismiss me like this. Don't you think you owe it to me to tell me what's happened?" She said this in an unfamiliar voice. As Bethany would relate it to Ray later, it was a meek voice filled with love.

And it worked. All of a sudden, Artie's reserve melted, and he had to wipe the tears that started streaming down his face. "Oh, Mary, it's my grandfather. He died! And I wasn't there for him. He died all alone!" The wail that followed was perhaps the most sincere expression of emotion that Mary had ever heard. Bethany's gasp added to the moment as she let out her own wail.

"Oh, my dear heavens! But what happened, dear? How did you know he died?" Mary put her arms on his shoulders to help him calm down.

Finally, gaining control of his breathing, he said quietly, "I was driving to Aaron's from Derkins when I suddenly got this feeling that something was wrong with my grandfather. Of course I just pushed it out of my mind. But it came again a few minutes later, even stronger. I looked at my watch, and I knew that I didn't have time to go to the old-folks home and make it to dinner at the Glens'. So I thought to myself that maybe I should find a telephone and call you and tell you that I needed to go to my grandfather, but then I thought how crazy it would sound, a feeling and all, so I put it off for a few more minutes. Then it came the third time, and I knew I had to go. So I just turned the corner and went straight to the nursing home without telling Aaron or you or anyone. By the time I got there, I went running in and shouting to the orderly that I had to see my grandfather. That's when Nurse Harrington came up to shush me. I could tell the second I saw her face that my grandpa had died. I could just see it in her eyes. And then I kind of went crazy, yelling that I had to see him. At first they wouldn't let me, but I just kept insisting until they took me to his room. The people from the mortuary were there, but I just pushed them aside. But there was nothing that could be done. He was just lying there, his face all gray and cold." Artie shuddered at the thought. "They told me that he came around enough to ask for me, just before he died. But they couldn't find me, because we weren't home. But I heard him—I heard him in my mind. I know I did. But I didn't know what to do. I didn't want to leave you, but I wanted to go find out what was wrong. But it seemed stupid that I'd hear something in my mind, and I thought it was just my imagination. But then I had to go . . ."

Mary pulled Artie to her shoulder again. This time she allowed his sobs to continue until they had plenty of time to exhaust his emotion. "I'm so sorry," she kept repeating softly in his ear, "I'm sorry you didn't go when you first felt prompted."

"But, how could I?" he eventually asked. "I couldn't just leave you. You trusted me. And now I've broken your trust and my grandfather is gone and I didn't get to say goodbye. I wanted to call you from the mortuary, but I was afraid."

"Afraid? Afraid of what?"

Artie dropped his head, and his body stiffened. "Afraid you wouldn't want me since I didn't do what I was supposed to. Or that you wouldn't let me go to New York to discipline me. I knew I should call, but I didn't want to. As the time passed, and they got ready to take him to the mortuary, it got harder, so I just decided to drive home. That's when the police pulled me over."

"Arthur. I'm only sorry that you didn't trust me a little more." That was hard, so she softened her voice and continued. "But I'm more sorry that you lost your grandfather. You were a loving and good grandson, and he had every right to be proud."

"What do you mean you feel bad that I didn't trust you? I'm the one who broke the rules."

"We can talk about it more, later, dear. But one of the things that family members do is trust the others to *understand*. You should know by now that if you had feelings like this, you could have gone to the home and called me from there, just as you were prompted to do. And of course I'd have come to join you immediately. There's no dinner in the world that's as important as your grandfather. And you should also trust me that I'd never want you to leave. Now that I understand what happened, I'm not angry at you for going where your heart told you to go. I certainly wouldn't abandon you for that. I didn't take you on to stay with me only when things go right. But perhaps we haven't known each other long enough yet for you to feel confident about things like that. Perhaps . . ." and now it was her voice that tightened up, "perhaps I've been too firm with you so that you don't really know how much I love you. I do love you, you know . . ."

Well, that started the tears flowing again—from Artie, from Bethany, and from Mary.

"We all love you, Artie," Bethany added. "You're part of our family. And we're so sorry this has happened to you."

Finally, after this new round of emotion worked its way out, Artie said quietly, "I don't know what to do. The people from the mortuary want me to tell them what to do, but I don't know . . . ."

"Would you like me to help you arrange his funeral and to take care of all the other details that are likely to come up in the next few days?"

Artie nodded. "They said I don't need to come in until tomorrow morning."

"Then I'll go with you tomorrow morning. I'll call the school and tell them what's happened."

Artie's body softened in the couch, his emotional energy spent. "Would you mind if I went to bed now?"

"Not at all. I hope you can get some sleep."

"Thank you. Both of you." Standing up, Artie started toward his bedroom, but then turned suddenly and changed direction toward the kitchen door.

"Where are you going?" Mary asked in surprise.

"The cars. I should put the truck away and make sure all the doors are locked. That is . . . if you want me to."

Mary reached down and picked up the keys and then held them out to Artie.

"Then it's okay?"

"Of course. You have your chores, and you should do them. I wouldn't expect anything less."

Artie nodded, and then he was out the door.

"I said it, didn't I?" Mary asked quietly.

"Said what?" asked Bethany.

"I said that I love him."

Bethany smiled. "I'm glad it's out. Now we can act like a proper family to the boy."

* * *

"It was a nice funeral," Joey said.

Artie was walking home from the cemetery with Aaron and Joey.

"Pastor Wyndham said some really nice things, and I thought it was neat that Ray talked about his life. I didn't know he did all those things like mining and cutting timber and stuff." Aaron added this quietly, not knowing exactly how Artie would react.

"Nobody knows that. Nearly everyone just thinks of him as an old man. It was Mary who said that Ray should give the talk. He knew my grandfather before he got sick, and I told him a lot about him. He did a real nice job . . ." He corrected himself. "A really nice job."

"Ray's kind of like family, isn't he?" Joey asked.

Artie nodded. "I wish he was family. I don't have one now. At least not any that I'm related to."

"So are you going to leave town like you talked about before?"

Artie stopped and turned to look directly at Aaron. "What?"

"A long time ago you said that when your grandfather died, you were going to go to California or someplace? Are you going to do it?"

"You can't go," Joey started to say, but Artie shushed him.

"No, I'm not going to go. I said that back when I was living with the Boones. Mary needs me. And Ray said he'll help me go through my grandpa's things . . ."

"I'm glad," Aaron said simply. "I hoped you'd want to stay."

They walked in silence for a while. Artie had a lump in his throat that hurt so bad he felt like he'd never be able to swallow again.

They walked along in silence for a bit, although Aaron cleared his throat a couple of times. That usually meant he wanted to ask a hard question, and Artie braced himself. But it turns out that Aaron had something to ask Joey. "So is it true what I heard about your house?"

Joey's face clouded up. "Yeah, it's true."

"What about your house?" asked Artie.

"I didn't want to say anything, since your grandpa just died. But my dad's been out of work so long that they're making us move out."

"Not they—it's Boone. David Boone is making you move out." Aaron's voice had a hard, angry edge to it.

"What? He wouldn't do that? Why would he do that?" Artie was indignant.

"Why? Because he's a banker. He doesn't care about people or families. He just cares about getting his monthly payment. Even though the Westons have paid him enough money to make him rich, if they miss a couple of payments, he throws them out, just like that! It really stinks!" Aaron's voice had taken on an intensity that few people ever got to hear. Artie had experienced it a few times, like when he'd stolen the candy bar, and it was kind of frightening.

"So what are you going to do?" Artie asked Joey. He was worried about the Westons, but he also wanted Aaron to stop talking about Mr. Boone.

"I don't know. My dad won't even talk to us. He just sits there in his chair not saying anything, or he goes out and doesn't come home until after everybody has gone to bed."

"But where are you going to live?" It was still pretty cold outside, particularly at night, and he couldn't imagine the Westons without a house.

"He should go live in the Boones' house," said Aaron. "We could arrange to throw them out and see how they like it." In the back of his mind, Artie remembered that Aaron's father was something called a Socialist, but he didn't know exactly what that meant. But he did know that it meant that Aaron sometimes had strange ideas like this.

"All I know is that Mr. Boone didn't look very happy when he came and told us we had to move. My mom was crying, and my dad just stood there, and Mr. Boone was apologizing all over the place. But then he kind of got mad when my dad started asking for another month . . ." Joey's voice choked up at the humiliation of it.

Aaron shook his head. "It stinks."

Joey was so distressed at this point that his thin little body was trembling, as if it was cold. But it wasn't cold.

"So what about . . ."

"I don't know where we're going to live! So don't ask." That was as angry as Artie had ever seen Joey, and it really shook him up.

"Maybe you could live with your grandparents . . ."

"I don't want to talk about it. Is that all right with you guys? I don't want Aaron mad at Mr. Boone, and I don't want you trying to think of all the places we can live. That's up to us to figure out.!"

"Sure," said Artie quietly.

* * *

Artie sighed. Then he got a nervous look that often indicated he wanted to ask a question.

"What is it?" Mary asked.

"It's just that I was wondering . . ."

Mary put down her book. "What were you wondering?"

"Well, I was just wondering what's going to happen to my grandfather's house."

Mary's heart skipped a beat. She'd already considered the possibility that Artie would want to move back into his old home, even though it was impractical. She knew that he was sentimental, and she didn't want to have to be the one to tell him that he couldn't.

"What will happen is that the court will appoint an executor for your grandfather's estate."

"Estate? He wasn't rich."

"Everyone who owns property has an estate. Some are bigger than others, it's true. But still, someone has to pay any bills that your grandfather left and then distribute the property."

"So they may have to sell the house to pay his bills?"

"I certainly don't know that, for sure. My sense is that your grandfather had enough other assets to sell to cover his bills. I know that you thought he was poor, but I think he was more confused. Chances are that you will inherit the house. While you're not old enough to legally own property, it can be held in trust for you until you are old enough. Or the trustee can sell the house and set the money from the sale aside for you. I'm sure you can help the trustee make that decision. What are you thinking about the house? Are you thinking of moving in there?"

"What?" Artie shook his head in confusion. "No. I mean, not unless you want me to. It's just that, well, Joey. I mean his family."

"What about Joey? What's happened to his family?"

"It's just that I learned today that they're losing their house to the bank. Mr. Boone foreclosed on it, and they have to move out. I don't think they have any place to go, and I've been thinking that since I live with you, it doesn't make sense for the house to sit empty like it does. I try to take care of it, but with all these people out of work . . ."

Mary was inestimably relieved that he wasn't thinking of leaving. "So what exactly are you thinking you'd like to do for the Westons?"

"Well, what if I just gave it to them? They need a place to live, and I don't need that house, and all."

"That's a very generous impulse. But I don't think I'd do it quite that way."

"How would you do it, then? Or is it just a bad idea?"

"I think it's a very good idea to help the Westons. But I think I'd rent the house to them at a very low monthly cost, rather than just give it to them. Then when things get better, they can increase the rent or even buy the house from you if you want to sell it to them. You could even give them credit for all the rent they pay against the purchase price of the house."

Artie narrowed his eyes, a sure sign that he was pondering. "But I don't need the rent. And they're in a pretty tight spot."

"The point is not whether you need the money but rather that Mr. Weston probably needs to pay rent so that he still feels like he's the breadwinner for his family. There's nothing quite so discouraging to a man as having to rely on a handout."

Artie nodded. "I think I get what you're saying. If I give it to him, he'll feel guilty or something. But if I charge him rent then he gets to feel like he's paying for what he gets."

"Exactly. But a very low rent that he can afford with the spot work he gets. It's funny, but people actually end up resenting you when you do them a favor with no way for them to repay you. This way you're doing Mr. Weston a favor by charging him lower-than-market rates for rent, but he can pay you back by increasing the payment later on or by buying the house. I really think he'd appreciate that approach a lot more."

Artie furrowed his brow. "I like your idea. Joey said that his dad has been really quiet lately, like he's sad. It probably wouldn't do him any good to give it to him, just like you say. But we could rent it to him for real cheap."

"Really cheap, dear."

"Yes, really cheap." Artie was thoughtful for a few more moments. "About this executor thing . . . who do you think they will give the job to?"

"I don't know, I hadn't thought of it."

"Could it be you?"

"Perhaps. Although I think Ray is a more likely candidate. Perhaps we could call Judge Farnsworth tomorrow and suggest it."

Artie was excited now. "That's a great idea. Then we could talk to Ray about our idea. Maybe you could help me write up the papers or whatever? Mr. Weston would probably want something in writing."

"Of course. Let's talk to the judge first, and then, when the time is right, we'll invite Joey's father over to our house without his family so we can talk to him about it in private."

"Okay. But they only have a couple of weeks before they have to get out."

"We'll get things moving as quickly as possible, then. I promise."

Artie settled back in his chair. "It's very sad that my grandfather died. But the funeral was really nice. Ray did a great job, just like you said he would."

"It was very nice. I'm glad there were so many people there."

"Me, too." He was quiet again for a few moments. "It's sad that he died, but this thing about his house is good, isn't it?"

Mary smiled. "I think that since you no longer need the house, your idea is very good."

Artie nodded. "Thanks, Mary. For everything." He stood up and started to his room. But he paused and rather impulsively came back to the couch, where he leaned down to give her a hug. "I love you," he said softly. And then before she could react, he was off and out of the room, leaving Mary to wonder at this interesting turn of events.

CHAPTER 18

Boone on the Warpath

March 1934

"You better watch out, Artie. I hear that Mr. Boone is going to call the police on us."

Artie turned sharply to Joey. "What for? We didn't do nothing . . . I mean, anything."

"Somebody let the air out of one his tires this morning, and he had to pump it up in his suit. I guess he was furious."

Artie laughed. "I wish I could have seen that. But why blame us? Ray gave me a ride to school . . ." Then the smile faded and he looked at Joey darkly. "You didn't do it, did you?"

Joey coughed, which was his way of showing that he was nervous. "Of course not. I get in enough trouble without crossing him. I walked to school with Jeff and Tim."

"It's just that he's been pretty mean to your family."

"I didn't say he didn't deserve it. But I still didn't do it."

Artie felt bad for being suspicious when he saw the crestfallen look on Joey's face.

At this point Aaron had joined up with them.

"The way he's been accusing people—mostly you two—he deserves whatever he gets!" said Aaron.

Now Artie looked at Aaron a bit suspiciously. He was still the best student in the class and still revered by all the adults. But there was clearly a darker side to Aaron Nelson.

"Do you have anything to do with all this?"

"Me?" Aaron feigned mock indignation. "Why, you know that I'm a 'fine young man' who would never dream of doing such things."

"Uh, huh."

"Actually, I wish I had done some of those things just to teach him a lesson. But unfortunately I'm a coward—I do have a reputation to protect, and for some stupid reason, that's important to me. Still, whoever's doing it is getting pretty bold."

"And pretty mean," Joey added. "Some of the stuff is really pretty bad."

"So has anybody told Mr. Boone that we aren't the ones doing these things—particularly today?" Artie asked.

Joey nodded. "I think Monica told him she saw you riding with Ray. But he doesn't believe her."

Artie shook his head. "We don't stand a chance if he doesn't believe his own daughter." He was thoughtful. "But since we didn't do it, who did? Somebody has really been giving him trouble. And who's been telling you all this stuff?"

"Tim Lewis. His dad and Mr. Boone are friends and they talk all the time. Also, Monica talks to Tim sometimes. From what she tells him, she can't stand her father, either, and thinks he's going a little crazy."

Artie blushed when he heard it was Tim. "Does Tim believe you, or does he think we did it too?"

"He believes me. He thinks somebody's trying to set us up."

Artie felt his heart slow down a little. Tim was Stephanie Lewis's twin brother. It made him heartsick to think that her father was a friend of Boone's.

Which is why he was so surprised to hear a voice from behind them call out, "Hey, Artie. Joey! Wait up!" If Artie thought his heart was pounding a minute earlier when he was upset about what Mr. Boone had said about Ray, he thought it would pop out of his chest now.

"Hi, Stephanie!" Joey called back.

Artie watched as she came running up to them, holding a stack of books in her arms. Instinctively he reached out his hand to take them from her. It wasn't right that someone like Stephanie should have to carry that many books.

"I better not," she said. "I'd like to let you carry my books, but people might tell . . "

"It's okay. I didn't think you were even supposed to talk to me."

"I'm not. But I don't care." She hesitated for a moment, thinking about what she'd just said. Then she handed her books to Artie. "I hope somebody *does* tell my father. He and Mr. Boone have no right to treat you the way they do."

Artie found himself a little short of breath. The thought that he was now walking with Stephanie, carrying her books, was just too much to comprehend. Something about Stephanie made him so nervous he thought he'd die. But it was a good nervous, something he wished he could keep all the time.

He wanted to tell her just how much it meant to him that she would say something like that, even in defiance of her father. He wanted to tell her how happy he felt when she talked to him, even though he knew he didn't deserve it. He wanted to—he almost didn't dare admit this to himself—he wanted to take her books in one arm while holding her hand in the other as they walked to school. But of course that was impossible.

But all that came out was, "By the way, we didn't do it."

"Didn't do what?"

"Let the air out of Mr. Boone's tire. I rode with Ray, and Joey walked with Tim and Jeff."

She huffed. "I know all that. Tim told my dad, but he just brushed it aside. I wouldn't be surprised if Mr. Boone let the air out of his own tires just so he could blame it on you two. Neither he nor my dad want to know the truth."

Artie didn't know for sure what love was, but it had to be something like he felt right then. To actually have Stephanie defending him was more than he thought he could stand.

"Well, I better go. I don't want to be late for class." She reached out for her books. Unfortunately, it took a moment to register with Artie, so she laughed and took them from his hands. He blushed, but if Stephanie noticed, she didn't say anything. And then she was off—just like that. To Artie it was like somebody had just switched off a light in a room.

"She is a nice girl, isn't she?" said Joey.

Artie couldn't say anything. He'd heard about people being speechless, but right then he was. So he just walked on, trying to control his breathing. As they reached his classroom, he turned to Joey and whispered, "We've got to find out who's doing this stuff to Boone. You remember how last week somebody threw an egg on his window? And the week before that, pouring gasoline on some of his stupid flowers?"

"And the week before that, he caught us tipping his old outhouse."

Artie sighed. "Yeah, that was pretty stupid, wasn't it? That's why he blames us for all these other things."

"Tim's the one who thought that one up. Do you think he's the one doing all this?"

Artie shook his head. "I don't know. You know him a lot better than I do. What do you think?"

"I don't think so. Like today, he was with me. And his dad gave him a real whipping when he found out that he took part in the outhouse tip. I don't think it's him."

"Well, we've got to figure out who it is, or Mr. Boone may be able to make real trouble for us. I know Mary has defended me, but I'm sure that even she wonders sometimes. Ray is the only one who completely believes me."

"You called her Mary. You've never done that before."

Artie's face reddened. "Yeah, she told me the other day that Mrs. Wilkerson just took too long to say. So she said it would be all right if I called her Mary. She said that nephews and nieces get to call their aunts and uncles by their first names, so she didn't see why it wasn't all right for me to call her that."

"So do you call her Aunt Mary?"

Artie shook his head. "No, she said to just call her Mary. It's kind of hard and I end up calling her both names sometimes."

Joey smiled. "It's kind of nice, though, isn't it? It must mean she likes you."

"I suppose so." Artie tried to sound nonchalant.

"We'll find this person. I promise. I don't want old Mr. Boone messing things up with you and Mrs. Wilkerson."

Artie nodded. He didn't want that either.

CHAPTER 19

Boise to New York

March 1934

"Arthur, you and Ray will share a compartment while Bethany and I will have adjoining rooms in a suite. Mine is the largest, so you're welcome to come here during the day if you like."

Artie had never been in a Pullman sleeper car. Heck, he'd never been on a passenger train, so it was all a wonder to him. But he sensed right from the beginning that he wasn't experiencing what the normal traveler would. His first clue came when a virtual army of red-coated porters greeted them at the station to transfer Mary's steamer trunks to the luggage car. Since the trip was scheduled to take nearly six weeks she had a lot of trunks. It had taken Artie and Ray nearly an hour to ferry them all to the station. Then they'd been given priority service as they stepped up to the First Class window to complete their tickets. Next a conductor personally accompanied them to their sleeping berths, which Artie learned were cleverly designed compartments finished in teak wood and chrome that featured comfortable couches for sitting during the day and beds that pulled down from the walls for sleeping at night. Their personal porter made it clear that they could have food ordered in at any time they liked, or they were free to move to the dining car at preassigned times for their meals. Large plate glass windows in the compartment made it easy to see outside to the platform, and Artie couldn't wait to see what it looked like when they were moving.

But, as intriguing as their individual compartments were, Ray had already told him that it would be far more interesting to spend their daylight hours in the club car, where gentlemen played cards, and the ladies read books and chatted with one another. To Artie it was all amazing, and he couldn't wait to learn everything there was to know about rail travel.

"Arthur, did you hear me?"

"What?" Artie looked up startled. His imagination had carried him away, yet again. "I mean, yes, ma'am. Ray and I will be in one compartment, and you and Bethany will be in another."

Mary huffed. "Bethany and I will each have a separate-but-adjoining compartment. But you can join us in mine during the day."

"Oh, sure."

"Or you could take one of Mr. Jules Verne's spaceships to the moon if you prefer."

"That would be good."

Mary shook her head as Bethany burst out laughing. This was clearly not the time to give Artie any complex tasks.

"Why don't you go find Ray and check up on the loading of our automobile. Then I'm sure that he can show you parts of the train that I'm not interested in."

Artie did manage to hear this invitation, and with a quick thanks, he was off on a dead run for the freight dock, where he found Ray supervising the loading of the Cadillac into a box car. It was a tricky task that required the car to be maneuvered back and forth a number of times as it was worked through the door and into the narrow profile of the forty-foot train car. The look on Ray's face told him that things weren't going well, and Artie shrunk back to the side of the building when he heard Ray bluster for the freight handler to get the blazes out of *his* car and to let *him* do it. There was a quick huddle of railroad employees, and one said, "You'll have to accept responsibility for any damages to the automobile," and so forth. In a trembling voice, Ray assured them that if that was the case, he was about to save the railroad a small fortune, since they were far more likely to wreck the Cadillac than he was. Once they yielded control of the operation to Ray, he had the bulky automobile safely inside the railroad car in a matter of moments. He emerged triumphantly with jaw firmly set, a practice Artie had come to know was Ray's way of stopping himself from saying something cutting or sarcastic.

"Now, then, will you help me get the appropriate blocking and tackle so we can secure the auto?" Ray's voice was even and polite, but it still had power to send men scurrying for the ropes, blankets, and the wood blocks needed for the job. He then personally supervised the blocking of the wheels, covering the car with heavy quilts, and making sure that nothing else was left in the railroad car that could slide into the Cadillac and cause damage. After perhaps thirty minutes of heavy work that even Artie was allowed to help with, Ray stepped outside and watched reluctantly as the doors of the boxcar were pulled closed. He sealed them with a heavy padlock.

"Thank you, gentlemen," he said evenly, adjusting his cap and motioning for Artie to follow him toward the front of the train.

"Thanks for letting me help."

Ray didn't look down at him. "If we'd left it up to those idiots, the Cadillac would be nothing more than a pile of nuts and bolts by the time we reached Pocatello. By New York City, it probably would have rusted into a pile of scrap metal—I mean, did you see that open air vent on the top of the boxcar? The rain that could have come in on the automobile!" He had to stop talking—it made him so furious.

"You'd sleep with it if you could, wouldn't you?"

Ray looked at him sharply, at first thinking that Artie was being sarcastic. But when he saw that he was sincere, he smiled. "And you wouldn't?"

"Of course I would if they'd let me."

"Well, you can see why I'm worried, then. There's a lot of switching between here and New York City, which makes for lots of opportunities to bang the Cadillac around. What a disaster it would be to show up in New York City with a dent or scratch in the Cadillac. Can you imagine driving in New York City like that?"

Artie tipped his head to the side and narrowed his eyes. *So that's it,* he thought. *Ray doesn't want to be embarrassed in New York. This must be a really big deal to him.* Ray had pride, and somehow it made Artie feel good to think that they would arrive in the city in style. He knew for sure that Ray would see to that now.

"Well, here we are. Let's get on board and go to Mary's compartment for departure. She'll be all nervous about that. We'll stick with her 'til, oh, Mountain Home, which is about forty minutes, and then we'll make an excuse to go for a walk to get a drink and take a look around." Ray smiled mischievously. "Then who knows—maybe we'll have to accept an invitation for a card game in the club car? It wouldn't be polite to turn down an invitation like that, now would it?" Artie grinned. "That's where the real action is, you know." Artie was pleased that the excitement had come back into Ray's voice.

"How fast will we go?"

"At least sixty or seventy miles per hour once we get out into what I call the 'desolate zone' between here and Twin Falls." He got a faraway look in his eyes. "It's been so long since I've been through Nebraska and the flatlands. Who knows how fast this streamlined train can go. Just look at the front of this engine," he said while pointing to an identical high-speed passenger train on the adjacent track. As Artie surveyed the glossy black ceramic paint, he decided it looked like one of the art deco statuettes that Mary was so proud of in the library. The face of the locomotive was rounded in such a way that it offered little resistance to the wind and even the rivets holding the massive boiler together had been polished and rounded so they'd offer less resistance. These details effected a sleek appearance, giving the illusion that it was in motion even while sitting at a standstill next to the passenger terminal.

Ray noticed Artie's intent look as he surveyed the engine. He was totally absorbed in what he saw, and Ray was very pleased to see his eyes stop and pause at the right points along the length of the locomotive's impressive frame. It meant that Artie was surveying the engineering involved in the design of the machine, and he could sense that Artie was trying to understand how everything worked together.

"It's really something, isn't it?" he asked the boy.

Artie didn't even react—he was so lost in thought. So Ray put his arm on Artie's shoulder, which caused him to look up. "Bet you'd like to know how all this works, wouldn't you?"

Artie nodded. "Yes, sir. But there's just so much to it. Look at all the valves and bearings and . . ."

"I thought you might find this interesting. If you're like me, you like to know how things work—particularly when they're going to be moving you around for the next 2,500 miles. So I got you this."

"You got me something?"

Ray reached into the leather satchel he'd been carrying over his shoulder and pulled out a large book. "It's an illustrated guide to railroad locomotives. It's got diagrams to explain how each and every part of the locomotive works to produce motion." He handed it to Artie without fanfare. "It's something that every engineer should have."

Artie's eyes widened to the size of saucers. "Ray . . . it's wonderful!" Artie took the book into his hands and smoothed the cover with his hand a few times just to prove it was real. Then Ray watched in satisfaction as Artie opened the book to the first page. Artie turned each page in order until he came to the first diagram. It was an annotated picture of the entire locomotive, with arrows and text boxes to label the major components of the massive machine. "Oh, my gosh," Artie said under his breath. He drew his hand over the facing pages. He looked up with such a look of wonderment in his eyes that it took Ray back a bit. He'd given many a gift in his life, but none had ever been received in quite this manner.

"This is . . . it's just that . . ."

"I know. It's something special, because it will help you figure this machine out." Ray knew exactly how Artie felt. He'd actually wanted to buy two copies so he'd have one himself.

"It's the pictures. They're so amazing."

Ray had been very careful when ordering the book to make sure it was highly illustrated. He knew of Artie's problem with reading. So he figured that having an illustrated book would make it easier for him to understand.

"Well, we better get to Mary's compartment," Ray said in a business-as-usual voice. He'd actually gotten a little uncomfortable with all the emotion this thing seemed to be generating.

"Okay . . ." And then quite unexpectedly Artie simply reached up and threw his arms around Ray. "Thank you, Ray!" He did this with such force that it knocked Ray back a step, but then, a bit uncomfortably at first, he put his own arms around the boy. Having never been a parent, this wasn't usual for him. But it felt good. Finally, after a few moments, he released his grip on Artie and gently put his hands on his shoulders to push him away. "Now then, it's off to Mary's compartment."

Artie stepped back and smiled. Then he carefully put the book under his left arm and followed Ray down the side of the train to their assigned car, where they boarded the steps of the train. When Ray knocked on Mary's cabin door, they were greeted with an "It's about time! The train was about to leave without you, for heaven's sake. Now wouldn't that be a sorry situation—two old women traveling alone to New York City!" Ray looked down at Artie who had simultaneously looked up at him. They burst into grins and then, just as quickly, wiped all expression off their faces as they stepped into the comfortable compartment that was to be Mary's home for the next five days.

* * *

"Wow! Would you look at those skyscrapers! And I thought Chicago was amazing!" said Artie. Both the Chrysler Building and the Empire State Building had been completed since the last time Mary and Ray had been to New York, and the sheer size and grandeur of these new additions to the New York City skyline was enough to leave them as speechless as Artie. The Empire State Building was truly spectacular with the airship mooring mast projecting to an astonishing 102 stories above the ground.

The view from the New Jersey Palisade, high above the western shore of the Hudson River, was probably the finest vantage point of all to take in the whole of New York City all the way from the financial district in Downtown to Midtown, where the new buildings had been erected, and then all the way north to Uptown, where hundreds of apartment buildings completed the chain of buildings.

"It's like looking at the Rocky Mountains near Denver," Mary said finally. "Except that these mountains are all manmade."

The ever-practical Bethany asked simply, "So how do we get over there. I don't see any bridges."

"We'll unload the Cadillac and drive into the city through the Holland Tunnel," Ray replied.

"A TUNNEL!" Bethany shrieked. The people standing nearby turned and looked at her anxiously, some likely coming close to a heart attack from the sheer intensity of the outburst. As it was, Mary jumped so far that she would have fallen had not Artie been between her and the steps behind them.

"Bethany! Hold your tongue. You nearly scared me right out of my skin!"

"But a tunnel?" Bethany said weakly. "Where it's dark and tight and crushing in on you."

"You're afraid of tight spaces?" Ray asked.

The look of terror in Bethany's eyes showed that she was.

"Well, it's like this," Ray said. "You have your choice of going through a tunnel for something a little longer than a mile with ninety feet of Hudson River mud, water, and ooze above you, or we could drive way up north and come across the Washington Bridge, where the river is two hundred terrifying feet below you. Personally, I like the idea of a tunnel, but I'll leave that up to you."

Mary shook her head in disgust at the way he was tormenting the poor woman as Bethany shrunk back in terror at the Faustian choice. Either way she had to sell her soul to the river god.

"I'll sit by you," Artie said simply. "You can close your eyes and hold my hand, and I'll tell you when we're through."

Bethany turned and looked at him appreciatively. It was obvious that his offer wouldn't stop her terror, but she was so touched at his gesture that she motioned for Artie to come over. After he took her hand, she started patting it. "You promise you'll sit close once we get our car?"

"I promise," Artie said.

Glancing back at the incredible skyline, Artie said quietly, "We're actually going to *New York City.*" The awe had returned to his voice. No one else said anything, but it was obvious they all felt the same way.

CHAPTER 20

New York City

April 1934

New York City in 1934 was a dynamic place, particularly at the approach of spring. While the stock market crash had foreshadowed a slowdown in new construction and had increased the city's unemployment rate dramatically, there were still millions of people who had jobs, and it seemed like all of them poured out onto Fifth Avenue at exactly the same time every morning.

At least that's the way it looked to Artie, who stood at the window of an elegant room he and Ray shared on the fifteenth floor of the world-famous Plaza Hotel. It was inspiring to look down on the moving mass of people, automobiles, and horse-drawn carriages that crowded the Grand Army Plaza at the front of the hotel.

In the three days that they'd been there, Ray had been more animated than Artie had ever seen him. While most people were intimidated by all the traffic and congestion of the New York City streets, Ray seemed to relish the challenge of driving in the crowd.

The phone rang. Ray picked it up, and Artie heard him say, "Of course, we'll be right over." Artie looked at Ray expectantly when he hung up the phone. "Mary is ready for breakfast. I guess she wants to go out for it instead of ordering room service."

"Really?" This was a variation on their routine. On the train out from Boise, Mary had always eaten breakfast in her compartment, dinner in the dining car, and seemed to split between the two for lunches. On the previous two mornings since they'd arrived in New York, she'd had breakfast served at the dining room table in her suite. "I wonder where we're going?"

Ray shook his head. "I have absolutely no idea. The woman is proving totally unpredictable. Sometimes we go to the most expensive restaurants in town, and other times she wants to eat a hot dog from a street vendor."

"I know! Did you see how much money she spent on our dinner last night?" Artie asked.

"Nearly three dollars apiece. The Oak Room here in the hotel is one of the most famous and expensive restaurants in the city."

"But three dollars when you could buy a five-course dinner on the train for thirty-five cents. Don't you think that's kind of an amazing difference?"

Ray smiled to himself. "Well, we could keep talking about how much food costs, or we could go get some. I prefer the latter."

Now it was Artie who smiled. Ray was always practical. Well, almost always. Casting one more glance out of the window, he looked at the elegant carriages lined up at the entrance to Central Park at 59th Street.

"Well, let's get going, then. I'm sure that Mary is annoyed right now because we've been fooling around so long."

Artie pursed his lips and nodded, grabbing his hat as he went past the hand-carved cherry wood table by the door.

As they arrived at Mary's suite, they were greeted by an impatient, "Well, you two certainly took your time." Ray cast an irritated glance at Artie.

"I'm practically starved," Mary continued. "Not that it would show in my waistline. We've only been here three days, and I've already put on ten pounds from the rich foods we've been eating, I'm sure!"

"If you don't mind my saying it, ma'am, it's all those chocolates you've been buying . . ."

Bethany cut this statement very abruptly when she caught the dagger look in Mary's eyes.

"So what are we doing for breakfast? Shall I call down for the car?" Ray asked. One of the hardest things Ray had been forced to adjust to was turning the car over to a valet as they went to and fro. But the only available parking for the Plaza was in a car park down the street, and guests of the hotel were not allowed to drive in there. Normally, if Ray had been a true chauffeur, he would have stayed in a different hotel while waiting to be summoned by his employer. In that event, he could have parked the car himself. But Mary did not think of him as a chauffeur, as evidenced by his rather costly room with a plaza view.

Officially he was there to help her decide on a new automobile, but Artie knew that her affection for him was deeper than that. He was her trusted advisor in many matters, and it was evident that she thought of Ray as a friend.

"We don't need a car for the breakfast I have in mind. We're going to walk."

"Walk?" At least Bethany didn't scream at this like she did so many other things that took her by surprise. "On *these* streets?"

"Oh, for heaven's sake. Millions of people walk on these streets each and every day, and they're perfectly safe. Besides, there's nothing quite like walking in New York City. The place is just brimming with energy."

Bethany didn't look convinced, but she didn't press the matter and they made a quick trip to the elevator, where the operator greeted them by name. The car made its way between floors, stopping occasionally to admit other passengers.

Out of the blue, Artie asked, "Did you always stay at the Plaza when you came here with Mr. Wilkerson?"

"Only once," Mary replied wistfully. "George preferred the Waldorf-Astoria. He said it was the grandest hotel in all America."

"Why didn't we stay at the—" he stumbled over the name *Waldorf.*

"Because they tore it down. To make room for the Empire State Building."

"They tore down an expensive hotel? Why would they do that?"

"Because in New York City the land a building sits on is far more valuable than the building itself. The builders figured they could make more money with a large business skyscraper than a hotel, so down it came."

"Wow!" Artie took a moment to ponder that. "So now the Plaza's the best?"

"For now, dear. But I understand that they're going to build a new Waldorf on Park Avenue. They're promising it will be even grander than the original." She turned wistful again. "Of course, I'll probably never live to see it, but still it would be nice." It had become obvious by that point that the trip to New York was crowded with many memories for Mary. Most of the time they made her happy, but sometimes she seemed sad.

Fortunately, Ray had a way of snapping her out of it. "Well, we're on the street. Where do we go for breakfast? I'm starving!"

"Me, too!" Artie added, subconsciously patting his stomach.

Mary lost the faraway look and replied firmly, "We're off to George's favorite delicatessen. You're about to get a New York City breakfast of pancakes, bacon, and eggs smothered in maple syrup along with some of the best hash brown potatoes you'll ever put a fork into. My husband used to say there was no breakfast in the world as good as a New York deli's."

"Hmph!" Bethany snorted. "I'm sure there's no better breakfast in the world than the ones that you used to fix for him. That wasn't really very nice of your husband."

"Don't take offense. I never did. There's something special about this place, as you'll see soon enough." And with that they turned left out the front doors of the hotel, passing under the giant flapping flags that were the trademark of the Plaza. They quickly made their way to 59th Street, where Mary indicated that they should turn right to cross Fifth Avenue. In a matter of a couple of blocks, they'd found their way over to a crowded little deli on Lexington Avenue, where, much to Bethany's surprise, she did indeed have the finest pancake breakfast of her life. Perhaps it was because you could watch the cook making it, perhaps because of the hot maple syrup, or perhaps just because it was in Manhattan. Whatever the reason, it was wonderful.

* * *

Mary's 1931 Cadillac was guaranteed to turn heads in Boise, what with its striking blue enamel paint and highly polished chrome. But in New York City, it was just one out of a thousand luxury cars that made their way up and down the crowded streets of the city. Not that it didn't get them the best service at restaurants and retail stores as doormen rushed over to help Mary and Bethany get out of the car wherever they stopped. It's just that in the mix of Rolls-Royces, Mercedes, Imperials, Auburns, Cords, Lincolns, and even the occasional Pierce-Arrow, the Cadillac was just one of a dozen marquee brands that allowed the wealthy and the aspiring wealthy to try to stand out in the crowd.

At any rate, in the hours and days following that first breakfast out on the street, Mary had put the Cadillac to the test in a frenetic round of visits to all the famous tourist spots, as well as to shopping and dinners in many of the ethnic neighborhoods in the city. Fortunately for Ray, the streets of New York were laid out on a grid pattern so that finding things was relatively easy. Keeping the Cadillac free of dents and collisions was another matter entirely.

"These people are crazy!" Bethany was fond of saying. Ray and Artie found it hard to disagree. But Mary always "pshawed" them, responding that crowded and noisy is the way a city really should be, full of life and bustle and energy.

"Is she crazy?" Artie once whispered to Ray.

"I think she's lonely," he replied.

"Lonely?"

"For her husband. He's the one who loved New York City. I believe if he'd lived longer, he would have followed Walter Chrysler's lead and built his own skyscraper here."

"Wow!" The wow was in recognition that the new Chrysler building, completed just a few years earlier in 1929, was one of the most strikingly beautiful buildings in the world. Its long, tapering central tower was sheathed in sparkling chrome, with gargoyles fashioned in the image of a Chrysler automobile's radiator cap projecting far out above the city on the 31st floor. To Artie, they resembled fierce birds of prey, extending out into the city to protect the building from evil spirits. But it was the pinnacle at the top of the building that garnered the most attention. The tower dome was made to resemble concentric arches stacked one on top of the other until they formed a sharply pointed spire that gave the appearance of a needle puncturing the very sky itself.

"Did Mary's husband really have enough money to do something like that? Build a skyscraper, I mean?"

"If he didn't, he would have found it somehow. George was a dreamer who somehow had the ability to make his dreams come true. He would have found the investors. He loved the trappings of success, and in today's world the only place to really show off one's wealth is right here."

Artie was quiet for a time. "She really misses him, doesn't she?"

Ray nodded.

"Did he love all the museums, like Mary?"

"I don't think so. But he liked it that she liked them."

After that first pancake breakfast at the Lexington Street deli, they had walked up to the Metropolitan Museum of Art. Mary loved the art galleries in the Met, particularly those that featured the Rembrandt and Hudson River paintings. Bethany favored the housewares section, where elaborate antique goblets and silverware were displayed from the palaces of Europe and the Near East. Fortunately, for Artie and Ray, neither one of whom could work up that much enthusiasm for a painting, there was the medieval armaments gallery, where ancient coats-of-arms, mail, and weaponry were displayed from the Middle Ages in all their regal glory.

"I don't know about those museums," Artie said quietly.

"What do you mean?"

"Those Greek statues—they don't have any clothes on!"

Ray smiled. "It's considered great art, you know."

"It's embarrassing."

"Think of it as a three-dimensional painting. Just imagine the skill it takes to carve out something as complex and smooth as the human body from a piece of rock. The men who created those statues had a rare and unique talent.

Besides, there's nothing wrong with the human body. It's God's greatest artistic creation, after all."

Artie nodded. Ray was surprising about things like that. Artie had expected him to agree that they were embarrassing, but instead Ray found a way to make them something special, even reverent.

"Well, we better hurry . . . I think Mary's saved the greatest surprise of all for today."

Artie scoffed. "What could be more exciting than climbing up the inside of the Statue of Liberty and standing on the torch?"

"That was something, wasn't it? But I think you're going to like this even more."

Artie shook his head. He couldn't imagine how his brain could hold anything else. Besides, what the adults found exciting sometimes didn't mean all that much to him. For example, he preferred a hamburger to the fancy food at the Russian Tea Room that cost twenty times as much. Yet going out to dinner seemed to be the thing that Mary looked forward to the most of all.

"So where are we going?"

Ray tipped his head. "It wouldn't be much of a surprise if I told you, now would it?"

Ray was not wrong about the surprise. It was the very best. As Artie stood on the small deck of the 102nd story observatory of the Empire State Building, he couldn't believe his eyes. It seemed like he could see forever in every direction. He'd decided that this must be what the world would look like from an airplane, with everything down on the ground just miniature little buildings, cars, and streets. They were so high up that it was almost impossible to see people on the sidewalks, and those that he did see didn't look even as big as ants.

"They look like little toy cars, don't they?" Artie said.

Ray nodded.

"What's that building over there?" Artie pointed south.

"The New York Life Insurance Company building."

"That's a very cool dome on top. What about that one?"

"That's City Hall?"

"And that one?"

"Do I have to tell you every single building?"

Artie smiled. "Not every single one—just the tall ones."

So Ray relented and gave him a quick tour of the city, as seen from this very unique vantage point. Then he stood silently staring at the city.

"What are you thinking about?"

Ray didn't answer immediately. He just gazed through the glass to the south. "I was just thinking about my life when I lived here. I was married to an actress, you know."

Artie's eyes widened. "Married? You never told me that!"

"Well, it's true. I'd come to New York City to work for Rolls-Royce of America. One of my jobs was to test the cars, so naturally everybody thought I was rich.

"You were married?"

Ray nodded. "She was a beautiful woman."

"So what happened? Did she die or something?" Artie immediately regretted saying that, because he knew it would make Ray uncomfortable if that's what had happened. But he had just blurted it out and now it was too late to take it back.

"No, she didn't die. She just got tired of me."

Artie wrinkled his brow. He'd never heard of something like that. In Boise, people just got married and that was the end of that. "She got tired of you?"

Ray turned away. "She said it didn't matter that I wasn't rich like she first thought I was. But it *did* matter. I think she was embarrassed whenever we would go out to one of her parties, and people would ask what I did for a living. When I told them I was an automotive engineer, they'd raise an eyebrow like, 'What's he doing here?' and it would embarrass her."

"So what did you do?"

Ray paused again before finally saying very quietly, "We got a divorce."

Artie had heard the word, but never up close. "Oh." Then, "I'm sorry I asked, if it makes you feel bad."

"It's all right. I had a great time while we were married. She was glamorous and fun and beautiful. I got to do things and meet people that I would have never met in any other way. But the truth is that we really didn't have a lot in common. I'm more of a Boise person than a New York City person anyway, so it's all right that it came to an end. But it's fun to come back."

"Does she still live here? Are you going to see her?"

Ray shook his head. "I honestly don't know. And I guess I don't care." He glanced down at one of the buildings close to the Empire State. "But I have thought about it. It makes me a little crazy to think that I'm here, and I'm not seeing her. The problem is that even after all this time, I'm afraid we wouldn't have anything to talk about."

Artie inhaled deeply. New York City was proving to be more interesting than he could have ever imagined. Ray had lived here. Mary had formed some of her very best memories here. Yet the place made them both lonesome. He decided that was sad.

"I'm sorry things didn't work out for you."

Ray attempted a smile. "Well, come on. We better get down to the 82nd floor. Mary is probably impatiently waiting by now, wondering where we are."

"Just don't make me go over to that railing again. I'm afraid I'd throw up or something if I had to look straight down on the street again."

Ray laughed. "That would be an unpleasant surprise for someone down there, wouldn't it?"

It took Artie a moment to figure out what Ray meant, but when he did, he burst out laughing.

"Thanks, Artie."

"For what?"

"For helping me remember the good things about New York. It's good to see all these places through fresh eyes again."

Artie didn't really understand, but he was glad that Ray was happy.

CHAPTER 21

The 1934 New York
Auto Show

They'd been in New York City nearly ten days by the time the Auto Show opened. They were invited to a special section of the Grand Central Palace held exclusively for the showing of deluxe luxury automobiles to people who could afford to buy them, if they were so inclined. Accordingly, it was a strictly by invitation-only affair that afforded serious customers the chance to spend as much time as they desired checking out the cars, meeting with the coachbuilders who would design and build their custom coachwork, as well as mingling with others who shared their passion for fine engineering and automobiles.

For his part, Artie was most amazed by the specially designed elevator that could lift the automobiles up to the second floor, given that many of them weighed more than 6,000 pounds. But that was just the beginning of the marvels.

Once inside the hotel, they had been personally escorted by E. L. Cord, to the showroom where canapés and drinks were served by tuxedoed waiters moving silently through the room of wealthy industrialists, real estate tycoons, magazine and newspaper owners, and Hollywood producers and movie stars. Cord was the president of Cord Corporation, which owned over 150 operating companies, including Auburn Automobile, Lycoming Engines, New York Shipbuilding, and, of course, Duesenberg Motors. He was one of the most famous industrialists of the age, and poor Bethany seemed always on the verge of fainting at each sighting of some famous person who came up to him and Mary as they made their way through the crowd. Mary always pooh-poohed her wonder, but it was quite clear that Mary enjoyed being recognized by the very people that Bethany was so enamored with.

For Ray and Artie it was the cars that caused their excitement. The best labels of both Europe and America made their appearance there, as evidenced by the oohs and ahs of the crowd.

"I like that one," Artie said, pointing to a fine-grilled automobile on a cherry- trimmed pedestal.

"That's a Mercedes-Benz from Germany," Ray responded. Artie nodded knowingly, although he'd never heard of a Mercedes. The next one to catch his eye was Britain's entry, the American-made Rolls-Royce, with its distinctive grill that featured the double-stamped RR at the apex of the radiator. At that point, they lost Ray for a few minutes as he was greeted by one of his old coworkers at Rolls. While he was chatting, Mary, Artie, and Bethany looked at the Minerva from Belgium, France's Renault, and the Isotta-Fraschini from Italy.

"I still like the American cars best," Bethany said decisively. "Particularly the Stutz Bearcat. Now *that's* a beautiful car."

"It's like taking a tour of the whole world in a single showroom," Mary said contentedly, not acknowledging Bethany's foolishness. Mary suspected that she was attracted to the novelty of the name more than to the car.

As they turned a corner, it was obvious that they'd reached the Duesenberg display, since it was the one with all the people. As soon as the little group from Boise, now joined by Ray, closed up it was obvious why. The Duesenberg so clearly stood out from all the other automobiles, with its distinctive chromium grill, two large headlamps, and rakish engine cowling that seemed to give it the appearance of motion even with the engine shut off. It was like a vision of auto-motive perfection, and it left people wordless. Whereas just a few moments ear-lier, they'd been admiring the Pierce-Arrows, Stearns-Knights, Franklins, Stutz and Packards, all those were now forgotten.

In spite of the fact that Mary was perfectly coiffed and dressed, she sudden-ly felt self-conscious. That she was gawking at the "Duesy," was a sure sign that she'd never seen one. So she fell back on her old pattern of dealing with ner-vousness by becoming curt. "Oh, for heaven's sake, close your mouth, Arthur. You're making a spectacle out of all of us. You, too, Ray. I know it's a sight, but we don't have to act like country bumpkins, do we?"

Ray had been so absorbed in taking in the details of the car that he hadn't considered how he might look to others. Since there were a number of engi-neers in the room who knew him from his days in New York and Detroit, he didn't want to look foolish any more than Mary did in front of her friends. So he just stood with his hands in pocket doing his best not to look conspicuous.

Plain-Jane Bethany was the only one who looked unaffected—primarily because she *was* unaffected.

"What do you think, Bethany?" Artie asked her in an attempt to regain his composure.

"It's a car. It's a nice car—I can see that. But it's got four wheels just like every other car that costs a fraction of what this one does. I don't see what all the fuss is about."

Artie glanced up at Ray, who just shook his head. Artie was about to say something snide to Bethany when he was startled by the sound of a masculine voice coming up from behind him. "Welcome to the Show. May I help you, madam?"

Artie looked up to see a trim little man in a dark suit, sporting the most perfectly manicured moustache he'd ever seen in his life. Artie wanted to ask Ray how the fellow did that but knew it was time to keep silent. This was confirmed when the man cast the most withering glance at Artie that he'd ever experienced—well maybe not as withering as some of the looks that Mr. Boone had given him—but it was still pretty obvious that the salesperson didn't like the idea of a teenager being there.

"You can help me if you're familiar with this automobile," Mary said in her most haughty voice. Artie was proud at how well she bristled at the fellow.

"I'm affiliated with Duesenberg Motors, ma'am, and I would be glad to answer your questions. How may I be of assistance?"

Artie couldn't tell if the man was sincere, or if he was acting condescending to Mary. The tone in the man's voice suggested it was the latter.

"Ah, Charles—I see you've met my dear friend Mary Wilkerson." Artie was thrilled to see the way that Charles's face colored when he saw who it was who said this.

"I'm afraid we were just in the process of introductions, Mr. Cord. Perhaps you could make me better acquainted with her." Artie loved how pleased this change in circumstances seemed to make Mary feel.

E. L. Cord went on to explain to his salesperson how he knew Mary and how he hoped that Charles would take as much time as she needed to get all her questions answered. From that point forward Charles was most accommodating. Once the conversation started back up, E. L. excused himself to go chat with yet another wealthy customer.

"I know the automobile itself is the obvious center of attraction, but perhaps we could step into this small alcove, where I can talk to you without all the clamor of the open floor." Mary motioned for the others to follow Charles, and soon they were seated comfortably, with yet more drinks and hot hors d'oeuvres set out on the table in front of them.

"While I can see that you know much of the history of the company already, perhaps I could take a few moments to refresh your memory of how the Duesenberg came to be the definitive American car?" Artie didn't like the ingratiating tone in the man's voice, but Mary seemed pleased by it, so he settled in.

"By all means. It's been a few years since I've been to New York, and I'd like to know the full story."

"Ah, yes. Well, as you know, Duesenberg Motors is one of the most august names in the automobile industry. But it took the genius of Mr. Cord to make it the leader in automotive technology that it is today by orchestrating a series of mergers, not just of companies, but of the finest and most brilliant minds in the industry." Charles was pleased when Mary nodded appreciatively, but Artie had to stifle a laugh when he saw Ray roll his eyes at the fellow's self-importance. "But it was the year 1926 that was to bring the firm international acclaim when Mr. Cord arranged to purchase the Duesenberg Motor Company. As you perhaps know, the brothers Fred and Augie Duesenberg were self-taught engineers who built some of the finest racing cars in the world when they were still very young. For example, they gained immediate prominence when they won the Indianapolis 500 in 1924, and again in 1925 and 1927. But the capstone for the brothers, at least during their racing years, was when their car, driven by Jimmy Murphy, became the first American automobile to win the French Grand Prix in LeMans. That set the Duesenbergs apart as *the* premier designers of quality engines."

"In other words, their automobiles are well engineered," Mary said.

"Precisely, madam. You're very perceptive. And I promise that I'm getting to the point. I only tell you about their racing success to set the stage for why their luxury cars are such a remarkable accomplishment."

Mary nodded for him to continue. "Unfortunately, the Duesenbergs' first attempt at breaking into the luxury car market was a failure in spite of the Duesenberg Model-A's remarkable technological innovations. But the coachwork was uninspiring and failed to gain much of a market. Quite frankly, their company was in trouble until Mr. Cord bought them out in 1926 and then immediately hired Fred Duesenberg as the chief engineer."

"But why would he buy them out, only to hire them back. That doesn't make sense."

"Mr. Cord's genius is for organizing and promoting, with a keen eye on engineering as well. Cord realized that if Fred Duesenberg were freed from the tedium of running a company, he could unleash all his creative energy and push to design a car unparalleled by any other. In fact, his direct charge to the brothers was to 'build the finest automobile in the world, without regard to engineering costs or constraints.' Can you imagine what a great opportunity that presented the brothers?"

"Go on," said Mary.

"It turns out that Mr. Cord was correct in his judgment. Without having to spend all his time on the responsibilities of day-to-day management of the company, Fred Duesenberg rose to the challenge in a remarkable fashion. The new Model J was first shown here at the New York Car Show of 1929. In the years since then, I think it fair to say that the Duesenberg Model J has become a sensation. The very act of owning one distinguishes the owner as a person of substance and discriminating taste. Turning to Ray, he added, "Perhaps you're aware that it's the first to use dual overhead cams, four-valve cylinder heads, and the first 4-wheel hydraulic brakes ever offered on a passenger car?"

"I am. Quite remarkable indeed."

"Of course, the Duesenberg is not for everyone. Rather, we seek owners who will spend the time and energy to custom design their car so that it is unique in all the world. Even though the mechanical components are all built to our most exacting specifications, there is a great deal of latitude in how the coach is to be crafted so that you can make a distinctive statement about who you are and what appeals to your sense of style and élan."

Mary nodded. "I am anxious to learn what styles are available as well as discussing the choices we have in coachbuilders."

"Currently there are fourteen, madam. They include such distinguished names as Derham, LaGrande, Rollston, Murphy, Willoughby, Judkins, and LeBaron."

"Ah," Mary said, nodding her head appreciatively. "The best of the best."

"Yes, ma'am. The very finest coachbuilders in the world."

There was a moment or two of silence as Mary considered things.

"Would you like to know some of the technical innovations that make the Duesenberg the finest automobile in the world—things such as the sealed mercury cartridges that dampen the natural vibration of the crankshaft, or the specially designed universal joint with eight rubber balls to provide the smoothest possible transfer of power to the drive shaft?"

Mary smiled. "I'll leave the technical details to Ray. He's the engineer in our group, and I will trust the two of you to settle all that. What I would like to do is to glance through your catalog and settle on the type of automobile we wish to purchase."

Charles did his best to act nonchalantly at the good news but didn't entirely succeed. "Very *good*, Mrs. Wilkerson. Why don't we go over to our main lobby, where we can spend as much time as desired reviewing the almost infinite variety of choices that await your informed judgment and discerning taste?"

This was too much, even for Mary, and Artie knew instantly that the huff in her voice meant that she'd had enough of Charles's pandering.

"Yes, then, why don't we do that. But perhaps you would be kind enough to review all those technical details you spoke of with Ray and Arthur while Bethany and I look through the catalogs."

Artie and Ray's smiles disappeared as they realized that the crafty old Mary Wilkerson had just pawned Charles off on them. "What a dirty trick," Ray wanted to say, but instead he just smiled and stood up to hold Mary's chair as she rose to her feet. "Perhaps while you're tied up, Charles, E. L. wouldn't mind spending a few moments giving me his thoughts on what would be best for me?"

Charles smiled weakly. "I'm sure he would, Mrs. Wilkerson."

* * *

Once he sized up the situation and how the group reacted to Charles, E. L. Cord had been wise enough to send him off on an errand so that he could personally involve all the members of Mary's party in the decision of which body style to purchase. E.L. remembered Ray from his association with George Wilkerson and had great respect for his judgment. As they looked through the catalog, Artie had been fascinated with the racers, which wasn't surprising given his age, but Ray was sensible enough to know that they were there to purchase a comfortable car for Mary.

"The phaeton is nice," Ray said, "but we have just enough bad days in Boise that you should have an all-weather car. I suspect the phaeton does well in California."

"I think that's quite right," E. L. responded. "Besides, you need something that shows the dignity and position that Mary has acquired."

"I'm quite sure that any Duesenberg we purchased would be instantly admired and envied in Boise. As far as I know, there isn't a single person in the whole state of Idaho who owns one."

"I'm sure that's right, Mary. When Fred perfected his design we placed an order for five hundred chassis. So far we've sold about half of them. I'm sure that yours will be the first in Idaho."

"So it comes down to three models," Ray said. "The limousine is big and comfortable, but very long. I'm not sure it would do very well on our narrow streets. That leaves the brougham and the cabriolet two-seater. What do you think, Mary?"

"I think they're both very sensible. But I'm not buying this car to be sensible. There's nothing I love more than riding in the open air."

Ray nodded. "So you're thinking a convertible."

"Yes. There's something elegant and refined about a convertible. I like seeing people on the street without a window between us, and feeling the sun on my face as we drive."

"Well, then, the convertible," E. L. said cheerfully.

"And it seems to me that if we're going to spend all this money, we ought to buy the supercharged version—the one with all that horsepower."

Ray's eyes widened. "But Mary—the supercharger brings it up to 320 horsepower. I can't imagine you'd ever like to go 130 miles per hour."

"A minimum of 130," E. L. corrected.

"Are you sure?"

"I'm sure that you and Arthur would like it. And I know that's what George would have bought. He would have said, 'Why go ninety percent of the way to the finish line, only to come up short.'"

Ray looked on in disbelief, turned to Artie who had a similar look in his eyes, and then they both burst out laughing.

"The supercharged convertible, then," Mary reaffirmed.

Cord smiled. "There's nothing like it in the world, Mary. Nothing even comes close."

While Mary was able to maintain a look of calm detachment, Artie certainly couldn't, and when he broke out laughing at this unbelievable development, both Ray and E. L. Cord joined him.

CHAPTER 22

Just When Things Are Going Well

After dropping Mary off at a fashionable dress shop on Fifth Avenue, Ray asked Artie if he minded walking down the street to a men's store so he could look for a sport jacket made out of "good old Scottish wool." It had taken more than a week getting all the details completed on ordering the Duesenberg, choosing the amenities to be included in the coach, and agreeing on delivery terms. Now they were spending their last few days in the city, and Mary wanted to place some last-minute orders to be mailed to her in Boise. The Duesenberg wouldn't be ready for a couple of months, and it had been agreed that Ray would travel to the Derham factory to pick it up when it was ready. The time required to complete the car also meant that rather than sell the Cadillac in New York City, they would ship it home to Boise, which gave Ray something else to worry about. All of which seemed to weigh him down emotionally. That, in addition to leaving his nostalgic New York City.

Because Artie could tell that Ray was in something of a melancholy mood, he readily agreed to go with him to the store, hoping it would cheer Ray up somehow.

They entered a small shop on 52nd Street, just east of Fifth Avenue. There were a number of customers in the single room, but they left shortly after Ray and Artie's arrival, leaving the two of them alone with the proprietor.

Soon Ray was engaged in a discussion with the clothier, talking about the relative merits of a plaid or tweed jacket, which left Artie free to wander. As he came upon a glass counter and display case, he noticed that the owner had left out a beautifully carved box, lined with red felt, to display a number of expensive looking cuff links. Even though he didn't have any shirts with French cuffs that required cuff links, in his mind's eye he could picture himself wearing one someday. Out of all the links in the box, he found his eyes returning to one particular set that featured a large ruby in each cuff link. The red, square-cut jewels were set in a gold mounting that was absolutely mesmerizing, and Artie found himself licking his lips at the thought of just touching them. Acting on impulse, he did put his hand out but quickly withdrew it. Then he put it out a little slower, as if he were actually considering purchasing them and just wanted to hold them up to the light. *That guy can't possibly know that I can't afford them. For all he knows, Ray is my father, and we're rich.* At least that's the story that he hoped the fellow would assume. Turning to glance at Ray and the proprietor, he found that they were now looking at a gray jacket with their backs to Artie. Before he even realized what he was doing, Artie reached forth and snatched the two cufflinks and slipped them into his right pocket. Very casually, he wandered to another part of the store. Pretending to look down at a rack of shoes he slipped the cufflinks out and turned them over in his hand until they caught a ray of afternoon sunlight. The jewels sparkled as if they were on fire. More than anything in the world Artie wanted to have them, to be able to take them out and look at them, and one day to wear them on an elegantly tailored shirt so that everyone could see.

Slipping them back into his pocket, he quickly turned to see if he'd been spotted, but he hadn't. For the next few minutes, he just sort of shuffled around, acting bored, but always keeping an eye out for Ray. He was thrilled a few minutes later when it sounded like Ray was going to wrap things up, because it meant he could make his way out with his treasure.

But in the very same moment that he contemplated his escape he also felt a cold dread invade his stomach when he thought, *What if the man notices the links are missing? What if he calls the police?* He looked up behind the main counter to see if there was a phone in the store, and his heart sank when he saw that there was. Ray would be disgraced right along with Artie. Of course, all of these things argued that the prudent thing would be to put the links back in the box. But even all of those very real risks together weren't compelling enough to make him move back to the counter. Instead, he fingered the cuff links inside his pocket. They felt warm and elegant.

But it's simply the wrong thing to do! When he thought that, his stomach did hurt, so much so that he moved back toward the display case. When he got there, it felt like his hands were burning and he was certain that he had to put the cuff links back. But then he realized that there was just no way he could get them back out of his pocket and into the felt-lined box without being spotted. It's a lot easier to snatch something quickly than to deliberately put them back.

After agonizing over this a few moments, he decided he had to try anyway. So as unobtrusively as possible, he slipped them out of his pocket. Unfortunately, he did this at exactly the same moment that Ray and the fellow started to walk his way. He was now at the decision point—put them back in his pocket or get caught red-handed with the cuff links. As he did with so many other things, he acted impulsively on the first thought that entered his mind. Rather than thrust his hands back into his pocket, which would certainly incriminate him, he continued to lift them to the counter while saying, with only a little tremble in his voice, "Excuse me, sir, but could I ask you a question?"

"Certainly," came the reply.

"I doubt that I can afford these, but they're probably the most beautiful thing I've ever seen." By this point he held his hand open on top of the display case with the rubies in full view. "Can you tell me how much they cost so that I can maybe get a pair someday?"

"Oh!" the man said moving swiftly behind the case. "I should never have left these out. I was showing another pair to the last customer when you came in." He quickly took them from Artie, eyeing him warily.

"I'm sorry if I shouldn't have picked them up . . ." Artie said this with a defensive tone in his voice. "I didn't know."

"No, no. It's not your fault. It's just that I prefer to be here when people are looking at our jewelry. No harm done." Quite distractedly the man wiped the cuff links with a soft cloth and then put them back in the mahogany box with the others. "Now, to answer your question. This particular set is more than a hundred dollars. Is that something your father here would be interested in getting for you?"

Artie didn't dare turn to look at Ray. "I don't think I could afford anything like that right now."

Ray spoke up. "I think perhaps we could pick out a fine necktie for him when I come back to pick up my herringbone on Thursday. But we're not quite ready for cuff links."

"Yes, well. I'm certainly glad you found a jacket that you like. We'll have it ready for you at 10:00 AM on Thursday."

Ray tipped his hat and used his eyes to motion Artie out the door.

Once outside, they made their way back to the Cadillac, where Ray held the door for Artie. Once inside, Artie found himself breaking out in a sweat as he waited for Ray to come around and get in. When he did, Artie almost blurted something out but managed to stifle his response. It was way too early to pick up Mary, so Artie worried about what Ray had in mind. On the one hand, Artie was trembling inside because of how close he'd come to doing something truly awful. The theft of a hundred dollars' worth of merchandise was enough to land someone in jail. But he also felt pretty good that he'd put it back of his own free will. That was a good thing. So his thoughts were all kind of jumbled. He didn't know if Ray had bought his story like the store owner did. All things considered, he had a lot of things to be worried about.

When Ray settled into the driver's seat, he said quietly, "I didn't realize you were in the market for cuff links." His voice was unusually low.

"I wasn't. I mean, I'm not. I just saw them and thought they were nice."

"You weren't thinking of—"

Artie turned on him sharply. "I wasn't thinking of stealing them? Is that what you were going to ask me? Why does everybody always think I'm going to steal something?" Artie huffed in indignation, angry that Ray would suspect him. It was the logical extension of his earlier bluff.

"What I was going to say is 'you weren't thinking of turning into a clothes horse, were you?' But your question is a pretty good one, too."

Artie's stomach flipped as he realized that he'd betrayed himself by reacting so quickly.

Ray settled back in his seat and closed his eyes. Which is when Artie knew that he was in trouble. He started preparing a mental defense as fast as he could when Ray surprised him by asking, "Can I tell you a story?" That was unexpected and he turned instinctively to look at Ray.

"I guess."

"Okay. See what you think. There was this young fellow in New Jersey who loved to get in fistfights. I mean he really loved it. He got in fights with anybody he could find, even though he wasn't the biggest or strongest kid around. It's just that he was the meanest. He usually won his fights because he didn't care if he got hurt or not. The fellow who worries about getting hurt is always going to lose in the end. If you don't care, then you're kind of invincible."

Ray paused and looked very deliberately into Artie's eyes. "Aren't you going to ask what happened to the young man?"

Artie looked at him with a wary glance. "So what happened? Did he get beat up really bad or something?"

"Actually, just the opposite. One day he got so worked up in a fight that he nearly killed a man. Even when the other guy fell to the ground, he just kept pounding and pounding him until his friends had to pull him off the guy's back just in the nick of time to save the fellow's life. The poor man went to the hospital with a broken nose and cuts on his face and neck, as well as some broken ribs. Everybody hated the person who did it for being so mean." Ray went quiet.

Artie knew he was supposed to ask a question or say something to keep the conversation going, but he didn't want to. He knew there had to be a moral to the story, although he couldn't guess what it was. Right then he wasn't in the mood for a moral. So he just sat there determined to outlast Ray.

But it was really tough to wait out, and the silence in the car was so overwhelming that Artie couldn't stand it. So he finally asked, "Well, what happened to you? I'm guessing that you're the guy who did all the fighting."

"What happened is that my own mother kicked me out of the house. She said that she wouldn't live with a bully and that I could go and sleep on a park bench if I was going to act like that."

Artie didn't reply. He was curious now, but he was also angry. It's one thing to be tempted to steal something and then give it up, and another to be lectured when you didn't do anything wrong. It was like Ray was spoiling his small victory.

Ray reached out and turned Artie's face with his right hand. Artie was a little frightened now that he knew about Ray's past as a fighter, so he allowed his head to be turned. "It's like this, Artie. I had a terrible weakness for fighting. I was so competitive that one day it was inevitable that I was either going to kill somebody or get myself killed. You saw how bad my competitiveness got during the race near Kuna."

"It kind of scared me."

"I know, and I felt bad when Henry had to snap me out of it. But when I get like that, it's hard to stop. I knew it was a problem even when I was young, but I kept on going until I hurt that fellow. Even then I justified it to myself that he'd agreed to fight me, which meant that whatever happened was fair. But when it hurt my own mother, that's when I knew that I had a problem."

"It sounds to me like it was the other fellow who had a problem. He shouldn't have agreed to fight you if you were that much better."

Ray sighed. "Artie, we have to get this out and into the open right now. I don't want you to keep giving me lip and pretending that I don't know what's going on. I saw you slip those cuff links into your pocket. I was looking into a mirror when you did it, for crying out loud! If you hadn't put them back by yourself, I would have turned you in to the police."

Artie turned on Ray, his eyes flashing. "You would have called the police? I thought you were my friend!"

"I am. That's why I would have called the police. It seems to me that you've come to the very same point with your problem that I was with mine. Stealing those jewels is about the same thing for a thief as almost killing that man was for a fighter. Those cuff links are expensive enough that it would have been grand larceny. It's one thing to steal because you're hungry, quite another just because you feel like it. That's about as low as a man can go."

"So what are you going to do?" Artie wanted to scream at him that he did put them back, and not because he was afraid of being caught but because it was the right thing to do. It seemed like no matter what he did, people still thought the worst of him.

It was like Ray was reading his thoughts. "It's like this. I don't know why you put them back. I'd like to think it's because your conscience told you that stealing is wrong. But even if it was just because you were worried about getting caught, you did the right thing. I'm proud of you for doing that."

Artie took a couple of breaths before replying. "But that's not enough, is it?"

Ray exhaled slowly. "No, it's not enough. Can you look at me again?" This time he said it softly, so Artie finally raised his gaze to meet Ray's. He didn't want to, because now he was embarrassed and humiliated. Ray was probably the one person he admired most in the world, along with Aaron, and now Ray knew that Artie was a criminal at heart. He was so afraid that this would ruin their friendship forever. Ray might not even trust him to become a driver. So even though he put the cuff links back, the reality of the fact that he was even tempted still had terrible consequences to it.

"A lot of people were angry at me after I hurt that guy. But a few of them stood by me. Some, like my mom, made me face up to the kind of person I was becoming. It was because of her that I was finally able to change. And the interesting thing is that she never held it against me. In fact, it seems like she loved me even more because I did something really hard—I changed my ways."

That hit Artie really hard. If he understood what Ray was saying, it was that Ray would still love him, even though he'd caught him almost in the act of stealing.

"So how did you change? I've tried, but I don't seem to do so good at it." He looked up at Ray quickly and then dropped his eyes. "I thought I'd beat it before I went into that store. I haven't even thought about stealing anything for months now, let alone since we've been in New York. And then all of a sudden I saw those cuff links, and before I knew it, I was putting them in my pocket. It scares me."

Ray took a deep breath. "I don't know if this will work for you, but I did three things. First, I had a good talk with myself to figure out just what kind of a person I wanted to be. Was it to be a bully, who was always angry and mean, or did I want to be a decent person who carried his own weight in the world and who helped others when they needed it? Second, I had to figure out why I wanted to fight. I had a lot of anger inside of me because my dad had left us when I was only six years old, and we'd struggled ever since. And I was angry at my older brothers who used to kick me around and treat me like a baby, even when I started to grow up. And I was angry at our landlord, who used to threaten my mother with eviction just because he enjoyed seeing her cry. There were so many people I was angry at that I didn't know how I could let it all go. But I wanted to let it go. I told myself that day that I needed to let it go . . ." His voice trailed off.

"So how did you do it?" The defiance was gone out of Artie's voice now, and he sounded like a boy, not a tough guy.

"That's the third thing. I finally admitted that I needed help. I needed God's help, and I needed other people, like my mother."

"You needed God?"

"I know, I know . . . nobody thinks of me as a religious man because I don't go to church. But I found God on the day that my mother threw me out of the house. Probably because I needed Him so badly. I said a prayer. Not just words, but a real honest-to-goodness prayer. After apologizing for all the people I'd hurt, I told God that I knew I had a problem that was bigger than me and that I couldn't fix it by myself. So I asked Him to help me."

"Did He help you?"

Ray nodded. "He did. I think that's where that peaceful feeling came from. It was like He reached down and took all that off my shoulders. When it was gone, I could start to live the kind of life I wanted to live. I haven't been in a fight since—even though there have been a lot of times I've wanted to." He smiled, thinking that perhaps it was time to lighten the mood, a bit. "Heck, there have been a lot of times that I should have gotten into a fight because the other fellow deserved it. There's been more than once that I've wanted to slug that David Boone because of the way he treats you."

"What?" Artie's eyes widened. "You wanted to hit Mr. Boone?"

"But I didn't. Because I made a deal with myself a long time ago that I wouldn't."

This would have been a good time for Artie to say something—to make the same kind of promise that Ray had made. But even though his anger was dissipated, and even though he was really scared at how close he'd come to really messing things up, he wasn't sure he was ready to promise that to himself. For all he knew, it might come back just like it had today. So he decided to put his cards on the table.

"The truth is that I don't know why I steal, so I'm not sure how to give it up. It almost seems bigger than me. I do get angry, and sometimes I feel like I ought to get something just because I went without stuff for so long. But that doesn't account for it really, particularly now that I live with Mary. She has more money than a fellow could ever hope for, and she takes care of everything I need. Even so, I still get tempted."

"I think I have an idea of what makes you act this way, even though you no longer need to steal for food."

"You do? What is it?"

"Of course I can't see inside your brain, but if you're as much like me as I think you are, then at least one of the reasons you do it is because you like the excitement of stealing and the fear that comes from being caught."

"The excitement? You've got to be kidding. When I'm stealing something, I get so scared, my heart pounds like it's going to jump right out of my chest."

Ray nodded. "So that's it, then, isn't it?"

"What? I just told you that I get scared when I do it. Not excited."

"Oh, come on. Don't you see that anger was my excuse for fighting, but it was the excitement that made me do it? There's no feeling in the world like getting your heart pounding hard and feeling the rush of adrenaline that floods into your body when you're facing danger. When everything else was going wrong in my life, fighting was the only way that I could make myself feel like I was really alive. It was the one thing I could control. For me it was getting into fights. For you it's the fear of getting caught. But the feeling is just the same."

Artie pondered that for a moment. He could see how stealing was something like a game, maybe even an exciting game, where it was him against the store owner. He really did feel something of a thrill when he got away with it. Maybe that was part of it. Maybe he used all those other reasons as excuses when the real reason is that he just liked it.

"Here's the deal, Artie. You've got to decide who you want to be. You can't have it both ways. You can't be a good, law-abiding citizen and at the same time have the thrill of trying to best others by stealing from them. So you have to decide which one you want more. And then you have to make a deal with yourself and pray to God for strength to stick to the deal."

Artie leaned his head back in the chair. For the first time in his life, it felt like things had started to come into focus.

"There's one last thing that maybe you haven't thought about. While I'm sure you had good reasons for stealing at one time, those reasons are gone. You have a family now, one that can take care of you, not the other way around. Mary loves you, Bethany adores you, and . . . and I care about you, too. Maybe it's time to stop thinking of yourself as a picked-on kid and start thinking of yourself as a member of a family."

Artie sighed. He knew that everything Ray said was true. More than anything, he wished he could go back and replay that moment so he didn't embarrass himself in front of Ray. But Ray had embarrassed himself by talking about the bad things he'd done. Maybe that was his way of making it all right for Artie to talk about his problem.

"Will you help me, Ray?"

Ray nodded. "I was hoping you'd ask. What can I do?"

Artie didn't know how to say what he wanted. It was all jumbled in his mind. "I want you to watch me and to stop me when I'm tempted, but I also don't want you to always be thinking the worst of me. I need help, but I'd also hate it if I thought you never trusted me. Of course that doesn't make sense, but—"

"I think it makes a lot of sense. For me it was my mom who helped me. Once she finally let me back in the house, I told her what I wanted to do. She promised to help me. And she was great in how she did it. Somehow she always made me feel like she had confidence that I'd make the right choice. But when somebody did something really rotten to provoke me, she'd step in and help me out—sometimes by standing up for me, sometimes by just shaking her head ever so slightly so that I'd know it was time to back off, and sometimes she'd just step in and say, 'Ray isn't going to fight right now. He should knock your blooming head off, but he's not going to because he's too big a man for that. That one always worked." Ray smiled. "She stuck by me until I finally left home. The main thing is that she always made me feel like she trusted me."

"So do you think you could ever trust me?"

"I think I did that earlier today in the store, don't you?"

Once again, Ray had taken Artie by surprise. "I guess you did, didn't you? You could have called the police right away, but you waited long enough for me to make it right."

"Exactly."

Artie smiled. "Thanks, Ray." He took a deep breath. "I'm going to do it. I'm going to ask God to help me stop. But I'm scared of messing up."

"That's all right. Being afraid can help." Ray reached down and started the car.

"Where are we going?"

"It seems to me that this decision of yours deserves a celebration. I was thinking that we ought to get at least one more milkshake before we leave the city."

"In that malt shop in Central Park?"

"Central Park? You've got to be kidding, That's ten blocks away, and we've got to be back here in less than an hour to pick Mary up."

"But you're the one who said they have the best milkshakes in all of Manhattan. 'Worth driving clear across the country for!' as I remember it." Artie grinned.

"Why you little brat!" Ray slugged him good-naturedly. Even so, it hurt, and Artie realized that it was probably a very good thing that Ray had given up fighting a long time ago, or he really would have killed somebody.

"Well?"

Ray sighed. "Hoisted on the petard of my own words. Off to Central Park, then."

As they pulled into a parking spot next to the park, Artie somehow felt better than he'd ever felt in his life, in spite of the bad events of the day. As he joined him on the sidewalk, Ray said, "Remember, you need prayer to make this work, too."

Artie nodded solemnly. He'd already started saying one in his mind.

CHAPTER 23

Family

May 1934

Artie was nervous. They'd arrived in Boise the previous night at eleven. By the time they got home and settled in, it was after one in the morning before anyone fell asleep. Now it was Sunday morning. He'd missed the early-morning worship service because he simply couldn't force his eyes open, but he was anxious to get to Sunday School. He wanted to talk with the pastor again. The problem was that Mary was still sleeping, which she undoubtedly needed, and Ray had been given the day off. So Artie didn't know if he should wait for Mary in case she woke up or if he should start walking by himself. He didn't dare take the pickup without permission. It would take at least forty minutes to walk, and it was quickly approaching the do-or-die moment.

Just as he was about to take off, he heard Mary stirring, so he rather impatiently returned to the living room to see if she'd like to go with him. A few moments later she came out in her bathrobe.

"Good morning, Arthur," she said with a yawn.

"Good morning, ma'am."

Mary looked at her watch. "Oh, dear. You're dressed for church, and I'm going to make you late, aren't I?"

Artie smiled weakly. He didn't want to press her.

"Maybe I'll let you go by yourself this morning and catch up with you tonight."

"Are you sure?"

"Yes. I am definitely too tired to hurry now. Ray can give you a ride."

"He has the day off."

"Oh. Well, now what do we do?"

"It's no problem. I'll just walk or ride my bike."

"No, you can take the Ford. I trust you with it. I'm sorry I'm so sleepy."

This time he smiled more easily. "It's fine. I'll be home after Sunday School."

Before Mary could reply, there was a rather severe knock at the door. "Good heavens. Who can that be? Will you get it, Arthur?"

Artie went to the door where he found two policemen standing. "Hello, Artie," the first one said. "We need to come in."

Artie's stomach lurched, and he felt his legs go a little weak. As Artie stepped aside, the two men stepped into the entryway. Artie motioned to the parlor. "Who do you want to see?" he asked weakly.

"We need to talk to both you and Mrs. Wilkerson."

At this point Mary stepped out of the shadows. "And what brings you by, Officer McKenzie?"

"I'm afraid we have to talk, Mrs. Wilkerson. There's been a charge made against Artie, and as his guardian you need to help us sort it out." Mary bit her lip and motioned for them to sit down.

"Now what is this all about?"

McKenzie cleared his throat. "It seems that David Boone has filed a complaint against Artie. His home was severely vandalized—the plate glass in his parlor window was smashed in—and he blames Artie. We're conducting an investigation." When he saw Mary's expression, he quickly added, "Mr. Boone has been subject to numerous attacks, and something has to be done for him."

Mary tipped her head back and looked down her nose at the two officers for a moment. Then, very steadily, she asked, "And when did this vandalism take place?"

"Thursday night. We tried to contact you Friday and yesterday, after Mr. Boone came in and leveled the charge, but we couldn't find you at home."

"Were there any witnesses to the event?"

"No ma'am. But Mr. Boone asserts it has the telltale signs of the previous attacks, which is why he's sure that your boy is involved."

In spite of the present controversy, Mary somehow found that she liked the phrase, "your boy." It caused her to glance over at Artie, who, even though he was looking down at his feet, looked like he might have liked the sound of it as well. As she thought about it, she was also pleased that Artie hadn't blurted out the truth of his whereabouts on Thursday, as he certainly would have done when he first arrived, but rather that he trusted her to take control.

"So the attack took place Thursday night, and there were no witnesses."

McKenzie looked a bit exasperated. "That's what I told you."

"Perhaps it would interest you to know that Arthur was with me in Denver on Thursday night. We didn't arrive home until last night at eleven. So, it's quite impossible that he did this act."

McKenzie blanched. "I wasn't aware of that."

"Well, then . . ."

"Not so fast, ma'am. Mr. Boone has asserted that it's possible Artie may not be directly involved but that he uses his influence with others to carry out these attacks on his behalf."

Mary took a deep a breath and raised her hand to quiet Artie, who she could tell was now at the bursting point. "And whom does he suggest is Arthur's accomplice?"

"Joey Weston, for one. And Aaron Nelson, for another."

Mary nodded, and then her gaze hardened. "Now listen to me, Ian McKenzie. I feel very bad for David Boone that these attacks take place. I can imagine how distressing they are. But Arthur is innocent. Since we have been away from home for more than a month, it's impossible that he's involved. Certainly you'll agree that it doesn't make sense that he had the foresight to plan an attack on David Boone way back before we left town, particularly to coincide with his return. And since the Weston's don't have a telephone, it would be impossible for Artie to communicate with him in the interim."

"Yes, well . . ."

"Besides that, Ian, you and I both know that young Joey doesn't have the wherewithal to do something like this on his own. He's a follower, who may go along with Arthur when in his company, but he certainly wouldn't do this on his own initiative, even if it had been suggested to him. I can't imagine that you would impugn Aaron Nelson." Artie noticed how her use of McKenzie's first name made it seem like he was a small child being lectured by an adult.

McKenzie turned to his companion. "It seems like this new information pretty well clears this up . . ." The other fellow nodded. Turning back to Mary, he said, "I'm sorry we bothered you on a Sunday morning, Mrs. Wilkerson. But you can see that we need to follow up on these complaints."

"Of course. I'm glad that you're so diligent." She stood up to show them to the door. Just as they were about to exit, she leaned toward McKenzie and said something that Artie couldn't hear. The officer's face colored, and then he left.

Mary returned to the sitting room where Artie sat, his shoulders slumped. "You're angry, aren't you, Arthur?"

He continued to look down. "Yeah, maybe a little."

"I'd be very angry, too, if I were you. You've been unjustly accused."

Artie looked up but didn't say anything. But there was fire in his eyes.

"What are you going to do?"

"I shouldn't do anything." He said this without conviction.

Mary sighed. "I'm going to ask you do something very hard. At least it would be hard for me." She held his gaze. "I want you to promise me that you will not do anything to retaliate against David Boone. No toilet paper, no eggs thrown at his windows. Not anything."

Artie looked surprised, as well as wary.

Mary confirmed, "Yes, I know about all those things. But here's why I want you to promise me—and to trust me. At this point we know that someone is harassing David maliciously. Consequently, he's suspicious of everyone, but most particularly of you. If you do anything to retaliate and get caught doing it, you will simply justify his suspicions about you and give him even more reason to file complaints."

"But it's not fair. He's on my back all the time, and I'm not guilty."

"Precisely. So let's keep you not guilty. Then, when he makes other spurious charges, I can back you up. But for me to do that, you have to be trustworthy. I have to know with absolute certainty that you are not harassing him. Only then can I stand up for you." She looked at Artie steadily. "Can you make that promise, no matter what he does to provoke you?"

Artie shook his head as he thought about it. This was all pretty hard. He had enough to worry about with his promise to Ray about stealing, and now Mary wanted him to make another one—one that was frankly much harder to keep than promising not to shoplift. But Mary *had* stood up for him. She deserved something in return.

"Okay. I promise."

Mary bit her lip. "All right, then. With that promise to stand on, I think I can assure you that David Boone will stop harassing you. But it will only work if you don't do anything."

"What will you do?"

She frowned, ever so slightly. "You let me worry about that." It was obvious that an idea was forming in her mind. She looked at Artie again. "Do you still agree? Are you really up to this challenge?"

Artie nodded slowly for a moment or two while thinking about it. Finally he said, "Yes. I'll leave him alone, no matter what he does to me." Then, as an afterthought he said, "I just hope it works."

"If it doesn't work, we'll come up with another strategy. Maybe I'll help you tip his old outhouse." That made Artie laugh. He could just picture Mary Wilkerson with a roll of toilet paper in her hand. "I think he took it down. They have an indoor bathroom now."

Mary nodded. "You know what I mean."

"Yes, ma'am."

"Now, I think you were going to church. You better hurry. Have you had breakfast?"

Artie dropped his head. "I couldn't go to church now, ma'am. Mr. Boone will be there, and when he hears what you said to the police he'll be even angrier than usual. Who knows what he'll say to me in front of people. I . . . I . . ." his voice faltered and Mary could tell the anger was returning.

"You just don't want to face him right away? That's all right, then. It will be good for you to have some time to master your feelings. Of course, normally I would insist that you go there just to show David Boone and his friends that we're not going to be intimidated. But perhaps it would be better if we waited until tonight when we both can go. In the meantime, maybe you wouldn't mind reading to me from the Bible this morning. We'll hold our own Sunday School. We could start up in half an hour, once I've had a chance to get ready."

Artie took a deep breath and inhaled slowly. It's hard work, he thought, to make all these darned promises. It was a lot easier just to act by himself. But now that he was part of a family.

* * *

People's heads turned as Mary Wilkerson walked into the bank. She always moved with a confident air, but today there was a purposefulness to her stride that made some customers step back to get out of her way. She ignored the greeting of one of the tellers, which was also very unusual, as she pressed her way directly to David Boone's desk. His head was down, and he was apparently so deeply focused that he was the one person in the bank who hadn't taken notice of Mary's arrival.

"David. We need to talk," she said with an icy tone.

Boone jerked his head and looked up in surprise. "Why, hello, Mary. Do you need help?"

"Yes, I do. I need to make a withdrawal."

Boone grimaced. "I'm sure one of the tellers will be glad to help you."

"I want you to help me."

His countenance darkened, but he motioned for Mary to sit down. "Now, what do you need, Maty?"

"Mrs. Wilkerson, please. I'm here to close my account. I want you to help me move it to First Security."

Boone's face blanched. "Close your account? But you can't do that." He paused. "I mean, which account?"

"All of them. I'm taking all of my money out of your bank."

Boone looked as if he was being strangled. "But, Mary—Mrs. Wilkerson, you know how things are. A withdrawal like that could cripple us."

"I'm aware that this may cause distress. If you need a few days to have cash brought in from Salt Lake City, it will be fine."

Boone shook his head. "But . . . but . . . why are you doing this?"

Mary fixed him with a steady, unblinking gaze. "Because I believe a person should only bank at a place that is acting in the best interest of their customers. Unfortunately, I no longer believe that to be the true in my case. So I'm moving my money."

"But I don't know what you mean."

"Oh, I think you do, David. You continue to harass Arthur, even when you know he is innocent."

"I do *not* know he's innocent."

"It was intolerable of you to send the police to our house when you, of all people, knew that Arthur was with me in New York City. You helped me arrange the cash needed for the trip, and you knew perfectly well that we weren't home when this terrible thing happened to your house."

"Mary, I appreciate that you are Artie's guardian, but that has nothing to do with our banking relationship!"

"It has everything to do with it. In the first place, I am not just Arthur's guardian. I am his family. And he is mine. I did not accept him into my home on a contingency basis. He is not in foster care that I can revoke whenever I choose. He is there for as long as he cares to live with me." In spite of her efforts to remain steady, there was a brief catch in her voice that betrayed the love that she felt for Artie. "And I hope that he chooses to stay there for a very long time."

"I didn't mean . . ."

Calming herself, Mary reasserted control. "I honestly don't care what you think of me or Arthur. But I will also not tolerate your continued interference. I am working as diligently as I can to reform the boy, and each time you publicly humiliate him, you make the task harder."

"I can appreciate that. But this remains a personal matter that I should work out with you."

"It is not just a personal matter. It involves our professional dealings as well. I will only leave my money in a place where I trust the employees. And this betrayal on your part, when it is so blatantly obvious that you accused Artie even when you knew of his irrefutable whereabouts, convinces me that you are not trustworthy."

"How dare you!" Boone half-stood from his chair as if he wanted to verbally assault Mary. But then, just as quickly, he seemed to slump. Perhaps he'd remembered that as their largest depositor, Mary *could* single-handedly put the bank at risk of collapse. Gripping the sides of his chair, he forced himself to sit back down.

"I'm sorry, Mrs. Wilkerson. I should not have acted like that. You are right to criticize me. But before you act, can we please talk about this?"

"I'd like to."

Boone fumbled for a few moments. It was usually his role to put people on the other side of the desk on the defensive as they asked for a loan, for additional time to make a payment, or other such things. But now he was the one who was being challenged. Clearing his voice, he said, "I don't know what to say. Someone has been making my life miserable—intolerable. You just can't imagine the strain it has been." He looked up uncomfortably. "It's just that everyone knows that Artie doesn't like me. That he . . . that he resents me. After all," and this had to be the hardest thing for him to say, "I *did* take him on contingency."

Mary settled in her chair just a bit. Finally, Boone was being fully honest and opening himself up.

"I've had my home violated, too, and so I appreciate how you feel. Fortunately, it hasn't been an ongoing assault, for me, which means your situation is even worse. I truly empathize with you. But you are picking on Arthur because he is an easy target. Your anger at the boy clouds your judgment. Maybe if you could get over your obsession with Artie, you and the police could start looking for the real culprit."

She could see that he wanted to contradict her, but refrained because of her threat. She had hoped to use it as a way to open up the dialog, to convince him, but his expression now showed that it was impossible. So she'd have to settle for less.

"Here's the way it is, David. I will leave my money here for the time being, although I will begin to transition some of my assets to other banks for diversification purposes. I think even you will agree that that is prudent."

Boone nodded.

"But you have to come to grips with your obsession over my boy. I will punish him when he does something wrong, but I will not stand idly by when he is accused falsely. This will not happen again, or I will take all the options available to me to stop it. Do I make myself clear?"

"Perfectly." Boone's face was hard now.

"Good. Now I will wish you good day." They both stood, and Boone extended his hand, which Mary took. It was an awkward but necessary ritual to seal the exchange.

"And David, I would like you to transition my remaining business account to First Security. It's relatively small, but I have been neglectful of my money. I will take a far more active interest in it from this point forward."

"Of course. I will see to it."

"Thank you."

With that, Mary left the building with the same forceful stride with which she'd entered it. But when she got outside and climbed inside the Cadillac, Ray couldn't help but notice that she looked very small as she sat back against the seat. And then he saw her put her face in her hands. Even though her business was not his to interfere in, he'd stepped inside the bank to a place where he could overhear what she was saying to Boone. If she hadn't done something, he would have.

"I know how you feel, Mary," he said softly as he walked around the car to get in the driver's seat. "I feel the same way about the boy." He closed the door and started the engine.

CHAPTER 24

The Grand Arrival

June 1934

Ray was gone a total of three weeks traveling to Philadelphia and back to Boise. To the people he left behind in Boise, it seemed like an eternity.

The reason it took Ray so long to pick up the car is that once he got back to Philadelphia, he had to do a thorough inspection of every single element of the car to make certain it fulfilled expectations. Since there was no authorized Duesenberg dealer anywhere in the state of Idaho, or even Oregon for that matter, it was vital that everything be in good order before he took delivery of it.

That included a number of test drives in the Philadelphia area with technical staff from Duesenberg Motors and some of the master craftsmen from the Derham Coach Company. And it was a good thing they did, too, for on one drive down the Main Line—the stretch where the highway parallels the Schuylkill River—Ray and one of the engineers had almost simultaneously detected a slight rubbing sound. When they pulled over to investigate, they found that one of the body joints that connects the coach to the chassis had been installed incorrectly, which had left one of the rear fenders rubbing against the tire. Of course the Derham men were embarrassed by this mistake, but repairs were quickly effected to put the car in good order.

After perhaps ten days of working with it, including adding the final personalizing touches that made Mary's car distinct from every other, Ray finally signed the paperwork to accept delivery. It was also at that time that he made the final payment on the car, Mary having previously wired enough money to a bank account in Philadelphia that Ray was authorized to sign on. As he handed the check over, he had to gulp. Even though he'd worked for Rolls-Royce, it was still something to see a total of $21,500 pass into someone else's hands. But the car was magnificent, and he hoped that Mary would like it. While the Cadillac was painted a deep royal blue, the Duesenberg stood out in a rich burgundy with coal-black fenders and trim. The effect was striking, with the black lines flowing back from the front of the car and down to the floorboards in a sweeping gesture that added to the natural grace and styling of the car. The enormous custom-made trunk that was strapped to the platform behind the passenger compartment was made of black, oiled leather, with brass trimmings. Gleaming, polished chromium was displayed in abundance all around the car, including the taillights. Ray concluded that it would be something of a nightmare to keep everything polished, what with the dusty summer roads of Boise, but he also knew that he and Artie would find endless hours of satisfaction cleaning and polishing all the intricate door panels and accessories.

Ray personally supervised the loading of the car in Philadelphia, with a remarkably similar dialog with the railroad workers there compared to the one that had taken place in Boise many months earlier when they set out for New York, except that the Philadelphians bantered back a lot more forcefully than the Boise porters had. Someone unfamiliar with the east coast style could easily have been intimidated, but for Ray it was just old hat, and he jousted with them vigorously until he got what he wanted.

The train pulled into Boise on June 12, 1934. He was gratified to see that there was a small party of enthusiasts waiting at the station, led by Artie, who started waving his hat as soon as he saw Ray through the window. In fact, there was an unusually large crowd out that day, which suggested that there would be a lot of passengers disembarking. As the train lurched to a stop, Ray made his way to the door at the rear of the railroad car, thanked the porter, and then descended from the train and onto the Boise platform. He was pleased with the little cheer that went up from those who had assembled to greet him, and even more pleased when Artie came running up to give him a hug.

"You're home!" Artie shouted as he threw his arms around Ray. Never having had children of his own, this was something of a surprise, and the force of Artie's body knocked him back a step or two. But even though it was still a bit unfamiliar, he returned Artie's hug and then said, "I honestly think you've grown six inches while I've been gone. And it's only been a month!"

"I hope your journey was all right," Mary said brightly.

"Fair enough."

"But what about all that money I gave you. You weren't supposed to show up empty-handed, you know."

Artie and Aaron laughed.

"Why, ma'am," Ray said in a perfect deadpan, "I know I was supposed to buy a car with all that money, but there was this fellow who sold me a handful of magic beans. I thought you'd be happy."

That one took everyone so completely by surprise that even Mary burst out laughing.

"Beans! I'll send you up the beanstalk for good, Ray McCandless!"

Before Ray could form a response, however, Artie let out a shout. "There it is—there's the switch engine that's going to detach the freight car. Can we go watch, Mary?"

At this point, all eyes turned toward the back of the train, and Ray huffed, "I better get back there and supervise the unloading. I've had to check on the darned thing at every single stop across the United States. I wish George would have decided to settle in Philadelphia instead of Boise. It would have been a lot less trouble than fighting the cursed railroad. Either that or I should have just driven from Pennsylvania."

Of course the reason that Ray didn't just drive the Duesenberg out to Boise is that the roads were simply too irregular and beaten up. The torture it would have been on the car to go through all the muddy roads that separated Pennsylvania from Idaho would have marred the fantastic coachworks of the car. Not that the Duesenberg itself would have had any trouble—it was built to take anything the open road could throw at it—but this was intended to be a refined car, a city car, and not one to brave the wilds of Tennessee or Nebraska. So travel by train was the only way to assure that Mary would get a brand-new, unblemished car.

"Well, get going, then, and come to the front of the station when you're ready to pick us up. You go too, Artie. Yes, and you too." She motioned to Aaron and Joey. The three boys jogged off happily after Ray. The car could have been a new Flash Gordon rocket ship based on the way Artie had built it up to Aaron and Joey. They honestly had no idea what to expect, although Aaron suspected that Artie had exaggerated the whole thing.

It didn't take long, however, before Aaron had to swallow his suspicions. As Ray personally backed the heavy car out of the boxcar and onto the loading dock, the sounds of the crowd , including the railroad workers helping him, drew hushed oohs and ahs that at once pleased Artie and at the same time left him rather speechless. The display cars at the Auto Salon had been sleek and stylish, but this car was downright elegant. He loved the colors. But it was the chrome radiator that sealed the deal, and the crowd burst into spontaneous applause as Ray backed down the loading ramp and onto the street.

"Well, then, come on, boys. Let's go get Mary and Bethany!" Ray called out. As they drove around to the front of the Spanish-style depot, with the extensive lawn and reflecting pools extending down to Capitol Boulevard below them, Ray was surprised to find that the large crowd on the platform wasn't there to greet other passengers. The people were there to see the Duesenberg. "What is all this?" he muttered. "How did all these people know we were coming?" He turned and looked at Artie suspiciously.

"Guilty! I'm the guilty one! I told Aaron, and he told his family, and Joey told his, and Mary told the pastor, and the pastor told the congregation, and the mayor's secretary is a member of the congregation, and she told him, and the mayor told the city council, and the city council told everybody they know . . ."

"I get the point, Artie!" Ray tried to be tough, but he was frankly moved as more than a hundred people parted to allow the Duesenberg to pull up in front of the elegant depot, where Mary stood beaming, with Bethany smiling shyly behind her. He put the car in neutral, turned the engine off, and set the parking brake. Then, to his surprise, he stepped out to a round of applause. At first he was discomfited by the attention, but when he saw Mary smile ever so slightly at him, he decided to yield to the moment and he tipped his hat to the crowd. "Well, then, he said, why don't you all come up and take a look!" And with that, the crowd descended like a group of artists discovering a new Picasso painting. They circled and paused, reaching out to stroke the chrome and rub their hand on the enameled doors. Of course Ray winced each time he saw another handprint, but he knew that this is what the crowd needed. It was obvious to everyone that this wasn't just Mary Wilkerson's car. It was to be Boise's car.

"Who would have thought that they'd be so taken by the car?" he whispered to Mary as he stepped up close to her. "It's like they think it's their own."

"It is theirs. Don't you see that gaining a Duesenberg is gaining a new kind of status for Boise itself? We now have something that the big cities have—a symbol of the very best that man can make. I think it makes people proud and hopeful. At least I know that's how I feel."

"Why, Mary Wilkerson, is that what you had in mind all along?"

She sniffed. "Of course, I didn't know if people would take to it, but I hoped they would. One of the things George taught me is that a city has its own personality and that it takes leaders to bring out its best. If a town has pride in its people, then its citizens will naturally accomplish more, because they have confidence in themselves. It seems to me we've been beaten down so much lately, so I hope people take confidence from this."

"Well, if it's a show they need, let's give it to them! Artie, Aaron, come help Mary and Bethany into the car!" With that, Artie stepped forward and gave his arm to Mary, who graciously accepted it. She looked like a queen as she stepped gracefully into the back of the magnificent car.

"Would you mind riding up front with Ray," Mary asked Aaron and Joey. "I'd like to speak with Arthur on our way home."

The boys eyes brightened considerably. They didn't know for sure whether they were even going to get a ride. Now they got to ride up front where they could see more easily. They would be the ones whom people saw as they drove through town. "Sure!" Aaron replied. If Artie was disappointed, he didn't show it. Instead he helped Bethany step up into the coach, and then he pulled the door behind him as he settled in between them on the seat.

"Well, what do you think, Arthur?" Mary asked.

"I think it's even better than I remember." Then, before Mary could say anything else, he let out a "Wow! Do you see that! There's an instrument panel back here in the passenger compartment. How neat is that?"

"I think it's a magnificent idea," Mary said. "That way I can check up on you and Ray as we're going down the road."

That gave Artie a sick feeling when he realized that she would know instantly if Ray was speeding, but then he caught on something. "Did you say Ray and *me*?"

"I said you and Ray. Why wouldn't I say that?"

"But does that mean you'll let me drive this?"

Mary inhaled. "Of course it will be up to Ray to teach you, but I don't see why not."

"Wow." That was it. Even though the English language contained more than a hundred thousand words, that was the only one that Artie could come up with. But the expression on his face was far more eloquent than his words.

"Okay to go, Mary?" Ray asked through the speaking tube that separated the driver's seat from the passenger section.

"Of course, it's all right. This is embarrassing to have all these people watching."

"As if she didn't invite them," Ray said under his breath to Joey, who was seated in the middle of the front seat.

"I heard that, Ray McCandless. You can watch what you're saying!"

Rather than respond, Ray engaged the powerful starter motor, and the huge Straight-8 engine came throbbing to life. The sound was deep and reassuring, although inside the car there was hardly a vibration to be felt. Then he slipped the car easily into gear and the Duesy started rolling toward the boulevard. As he quickly came up to speed, Artie was astonished at how smooth the acceleration was. "She'll go up to ninety miles per hour in second gear, you know!" He said this a little louder, since the sound of the wind coming back across them was quite noisy.

"Go ahead and roll up that window, if you will, Arthur. I don't want my hair to get blown."

Mary reached out for the speaking tube. "Try not to go too fast, Ray." She bristled a bit when she saw him shake his head slightly. "I don't mean you have to go slow. I know we need to give the Duesenberg its head. Just don't go ninety miles per hour in second gear, for land's sake!"

Ray nodded. "No more than seventy or eighty, I promise!"

Mary huffed.

Once they were on their way, she turned to Artie. "Now, we're not likely to encounter a crowd again until we get downtown. In the meantime, there's something I need to talk to you about. You don't need to give me an answer right now until you've had time to think about it, but I do want to raise the issue."

"Ma'am?" Suddenly Artie had a sinking feeling in his stomach.

Mary started fussing in her purse, somehow perplexed. She cleared her voice a time or two, which raised Artie's anxiety even further. It was obvious that she was nervous.

"Yes, well. Now that you're alone, without any of your natural family . . ."

Artie's face fell, which flustered Mary even more.

"I mean, since your grandfather has found his rest, I have had something on my mind. As you know, I have no children. For that matter, I don't even have any nieces or nephews, except for two no-account nephews of George. I've had it in my mind that when I die, I'd like to leave you a little something, but as it stands now, those two boys could make trouble."

Artie looked more confused. Which made Mary even more discombobulated.

"Well, Arthur, it's like this. For legal reasons it makes sense that I . . . that I . . ."

"Oh, just say it Mary!" Mary turned and looked at Bethany, the anxiety showing in her face.

"What she wants to say, Artie—"

"What I want to say, Arthur, is that I'd like to talk to you about adoption. It isn't to take anything away from your grandfather, or your dear grandmother and parents for that matter. It's just that we love you, too, and I would like to make it formal. That is, if it's something you'd like."

Artie was speechless.

"There, you see how you've upset him by forcing my hand, Bethany. Some things require finesse—a paring knife, not a cleaver!" By posing this invitation to Artie, Mary had made herself vulnerable, an unusual situation for someone as buttoned-up as she. She'd opened her heart. *What if the boy doesn't return the feeling?*

Artie erased Mary's concern by simply reaching over and embracing her. This took her by so much surprise that she at first resisted, but then she put her arms around Artie. "Of course I'd like you to adopt me," he said. "I'd like that more than anything in the world. But not because I might get some money or anything. But because I like living with you."

Mary found it hard to speak, but she was able to nod slowly. "Well, that's what you have then. It seems we both need a family, you and me" She straightened up as Artie let his embrace relax. Then he smiled at her.

"I just said those things about making it legal so that you'd have a way to back out if you didn't want this. My real reason for wanting to adopt you is that I've come to love you, Arthur. Our house it so much happier since you've come to live with us."

"I love you too, Mary. And I don't think my parents or grandparents would mind. Do you?"

"No, I don't think they'd mind. I think they'd be happy for you."

Mary, Bethany, and Artie all took a deep breath and then let it out slowly. When they realized that they had done it simultaneously, they burst out laughing.

"Well, this really is a day for celebration, isn't it? Our Duesenberg has arrived and we get to be a family. Perhaps we should go out to dinner tonight!"

Artie was about to agree when Aaron turned and pounded on the window that separated the front seat from the back, even when the top was down.

"What in heaven's name?" Mary exclaimed. Then they saw that Aaron was pointing out to the street. When they looked out, they saw that a crowd had gathered at the corner of Grove and Capitol as they approached the state capitol. People were waving, shouting, and pointing. Artie laughed happily when one man picked up his two little children and put them on his shoulders so they could see the beautiful new car.

Someone even shouted the phrase "It's a real Duesy," which had been made famous in Hollywood circles.

"You'd think they'd never seen a fine automobile," Mary said sternly.

"Begging your pardon, ma'am, but no one in Boise has ever seen a car like this! It's the grandest car ever made!" Joey said.

"Well, then, if that's the case, it's about time there was a Duesenberg in Boise. New York can keep its Fifth Avenue. We'll turn Warm Springs Boulevard into our own Park Avenue." Mary had started to feel quite grand herself. "Who knows, maybe I'll build a skyscraper just like Walter Chrysler." Then more quietly, "Or maybe not." Just thinking about it made her remember the $20,000 hole in her checking account. Then she smiled. Who cared about $20,000? Mary Wilkerson had a son.

CHAPTER 25

Racing and Touring

August 1934

It was nearly two months before Ray trusted Artie to drive the Duesenberg. It's not that it was such a different driving experience, given that the Cadillac had a V-16 engine that weighed every bit as much as the Duesy. And while the mechanical elements of the car were extremely stiff and rigid, that simply increased its stability in turns and at high speeds, (not that Artie was allowed to drive it at high speeds). The Boise roads just weren't good enough to risk damage from flying rocks and gravel. Ray did talk about the day he drove it well past 130 miles per hour on the test track in Philadelphia, where the track was paved, and road conditions were excellent and controlled. That left poor Artie just dreaming about what it would be like to experience that sort of speed. But to his credit, he never complained about it. Instead, he drove the Duesenberg in such a dignified fashion that it earned him kudos from Mary the first time he took her out driving. For his part, Ray seemed to like having a backup driver so he had more time to pursue his own interests.

With all the practice he'd had of late, it wasn't surprising to Artie when Ray asked him one Tuesday, "How would you like to go driving Saturday afternoon?"

Artie glanced up at Ray. He had been busy polishing the chrome on the rear panel of the Duesenberg. "Sure! Where are we going?"

"I thought we might take my Chrysler out to the race track. I've been hankering to stretch my driving legs a bit."

Artie laughed. "Sure, that sounds great."

What Artie didn't figure out from that little interchange is that Ray planned to reward him for his good behavior. Which is why it came as such a surprise when Ray drove up on Saturday and, slipping out of the driver's seat, motioned for Artie to take the wheel.

"So what's this about? You've never let me drive the Imperial before."

"I know. It's just that I thought it was time we finally teach you something about driving fast. You've got this city driving down pat. In fact, your driving is so dull that you could bore the paint right off a wall."

"And whose fault is that?" Artie asked indignantly.

"Don't get mad—it's what's expected of a chauffeur. And if I ever find you driving that Duesenberg or Cadillac faster than the speed limit . . ."

Artie put up his hands. "I know, I know—I'll never live to see seventeen."

Ray nodded appreciatively. "So you have been paying attention. But just because I want you to treat Mary's car with kid gloves doesn't mean that's the only way a man can drive. The Chrysler's a very different proposition. It is meant to be driven, and to be driven hard. And do you know the other big difference between the Chrysler and Mary's cars?"

"What?"

"I own it!" Ray smiled mischievously. "So why don't you drive me, in your very best city fashion, right out to the race track. Then I'll give you the lesson of a lifetime."

Artie burst into a grin and started the engine. The most noticeable difference right off the bat was the sound. The Chrysler Imperial had a deep-throated voice caused by its high-performance muffler. Simply stated, the muffler created less back pressure against the flow of exhaust gasses. That enhanced performance but at the price of increased noise. The second thing he noticed is that the steering was much more tactile than the Cadillac or Duesenberg and responded instantly to his steering. In fact, everything about the car felt more rugged.

"Are all Imperials like this?"

"Like what?"

"You know . . . so, so muscular? This is like handling a rodeo horse."

Ray laughed. "And the Caddy is like driving a Shetland Pony!"

"Exactly!"

"Nah—most Imperials are as big and soft and slushy as the Cadillac. I've done a lot of custom work on the engine and the suspension to get this one trimmed up for racing."

They had reached the fairgrounds, and Ray motioned for Artie to head for the gate. No one was on the track, and the gate was closed. But Ray had the combination to the padlock and quickly had the gate open. "All right," he said, climbing back in, "here's what you're going to do. I want you to start out around the track at a nice, easy pace. Slowly bring it up to, say, fifty miles per hour until we've circled it at least twice. I want you to get a feel for the surface and for how the car handles on turns. Then, when I give you the signal, I want you to speed up on the straightaway until you get to seventy or seventy-five. Then, before we enter the turn at the other end, I want you to back off a bit so you lose some speed.

"So I can go slower through the turn."

"Absolutely not. So you can accelerate through the turn."

"Accelerate?"

"Exactly. The simple fact is that you have a lot more control of a car that's under acceleration than you do with one that's not under power. So you have to learn to judge your turns so that you can always power through them."

"Wow! I didn't know that."

"Which is why you've never been allowed to go fast. But today's the day."

So Artie did as he was told, going through the practice runs, first at fifty, and then clear up to seventy-five. The difference in how the car responded was pronounced. In some ways, it was much easier to handle at a high rate of speed since the response to a steering command was executed instantly. But if there were any irregularities in the road, the car would bounce off them, almost taking to the air, which meant Artie had no control for a moment or two. He quickly figured out that that could be fatal if he was in a turn.

"All right, you're doing a good job. Try to hold it to at least sixty-five miles per hour through the next turn, and then I want you to floor it!"

"Floor it?"

Ray smiled. "Floor it! Just as soon as we come out of the turn, I want you to pour it on. Give it everything you've got until I tell you to decelerate. And then I don't want you to brake—just take your foot off the accelerator so we slow down before heading into the turn. My guess is that you can get up to at least ninety on the straightaway. We'll need to be down to seventy before we enter the turn. So you won't have the top speed for very long."

Artie took a couple of deep breaths. "All right!"

Ray gave him the signal, and away they went. As they came out of the first turn, Artie punched his foot on the accelerator and couldn't help but burst out laughing when the acceleration whipped his head back. He had no idea that the Imperial had that kind of power in third gear. Confidently the needle on the speedometer started to climb, almost in tune with the increase in Artie's heart rate. He power-shifted into fourth gear while keeping his focus straight ahead with both hands gripping the wheel. He didn't dare take his eyes off of the forward position as he held the steering wheel absolutely steady with both hands.

In fact, his concentration was so intense that he nearly jumped out of his skin when Ray shouted, "That's it—you're at ninety!" But even though startled, Artie didn't flinch. He just held it nice and steady. For a matter of just a few seconds, he felt the thrill of traveling faster than he'd ever done in his life. Well, faster than he'd ever gone while he was in control. It was possible that Ray had gone at least that fast in their Grand Prix race.

"All right, let her coast!" Artie still hadn't looked at the speedometer, so he indulged in a quick glance down and was delighted to see the needle stuck squarely between the 9 and the 0. And then he took his foot of the gas.

In retrospect, that may have been a mistake. Perhaps he should have backed off a little more slowly, but with the sudden loss of power, the car unaccountably started to shimmy, and Artie found his arms shaking violently as he did his best to hold their position.

"Give it some juice!" Ray shouted. His voice wasn't exactly frantic, but it was urgent.

Artie pressed on the accelerator, and the car quickly stabilized. "All right, but you've got to start backing off, or we'll never make it through the turn. Slow down as fast as you can while maintaining control, even if you do get some shimmy."

Artie backed off a little more gently than the first time, but even so, the car started to behave somewhat erratically. He felt he had to continue to slow down since the end of the track was coming very quickly. He knew that on a dirt surface, he'd be in real trouble if he went into the turn too fast. So he continued to back off on the gas, doing his best to hang on to control as the car slowed through eighty miles per hour. That was the speed at which the shaking was the most violent. Fortunately, as he dropped toward seventy, the shaking stopped, and he was able to enter the turn only a little hot.

"Nice and easy on the turn, give it just a little bit of power for stability." Artie was surprised to find that at the speed he was going, it took just the slightest pressure on the steering wheel to stay properly lined up through the turn. As he successfully pulled back to the straightaway going the opposite direction, he was pleased to see that he was still going just seventy miles per hour, the same speed at which he'd entered the turn. This meant that he'd given the car the ideal amount of power, since the change in direction consumes power, which he had managed to offset exactly with his extra acceleration.

"Wow!" he shouted as they came back onto the straightaway. "Should I do it again?"

"No! I want you to slow down to twenty as quick as you can. Once you get below fifty, use your brakes if necessary."

Artie didn't understand but did as he was told. As they slowed down to twenty, he had the distinct feeling that the car was crawling, and he honestly thought that he could probably get out and walk that fast. Of course, that was simply an illusion, created by the difference in the speed they'd been traveling at, but it still felt slow.

"What's up? Did I do something wrong?"

"No, it wasn't you. It's the car. Go ahead and pull of the track and bring it to a stop in the car park outside."

After exiting the gate, Artie brought the Imperial to a stop so that Ray could close and lock the gate again. He happened to glance over at Ray as he was getting out of the car, and he was shocked to see that Ray's hands were trembling and that he seemed a little wobbly on his legs. That caused Artie's stomach to lurch. It made him so nervous that he turned the ignition off and got out of the car.

"Were we in trouble out there?" he asked urgently when Ray returned.

Ray shook his head. "We could have been. I don't know what caused the problem—it could be a wheel out of balance or maybe a bad alignment, but at that speed, anything can be dangerous."

"Particularly with a brand new driver." Artie's voice was unsteady.

Ray looked up from the wheel well, where he'd kneeled to look at the front passenger tire. "I've got to admit that even that crossed my mind. But you did your part about as well as anyone could. You didn't panic, maintained good control, and followed my directions precisely."

"I don't think I knew how bad it was."

"Well . . . that's probably a good thing. At any rate, how did it feel—I mean when you hit top speed?"

Artie burst into a grin. "It felt great! Thanks for this."

"You're welcome. It's all right. We'll do it again when I get this thing fixed. In the meantime, maybe you won't mind if I drive back?"

"Course not." Artie went around to the passenger side as Ray circled the car to get in on the driver's side. Artie noticed that even now Ray's hands were still trembling, though not as badly as they did earlier. As he settled into the passenger seat, he pondered the very close call they'd just had. It was kind of scary. Still, they'd lived through it, and it had been an amazing experience.

CHAPTER **26**

Old Friends

The problems for David Boone continued unabated. A can of paint thrown against his siding, a long and deep scratch in the paint on his car—almost certain to cause rust—and perhaps most ominous of all: slashed tires.

"Arthur, do you have any idea who is doing this to Mr. Boone?" Mary had posed this question after yet another police interview. It wasn't that Boone was singling Artie out anymore. He had learned better than that. Rather, he seemed to be casting a net on anyone and everyone under the age of twenty. Still, Artie's reputation hadn't entirely subsided with the police, and they continued to think of him and Joey as prime suspects, even on occasions when they could establish an airtight alibi. Artie tended to panic when something happened and he didn't have anyone to verify where he was. It had even put a strain on his friendship with Joey, since some people seemed to think that they must be up to no good whenever they were together. The primary spokesman for this line of reasoning was Mr. Lewis, Stephanie's father, who had forbidden her to date Artie. Which was all right, of course, since Artie wasn't quite ready to start dating. Still, he liked Stephanie, and she seemed to like him, and it was awkward to always have to worry about what her dad was thinking.

"Arthur! I asked you a question."

Artie managed to pull one of his famed rabbits out of the hat. His mind had been wandering when Mary asked him her question, but somewhere in the creases of his brain it registered enough that he could respond instantly. "No, ma'am. I don't. Believe me, if I did know who was doing this, I'd rat on them. Kids are scared to even be seen with each other for fear they'll get blamed for something."

"Well, it's very puzzling. I can't imagine who would have it in for David in such a mean and vicious fashion. You're sure you don't know anything?" Obviously it had put a strain even on her trust, which kind of hurt Artie's feelings. But rather than say something, he just shook his head.

Unfortunately, David Boone turned out to be just one of Artie's problems that summer. The second came quite unexpectedly one night in June while Artie was out in the garage working on the Ford pickup. He'd been studying auto mechanics in school before the summer recess, and Ray had turned over all the routine tasks of maintenance to Artie, such as changing the oil; replacing spark plugs, hoses, and belts; and other minor repairs. He'd gotten good enough at it that he was changing the spark plugs on the Ford without any supervision.

On that particular night, he was deep in contemplation on how to extract a poorly placed spark plug when he was startled by a male voice.

"So if it isn't Little Orphan Artie himself. Living with Mary Bigbucks! How are you doing, Artie?"

The shiver that ran up Artie's spine made the hair on his neck stand straight out, like a cat that's just been challenged. Whirling around, he found his worst fear confirmed when he saw standing there before him none other than Reuben Kinley and a huge stranger. Reuben looked more menacing than ever, particularly since he was in his prison garb. His head had been shaved, which added to the sense of menace. But as bad as Reuben looked, the fellow next to him was even worse. A good thirty pounds heavier than Reuben, who was at least twenty pounds heavier than Artie already, the fellow had massive biceps and stood well over six feet four inches tall.

"Meet Tom. Tom, this is Artie."

"Where's Jake?" Artie asked nervously, trying to stall for time to figure out what he could do to get out of this.

"Jake is a sap. Once he got in prison, he lost all his nerve and has become a model prisoner. Even beating him up a couple of times hasn't seemed to help." The look in Reuben's eyes was maniacal.

As Artie shuffled uneasily, Reuben smiled. It was obvious that he was relishing Artie's fear. Artie just dreaded hearing whatever it was that caused Reuben to stop by. One explanation might be that he simply wanted to come and beat Artie up for turning against him on the night of the robbery. Of course there was another possibility, but Artie didn't want to think about that.

"So what are you doing here, Reuben?" Artie tried to be nonchalant. "Did you finish your term?"

"That's good. Just as clever as ever." Suddenly he slugged Tom on the arm. "Hey, did you hear that? I'm a poet—*clever as ever.*"

Tom didn't get it. Or at least it didn't make him smile.

"No, I'm not officially out. You might say Tom and I are on laundry detail. It's just that the prison didn't know that we'd be coming out with the laundry."

Artie nodded. It was a jailbreak. And they wouldn't have stopped by just for the fun of beating Artie up. They undoubtedly wanted cash—Mary's cash.

"Well, it seems to me you shouldn't really spend your time hanging around here, then. The prison's not too far away, you know."

"Yeah, I know how far it is. And you know why we're here. We need cash and your old lady has got it. So you're going to go in there and get some."

"Mary keeps her money in the bank. Ever since you beat her up, she doesn't keep any money in the house at all. She writes checks." Artie did his very best to maintain his bluff. The truth was that Mary had moved the gold out, but she still kept a sizable amount of cash on hand for fear that one of the banks would fail. Artie didn't know where all of it was stored, but he had an idea. "But I have some money—nearly fifty bucks that I've been saving. I'll get it for you if you want."

"Oh—Call has fifty whole dollars. And just how far do you think that would get us, you moron?"

Enough time had passed by then that the initial shock and fear had worn off, and Artie was managing to maintain his composure. He knew that these two could kill him if they put their mind to it. But more than anything, he had to keep them from hurting Mary and Bethany. So all the time he was talking, he was trying to think of some tool he could use as a weapon. He was sorry now that Mary hadn't followed up on Ray's idea to put a telephone out in the garage. If he could get to a phone and knock it off the receiver, the operator could hear what's going on and send the police.

"Look, Call, we didn't stop by for a lousy fifty bucks. From what we hear, that old biddy in there has millions!"

"What gives you that idea?"

Reuben shook his head in disgust. "The newspaper—idiot! As far as I know, she has the most expensive car in all of Idaho."

Artie was enormously relieved that Ray had taken the Duesenberg that night. At least it wasn't there for those two to steal or damage.

"Listen," Artie said suddenly. He'd had a burst of inspiration. "I know fifty dollars won't get you very far. But maybe fifty and a truck with a full tank of gas would."

"Really? That's not a bad idea, Artie. I like your truck there. It is *your* truck?"

Artie recognized the sarcasm in Reuben's voice. "No, it's Mary's. But you can have it. And the sooner, the better, since they'll probably figure out that you're missing any minute."

Reuben threw a punch at Artie, who managed to dodge him, angering Reuben. "You let me worry about when we're leaving," he said, picking himself up from where he'd slipped on some oil. "But you're right that we've wasted enough time here. I just sort of liked seeing your pretty-boy face one last time." With that, Reuben pulled out a ragged knife that he seemed to have fashioned in prison. "Too bad it isn't going to stay that way—that is, unless you help us get to some of the old woman's money. I know she has more. You're just trying to hang on to it for yourself."

"And what if I don't help you?"

"Then we're going to cut you up, and then we're going to go in and do even worse to her. That's what's going to happen. I let you come between us last time, but I won't do it again." Now he lunged part of the distance, sticking the knife out with a thrust. Artie jumped, and Reuben laughed. "So what's it going to be? Scars for the rest of your life, or are you going to help us?" Then, in what might be the one olive branch Reuben had ever extended, he added, "For that matter, you can come with us. With that much money, we'll go to California or someplace worth living. You won't have to take orders from anybody—not me, not Mary Wilkerson, not anybody. What do you say, Artie?"

Somehow Artie had always known that a moment like this would come. Since his talk with Ray in New York, he'd passed on hundreds of opportunities to shoplift or do something petty. So often, in fact, that he hardly even noticed things like that anymore, and he was finally starting to feel like maybe he had beaten the thing. But in the back of his mind, he knew that something was going to come back to haunt him and force him to face his old self. He decided that this was the moment. He had to choose.

His mind raced through all the possibilities. Was it bad to help Reuben get some of Mary's money so that he'd leave her alone? After all, he'd have a hard time protecting her all by himself? But then he wondered if, as rotten as Reuben was, he would use Artie to get the money and then hurt Mary anyway to get revenge. In the end, he decided it didn't matter. He was going to do his best to protect Mary.

Like a cat poised to leap, he lunged straight out for Reuben with a yell, at the same time reaching out with his right hand to grab the tire iron lying across the front bumper of the Ford.

For a moment, his plan of attack worked. The speed of his attack took Reuben completely by surprise, and he was able to whack him a pretty good one with the tire iron. But things turned against him very quickly after that. The force of Artie's own attack drove Reuben's knife into his left arm. The pain seared through his arm and caused him to wince in such a way that he wasn't able to bring the full weight of his body against Reuben. Besides, it was one thing to go after Reuben, but there just wasn't enough of him to take on Tom at the same time. And Tom, who was much slower to react, hadn't been as taken by surprise as Reuben. Well, maybe he was surprised, but his reflexes were so slow that he hadn't fallen back, like Reuben had. So he was still free to pile down on top of Artie, who had tumbled on top of Reuben.

"I'll kill you, you little rat!" Reuben screamed, rolling out from under him. Fortunately, the knife had been knocked from his hand, so Reuben scrambled now to get it while Artie did his best to wriggle free from the lump named Tom that was crushing him. Nothing he did seemed to make an impression until he accidentally lifted his left arm, covered in blood. When he happened to smear some blood on Tom's face, the giant let out a scream and rolled off Artie like a walrus scrambling to get into the water. "Blood!" he shouted. Apparently he was a giant who couldn't stand the sight of blood.

With Tom off him Artie sucked great quantities of air into his lungs. He'd faced the very real possibility of suffocating under Tom's bulk.

But of course his liberation from one problem just presented another. Reuben now had a clear shot at attacking him, and he didn't waste any time. "Say your prayers!" Reuben shouted as he lunged towards Artie, who was now attempting to scramble into a sitting position. As Reuben lunged, Artie rolled, but Reuben had anticipated this and Artie felt the knife slice across his face. Naturally he cried out in pain, but kept rolling to avoid Reuben's upraised hand. Unfortunately for Artie, Reuben had managed to immobilize his right hand under Reuben's right leg, and he wasn't sure he'd have enough strength in his left arm to deflect the next blow. He winced as Reuben's arm started down, but he couldn't pull free.

That's when the air was shattered by a terrific CRACK!, punctuated immediately by a cry of pain from Reuben who fell forward onto Artie, the torso of his body coming down hard on Artie's face. When he lay there for a moment Artie thought he might be dead, but then Reuben rolled off to the side, crying out in pain and holding his bloodied right hand with his left hand.

"What did you do, Tom," Reuben shouted furiously, but when Artie was able to look up he saw that Tom was backing against a wall while Ray moved forward menacingly, a pistol in his right hand pointing directly at Reuben.

"Who the—!"

"I'd be nice, if I were you," said Ray steadily. "And I'd get myself up and against that wall with your friend." He waved the gun in the direction he wanted Reuben to go. For his part, Reuben sort of slid his way over to the wall and then stood up, still cradling his hand. As Artie followed his movements, he could see that Reuben's hand was a bloody mess. Ray must have hit it directly.

"I'm going to bleed to death here," Reuben cried out. "Maybe you could do something!"

Ray ignored him. "Artie—are you hurt?"

Artie pulled himself to a standing position, holding his left arm. His face hurt much worse than his arm, but he'd brushed it with his hand enough to know that the wound there was just superficial while his arm was in real trouble.

"I'm okay. How did you . . . what brought you?"

"Never mind that now. Come over and stand by me."

Artie moved painfully over to Ray.

"I need you to go into the house and call the police. I'll keep these two at bay until they get here. Stay inside with Mary and Bethany, and get your arm wrapped up."

Artie hesitated. "Go, Artie! We need the police here right now."

As if to prove the point, Reuben made a slight movement to the right. He shouldn't have. Ray shot off another round, right between Reuben's legs.

Reuben let out a horrible obscenity at Ray, who kept his cool.

"I told you stay against the wall. I won't tell you again."

"You could've killed me, you old buzzard! Or maimed me!"

"Next time I will." The tone in Ray's voice made it very clear that he wasn't kidding.

Artie couldn't remember if Ray had shot two or three bullets. But the pistol had a clip that carried just five bullets. So Ray could be in trouble if the two of them bolted in different directions.

"I said get going, Artie. We don't have time for this."

"Ray, I don't think I should leave. There are two of them, and even though you have the gun, they're experienced criminals."

"I'll kill them if they make a move. I know that sounds terrible, but they were going to kill you." Reuben's sneer made it clear that he would still like to kill Artie.

"But one of them might still come at you."

"We don't have time for this! What do you propose?"

Artie looked around the room frantically. Tying them up wasn't really an option, since there'd be two people to cover while he tried to tie the knots. With his arm injured, he couldn't do it anyway.

"Well?"

"Maybe you could both just let us go, and there won't be any trouble."

That made Ray's face flush, and he brandished the pistol in Reuben's direction.

"I know! Let's lock them in the old coal bin. There's nothing in there—you made me clean it out last Saturday. And there's no way they can get out. We can lock it when they're inside. Then you can stay and guard them, and I'll go in and call. Will you do that Ray?"

Ray cast a quick glance to the coal bin. It hadn't been used ever since Mary put a supplemental oil heater in the garage a few years earlier so that Ray wouldn't have to tend a coal stove. Ray took a deep breath and exhaled slowly. The rage that burned inside him started to cool just a bit.

"Let's do it." Turning to Reuben, he said, "You should say a prayer of thanks that Artie was here tonight. You see, since you beat up Mary Wilkerson before . . . Well, let's just say that if Artie hadn't been here, I'd just have shot you as soon as I looked at you. And I'm a very good shot."

That was what Artie had feared most. He knew how angry Ray had been that he hadn't been there to protect Mary. He'd fumed about it on more than one occasion. It was more than an idle threat that Ray might have done something terrible to Reuben. And then Ray would have had to live with that all the rest of his life.

"What about my hand?" Reuben asked bitterly.

"Personally, I hope it gets gangrene," Ray replied. "But for right now I don't care a thing about it. Just get yourselves into that bin." Slowly, Reuben and Tom made their way to the coal bin. You could see the hate in Reuben's eyes as he backed into the dark room.

"If you try anything while Artie's closing the door, I *will* shoot you dead," Ray said evenly. "So just to make sure a terrible accident doesn't happen, I suggest you back against the far wall in the bin where I can see you."

The two backed against the wall, Reuben attempting to tighten his sleeve around the wrist on the injured hand.

"Now, Artie. Quick!"

Artie slammed the door shut and slid the bolt closed faster than he'd done anything in his life. The pain it caused his left arm was terrible, but he didn't want those two to reach out and grab him. Fortunately, all went well.

"Okay, now go in and get help."

"All right." Artie started forward but stumbled terribly. "I guess maybe I'm not feeling so good."

Ray moved quickly to where Artie had sort of settled to the ground. "Here," he whispered urgently while grabbing an unused cleaning rag. "Let me tie this around your arm to slow the blood." All the while he was doing this, he kept turning to check the door of the coal room. The door itself was pretty flimsy, with the planking of the walls made only of one-by-fours. He whispered so that Reuben and Tom wouldn't know that he was diverting his attention, or they might have forced the door.

"There. Now I know it hurts, but you've got to get to the house! Get there as fast as you can. Then send Bethany out to let me know you made it."

"All right." Ray helped Artie up, who stood there for a few moments to let the blood stabilize in his head, and then he moved as quickly to the house as he could.

"You can do it, Artie!" *You've got to do it!*

Artie stumbled his way across the gravel sidewalk up the stairs. To his horror, he found that the door was locked, so he started pounding with his right arm as hard as he could. But the light stayed out on the porch.

Next he tried shouting, but it was hard. His head was throbbing. "Bethany! It's me! It's Artie!" Then he pounded again. After what seemed like an eternity, the light came on.

"Arthur, is it really you?" He heard the fear in Mary's voice.

"Yes, ma'am! I'm hurt. And Ray needs you to call the police."

The door swung open, and Mary cried out in alarm. "Oh, my, you've been cut! Bethany, come here immediately. Come help me!"

"The police. You've got to call the police! Ray needs help," Artie said.

"They're already coming. We heard the shots and called them immediately. I didn't want to open the door for fear of who might be there. I'm sorry I didn't leave it open for you. What's happened? Is Ray hurt?"

Artie shook his head. "He's fine. It's Reuben and another escaped convict. They wanted to steal some money." His voice sounded funny, even to him. He'd never quite felt like this. His head was swimming.

By now Bethany had arrived, and after she let out her cry, she immediately lifted Artie up and dragged him into the kitchen, where she quickly washed both his wounds and started to bandage them properly. Artie was aware of a blinking red light through the window, and he heard Mary shouting out to Officer McKenzie as she went outside. A few minutes later, he heard the sound of two dull thuds and then he heard the police cruiser start up and leave.

All this time he'd been sitting on the floor of the kitchen, slumped against a wall. He was glad that he hadn't lost consciousness. He was also distressed that he'd made such a mess, with blood trailing its way from the back door to the kitchen sink cabinet where he was sitting.

"We need to get him to the hospital!" said Mary urgently as she came in. "Ray's got the car ready. You need to help me Bethany!"

"You can't lift him!" Bethany protested. "Let me do it." Artie wasn't able to help all that much, and he was too tall for Bethany to handle by herself. So Mary Wilkerson reached down and quite firmly lifted Artie up and onto his feet. It seemed almost superhuman. They got him out to the doorstep, where Ray had come up to help. In a matter of moments Artie was stretched out on the backseat of the Duesenberg, slowly losing consciousness, while the two women knelt beside him.

"I forgot to tell Bethany to come out and tell you I made it to the house…" Artie's words trailed off, the final ones nothing more than a mumble.

It was in that condition that he was taken into the hospital. An hour later, he was the recipient of more than thirty stitches on his arm and face. He was also sound asleep, fully anesthetized so that he wouldn't jerk while the doctor sewed up his face.

A little after midnight, Ray, Mary and Bethany stood by his bed watching him sleep. Officer McKenzie had already been by to take Ray's statement. Also, Bethany had managed to retell what she'd heard from Artie with sufficient clarity that—in addition to what he'd heard from Ray—McKenzie was pretty certain that Reuben would be charged with attempted murder, assault and battery, grand theft auto, and a number of other counts. That, on top of his escape, pretty much assured a long incarceration—if not life in prison.

"Good riddance," said Ray. His hand trembled as he said this, perhaps because he knew how close he'd come to killing the man. It had been the most difficult thing of his life to restrain himself—all the old fighting instincts having raged back in their full fury.

"It's odd that Artie was the one who restrained me," he said quietly under his breath as the scene replayed itself in his mind.

"What was that?" Mary asked.

Ray turned abruptly. "What? Oh, nothing. I was just talking to myself."

Mary's face darkened. "No you weren't, Ray. You were talking about Artie."

"I just said that he showed real poise in that situation. Of course it was pure luck that I decided to bring the Duesenberg home at that moment. But when I saw what was happening, I was amazed at how well Artie was handling it. Plus, you heard what Bethany told us about how Artie had tried to bargain with his own money as well as letting Reuben take the Ford. That was pretty quick thinking for anyone, let alone a teenager."

"They could have had every dime I have in the house and the bank if they would have just left him alone. Artie should have let them have all of my money."

"That wouldn't have solved anything. They would have taken all his money and all of yours and still have hurt or killed all of you. They wouldn't have wanted any witnesses and Reuben hated all of you from the last time he was here, so, Artie wasn't just defending your money—he was defending your lives."

"I know . . ." Mary's voice caught.

They remained quiet for a time. Artie was so totally at peace now.

Finally, it was Mary who broke the silence. "Ray, I haven't asked you about New York City, because I felt it must be private. But now, with Arthur hurt, I'd like to know what happened."

"What do you mean? Nothing happened in New York."

"Yes, it did. Something happened between you and Arthur. It happened that day Bethany and I went shopping. The boy was happy and cheerful when you dropped us off and sullen and frightened when you picked us up. He wasn't his usual cheerful self the entire trip home. What happened?"

Ray took a deep breath. "I can't tell you. Artie and I have a deal. But I can tell you that it was an important turning point for Artie. He left the boy he was behind him that day—the one who was prone to getting into trouble and doing things he shouldn't. Since then I've felt that his commitments that day were sincere. Now, after today, I know that they were. As far as I'm concerned, we can stop worrying about him. He's going to turn into a very fine man, Mary." Ray found himself in the unusual position of choking up a bit.

Mary patted his hand. "I'm glad. I've felt a change, too." Then she stepped around to the head of the bed, where she gently smoothed his hair. He was so deep asleep under the effects of the anesthesia that he didn't even stir.

"I plan to adopt him, you know. Did he tell you that?"

"Only about fifty times." Ray smiled. "Who'd have thought . . ."

"Yes, who?" Mary patted Artie's cheek and then leaned down and kissed him.

"You two go home. I'm going to sit here by him until he wakes up." When they protested, Mary shooed them outside with her hand.

CHAPTER **27**

An End-of-Season Picnic

October 1934

By the second week of October, Artie's arm had healed enough that he was driving again. The doctor had told them that he was very lucky that Reuben's slash hadn't severed any tendons, although one of the muscles in his upper arm had been damaged. The most impacting effect of the injury was that he couldn't raise the injured arm any higher than his head. But that was a small price to pay, after all, for defending the rest of his body. "I'm too short to play basketball, anyway," he'd joke when people expressed sympathy.

On this particular occasion, Mary had summoned Artie and Ray to the study. Somehow it always felt like they were being subpoenaed to appear before the Supreme Court, since Mary would never tell them in advance what was on her mind. Even though she'd softened a lot in the past two years, she still loved to be in control of a situation. Artie made sure that he timed his arrival to co-incide with Ray's. He didn't know if they'd been doing something with the cars that Mary didn't like, or if she was going to tell them she was selling something. The possibilities were pretty much endless.

After motioning for them to sit down, she huffed, "Oh, for heaven's sake, you don't need to look so serious. This isn't anything important. I just need you both here so we can make a decision."

"A decision on what?"

Mary's eyes narrowed. "A decision that is mine to make but that I thought you might want to advise me on."

Ray surrendered. This was to unfold at her pace, not his.

When she saw Bethany peeking around the door, she said, "Oh, for pity's sake, Bethany."

"It's just that the last time you did this, we ended up going to New York City."

Mary relented. "Well, the truth is that this is about a trip. But I wouldn't go grinning all that wide. I just want you to help me think through how we can help people get up to the church social that's been scheduled at the clearing next to the lake at the diversion dam on the Boise River."

"A dam?" Artie said excitedly.

"Not much of one," Ray replied. "It's just large enough to divert water from the river into canals. The really impressive dam is further up the river, called Arrowrock Dam. Now that's a real engineering marvel."

"Yes, well, I'm sure that would be very interesting, but we're certainly not going that far for a picnic. It's enough of a journey as it is on these rough roads just to get to the diversion dam. The problem is that so many people have lost their automobiles in this infernal depression that it's going to be hard to find a ride for all of them."

"It seems kind of late in the season for a picnic."

"Yes, and the elders might have to call it off. But the weather is unseasonably warm, and wouldn't it be a great way to celebrate before winter sets in."

"Well, we can always take the Cadillac," said Ray. "It will get dusty, but that wipes off."

"I already invited the pastor to drive a car full of people in the Cadillac."

Ray's eyes narrowed. "You're not thinking of taking the Duesenberg up there, Mary Wilkerson!"

"And why shouldn't I? It has the power to climb the hills, doesn't it?"

"But those are rocky roads. It will be filled with dust and it could get rock chips in the paint! I won't hear of it."

Of course that was absolutely the wrong thing to say, and Ray knew it the instant the words had left his mouth. He wished the conversation was like a 78 rpm record so he could just turn the platter backwards and say it differently. But he couldn't.

"Ray . . ."

"I'm sorry, Mary. Of course it's your car. But they just aren't the best roads."

"Just a few moments ago you were saying it was fine to take the Cadillac."

"It is fine—the Cadillac is several years old—and you . . . well, the Duesenberg is different. And you know it."

Mary softened. "I know. It worries me, too. But it can carry five people comfortably plus two children if needed. The Cadillac can carry six. I thought that if you drove the Duesenberg and Arthur drove the pickup with supplies, we could make a big dent in the problem. And with you doing the driving, you'll know how to protect it."

Ray frowned, but he knew the decision had already been made. "I'd let your church use my Imperial instead of the Duesy if it wasn't up on blocks for some suspension work."

Mary took this as Ray's concession, so she moved on. "Would you be all right driving the truck, Artie? I suppose that Aaron or Joey could ride with you to save space in the other cars."

"Sure. I can drive the truck."

"The roads can be quite treacherous, and with your arm . . ."

Artie shook his head to convey his disgust that there might be roads that were too difficult for him. He felt that he had more than proved his virtue and skill as a driver, but Mary was sensible enough to realize that he was still a teenager. And from time immemorial, teenagers had been invincible. But Mary decided not to press him.

"Well, then. We need to assemble next Saturday at 9:00 AM at our church. They have all kinds of games planned and wonderful food. Bethany's in charge of desserts, so we know those will be worth coming for." She looked around the room. "So it's settled, then?" Everyone nodded. They were off on yet another adventure, albeit a bit more modest than the earlier one.

* * *

"Why are you staying so far behind Ray? I can hardly even see him up ahead," Aaron asked.

"The only way Ray agreed to take the Duesenberg was if he could be first so that he wouldn't have to eat anyone else's dust. Ray's second condition was that I had to be second in line behind him so that no car could attempt to pass him. And his final point was a promise that he'd kill me if I followed too closely. I guess he's paranoid that I might not stop in time or something."

Aaron shook his head. He knew that Artie idolized Ray, but he couldn't see why. To him Ray was something of an old grouch who took his cars far too seriously. Still, he had made a positive difference in the way Artie acted, and Ray was never mean or grouchy with Aaron. It was becoming pretty clear that Artie would somehow follow in Ray's footsteps with regard to automobiles—perhaps as a mechanic, or maybe even as a salesman. Artie was good with people and could probably do really well selling cars. Aaron just hoped that he wouldn't become a race car driver since that was a pretty rough crowd.

"The river's running really high for October, isn't it?" Aaron asked.

"Ray said they've opened up the Arrowrock Dam since the year's been a lot wetter than normal, and they want to have storage room in the reservoir for the winter snow melt."

"Well, it's a beautiful area."

Artie cast a glance down to the river. Because it was a bit cloudy that day, the water was running a dark, bluish gray color. One of the other things that Ray had taught him was that water picks up the color of the sky. So on a cloudless day, it would be light blue. On a fully overcast day the water looked gray, and so forth.

"I guess it's pretty," Artie replied. "I like all the trees. The hills are so dry this time of year that it's just all brown and dusty. But then there's the river, and you get all sorts of brush and trees growing along the bank." They drove on silently for a time. The road was in really poor condition and required Artie to concentrate.

"It was great of Hank to cover for us at the Egyptian," Artie said after they reached a level spot.

"Yeah. He's a pretty regular guy, really, even though he can be grouchy sometimes."

In fact, it had taken a small miracle for both Aaron and Artie to get the day off since Saturday afternoon matinees at the Egyptian were the most profitable show times of the week. Fortunately, Hank had agreed to work the whole day by himself as long as Aaron and Artie promised to take extra shifts during the following week.

Even though Artie was fully engaged in driving on the rough road, Aaron's mind wandered as they bounced their way along the dusty road. But he was jerked out of his thoughts as the little truck lurched over a fairly large mogul in the dirt road where they had climbed up and away from the river for a bit.

"Wow! This road really is rough. I can see why Ray was so reluctant to bring the Duesy up here."

Aaron tried to agree, but the passenger front tire dropped into a hole and then bounced out. The shock of this was so severe that both boys hit their heads on the ceiling. They turned and looked at each other and then burst out laughing.

"Ray's going to be absolutely crazy by the time we get there."

"That's for sure!" And they laughed again.

With the next turn the river road narrowed at a spot where it perched precariously above the turbulent waters of the river. Artie had both hands on the wheel and was giving his full concentration to the task of driving. One slip could be deadly if they were to get too close to the edge and slip over, since there would be nothing to stop them from rolling right off the edge and into the water.

The drive was so tense that at one point Aaron was not even conscious that he was holding his breath. But when they pulled free of a particularly narrow spot and the road started to slope down into a fairly broad plain, he found himself exhaling slowly. It was also at that point that he discovered that his hands had been digging into the sides of his legs.

"That was a little too close," he said.

Artie turned and looked at him, almost pale. "I had no idea it would be like this. It seems like a crazy place to have a picnic."

"It was smart of you to stay as close to the side of the hill as you could."

In another quarter of a mile, they made a turn to the right and suddenly the dam came into sight. It was only twenty feet high or so, but the water coming over the spillway made for an impressive waterfall and since Artie had never seen a dam in his life, he was ecstatic. Artie pulled the truck over to the side so they could get out and take a look.

"Kind of neat, "Artie said. "I wish we were going up to the big dam."

"Arrowrock? It really is something. It was the tallest concrete dam in the world, you know, at least when they built it. I've only been there once, but it has these huge valves mounted high up on the concrete side that shoot water out for at least a hundred feet or so. I was just a little kid when we went up there, but I thought how exciting it would be to get shot through one of those valves and going flying out into the air before falling into the river below the dam."

Artie laughed. "You know that would have killed you . . ."

"I know. But it's kind of fun to think about."

"I wish I could see it. But if the road up to that dam is even half as bad as this, I don't want to go."

"I think it's even worse."

"Well, I'm glad we're here, then." Artie took one more look at the spillway and then said, "We better get going before Ray gets mad." So they piled back into the truck, and Artie started it up. In just a few minutes he'd pulled up behind the Duesenberg, which was parked by the side of the small lake above the diversion dam. The people who had ridden with Ray were already out of the car and down by the edge of the water. It was surprising how placid the lake was, given the turbulence of the river below.

Ray had pulled the Duesenberg under a shade tree, and he was busy dusting the car down with a large oiled feather duster that he carried for just this purpose.

"Doesn't he know that it's just going to get dusty going back down the road?" Aaron asked as they got out and started taking the tarp off the back of the truck.

"He just wants it to look as good as possible while it's sitting here. Ray believes that a good car man always keep his vehicle in the best possible condition he can, no matter where's he at or how long he's going to be there."

Aaron nodded. Even though it seemed a little silly, he admired Ray's dedication.

After that, it took perhaps half an hour for all the other cars and trucks to make it up to the picnic spot. No one parked too close to Ray for fear of incurring his wrath. But before long, everyone had unloaded the vehicles, started the cooking, and set up the tables and a cooking fly to keep the sun off the food. Meanwhile, most of the kids had gone out into the lake on an old log raft that was left there for just that purpose.

"Coming into the water?" Joey asked excitedly. He'd ridden up with the pastor in the Cadillac. Artie readily agreed, but Aaron held back.

"I don't think so," he said hesitantly. Only a few people, including Artie, knew that he had never learned to swim. Even though there was the raft, he worried about what would happen if he fell in. So he declined and hung around with the adults instead.

Mary found a spot to set out her umbrella and chair, and after settling in, she proceeded to watch the events unfold as everyone enjoyed a grand time in the water, playing games, and eventually eating the abundance of food that had been prepared.

A little after three, the western sky started clouding up. When the wind picked up, the pastor ordered everyone off the lake, and people started to clean up and start packing for the return trip. By around four, the sky was totally dark, and the first thunderclap was heard in the distance. The lightning flashes that started crackling in the nearby hills accelerated the process of cleaning up but not nearly as much as the torrent of rain that suddenly descended on everyone. People were scurrying around the cars with parents hurrying drenched children still in their swimming suits into the backs of the cars while the adults rushed to cover the boxes of food with tarpaulins and to get them strapped down inside the truck beds.

Of course Ray had put the roof up on the Duesenberg at the first appearance of the clouds, so it was snug and secure, but the rain was going to make for a difficult drive down the canyon, particularly since the wipers on the vehicles just weren't that effective against a cloudburst.

"We better get out of here!" Ray shouted to Artie. The road had been difficult enough to traverse when it was dry. But now it was quickly turning to mud.

"Better get out of here is right," he muttered, and he climbed into the cab of the pickup truck.

Once again Ray led out, followed by David Boone driving his 1930 Model-A Ford, followed by Artie in his truck. Boone had crowded in front of Artie in spite of

Ray's displeasure. The convoy snaked behind them with two more trucks, three cars, and finally, the pastor driving Mary's Cadillac.

"Did you take that a little fast maybe?" Aaron asked nervously. He seemed to become more anxious as the condition of the road worsened. They'd just slid around the first corner at the top edge of the dam as the road turned right toward the first switchback. The increasing water cascading down the face of the dam emitted an ominous roar as it raced down the concrete spillway and into the turbulent river below.

"I didn't mean to take it that fast," Artie replied. "It's just that it's so muddy that it's hard to keep control." Artie's white knuckles on the steering wheel proved that he wasn't taking the experience lightly.

"Oh, my gosh!" Aaron said suddenly. "Did you see the Duesenberg?"

Artie nodded. The heavy car had just spun out on the turn at the base of the dam as it started to head downriver. Even with Ray's expert driving, he had come within perhaps three or four feet of the edge of the riverbank. When David Boone also had trouble maneuvering the tight turn at that spot, Artie muttered, "This is awful."

Fortunately, Artie was able to slow the truck enough that he made the turn without slipping, but with so little weight over the back wheels, there was a heart-stopping moment when he thought he'd get stuck in the muck. That would be a disaster, since no one could get around him, and the chance of the cars behind him sliding in to him or into each other would be greatly increased, not to mention their getting stuck in the mud, too. As the wheels started to slip a little more, Aaron prepared to jump out into the rain to give them a push if needed, but at the last moment, Artie was able to use the clutch in such a way that kept them moving. There was enough of a slope to the road that gravity took over, and they were on their way again.

For the next twenty minutes, they continued at a snail's pace, the rain seeping in and around the edges of the windows while a mist built up on the inside of the glass from all the moisture in the air. "This is nuts!" Artie said in exasperation, while trying to wipe a spot in front of him. "I can't see a thing." This prompted Aaron to take out a handkerchief and to vigorously wipe both sides of the window. He also had the common sense to roll his window down, even though that meant that his arm was instantly drenched in rain.

As they approached the turn that would take them from the river for a couple of miles, the rain stopped, which brought an immediate sigh of relief. And then, as is often the case in a fickle desert rainstorm, the late afternoon sun burst through the clouds for a few moments, blinding them. As Artie winced at the light, he did his best to keep the truck moving in the right direction, lifting his healthy arm to shade his eyes. Fortunately, even though crowded up against the hillside on the passenger side with the river bank sloping down to the left, he was able to keep the truck steady in the road before a slight turn to the left provided some shade.

"Nice job," said Aaron.

Artie looked to the swollen river to his left. "Thanks. I had a lot of motivation." The sweat on his forehead evinced of just how difficult the drive had become. "One wrong turn and . . ."

Perhaps fifty feet ahead, Mr. Boone had come to the point where he had to make a sharp right turn at a promontory that rose up sharply above the river on his left. The river narrowed as it made a slight turn to the right. Even so, the bend was precarious enough that if the road continued straight ahead, it would plunge straight down into the river. Instead, by making a sharp turn to the right, the road pulled away from the river for perhaps a mile or two before descending back down to water level once the stream spread out in the wider valley.

Unfortunately for David Boone and the occupants of his Model-A Ford, the turn to the right brought them out of the mountain's shadow, exposing them to the full glare of the sun at precisely the moment when the driver really needed to be able to see the road and where to make the turn. Ray had anticipated the problem and had slowed almost to a crawl, well prepared to shield his eyes while making the turn. But Boone must have been distracted, because to Artie's and Aaron's horror, they saw his car slide sideways, jerk suddenly to the right as Boone tried to correct the error, only to tumble over the edge of the precipice.

"Oh no!" shouted Aaron as he jumped forward in his seat, reaching out with his arms as if he could grab hold of the car and keep it from falling.

"Oh, my…!" shouted Artie as he closed the distance. As they came to the turn, he nuzzled the Ford pickup right up against the side of the hill and was already half out of the truck when he shouted to Aaron, "Come out my side. And grab some ropes out of the back!"

Artie had no idea what to expect as he ran up the road to the spot where the Model-A had disappeared over the side. In his mind, he could picture the car disappearing beneath the waves of the river, and he wondered what he would do to save the passengers. But as he came up to the edge, he was relieved to see the Model-A tipped on its side, perhaps forty feet down the side of the cliff, inches above the water line, but held precariously in place by an old spruce tree that was bent nearly over by the weight of the car that had crashed into it. Inside he could see people waving and screaming, but no one was attempting to get out. It was obvious that any sudden movement could rock the car either forward or back in such a fashion that it would slip off the tree and into the water.

"Hold on!" he shouted.

"Artie, we've got to stabilize the car or they could all lose their lives." Artie felt an incredible wave of relief at the sound of Ray's voice.

"But how? What can we do?"

"Look at me. I'm going to ask you to do something very dangerous."

Artie turned and looked directly at Ray, whose face was flushed. "What do I need to do?"

"I need you to take a rope down there and secure it to the back bumper. I'm going to secure the top of the rope to the front bumper of the Duesenberg. Then, once we have a good connection, I'm going to back the Duesy to the point that there's tension on the rope. I want you carry a second rope—a much longer one—that you'll use to effect the rescue, and a third one to tie around your waist so we can support you. Can you do it?"

Artie had never been asked such a question in his life. He had no idea in the world if he could do it. But he knew that he would try.

"Sure. Let's go."

"Hold up!" Ray's voice was trembling. "We can't do this half-cocked. It's got to be done methodically and carefully. First of all, do you think your arm is strong enough to do this? It's only been two months. We can send Aaron, although he's a lot heavier."

Artie considered the question carefully. "I can do it."

Ray nodded. "You've got to do this my way. Do you understand?"

"Yes, sir." Artie didn't really understand, because it seemed like there was no time to lose, but he knew that Ray would do this in whatever way was most likely to succeed.

"I want you to go get three ropes. There are two that I know of in your truck and one good strong one in the Cadillac. Go!" And Artie ran.

Ray then proceeded to call down to the people in the car, who were hysterical. He managed to get them to be quiet, urging that they remain absolutely motionless until the car was secured and promising that they'd get everyone out safely if they didn't lose their heads.

"What about Brother Boone?" one of the girls shouted.

"What about Mr. Boone?" Ray replied. "Is he hurt?"

"He's not moving or saying anything. He must have hit his head on the steering wheel. There's blood." At that the clatter from the passengers started up again, and Ray had to shout for everyone to remain still.

"We'll get Mr. Boone out last. But for now we've got to go to work. Everyone must stay absolutely still."

The other cars in the caravan had pulled up, and men had come running up to try to help. Some were ready to climb over the side until Ray was able to convince them that the chance of someone slipping and then sliding against the car was the greatest hazard of all. One false step and everyone could be lost.

"So what are we going to do?" one of the men asked defiantly.

"What we're going to do is listen to Mr. McCandless," Pastor Wyndham replied evenly. "He's in charge!" No one bothered to ask why he was in charge—they just accepted that he was.

"So what do you have in mind, Ray?"

Ray quickly explained to the pastor and all the others what he was going to do.

"But you should send a man down. We need someone with strength. Artie's still a boy."

"Artie is still a lightweight. We have to approach that car as gingerly as possible. You can see how much mud there is, and I don't know how long that tree will hold. The last thing we need is for someone to lose their footing, plow into the car, and watch everyone go into the river."

Pastor Wyndham sighed. "Of course you're right. How can we help?"

Ray explained the plan then took off to back up the Duesy. He explained that it was the only car in the lot with enough power to hold the Model-A in position. While he was doing this, Pastor Wyndham quickly tied the lightest-weight rope around Artie's waist and did his best to pass along Ray's plan, as well as his cautions about not going too fast, even though the situation was dire. "You need to maintain control, Artie, so that you approach the car carefully." He then explained how to tie the rope around the bumper in such a way that it would hold when put under tension.

Once Ray had the Duesenberg lined up, Artie tossed the heavy rope over his shoulder and gave Ray a wave. He stepped over the edge of the embankment as the men in the party started to play out the rope, allowing Artie to work his way down the slope. The muddy ground was treacherous, and he slipped more than once as he did his best to figure out how to keep his footing in the muck and gravel. Fortunately, the men belaying the rope were strong, and they were able to hold him each time he slipped. Eventually he made it down to perhaps three or four feet from the car, at which point he signaled for them to hold.

"It's going to be okay," he said in a quiet voice to the people in the car. There were three teenage girls, as well as David and Olivia Boone. "We've got a plan, and it's going to work. Will you do what I say?"

This was a pivotal moment. Artie was not the most popular person in the world at the Boone residence and had never given any reason for people to think that he could take responsibility for a rescue. But Olivia Boone nodded and said that they would follow his directions exactly.

"Good, then here's what we're going to do." He explained Ray's plan for the three ropes. They immediately understood the function of the rope to the car— that was just common sense—but the rescue rope was tougher to explain. "It's like this. I brought down both ends of the rope with me, and they're holding the center up at the top. I'm going to tie both ends around your waist when it's your turn to be rescued so that the rope forms a loop. Then the men up top will pull you up by pulling on one side of the loop as I take up the slack down here at this end. That way, when the first one is rescued, I can simply pull the two ends back down so we can tie them around the next person.

"Why not just tie it to our waist and pull us up?" one of the passengers asked.

"Because there'd be no way to get the rope back down. It has to be a loop. Besides, the loop will make it more stable for you as you climb up by having me hold it down here."

He motioned to the men to play out some more rope as he inched his way toward the back of the car.

Closing his eyes to picture the knot that the pastor had shown him, Artie sat down on the muddy slope so that he'd be as stable as possible as he touched the bumper of the car. Working extremely slowly, he slipped the rope between the bumper and the back of the car, looped it over, and then slipped the end through the loop he'd formed to complete the self-tightening knot. If tied properly, it would simply grow stronger as more tension was applied to the rope. It wasn't as hard as he'd expected, and the car was more stable than it looked.

The sound of the river was a distraction. The cloudburst must have poured a hundred thousand tons of silt into the river from all the streams and gullies that fed into it, and as torn branches and other debris piled up at this narrow point, the river roared with an angry voice, punctuated occasionally by the sound of splintering wood as a tree branch or uprooted sagebrush crashed into the rocks just a few feet below Artie.

Another concern that tugged at his consciousness was that the river was rising. Water was already lapping under the front wheel on the passenger side. As loose as the soil was, that was a very bad omen.

Finally, when he was absolutely sure that the knot was secure, Artie signaled for the men to pull him back away from the car, and then he shouted for Ray to back the Duesenberg up. It had to be tough for Ray, since he couldn't see the Model-A from where the Duesy was situated. Instead he had to rely on the pastor to pass along information.

It took a few moments for all the hand signals to work their way through this little chain, but then Artie saw the slack in the rope start to disappear, and in just a few more moments the rope lifted up and off the ground as the tension finally started to pull against the Model-A. As the rope continued to tighten, it started making an odd sound, and for a moment Artie thought it might not hold. Then there was something of a grinding sound as the Model-A took the strain. The car started to move ever so slightly toward Artie.

"That's it! You can stop!" Artie was concerned that if they pulled too hard, the rope would have to carry the full weight of the car, which it wasn't strong enough to do. Instead, they needed to let most of the weight rest on the tree while using the rope to provide a stabilizing influence on the car as they executed the rescue.

When Pastor Wyndham motioned to Artie that they were ready to start the rescue, Artie worked his way ever so carefully to the passenger side door, the one facing up the hill, and gently tried to open the door. Of course it was very heavy pulling against gravity, and he couldn't get it open.

"Let me help!" Mrs. Boone said, and Artie watched in admiration as she positioned herself to use her feet to push against the door from the inside. With Artie pulling and her pushing, they got the door to open and start to swing.

Pleased with their success, Artie got ready to swing the door all the way forward when it lurched suddenly at the point where it passed the midpoint of the arc. The gravity that had been holding it shut brought it crashing against the spare tire mounting toward the front of the car. The car rocked from the force of it, and the girls screamed. Artie's heart missed a couple of beats before it was clear that the bump wasn't enough to dislodge the car.

"Who's first?" asked Artie. One of the girls said she was too afraid to ever go, and the other two wanted to go first to get out of harm's way.

The passengers discussed it like this while Artie became increasingly impatient.

"Please! Somebody, let's go!" Artie was sure that the pastor would have been calmer if he was the one down here, but Artie was pretty spooked by all this and just wanted to get it done.

"You go, Jenny!" Mrs. Boone ordered. Tentatively, the girl crouched forward from the back seat, allowing Artie to take her hand, and then she emerged from the car to the ground. Artie deftly tied one end of the rescue rope around her waist and then tied the other end up under her shoulders.

"Okay!" he shouted to the men above, and slowly they started pulling on one side of the rope, with Artie taking up the slack at the bottom end. They pulled Jenny up and away from the car. Although she stumbled nearly all the way to the top, she was so lightweight that the men could easily steady her until she was finally safely on the road. Both ends of the rope were with the pastor while Artie was holding the midpoint at his end. He felt the rope go slack as they untied Jenny, and he watched as the pastor quickly tied the two ends of the rope together and started feeding it hand over hand back down to Artie. In no time, the ends were back, and he assisted the second girl. By the time it came time for Mrs. Boone, he felt like an old hand at it and was quite confident of his ability to get her out.

"But what about David? You can't lift him all by yourself. He's too heavy inside the car."

Artie hadn't even thought about that. He had only worried about getting the women out.

"I don't know." Artie hesitated, trying to think of a plan.

"Maybe I could go up with him, sort of holding him," she suggested.

"No, no, I don't think that would work. That would be a lot of weight on one rope. I wouldn't know how to tie knots around both of you anyway."

"Well, then, let me at least help get him out on the ground and then you can tie a single loop around him for the men to drag him up. If you put the rope under his shoulders, maybe you can come up at the same time, holding his head."

Artie nodded. That was a good plan. "You'll need to go up first and explain it, so they'll know what we're doing."

"Okay." With that, Olivia Boone managed to get out of the side of the car and onto the ground with Artie's help. Artie quickly tied one end of the rope around her waist and then went and secured the other end of her safety rope on a small tree nearby so that she'd have something to work against as they pulled David Boone out. It was hard, but they managed to get his limp body to the upper edge of the seat. Artie was glad to see that he wasn't bleeding too badly.

"Leave him there. It will be easier for me to get the rope around him than if he's on the ground," Artie said.

"Whatever you think is best."

Artie went over and brought the second end of the rope back to Mrs. Boone, where he tied it around her. Then he gave the signal to the men up above to begin.

As she started to lurch up the hill, she gave Artie a quick kiss on his head. "Thank you, Artie. You're a very brave young man."

In spite of the circumstance, he blushed. "Thank you, ma'am." And then she was off.

As Artie started reeling the rope back down, he felt very alone. Up to this point, he'd had Mrs. Boone to talk to, but now it was just him and the unconscious David Boone. He noticed that the river was continuing to rise, which was an increasing source of anxiety. Even with the tension Ray had applied to the back of the car, the front wheel was now submerged in perhaps three or four inches of water.

Finally, the knot made its way back around, and very gingerly Artie made his way back to Mr. Boone. As he lifted his body up and forward in the seat—so he could get the rope under and around his chest—Mr. Boone's body fell forward, startling Artie right out of his wits. He feared that the weight of Boone's body flopping like that would be enough to dislodge the car. But it didn't—at least not yet. It was harder from that angle, but he was able to get one end around and tie it into a knot. Then he slipped the second end around and right up under his armpits. The plan he and Mrs. Boone had agreed on was that the men would pull on both sides of the rope so that they'd have maximum control. A second group would pull Artie so that he could support Mr. Boone's head.

When everything was ready, Artie gave the signal, and the two groups of men started pulling. They were strong enough to jerk Boone right out of the seat, and Artie had to scramble to keep his head from flopping and hitting the ground as he and Mr. Boone began their rocky ascent.

When Artie and Boone were approximately halfway up the cliff there was tremendous buckling sound as an uprooted tree came tumbling around the riverbend and crashed into the tree securing the Model-A Ford. The force of the impact, combined with the weight of the car against the tree and the erosion of the soil around the roots, was substantial enough to dislodge the spruce, which groaned as it tumbled into the river.

As the full weight of the Model-A came to bear on the rope, Ray sensed that something was wrong, and to compensate for the additional strain, he released the clutch and gave the Duesenberg more power to apply additional tension against the rope to hold the Model-A in position. It wasn't entirely to protect the Model-A, though, since the Duesy had started sliding toward the edge of the cliff.

At first, Ray's tactic seemed to work as he stabilized both cars momentarily, but eventually the strain on the rope was too great, and it snapped with a whip-saw motion that slapped Artie straight across the chest. The men holding Artie were surprised by the sudden release in pressure, and many of them stumbled backwards, some losing their grip on the rope as they did. Artie started to slide toward the river, but fortunately the pastor managed to keep his grip so that Artie didn't slip more than a few feet before his rope tightened. But even though the immediate danger was stayed, the force with which the broken rope had slapped Artie was so intense that it had hurt him badly.

Even in his pain, Artie watched in fascination as the Model-A Ford turned on its side and slid into the maelstrom of the river. In a matter of just a few moments, all but the roof disappeared beneath the water, accompanied by a terrible grinding and crunching sound.

Meanwhile, David Boone's head slumped backwards without Artie there to support it, but at least the snapped rope had missed him. One of the men pulling him simply took matters into his own hands by sliding down the slope of the hill until he reached Boone. He then used one arm to support Boone while using the other to hold onto Boone's rope as the men above pulled the two men up to safety.

But the worst consequence of the broken rope was what happened to Ray and the Duesenberg. When the rope snapped, the Duesy lurched backward, crashing into the side of the rock wall on the protected side of the road. It hit with enough force that a shower of rock came tumbling down onto the roof of the car. That would have been bad enough, except that in the supersaturated condition of the soil, the loosened gravel allowed a small boulder to crash down on the passenger side of the Duesenberg near the rear wheel. The tire blew, creating a sound equivalent to the firing of a small cannon. Ray jumped out of the car, cursing. At first his shock and anger was directed toward the damage to the car, but when he saw the men hauling Boone over the edge without Artie, the realization of what had happened dawned on him and he ran to the edge of the cliff. When he saw Artie hanging limply, Ray quickly took charge.

"I'm going over the side. Be prepared to pull both of us up."

One of the men said, "We've got him. Don't go down there and make it worse."

But Ray wasn't in a frame of mind to listen, and he slid down hand-over-hand until he reached Artie.

"Are you okay, boy?"

Artie looked at him with glassy eyes.

"I can't breathe," he rasped. "I can't get my breath."

Ray shook his head. "I'm so sorry this happened. They shouldn't have brought you up that way. Any fool could see that!"

"Can we get some help down here? Like, now!" Ray yelled.

"Hold tight, Ray. We're going to throw a rope down to help you," cried the pastor with a tinge of desperation in his voice. It was taking some time to get the rope off David Boone so it could be redeployed to help Artie.

"Right now would be good," Ray said under his breath.

"Here it comes, Ray!"

The rope landed with a thud, and Ray crawled over to it. Quickly tying it under his shoulders, he shouted, "Pull us up!"

He scrambled back to Artie, where he did his best to support Artie's head as the men above started pulling. The men dragged them up the face of the steep slope, finally pulling them up and over the edge. As soon as they were over, Ray jumped up and moved toward the truck while shouting out orders of what was needed to get Artie to the hospital. With both the Duesenberg and the Model-A out of commission, Ray ran back to the pickup and started throwing things out of the bed. "Can you help me, Aaron? I need to get this clear so we can get Artie and Boone to the hospital."

Aaron moved quickly to help him.

"Ray," Mary said as she came up to him, "you need to calm down. A lot's happening, and you're getting too excited." It was good advice, but Ray didn't even acknowledge Mary.

"Ray!"

Finally he turned at her.

"Ray," she said more softly, "you need to keep your wits!"

"I am keeping my wits. Artie's ribs have been broken. He may be suffocating. We need to get going right now."

"I understand that. But in view of things . . ." she said hesitantly, "perhaps it would be better if you let others take the lead."

Ray turned and looked at her then to Artie. "This is my responsibility. I sent him down there, and now he's hurt. I need to help him breathe before we move him."

Mary shook her head in concern. But she realized that it would only increase Ray's tension if she tried to interfere, so she backed off as he approached Artie. Ray was doing his best to stay calm and collected. But as he drew near to Artie, there was an ominous change in Ray's face as it changed from flushed to gray.

"You've got to sit down!" Mary said as she caught up to him. By now the pastor had started to move to Ray as well. Clearly, something was wrong.

"I do need to sit down," he said breathlessly, and suddenly Ray slumped to his knees and then fell forward. "My chest . . ."

"Ray!" Mary and Artie called at the same time.

"Oh, my good heavens . . ." said Pastor Wyndham.

Mary and some of the men who had helped pull Ray and Artie up came running over to Ray.

"My chest . . ." Ray said weakly as they turned him over.

"Ray! You listen to me, Ray McCandless—we need you right now!" Mary said this to try to focus his concentration. But Ray was in no position to hear her.

"Mary!" Artie cried helplessly.

"Oh, dear. Will you help Ray, Pastor?"

"Of course. Go to the boy."

Mary scrambled over to Artie, where she sat down on the ground next to him and gently lifted his head onto her lap.

"What's happening to Ray?" Artie asked desperately.

Mary took a deep breath. From Artie's color, she could tell that he was in real trouble. She had just a second or two to decide whether to tell him the truth, risking a panic attack, or to deceive him temporarily. She decided that in view of all that had passed between them, she owed him honesty.

"Ray is having a heart attack. The strain of all this was too much on his heart."

"A heart attack! Then we've got to do something."

"What can we do? There's nothing that can be done."

"But we've got to get him to a doctor." Artie's chest was heaving now, and Mary could tell that each breath was excruciating.

"Arthur," she said gently. Then she took his hand in hers and started stroking it.

"No!" Artie said, struggling to sit up. "He can't die. He can't! You've got to do something. Please, Mary, please!"

"Arthur. Ray loves you. You know that, don't you?"

"But he's going to die. You're all going to let him die."

"God is going to help Ray now. There's no one here who can help him. I can't. Nor could a doctor. There's no way known to medicine to start a heart when it's stopped beating. But everything will be fine."

"Oh, Mary. Ray can't . . ." Artie choked up.

"I know. I don't want it either." Mary looked over to where Ray's body lay listless. It was the most powerless feeling in the world to watch a man die and to know that there was nothing that could be done to prevent it.

"Can I talk to him?" Artie started to struggle, but Mary held him back.

"You can talk to him in a while. You should say your good-bye. But not now. Not for a few minutes. You need to calm down."

"Did he die?" Artie's eyes grew even wider. By now Aaron had kneeled at his side as well.

"Aaron, what's happening?"

Tears dripped down Aaron's cheeks. And then Artie started sobbing. In spite of the terrible pain the convulsions caused, he continued to sob. "Why did this happen?"

Of course there was no answer. There never was an answer. When Mary's husband George died, it was she who asked the question. Now it was Artie.

Quietly and gently Mary stroked Artie's face, wiping the tears away. Occasionally she had to wipe the tears from her own face.

"Why, Mary?"

"Because Ray has had a heart condition for many years. He knew that too much excitement could cause this. That's one of the reasons why he chose to become a chauffeur, rather than maintain the hectic schedule he had before."

Artie's eyes grew wide again. "But he never told me that?"

"Of course not. He didn't want you to worry."

When Artie's sobs started to subside, Mary said quietly, "We need to get you to a hospital. I want you to come in the Cadillac with me."

Artie nodded. His breathing labored. "Mary, you're not going to die, are you?"

"What?" She turned and looked at Aaron for an explanation. But he simply lifted his shoulders to show that he didn't understand, either. "What do you mean, Arthur? I'm not hurt."

"Everybody who has ever loved me has died. You're not going to die, too, are you?"

Mary nodded. Shock and despair were overwhelming the boy's system. How could he make any kind of rational judgment then? His parents, his grandparents, and now the man who loved him as a son. The man who had meant so much to her as well. "It's a wonder that you can endure such tragedy," she said quietly. Then, looking down at him, she said, "I'm not leaving you, Arthur. Not for a very long time."

Artie struggled to take a breath, and Mary put her hands on his chest to calm his breathing. "I'm not going anywhere, dear. I'll be here for you. I promise." After a few shallow breaths, Artie at last relented and closed his eyes.

"Dear God," Mary said quietly, "please help me keep that promise. Please."

Mary looked up and signaled to the pastor that it was time to proceed. With that he brought the Cadillac up to the front of the line. Gently Aaron and the pastor lifted Artie into the spacious backseat of the car, resting his head on Mary's lap. Then another set of men lifted David Boone onto some blankets that had been spread on the floor of the Cadillac.

"Aaron," the pastor asked, "would you ride up front with me? I may need some help if one of them wakes up on the way."

Aaron nodded and then climbed into the car. As he climbed in, he happened to glance at the Ford pickup truck, and he winced at the image of men lifting Ray's body into the back of the truck, which was now parked directly in front of the wrecked Duesenberg.

Once Ray's body was settled into position and respectfully covered with a blanket, Pastor Wyndham climbed in and started the motor.

Chapter 28

An Important Revelation

September 1934

"But I have to go, Mary."

Mary turned to the doctor, who had just broken the news to Artie that he should stay in bed, rather than go to Ray's funeral.

"It's very important to the boy."

The doctor looked at Artie, then to Mary, then back to Artie. Then he sighed. "Fine. But I want to tape your ribs, and you have to promise me that you won't try to lift anything. And I don't want you going out to the cemetery. The road is way too rough."

"I'll be careful."

"You can't let him get excited, Mrs. Wilkerson. It's not even his ribs that I'm so worried about as much as the punctured lung. If he strains it, it's likely to start bleeding again."

"I understand. I'll make certain he stays quiet."

The doctor turned back at Artie. "I'm very sorry you lost your friend. My own father died when I was about your age. It's very hard to get over it. From everything people have said about him, Mr. McCandless must have been a really terrific fellow."

"He was the best," Artie said quietly. "There's nobody like Ray."

"Well, you should go to the funeral then to tell people about him. He deserves it. Just promise me that you'll go straight home and go to bed after that."

"I promise." "Well, then, Mrs. Wilkerson, I'll sign the release papers so he can check out of the hospital. I'll stop by the house later tonight to check on him. I assume these two young men are here to help you?"

Mary acknowledged Aaron and Joey, who had arrived a few minutes earlier. "I'm sure one of them will be glad to drive us home, and my cook can go out for anything we need." She paused. "Still, it will be good when Arthur can get back to being my driver." She did know enough about grief to realize that she had to transfer responsibility to Artie as soon as possible. That would help him more than anything else.

"Well, hopefully that won't take too long." Turning to Artie, the doctor added, "You're going to heal from the injuries, Artie, so at least you don't have to worry about that."

"Thank you."

The doctor gathered his things. "I'm off to see David Boone. He's going to have a harder time, I'm afraid."

"David! I'd forgotten. Arthur, before we check out I think we should go see him."

"Why?" Artie asked in alarm.

"Because he suffered a serious injury, and it's the least we can do as neighbors." Artie didn't look convinced. "Everyone who was there has been traumatized by this accident. I just think it would be a nice gesture."

"Fine," Artie mumbled.

* * *

"May we come in, David?"

David Boone frowned but then motioned for Artie and Mary to come in. Boone's wife and daughter were there.

"We just stopped by to see how you're doing and to wish you a speedy recovery," Mary said. There was an awkward silence.

"I think you should tell Artie thank you, David. He risked his life to save us," Mrs. Boone suggested.

Boone glowered at his wife but said nothing.

Olivia looked at Mary and Artie. "He's been like this. Please don't take offense. It's just that he's been hurt . . . I know that he's grateful." She turned to Artie. "We all are."

Mary looked back and forth between the Boones, and her temperature started to rise. "Well, then, if you have nothing to say, please accept our best wishes, and we'll be off," she said brusquely.

Boone, recognizing that she was peeved, responded through clenched teeth "I'm grateful." "But . . ."

"But what?" Mary responded, betraying the irritation in her voice.

"But you shouldn't think—"

"David!" his wife said sharply.

Boone's shoulders slumped, and he looked away.

"Perhaps there's a better time, Mrs. Wilkerson." It was obvious that Mrs. Boone wanted the encounter to come to a quick end.

"No, I want to hear what David has to say," Mary said firmly, her eyes narrowed.

"But this isn't a good time. Artie is ill, and . . . David is out of sorts."

"I don't need you talking for me!" Boone yelled. "I *am* grateful. I know that Artie put his life at risk. But now everybody talks about how I should bury the hatchet with him. The pastor has said so, my wife says it, everyone thinks it. But it remains true that he's been vandalizing my property for years, and now I'm just supposed to overlook all that? Well, call me ungrateful, but somehow I'm not on that bandwagon just yet, even if he did drag me out of that miserable old car of ours."

Artie wanted to protest and started to get up out of the wheelchair, but there was a stabbing pain in his side from the sudden exertion, and he slumped back down. Mary looked at him in alarm, but Artie just dropped his eyes and bit his lip. More than anything in the world, he just wanted to get out of there. As he settled back into the chair, the fire died down as quickly as it flared up, and Artie was surprised to find that he wasn't really angry at Mr. Boone, even though he was sick and tired of being falsely accused. But right now he just didn't care. With Ray gone, it seemed like all the color had drained out of his world, and it took too much energy to get angry.

Mary was not in the same frame of mind, however. Not nearly.

"How dare you! You know perfectly well that Arthur has alibis for nearly everything that's happened to you. We already talked about the time you accused him when he was still in New York, for heaven's sake."

"Yes, we talked about it, didn't we? That's when you decided to blackmail me by threatening to pull your money from my bank. Well, I don't buy it. The boy is a delinquent and always has been. But now, after one single incident, he's suddenly a hero. Perhaps you can forgive me for having a contrary opinion."

"Blackmail? How dare you!"

"Stop it! Both of you stop it!" The outburst from Olivia Boone was so fierce and so unexpected that everyone in the room looked at her with mouths agape.

Artie was sure that the nurses had heard her bellow all the way down at their station at the end of the hallway. Mary quieted down in the face of her wrath, but David Boone turned on her with fire in his eyes.

"Olivia, you be quiet. We have nothing more to say to these people."

"You'd like it that way, wouldn't you? You'd like it if Monica and I allowed you to continue your deception. But enough is enough. You have made these boys suffer long enough, and it's time to bring it to an end."

"I warn you, don't say another word!" David Boone's face was flushed with anger, and he started coughing. The danger to his health was real enough that Olivia's face blanched, and she went quiet. When he got control of himself, he said very evenly, "I think everyone should just go now and leave me alone. I've said what I have to say about Artie, and I'm not interested in a fight with Mary Wilkerson. It doesn't matter what I say, anyway. She defends the boy even when it's clear that he's no good, and I simply can't deal with it all right now."

Mary was about to explode, but Boone's daughter Monica got there first. "Isn't it time to own up to the truth? You have blamed Artie and Joey all this time and now you're too proud to admit that you were wrong. Well, Mother's right—you do owe them an apology."

The turn of events in the conversation was proving hard to follow. Surprisingly, Boone didn't react this time, perhaps because it was so unusual for the normally docile Monica to challenge him.

But Mary reacted. "What do you mean? What have you learned about this terrible vandalism?"

"Do you want to tell her, father, or should I?"

Boone huffed and waved his hand to indicate that he didn't care.

Monica proceeded. "Fine, then I'll tell you all what we learned just last week. It turns out that father terminated an employee from the bank because they got in an argument over pay. While everyone admits that the man had his flaws, my father was anything but kind in the way he let him go. At any rate, he's been struggling with unemployment ever since, and apparently he didn't want to suffer by himself. So it's this man who has been doing the truly awful things to our family. The police caught him in the act of setting some flammable materials behind the bank and arrested him. Eventually he confessed to everything."

"You mean this man would have burned down the bank?" Mary asked, astonished.

Monica nodded. "Apparently so, Mrs. Wilkerson."

"But, why did it take so long to find him?"

"I think it's our fault," Monica replied. "I think it's because Artie and his friends occasionally did something that kept our attention on them. One of us should have thought of this man much earlier, but father was so convinced that it was Artie that we never even considered anyone else."

"But why didn't you tell us all this when you learned it?" Mary asked.

At this point, David Boone was completely ignoring the conversation, even though he was lying there in his hospital bed. Having his family challenge him was so unusual that he was completely subdued, at least for the moment.

"Because David wouldn't let us," Olivia said quietly. "He said that the boy was still guilty and should be made to feel the weight of what he was doing."

"But to call the police on him . . . to make me suspect him . . . to cast doubt on his friends? It's outrageous!"

"Outrageous? What's outrageous is that Artie Call, community miscreant, now stands to inherit a fabulous estate, drives outrageous cars, and is the darling of everyone in our church group. What's outrageous is that someone who fully deserves to be incarcerated is now the most fortunate person in Boise." David Boone made no attempt to conceal the frustration in his voice.

"But David, you took him into your own home to help reform him. I'd think you'd be grateful that he's improving."

"Father isn't like that," Monica said coolly. "He prefers to be the center of attention—the source of all wisdom and virtue. It's hard for him to share the spotlight with someone like Artie."

"Really, Monica, that's a little harsh," Mrs. Boone interjected.

"Is it, Mother? When was the last time he said a kind word to you? When has he ever said anything supportive of me and my life and *my* ambitions?" Her voice caught momentarily.

"That's enough!" David Boone said this so emphatically that it forced him into another coughing fit.

Olivia Boone turned to Mary with a desperate look in her eyes. "Please, Mrs. Wilkerson. This is very hard. Perhaps you should go . . ."

"Yes, it's clear that we should. I'm sorry for all that has happened." She turned to David Boone, wanting to shout at him for all the needless pain he'd caused, particularly once he had learned the truth of the attacks. But one look at the stricken man was enough to tell her that nothing she could say could add to his misery. As bad as it was to be injured, to be embarrassed was exquisitely more painful for a man like David Boone. Having accused Artie once he could never back down, even though his pride had now brought him to this awful moment.

"Come on, Arthur. We need to get out of here. It turns out that there is more than one kind of infection in this hospital that we need to avoid." With that, Mary turned Artie's wheelchair and firmly pushed it out the door and down the hallway, Aaron and Joey trailing behind them. A stranger who didn't know Mary would never guess, at that unhappy moment, that she was seventy years old, for she looked very much like a young lioness protecting her young as she strode quickly down the linoleum.

"I knew that it wasn't Artie," Aaron said animatedly. "I just knew it!"

"But you didn't know about me, did you?" Joey asked quietly.

The look on Aaron's face confirmed his suspicion. "Well, you had every reason to be mad at him . . . what with Mr. Boone repossessing your house."

"There's no need to explain," Mary interrupted. "That's the problem with something like this—in the end, everyone suspects everyone else. I'm very glad to know that you were all innocent. I wish I could say I had that confidence all along. But now we know, and David Boone should be ashamed that he didn't apologize as soon as he learned the truth." Under her breath, she said, "Very ashamed. To think that he's jealous of a boy . . ."

Somehow it pleased Artie that Mary was angry on his account. That was a sign of love, wasn't it? And even though he had no affection for David Boone, he felt sorry for him now. It turned out that he had a real enemy, and yet he had driven off everyone who would normally support him, even his own family.

"Thanks, Mary."

She looked at Artie in surprise. "For what?"

"For standing up for me."

CHAPTER 29

The End of a Season

October 1934

As 1934 drew to a close, it turned out to be the year that put the word *Great* in Great Depression. The stock market crash in October 1929 had clearly ended the giddy days of the 1920s. But even though it ushered in higher unemployment and slower growth, the economy continued to move forward in such a way that people always nurtured hope that things would get better. But in 1934, the Federal Reserve put the final stake in the heart of any hoped-for recovery by severely restricting the money supply just at the point that the economy was poised to expand, worried by the phantom fear of inflation. As banks called in loans, foreclosures increased, businesses collapsed, and the unemployment lines grew. In some way or another, virtually every person in America was touched. David Boone was one of them, as his bank folded and he joined the ranks of the unemployed. The social stigma of that was too great, and he and his family simply disappeared one night. Some said they went to Seattle, others to California, and some even to New York. Aaron's father lost his job, as well, which meant that the money Aaron earned at the theater became devoted to food instead of spending money.

But it wasn't all bad. Joey's father found a job working for one of the many government agencies that the Roosevelt Administration created to try to get people back to work. And some people said that families had never been as close as when they were all working together to get through the tough times. Adversity is like that—it brings out the worst in some, the best in others.

And it turned out that 1934 proved to be a great year for Artie Call. Once Mary had assured him that most of her money was still safe, even though she lost some when David Boone's bank collapsed, he simply decided to relax and enjoy the life that Mary wanted to share with him.

Which is why he found himself in his room one evening struggling to get his necktie in a proper knot. Having not quite successfully mastered his tendency to use cuss words when faced with frustration, he was quietly lecturing the tie in some colorful language when Bethany called out to him, "Artie! Aaron's here!"

Artie took a deep breath and told her to send Aaron to Artie's bedroom.

Instead of a usual greeting, the first words out of Artie's mouth when Aaron came in the room were, "Can you do anything with this darn tie?"

"Me? It took me five tries to get mine tied right." But when he saw just how poorly Artie was doing, he took the tie and started to work on it.

"I can't believe Mary's letting us take the Cadillac," Aaron said cheerfully. "We're going to be the envy of the whole school."

Artie smiled. "I think that's what Mary's got in mind."

"Stephanie should be pleased. By the way, how did you ever get permission from her father to take her to the prom?"

Artie shrugged. "Ever since they found out who had been doing those bad things to Mr. Boone, he's been treating me pretty nice. I think it helps that Stephanie's mother told him that he should start being nicer to Stephanie, or she'd end up hating him. Of course, she wouldn't really, but it got the job done."

"Well, it must be nice to have him on your side finally."

"It's hard to believe, isn't it? Ever since the accident, people who used to tell their kids to stay away from me are now treating me like a hero."

"Lucky they don't know you as well as some of us . . ."

Artie slugged Aaron in the shoulder. "Say what you want, but I'm going to the dance with the most beautiful girl in the school, and she's glad to be going with me."

"It's true that she's beautiful. But I might have to argue with you about who's the most beautiful."

"I know . . . you've got a great date, as well."

"There! That's as good as I can get it. We don't have any more time to waste on a stupid tie, so just put it on."

Artie grabbed the tie and slipped it over his head. Then he straightened his coat jacket, checked his shoes to make sure they weren't scuffed, and turned and presented himself to Aaron.

"Very nice. Now can we go?"

Artie grew serious. "Before we go, there are two things I want to talk to you about."

Aaron looked at his watch. "Can't it wait?"

"No. I'd be too nervous."

Aaron sat down on Artie's bed. "Well, what is it?"

Artie shifted uncomfortably. "You're coming Saturday, aren't you?"

"Yes, I'm coming Saturday, just like I told you I would a dozen times."

"Good. You know how Mary wants me to go to some eastern school when I graduate?"

"Yeah."

"Well, she's going to pay for it."

"Uh, huh. That's no surprise."

"Well, here's the thing. If you could go to any school of your choice, where would it be?"

Aaron's face flushed. "Don't even ask that. You know I can't go to any school I want. We can't afford it."

"Just suppose you could. In your wildest dreams."

Aaron shook his head. He had worked really hard not to be jealous of Artie. For his part, Artie had never made an issue of Mary's money. But it was always there. So this wasn't the best thing to talk about.

"Come on—where?"

"I'd go to USC!"

"USC?"

"University of Southern California!"

"Oh. Why?"

"Oh my gosh. You've known me this long and you don't know? Because they have a whole program dedicated to movie making. They teach you how to direct movies, how to finance them, how to produce them. You know that's where I'd go."

Artie was quiet for a moment. "How much does it cost?"

Now Aaron's face really reddened. "A lot more than I've got! Now stop it, I don't like this."

"Ray left me everything—all his savings, his house, everything. I even get the Chrysler."

"So?" It was harder than ever not to be jealous, a feeling that Aaron didn't like at all.

"So I don't need it. I don't even like going over to his house, because it reminds me of him."

"Yeah, well, so give it to Mary, or to the Church."

"I want to share part of my inheritance with you. I'm sure there's enough money to get you through USC."

Now the color drained from Aaron's face, and he had trouble controlling his breathing. "But I couldn't. I mean, I don't think people can do that."

"Of course they can. I've already talked to Mary about it. She's my guardian, so she has control over all the money until I'm old enough to get it. We both think it's a great idea to send you to wherever you want to go."

"But . . ." Aaron's voice was unsteady.

"Here's the deal. When nobody else in the world wanted to be my friend, you and Joey stood by me. Why shouldn't I do something nice for you guys?"

"But USC . . ."

"I'd feel great if you'd let me help."

"Maybe we could call it a loan."

"If that's what you want to call it, that's fine. But I'd just as soon do it and be done with it, no strings attached. I don't want you owing me money. "

Aaron was speechless.

"What do you say?"

Aaron looked up slowly. "I guess I say yes." Then a smile crept over his face. "You're serious?"

"Dead serious."

"Wow. I can't believe it—USC!"

Artie smiled. "I'm glad we got that settled. Now we've got to get going. The girls are going to think we've abandoned them."

"What? You're the one who started gabbing."

Artie grinned as they walked to the front door.

* * *

Judge Farnsworth looked up from his desk as people entered the room. "I didn't think I'd ever say this, Artie, but it's good to have you in court."

Artie smiled. As he approached his seventeenth birthday, he'd filled out a lot and had quite a striking appearance. He'd matured a great deal in three years, and not just physically. "Thank you, sir. I'm glad to be here as well."

The judge was surprised as the room continued to fill with Mary and some of her friends from church, Bethany, Judy and her family, the Nelsons, the Westons, and Pastor Wyndham and his wife. Before long the room was full.

"Well, it seems that you have a lot of friends."

Artie looked around the room and a wave of emotion swept over him. These were the people who had changed his life. "Yes, sir, I do." Mary's smile meant the most to him. But Stephanie's was close behind.

"Well then, let's get started." Turning to the court clerk, he asked, "Do you have the appropriate paperwork?"

"Yes, your honor. Right here." The clerk walked over and put a file in front of the judge, who quickly examined the pages in front of him. Looking up, he invited Mary and Artie to come forward.

He rapped his gavel and declared the court in session. Then, in a confident voice he started to read, "In the matter of the adoption of one Arthur William Call by Mary Wilkerson . . ."

Artie cast a glance at Mary and caught her in the act of wiping tears from her cheeks. She happened to turn at the same moment, and their eyes met. He stepped closer and put his arm around her waist.

Author's Notes

If I were a reader, I'd have some questions about this story. Here are a few with my best answers:

What happened to the Duesenberg after Ray passed away?

What I think happened is that the car sat damaged under a tarp for many years—the memories associated with it simply too painful to confront. But then Mary had it secretly restored and gave it to Artie and Stephanie as a wedding present. Later, after Artie's service in the U.S. Navy during World War II (and as the car turned classic), Artie used it as a showpiece to attract customers to the showroom of the Chrysler dealership that Mary helped Artie and Joey Weston purchase in Boise. A perennial favorite in the 4th of July parade, Boiseans came to love "their car," just as Mary Wilkerson hoped they would

Why did you decide to write about cars, and why the Duesenberg?

Why did I pick a Duesenberg? Because they were, quite simply, the quintessential American luxury and sports car. They pushed technology and styling to the very limit. I think my wife Marcella's reaction to Duesenbergs illustrates this. Through the years she has indulged my desire to go to antique auto shows and museums, giving a modest "hmm" or "I suppose," whenever I carried on about how impressive a particular classic Lincoln, Cadillac, or Franklin looked. But on one of these visits something unusual happened which caused me to take note. As we idled past a number of cars, she looked up and said, "Now *there's* a beautiful looking car . . ."

followed by her walking over to take a closer look. It was a Duesenberg. It happened again at a car show a few years later, and then again, until I realized there was a trend—of all the classic cars, the Duesenbergs are the ones that stand out. The fact is that a Duesenberg has styling and performance unlike any other, and it really is, in my opinion, the ultimate American motor car from the classic car era.

As to the first question, I wanted to write a book that featured cars because I grew up around them. My father, Reed Borrowman, worked as a traveling auto parts salesman for an auto parts warehouse in Blackfoot, Idaho. Even as a little boy, I loved going into "parts houses" that dad called on because I liked seeing the orderly rows of boxes and the shiny tailpipes and mufflers hanging from the ceiling, as well as inhaling the remarkable smells—that unique blend of oil and steel and rubber— that characterize car dealerships and parts stores.

In the 1950s, cars were increasingly powerful, and I learned every make and model on the road right up through my high school years. In fact, one of my best memories from childhood is when my cousin Mark Jensen and I, at the sophisticated age of twelve, walked five or six miles around Pocatello to go into every car dealership in the city to ogle and compare the various Lincolns and Imperials, Corvettes and Pontiac GTOs, and Chevrolets passing judgment on where each of these lined up in the panoply of fine automobiles. In retrospect, I'm awfully glad the dealers were patient with us.

All of which is to say that, like most Americans, I like cars and enjoyed this chance to write about the *classics*.

$22,000 for a Duesenberg doesn't sound like very much money – why was that such a big deal? A similar model to the one Mary bought in 1934 was recently purchased by the incomparable Auburn/Cord/Duesenberg Automobile Museum at the original Duesenberg factory showroom in Auburn, Indiana at a cost of more than $1,000,000! Not only are Duesenbergs classy—they're expensive, even seven decades later!

But then, they were expensive in the 1930s. Mary's Duesenberg cost $22,000 in 1934. That would be just a little over $350,000 in 2017, based on changes in the Consumer Price Index. If you use the Wage Earners Index, it would be the equivalent of nearly $950,000. So these truly were cars for kings and movie stars . . . and Mary Wilkerson.

Why write about the Great Depression?

In one way or another, each of my books has been about people facing up to adversity and finding personal triumph over fear. While the first seven books were written to pay tribute and honor to the men and women who were caught up in the great wars of the twentieth century, and who acted heroically when confronted by terrible challenges, I think the people who lived through the Great Depression faced a very different kind of adversity that is also worthy of tribute. While not facing bullets, they endured the grinding, sustained, and seemingly never-ending period of economic uncertainty and fear that drained hope and sapped emotional reserves. It had to be excruciating to face the very real consequences of unemployment, hunger, and uncertainty without becoming bitter or overcome by despair. And yet the people of that time, including my parents and grandparents, faced up to their problems and found ways to cope and to be happy in spite of the distress.

In fact, in many cases they found some of their greatest personal triumphs as they came to appreciate God and family in ways that those of us who grew up in more comfortable times can't fully appreciate. I don't know if you've thought of it like this, but nearly all the great stories about a particularly treasured Christmas come out of that era when to give a present represented real sacrifice, and to receive it was a treasure beyond compare. One cherished toy was all that many children could hope for. That may be a lesson that we have to learn in our generation.

ABOUT THE AUTHOR

Jerry Borrowman is a best-selling of author of co-authored autobiography, creative non-fiction, and historically authentic fiction. His first book, *Three Against Hitler* earned Rudi Wobbe and Jerry the **National Award from the Freedoms Foundation at Valley Forge**, which honors authors who promote the cause of freedom, (the first recipient of the medal was President Dwight D. Eisenhower). By using both fiction and non-fiction, his writing brings a new appreciation to hundreds of thousands of readers about the sacrifices and courage of valiant men and women in difficult situations.

Jerry likes to hear from his readers. He can be contacted on his website: www.jerryborrowman.com